Ebony Angel

Hope you have happy
hours reading this

Mary Burpee

Canada

The Publishers acknowledge the financial assistance of the Government of Canada through the Book Publishing Industry Development Program (BPIDP) for our publishing activities.

Library and Archives Canada Cataloguing in Publication

Burpee, Mary (Mary Josephine), 1918-
Ebony angel / Mary Burpee.

ISBN 978-0-88887-336-1

1. Ireland—History—19th century—Fiction. I. Title.

PS8603.U745E26 2007 C813'.6 C2007-901971-4

Cover design by Rory Degenhardt
Back cover photo: Jen Avaz
Printed and bound in Canada on acid free paper.

Ebony Angel

Mary Burpee

BOREALIS BOOK PUBLISHERS

Borealis Press
Ottawa, Canada
2007

Acknowledgements and Credits

Ireland, A History by Robert Kee
History of Ireland by Desmond McGuire
Granuaile: The Life and Times of Grace O'Malley c. 1530-1603 by Anne Chambers
Encyclopedia Britannica, 1957 edition
The unpublished memoirs of Harold Kennedy

Eileen Kennedy, and Doctor Sheila Hingston, for their encouragement and help with old Irish street names, etc.; Dr.Richard Hingston for his wealth of information about old sailing vessels; letters to the author from Col. R. S. Kennedy, D.S.O. and Major (later Brigadier) T. F. Kennedy

•

Thank you to my family for their advice and suggestions. And to fellow Albertans Jean Benfield, Mary Carson, Jean Cooper and Irene Gilpen who having read early drafts of *Ebony Angel* encouraged me to get it published.

Thank you too to publishers Dr. Frank Tierney, and the late Dr. Glenn Clever of Borealis Press who took a chance on an unknown author when they published my non-fiction books, *Musk Oxen of Gango* and *Horses Around My Heart.* And to editor Janet Shorten who said my manuscripts don't need much editing.

Dedication

I would like to dedicate Ebony Angel to all the descendants of George Alexander Kennedy, born September 4, 1822, in Dundalk, Ireland. He was an Irishman whose life left many questions unanswered.

Chapter One
A Convenient Hypocrite

"Katherine! What's wrong? Why are you pacing your room like a caged lion?"

The face of the young woman so addressed was a study in conflicting emotions. A mouth meant for smiling was set in grim, determined lines. Resentment smouldered in her blue eyes, giving them the glitter of the Irish Sea in a violent storm.

"I hate the English! That's what's wrong! I hate their laws! I hate what they're doing to the Irish! Sometimes I think I even hate my own father." A voice which normally held a cultured Dublin lilt was harsh and condemning.

"Katherine O'Connor! Don't speak that way! Not about your father. He's one of the most respected men in Dublin." A slightly older woman, whose large grey eyes were the only really outstanding feature in a pale face framed by an abundance of light brown hair, had spoken crossly. Now her eyes drifted with a hint of envy over her companion's willowy figure, and a face that, without the owner being aware of it, had the quality of making those she smiled upon feel singled out and very special.

"Then tell me this, Henrietta. Why did my father deny his Catholic faith and become a Protestant? Oh, I know. You'll say thousands are doing it. And you're right. They are. But they're doing it because it's advantageous to them, to their families, that's why. And you know it." Contempt changed a face of sculptured beauty into a mask of discontent.

"Katherine, do be reasonable. You're not a child. You're eighteen, old enough to understand that Irish Catholics aren't becoming Protestants without good reason."

"Yes, of course I know that! I know Catholics aren't allowed to own land, or property of any kind. They're forbidden to practise law, vote, hold public office, send their children to school, even to schools outside the country. They can't own a horse worth more than five pounds." The younger woman's mouth closed with an irritated snap.

"Well, Katherine, think about it. Would *you* be content riding any but the well-bred animals in your father's stable? I don't think so. You're never satisfied with anything but the best." Henrietta Kingsway had spoken as if in a rush to finish her say before she changed her mind.

Now her fingers absently traced the ivory marquetry on an ornate night stand, but an edge had crept into her voice. An edge that hinted she was categorizing her friend as a convenient hypocrite, one who created her own rules, then ignored them when it suited her purpose.

"Katherine, you know, as I do, that most Dublin girls would be thrilled if they had the privileges you enjoy."

"Lud Henrietta! Do stop preaching!" Katherine glared at her companion, snatched up an elegant silver-backed hand mirror from a dressing table and waved it as if intending to bludgeon the world into submission. "I'm not entirely stupid."

Then she lapsed into silence. When she spoke again her voice held a hint of uncertainty. "You know, Rietta, most of our Irish tenants are supporting Daniel O'Connell. Do you suppose he'll get the Act of Union repealed? The rights of the Irish Parliament restored? Do you think when Westminster hears about the huge crowds that come to hear him speak they'll decide to listen to what the people of Ireland want?" A disturbed frown lingered between her eyes as she finished speaking.

"Well, I pray O'Connell's magic for crowd control doesn't desert him. If it does there'll be more blood than water in your Irish rivers." Henrietta Ridgeway shuddered as if hearing the echo of a million British feet trampling on Irish graves.

Katherine, her eyes troubled beneath brows knitted in thought, stopped pacing. She swung herself up onto the big four-poster bed beside her friend and stared absently at hands clasping and unclasping, fingers intertwining, breaking apart, to intertwine again.

Henrietta's eyes followed them in hypnotic fascination. They reminded her of what she had read about red-sided garter snakes mating at a snake pit in the new world. Males, smaller than the females, were always the first to come out of hibernation. When they did they positioned themselves on the limestone rocks, and waited. Ready to pounce.

The moment a female appeared she was inundated by a pack of frenzied males who wound themselves around her in a writhing, squirming mating orgy. On warm spring days hundreds of males would rush to form wriggling, living balls around each receptive female until nothing but her head could be seen as she wriggled and squirmed in a sinuous attempt to escape her suitors. . . only one of which would be successful in copulating with her.

Copulation happens almost immediately. When it does there is an audible pop as that pair breaks apart, and then it's game over for the rest of the suitors. The successful male has blocked the female's urogenital opening with a copulatory plug. However, some males continue to cling to her, caressing her with a stroking motion of the head for another fifteen minutes. Only after they lose interest and move off to find a more likely prospect is the female free to slither into the hinterland to look for her first food in six months.

Henrietta had to mentally shake herself to drag her mind out of the snake pit when Katherine began speaking again.

"The Dublin papers are praising O'Connell for insisting 'negotiations, not violence, is the way to achieve reform.' Yet how long can one man control those monster crowds? Tempers are so volatile. A few rabble-rousers could trigger uprisings so bloody the Emerald Isle will turn red with gore. And it'll be the Irish peasants, those already ground into poverty under the heel of their English landlords, who will suffer most.

"Oh Henrietta! Why are men so blind? Can't they see fighting only results in more burnings, more murders, more floggings, more torture? Atrocities breed retaliation. And retaliation starts a still worse round of brutality. There is enough hatred now between the English and the Irish to last a thousand years. How much longer can it go on? Will it never end?"

As the younger woman finished speaking her eyes followed a trapped blue-bottle fly hurtling furiously around the room, droning angrily to itself as it bounced off walls and windows looking for a way to escape.

Suddenly a mercurial change swept over Katherine's face. "Patrick says O'Connell is right to insist 'Diplomacy and negotiations. . . not guns . . . are the answer.'"

At the name Patrick a smile had twitched briefly at grim lips, then left, as if afraid by staying it might betray a secret.

A moment later Katherine drew herself up as one who

has reached a painful but irreversible decision. The ramrod-straight body, the proud, resolute lines of her face, gave her the presence of a Grand Duchess ready to face her inquisitors with an aplomb that mustn't betray the inner tensions threatening to tear her apart.

But Henrietta saw. And was worried. "Katherine, why this diatribe now against laws designed to keep Irish Catholics firmly under England's boot? Those laws have been in effect for years. You can rant about them until the sun burns out, but nothing is really going to change. And you know it. So what's bothering you?"

Katherine face suddenly looked bleak as the death of hope.

Chapter Two
Shared Secret

Katherine, absently fingering a tendril of hair that having escaped its companions was curling about her face in a tantalizing fashion, sighed. The sigh, shuddering through her as a train leaving the station shudders down the long length of its spine, gave the lie to any suggestion of bravado. Her voice, when she spoke, was despondent, as if she was seeing nothing ahead but a lifetime tormented by hopeless regret.

"It doesn't matter what O'Connell does. It doesn't matter what anybody does. Nothing can help me. Not now. It's too late."

"Why Katherine O'Connor! Whatever do you mean?" Henrietta leaned towards her friend like a bloodhound discovering an exciting scent.

The younger girl hugged her body as if to ease the frightened ache within, and nervously moistened her lips. When she spoke her voice was brittle. "I've totally messed things up, Rietta. I'm pregnant. But if you breathe a word of it to anyone I swear I'll kill you."

"Oh Katherine! Who's the man? Peter Moriarty? It must be. Anyone can see he's mad about you. He's so tall and handsome. I'd swoon if he *even* looked at me that way. And they say his father wallows in money."

"No, it isn't Peter. Though I'll have to marry him now and make him think the child is his." Her laugh was bitter as she continued. "He's a gentleman, you know. And gentlemen don't bed ladies out of wedlock. His sort get their tumbles in the heather with peasant wenches. Girls too frightened to say "no" because to refuse could mean eviction, or worse, for their family. I tell you, Rietta, it's a rotten world." Katherine's face masked inarticulate resentment as she began striding around the room again.

"Then if it isn't Peter, who is it? I didn't know you had another suitor. Quick! Tell me! Before I explode with curiosity." Henrietta eyes dilated in anticipation of some forbidden and erotic news; her nerves tingled in a turmoil of excitement.

"Don't be a twit, Rietta. The man isn't my suitor. He's my father's groom."

"You mean? . . . You mean? . . .You mean you did *that* with a *groom*? Katherine O'Connor! How could you?" The words burst out like air from a pricked balloon.

For a moment Katherine's face looked empty, as if she had left it and gone to a place filled with exquisite memories. Memories she shared with a man not overly tall but tough as whipcord, his face and neck burnished by sun and wind to the colour of old saddle leather. A man with large, gentle hands, firm in their grip and always in control, whether it was managing a frightened horse or a beautiful woman. But it was the eyes, dark brown and flecked with splashes of green, that stared out at the world, challenging it from beneath a thatch of hair the colour of polished copper, that made the face distinctive. And when his arms were around her, his lips seeking hers, it didn't matter if he was groom or lord of the realm. He was her lover.

Then reality filtered back. Her words were crusted with impatience. "Why must you always be such a goose, Henrietta? He rides with me every morning. My father says he has to . . . because it's not proper for me to ride alone." Her laugh was brittle. "Anyway it isn't as though Patrick Tully is a regular groom. He'd be Chief of the Tully clan, with his own estate in County Kerry, if his grandfather hadn't joined the United Irishmen to fight for the rights of the Catholics."

"You mean he took part in that Wolfe Tone conspiracy at Bantry Bay in 1796? The one that failed when the French fleet was swept back out to sea by a violent storm? Goodness me! England hasn't had such an escape since Raleigh drove off the Spanish Armada." Henrietta's eyes were wide, her voice incredulous.

"It wasn't Raleigh, or the English, who bested the Armada. It was the weather. Just like the Wolfe Tone uprising." Katherine's voice was scornful.

"What happened to the rebels?" Henrietta, hunching down, looked almost afraid to ask.

"Without the help expected from the French the uprising amounted to little more than a few skirmishes around Grandon and Cork. The militia, supported by local yeomanry under the leadership of an obscure, small-time Grandon landowner — who the British promptly made an earl for his help — quickly gained control. It's what happened afterwards that clings like a dark and hideous memory in the mind of every Irishman."

"The conspirators?" breathed Henrietta, with the look of a frightened mouse. "Did most of them escape?"

Something slimy and unwholesome churned in Katherine's stomach, something she had to crush and control before she could speak. And when she did her voice came out numb and frozen.

"No. They had their lands confiscated. Some were shot without a trial. Those were the lucky ones. Most were brutally flogged before being allowed to die. Men who had taken no part in the rebellion were tortured in the hope they would betray friends who had."

Her hands were angrily clenching and unclenching, her eyes shooting fire and venom. "What had been Tully land for hundreds of years was given to an absentee landlord. A man who licks the boots of the English, who gave it to him, with never a damn about the land. Or the tenants. As long as his agent can squeeze the juice of life out of the peasants so he and his family can go on living like English potentates Ireland will never see the imprint of his boot.

"Patrick's father was killed too. At Ballingarry, in County Tipperary. Fighting for what he believed in. After that Patrick came to Dublin starving and in tatters, but he had a way with horses so he soon rose to the position of head groom."

As she spoke her face took on a softer look, her blue eyes turned dreamy. "You must have seen Patrick, Rietta. We grew up together. My father arranged for the governess to teach him as well as me and my step-sister. Miss Grimm was a Catholic, or she might not have done it so willingly, but Patrick was clever, so eager to learn, she claimed teaching him was a pleasure. He continued to share our lessons, even though my step-sister Sophia went to Father, whining *she* shouldn't be expected to sit in the same classroom as an Irish peasant."

"And?"

"He bellowed 'Go to your room! Don't let me see you again until you've found some iota of human kindness.' She's always blamed me for that. She's so vindictive it's scary."

"If you ask me she nurses grudges against everything Irish. Is it because she resents having to leave England? Or is there some other reason? It's the reverse of the Irish hating the English. Except the Irish have just cause. Whereas she . . . ?" Henrietta's voice trailed into silence.

Katherine regarded her friend with a reflective look, then nodded absently. "Yes, we Irish have many reasons to dislike England. And it isn't just because of unfair laws. When Patrick talks of the atrocities he's seen I wish I could shoulder a gun. Yes, I know you're half English and I know you'll tell me the Irish commit atrocities too. And you're right. They do. But why oh why can't both sides see all they're doing is fostering more hatred? All we Irish want is to be allowed to run our own country. Is that too much to ask?"

Henrietta looked suddenly bored, as if political problems were of only passing interest. Whereas affairs of the heart, especially when they concerned her best friend, were quite a different matter.

"Well, if you love your groom why not marry him? And leave Peter Moriarty for . . . ." Henrietta bit her tongue. At one time she had secretly nursed the hope that Peter Moriarty might offer for her. But that was before Stephen Cassidy had come into her life.

Now Peter's indifference didn't seem to matter. Anyway, Stephen was Peter's friend and as Stephen's wife, which she fully expected to become, Peter would still be in and out of her life.

"There you go being a twit again, Henrietta. Just because I love Patrick doesn't mean I'll marry him. You must know that. He's a Catholic. He has no rights as a citizen. Until recently he couldn't have sent his children to a proper school. Only to the secret hedgerow sort where priests risked their lives to teach the barest smattering of

Latin and numbers to Gaelic youngsters."

She fought a momentary impulse to stop speaking, then continued in a bitter voice. "Do you think *that* is what I want for *my* children? Patrick doesn't want it either. He'd like his sons (if he has any) to go to Trinity College so they could become lawyers and fight in the courts for the rights of the Irish Catholics. He believes more can be done in the courts than with guns and secret uprisings. But I'm not sure there's any hope there either. How can there be justice for the Irish as long as we live under British laws, dispensed by British judges?"

"Well, you should have thought of that before you got yourself pregnant."

Katherine tossed her head with such defiance several strands of hair escaped to frame her face. "Don't be so smug, Rietta. And don't preach. It's too late for that. Of course I won't marry Patrick. Do you think I'd give up everything Father gained when he embraced the Protestant faith? Don't be crazy. I might natter about Father's defection, but I'm too happy with my life to want to change it. Or I was until I didn't bleed last month. Now . . ." Her voice drifted into a reverie of indecision.

Then she straightened her shoulders with a look of strong determination. "But I've made a promise to myself. If Patrick's child is a boy I'll see he gets a chance to study law at Trinity College. And that is more than any other Tully could do for a son." Having said this, a self-righteous glow took possession of her face.

Henrietta squirmed into a more comfortable position before speaking. "I'll tell you one thing, Katherine. If I was lucky enough to have Peter Moriarty courting me it's not giving him second choice to Patrick Tully I'd be doing."

"Why Henrietta! I do believe you're wishing Peter Moriarty would offer for you. And you already spoken for. For shame! Whatever would Stephen Cassidy say if he knew? But don't worry, dear. I'd wager a ten-pound note you'll be happy with Peter's friend Stephen Cassidy. He may not be all that handsome, but he has a face that speaks integrity and concern for those less fortunate than himself."

A giggle bubbled from her lips. Her erstwhile serious face was transformed, suddenly showing a hint of mischief, perhaps even a touch of wildness. But her tone was practical.

"Why couldn't we have a double wedding, Rietta? Your marriage is next month. If I tell Peter a double wedding is what I want and if you tell Stephen you want the same, maybe they could hurry up the reading of the banns. A double wedding, why . . . " She hesitated as if suddenly seeing trouble ahead. "You don't think Stephen would mind, do you?"

"Of course not. Why should he? He's Peter's best friend." Henrietta's voice rang with poorly hidden pride. "Oh Katherine. I'm so proud of Stephen. A sea captain. And him not yet thirty."

Katherine didn't remind her friend that perhaps Peter's father and hers being major shareholders in the Granuaille shipping line might have had something to do with Stephen's meteoric rise to the rank of captain. Instead she grimaced sourly. "Father says the *Grace O'Malley* and her sister ship the *Corsair Queen* may soon have to carry convicts to the penal colonies in Australia."

Katherine was deeply resentful that ships named after her ancestor, Grace O'Malley, Ireland's intrepid pirate queen, should become prison ships taking Irish felons, to work as forced labour in Australian chain gangs. Many of them were convicted of no worse crime than poaching a hare or stealing a loaf of bread to feed a hungry child.

And all because Britain, while sanctimoniously voicing strong protests against black slavery, was emptying her over-crowded jails by sending convicts to forced labour in a penal colony half a world away. Many would never survive the horrors of months at sea in the stinking hold of disease-ridden ships where starvation was common and care was often non-existent. But perhaps those who died en route were the fortunate ones.

Katherine shut her eyes to try to block out what she had heard about the horrors and degradation heaped on prisoners unfortunate enough to be singled out to be "made an example of" by sadistic gaolers. Better for *them* to have died at sea. And many did choose death by their own hand rather than face the floggings that tore the flesh, destroying manhood and spirit. She breathed a silent prayer that no one she knew would ever be subjected to such torment.

Henrietta shot a quick glance around the room, as if to make sure no one was lurking in the shadows, then lowered her voice to a whisper. "Your pirate ancestor, Grace O'Malley, would have been proud of Stephen when he was on that smuggling run to France."

Deviltry danced in Katherine's eyes as she grinned at her friend. "She'd have been doing a rollicking barefoot dance on the deck of her flag ship, brandishing her broadsword and yelling encouragement to him like a triumphant banshee."

"I knew it! I felt sure she would have applauded Stephen every time he saved the Irish the need to pay the

English their export tax. That tax, levied on everything leaving the country through regular Irish ports, is so unfair. It's no wonder Ireland is such a poor country." Then Henrietta sighed, as if to resign herself to accept the inevitable.

"Now of course Stephen will carry whatever cargo the shipping line tells him he must. But if it's prisoners they'll get better treatment on his ship than on those dreadful floating hulks over-crowded with the starving jetsam from British and Irish prisons."

Katherine, looking as if the subject suddenly bored her, tossed her head in a way that emphasized every lovely curve and sensuous line of a body that combined strength with delicacy. A moment later she reached out to give her friend a conciliatory hug. "But you'll have to get accustomed to having your husband at sea for months at a time. That would never suit me. I want my man where I can get at him. Every night."

"Shush, Katherine. You sound like a harlot. If you really love a man I don't think waiting would be so bad."

"Perhaps you could wait and be happy doing it. Not me."

Henrietta, as if not wanting to continue that line of talk, said primly, "I've heard Peter will be opening a new branch of the Provincial Bank of Ireland in Grandon soon. Isn't that exciting? You'll be a big frog in a little puddle, having 'at homes' every month for women like the Earl of Grandon's wife and Lady Bingham from Mullagatooney Castle. La de da! Just think of it! Why, Peter might even decide to stand for election at the next session. If he does there's no telling how far he could go." She struck a theatrical pose and bowed dramatically as if to someone of considerable importance. "My oh my! Imagine! Wife of a

Member of Parliament, living in England. An absentee landlord. First thing I know you'll be wearing gowns from Paris."

For a moment Katherine looked vaguely impressed, then her mouth set in a firm, thin line. "Never! I'll never live in England. There'll be no agent making my tenants' lives a living hell. But what are we talking like this for?" Her voice took on an uncharacteristic tremor, a dark shadow flitted across her face as if some goading urgency had taken possession of her mind. "I'm not married yet. And if Peter finds out I'm pregnant I won't be."

Henrietta put her arms compassionately around her friend's slender waist. "I know, dear." Then she sighed reflectively. "If your Father hadn't thought it unsafe for you to ride alone none of this would have happened."

"Well, it has happened. And sometimes I even think I'm glad." Katherine stamped her small foot emphatically, but the hands vigorously twisting and untwisting a fine linen handkerchief hinted of inner turmoil. Yet when she spoke it was as if she had overcome any fears she might have had. "I'll tell Peter I've come to my senses. I'll marry him. And soon. So we can have a double wedding. But that doesn't mean I'll give up seeing Patrick." This ultimatum was accompanied by a short, brittle laugh totally devoid of humour.

"Do be careful, Katherine. What if Peter finds out?" Henrietta's eyes took on a frightened glitter. "I'd be scared to cuckold my husband . . . even if he was at sea for months."

"Oh, don't be such a fool, Rietta. Of course I'll be careful. After we're married I'll be a model wife. Until then I intend to go on riding . . . with Patrick." What was supposed to be a frivolous laugh somehow sounded hollow, as if it had been dredged up from the bottom of an empty barrel.

"Will you tell Patrick?"

"Of course not! He must never know I'm carrying his child. No one must know. Except you. And I've only told you because you're my best friend. And I had to tell someone.

"What if Peter finds out on your wedding night that you aren't a virgin?" Henrietta rolled her eyes in a dramatic fashion but there was a worried frown furrowing her smooth white forehead. "Gentlemen put a lot of importance on their brides coming to them as virgins."

"Oh pshaw, Rietta! You always think of the worst. I'll have dear old Peter so enraptured with my charms he'll be so hot and eager he'll be in and pumping before he knows what's happening." Then she gave a sluttish grin. "You forget m'dear. You're talking to a woman with experience."

"But the blood? There won't be any. You're not a virgin."

"Oh Rietta, stop being such an innocent. There will be, if I sneak my embroidery scissors into bed. Ever hear of pricking one's finger? There'll be more than enough blood for three virgins."

Having said that, Katherine crossed silently to a porticoed window richly draped in dark green velvet against the chill of a Dublin winter, and peered into the courtyard below where a few hesitant snowflakes were drifting down before settling stealthily on last summer's grass. "Ah, I must get into my riding habit. Patrick has the horses saddled and waiting. I gave Lucy the afternoon off. I didn't want her eavesdropping on our tête-à-tête, so be a dear and help me with the buttons, there are so many of them. But I can be thankful I'm not Empress Elizabeth of Austria. She wears such elegant riding costumes she has to be *sewn* into them. But before you help me into mine I'd better send a message to Peter to let him know I have something important to tell him this evening."

She grimaced as she walked to a 15th-century sycamore escritoire that stood near the window, its bronze inlays highlighted now by a pale sun that peered between scurrying clouds like a foggy myopic eye. Katherine ran her thumb experimentally over several quills before she found one to her liking, tapped its feather briefly against her forehead as if to brush away any cobwebs of doubt that might still be lingering, then sat down, dipped the quill in a pewter ink-pot, and began to write.

Neither girl heard stealthy footsteps stealing away from a heavy oak door, which seemed to have opened of its own accord.

Chapter Three
A Frightening Discovery

"Sure 'tis congratulations I be giving you, old chap. I hear 'tis a double wedding the colleens be wanting." Stephen Cassidy thumped his friend enthusiastically on the back as he pulled a flask of Irish whiskey from his pocket and offered a drink.

"Peter Moriarty, to be honest with ye, I never thought you'd pull it off. Not with Katherine O'Connor. Didn't think she was the type to settle to married life. Not so soon. Wouldn't have surprised me if she'd held out for an earldom. And she might have got one too. That colleen has a face to make the angels sing and she sits a horse prettier than anyone I ever knew. Not that I mean any offence, old boy."

Stephen, seeing the grimace darkening the angular planes of his friend's face, hurried on. "When news of your marriage gets out, Dublin matrons will hit the doldrums. Those with marriageable daughters have been eyeing you with the hungry look of a stalking tigress for years. If you ask my opinion, which you rarely do, Katherine is damn lucky to be getting you as her husband. With all the young rakes that pass for gentlemen these days her marriage bed could become a cold and lonely place."

Peter Moriarty's proud face, a face with the lean durability of chiselled mahogany, looked warm, relaxed, and very masculine as he bent to take a quick swallow from the proffered flask. He handed it back to his friend before pulling a white linen handkerchief from his pocket and carefully wiping his lips.

Having done that, he grinned in a conspiratorial fashion and the grin softened the angular planes of his face. "Thanks for your good wishes, old chap. I may not ask advice on affairs of the heart, Stephen, for I feel quite capable of handling that on my own, but I'd like advice about something else. But first my congratulations to you too. Henrietta Kingsway will make you a good wife. She's not one to strut off like a silly filly in heat the moment your back is turned. She'll be waiting for you no matter how long you're at sea." For a moment there was almost a hint of envy in Peter's grey eyes, then he thumped his friend vigorously on the back in the way of good friends.

"You're right, old chap. I am indeed a lucky man. My only concern is that with this Australia run I'll be at sea for long stretches. It'll be lonely for Henrietta when I'm away. Even though she assures me she'll have lots to keep her busy — she intends to have a baby son to show me when I get back — I'll leave happier knowing she has good friends like you and Katherine close by. But now what was the advice you wanted from me? Today I feel capable of giving advice to the gods."

"You know how much Katherine likes to ride. I plan to give her a mare for a wedding present. A well-bred animal that can go to my father's stud when" — here his handsome face turned red with sudden embarrassment and he stopped as if trying to decide on a discreet way to continue — "when Katherine gets . . . ah . . . ah . . . indisposed."

"Oh, you don't need to spell it out, man. You want a mare your wife can ride now, that can be sent to stud when she's bearing your children. No need to look so embarrassed, old chap. What you're referring to is commonly known as 'doing what comes naturally' or in more prudish society as being *enceinte.* And yes, it just so happens I do know of a fine mare, good bloodlines, gentle, well-mannered. Just the horse for you. And she's for sale for a song."

A look of sudden suspicion flashed across the well-chiselled lines of the taller man's face. "What's the catch Stephen? What's wrong with the mare? There's always something wrong if they're sold cheap."

"Nothing's wrong with the mare. It's what's wrong with the damned British laws we Irish live under. The fellow who raised her has the bad fortune to be Catholic and the integrity not to deny his faith to please the English . . . who as you well know have laws which, amongst other things, forbid any Irish Catholic, man or woman, from owning a horse worth more than five pounds."

"Hmmn. This mare sounds interesting. Tell me more."

"She's a grey showing Arabian or Barbe blood. Fine boned, intelligent head, good body, flinty hooves, proud carriage, legs with strong flat bones allowing lots of room for tendons. Barely three years old but well trained and gentle."

"Well, what're we waiting for? Let's order the carriage and go see this Pegasus and have her delivered tomorrow, if she's as good as you say." Peter stood up as he spoke.

"Sorry, old chap. I can't make it today. I have another commitment. But tomorrow?"

"Fine. Maybe the girls would like to go with us. Then Katherine can decide if she likes the mare. She has a better eye for a horse than I have. Somehow I never took to riding. Always thought it an uncomfortable way to get from point A to point B."

"Great idea. Asking the girls. See you tomorrow. Shall we say at ten?"

Then, as if it was an afterthought, Stephen turned to ask abruptly, "Your brother Albert. Will he be back from England in time for your wedding?"

"No, his year of fostering won't be up for another two months." Peter's smile was complacent. At that moment the warm glow from a big diaphanous sun smiled on his world. But not far away thin strands of smoke from struggling peat fires drifted slowly upwards. Like Ireland's destitute, they were momentarily expecting to be blown away, diffused by a bullying wind.

An eager sun was driving away the morning mists, putting warmth back into the winter air as a carriage pulled by two perfectly matched, but otherwise quite ordinary bay horses, bowled across the bridge spanning the Liffy.

Katherine, looking like a breath of Irish spring in a green riding costume (she intended to ride the mare to try her out before a deal was closed), smiled happily up at the tall man whose possessive grey eyes were busily devouring every delicate line of her body. The other couple, Stephen and Henrietta, were leaning slightly forward in their seats, talking quietly to each other as if there was so much to be said and too little time for saying it.

Soon the carriage was passing tiny hovels with the thatch falling off, and a general air of despair about them. Despair, like a contagious disease, seemed to hang over everything in a cloying cloud that fouled the air and shrivelled the sun.

Katherine was conscious of a feeling of apprehension she couldn't shake. These people were so poor. There was so much poverty. So much hopelessness.

Even the little children, with hunger-pinched faces and protruding bellies, and mouths that rarely had much to smile about, didn't run and play like normal children. They seemed weighted down with a terrible despondency that blighted their spirits and shrivelled their souls. Sad little gnomes, she thought, doomed to a life devoid of hope. Nor did the few scrawny pigs and cows tethered in a haphazard fashion here and there alongside the road look any better. They were pre-ordained to go to pay the landlord's rent.

Yet if a tenant was caught trying to get meat for his hungry brood by poaching a salmon or shooting a rabbit it meant eviction for his family. And a long jail sentence for him in one of Britain's stinking, disease-ridden hulks. Or perhaps it would be the clink and drag of ball and chain accompanied by the sadistic cut of a vicious whip as he sweated out his life blood in a work gang, carrying rocks to build an Australian road to nowhere. A place of floggings so vicious they tore away a man's flesh until the bones shone white, a place so full of blood and horror and hopelessness that death seemed a felon's only friend. And many took their own lives to gain it.

Yet the great men in Church and Government judged such cruelty necessary to dissuade others from a life of crime. Resentment burned like a hot brick deep inside Katherine, but what could one woman do about it? Except hope neither she, nor anyone she knew, would ever be sent there. Her body tensed as she realized with a unpleasant jolt that this was the second time those same fears had troubled her. *Did that mean it was a premonition of things to come? A warning? Of course not,* she comforted herself. *I'm not superstitious.*

While she was thinking this her thoughts were interrupted by Peter's amused "A penny for your thoughts dear?"

The tension that had been stretching her as tight as an over-stretched rubber band snapped and she flashed him a flirtatious smile. "I'm afraid they would be a poor bargain for a penny." Then, in a hurry to change the subject, she pouted prettily. "How could peasants living out their lives in squalor own the sort of horse you've been telling me about, Peter? It doesn't make sense."

"The chap who has the horse isn't the owner. He's acting as an agent. For a friend, I think."

"No. It's his brother," Stephen interrupted. "I'm not sure why the owner doesn't sell it himself. Maybe it has something to do with not being allowed to own a horse worth more than five pounds."

"That doesn't make a lot of sense either," said Henrietta almost as if speaking to herself.

No one bothered to reply. Perhaps because at that moment Stephen called out, "I think this is it," as they approached a place that looked better than most of the hovels they had passed. At least this hut had a new thatch, and the pig tethered to a nearby post looked, if not fat, at least well fed.

The woman who came to the low door with two small children clinging to her skirts looked strangely out of place. She spoke with the cultured voice of one who has known a different life. Her apron was clean. She flashed them a shy smile when she heard their errand and turned to call her husband.

A thin, broad-shouldered man soon emerged from a small lean-to shed leading a dainty grey mare whose feet seemed to spurn the ground. The man raised his cap respectfully from a head of tousled hair that gleamed in the sun like polished copper. "'Tis top of the marnin' I be wishin' ye."

Katherine noticed he had sad, unnatural eyes, brown if seen from one angle, emerald-flecked from another. Perhaps in reality they were neither, but opaque, mirroring the hills and bogs of Ireland. The man had a ruddy complexion that bespoke a lifetime of sun and wind, and a body so emaciated it seemed held together by nothing but skin and sinew. She thought for a moment she must have seen him before. But of course that was impossible.

The horse beside him was fit, well groomed and beautiful. And there was an obvious spirit of trust between man and beast. She nuzzled him affectionately as he began tightening the saddle girth. A moment later the man turned and seemed on the point of assisting Katherine to mount, as any gentleman might have done, when Peter roughly elbowed him aside, cupped his own hands, and expertly handed the girl into the saddle.

As Katherine took up the reins and moved away, easing the mare from trot to canter, then lifting her lightly over a nearby hedge, Peter's face glowed with pride. They made a good pair, a perfect blending of blood and beauty.

Stephen, who had been talking to the man, now stepped closer to Peter, murmuring in an aside, "She's good, Peter. A real steal at fifteen pounds. But I fancy you might get her for less. Her owner had her bred thinking that would lower her value to five pounds, so he could keep her, but no dice."

A puzzled frown lined Peter's aristocratic forehead. "I don't understand. Why should the mare being in foal lower her value?"

"Well, it wouldn't under ordinary circumstance, but the sire was a Connemara stud of unknown parentage."

At the words "unknown parentage" Peter Moriarty

looked as if he had been kicked in the stomach by an overworked mule. "You mean she's been serviced by . . . by a . . . by a scrub?" The words came out in a rush but they sounded muffled, as if they had fought their way up through a bale of wool.

"Yes." Stephen looked perplexed as Peter put the purse he had been opening back into his pocket, shoved it down deep, and kept his hand on it as if afraid it might somehow open and spill out sovereigns without his consent. With the other hand he waved to Katherine, signalling her to return. When she did he muttered, "There's no need for you to ride further. There'll be no sale. We're going back."

"But why?" she squeaked. "The mare's perfect. I love her already." She put one hand defiantly on the grey's neck as if to stop the man from taking her away. But when she saw Peter's granite-hard face she got the sudden feeling it might be politic to turn on the charm.

She flashed him a smile designed to make him feel nothing really mattered as long as he was by her side. Tantrums could wait until after the wedding bells. But the smile faded quickly, to be replaced by a puzzled expression as she heard Stephen protest, ""But you wouldn't need to keep the foal. Sell it to the knackers if it's that bad, but I'd give you good odds it won't be. Not with that mare's breeding."

"It wouldn't matter." The words were rasped out in little more than a grunt, but they held iron-strong determination. "I'll never buy any animal that's been bred to a scrub. This mare will always carry the taint of an inferior mating. You know how popular good Irish horses have become with the English?"

"Yes. Of course I know that. But what's that got to do with not wanting the mare? Next time around you can breed her to the best hunter-stallion in Ireland. Why, man, at the price you could get her for today you couldn't go wrong. I don't see any problem."

"It's not that simple, Stephen. Once inferior seed gets into the womb there's no knowing what effect it will have on a female's future progeny. It's too bad, of course. For the mare does indeed look like a splendid creature. But under the circumstances," and he sighed deeply, "I just can't take a chance on her. Here, give the man a sovereign. That should make up for his trouble showing us the horse."

Stephen, following the mare to the lean-to, wasn't sure if his friend's sudden generosity was to ease his own conscience or to mollify his betrothed. But he needn't have worried about what Katherine would think. There was such a straining tautness about her she was afraid Peter would hear her nerves screaming beneath her skin. Her innards felt as if they had suddenly become encased in flow-ice. What had he said? He wouldn't buy the mare because she was in foal to the scrub stallion of some half-starved peasant?

Sweet Mother in Heaven! Here she was, carrying the child of someone many would consider a peasant, and betrothed to a man who had just refused to buy a good mare because . . . . Oh dear God! What if he discovered her secret? She didn't dare even think about that possibility. The flow-ice congealed into a solid mass. For a moment her mind recoiled in such a purgatory of abasement she was afraid she might faint. Then her natural resiliency took over. A daring strategy began forming in her mind.

She smiled at the man beside her as demurely as a parson's daughter, "It doesn't matter, dear. I can borrow a horse from Father when I want to ride. And of course after we're married I expect you'll see to it that I don't have much time for riding anyway." And she blushed so prettily that if Stephen and Henrietta hadn't been close he'd have swept her into his arms and devoured her with kisses.

"Oh no, Princess. I'll get you a horse. An even better one. But it will have to wait now until we're married." She snuggled her head contentedly against the scratchy roughness of his coat, secure in the belief that the crisis was behind her.

The carriage turned and clattered back the way it had come. As it rumbled closer to Dublin a secret resolve began taking shape in Katherine's brain. In some strange, inexplicable way, she knew that the mare was linked to her own destiny. She felt as certain of it as if she'd read it in the Bible. If she didn't own that mare something dreadful would happen. To her? To her husband? To her family? That part was still unclear.

However, she was too shaken by what Peter had said, the grim look on his face, to risk implementing her plan yet. She'd wait until they were married. Maybe even until after the baby was born.

Stephen, with his arm comfortably around Henrietta, studied the pair on the facing seat with a curiously questioning expression on his face. But if anyone had asked him what was bothering him he couldn't, or wouldn't, have said.

Maybe that was because Darwin hadn't yet been to the Galapagos Islands. The world hadn't yet heard of evolution. The mystery of life, the reproduction process, was still largely shrouded in darkness, compounded by ignorance and myth.

Chapter Four
Pre-Wedding Doubts

Ordinarily Katherine would have knocked at the door of her father's study before entering. But not today. She knew on this, the morning of her wedding, he would be expecting her.

As she stepped over the threshold a venerable white-haired man rose eagerly from where he had been sitting, lost in thought, in a Biedermeier chair that looked strangely out of place beside the small peat fire. Now he moved towards her with arms outstretched, his face a mixture of poorly concealed emotions.

"Ah Mavourneen, 'tis expecting you I've been." A moment later she was cradled in his arms, her face pressed comfortably against his heart as one gnarled old hand, so translucent in age the veins stood out like over-fed worms, gently stroked her head. A sudden glitter of moisture sparkled on the old man's white eyelashes. "Sure'n 'tis not easy to be saying goodbye to me datter and handing her to the keeping of another man. 'Tis almost like losing your mother, bless her sainted soul, all over again."

Katherine sniffed back her own tears. But he seemed not to notice as he continued. "Your mother meant the whole world to me. When she was killed in that hunting accident I thought my life was over too. You were only six, yet that evening you crawled up on my knee, whispering, 'Jesus must have thought Heaven needed her more than we did. But don't worry, Father. I love you. I'll take her place.'"

"And you have, Mavourneen. In every way but one. And in recent years your stepmother has done her best to take care of that need. Before that . . . well, there were gossips who whispered Lucy's mother was more than a serving girl. Those with suspicious minds and clacking tongues did a mite of speculating but only my solicitor knew the truth. He had to know, because when Lucy's mother died giving her life, I promised myself the child would always have a home here, and when I'm gone she'll be provided for." He stopped, as if his mind was recapturing long forgotten memories that must be savoured before continuing.

"Sure'n 'tis every man's dream to sire a son to continue his line, but that wasn't in the fates for me, so now I'll wait for you to give me grandsons."

"Oh Father. I'm scared." The words were more wail than whisper. "What if I can't give you grandsons? What if I can't be a good wife to Peter? What if his love changes to hate? What if . . . ?" But she stopped before she finished that sentence.

"Hush, Mavourneen. 'Tis a case of bride-jitters you be having. Begorrah, child, Peter Moriarty is the luckiest man in Dublin, and 'tis knowing it I fancy he is." Then the old man sighed. "'Tis afraid I am of not having the right words to take your mother's place at a time like this, but me darlin colleen must remember no marriage is without some tears. Grace O'Malley had to cope with tears, and you who bear her blood will also cope. Peter is a good man and 'tis thinking I am there's too much light and laughter in your soul to give way to gloom for long. So come, wipe away those cobwebs of doubt. Give me a kiss. Go and let your stepmother and Lucy . . . and your step-sister too I suppose, help you into your wedding finery.

"Tonight I'll wager you'll show young Moriarty he married a worthy scion of Ireland." And his grey fringe of chin-whiskers twitched as if titillated by their own thoughts.

"That'll do, Lucy. Now shake out the dress." An approving smile creased Mrs. O'Connor's kindly face as she nodded to a serving girl, scarcely more than a child, who had been tightening Katherine's corset with such dedication that the young bride grumbled "Ouch! Lucy! Stop it! There's no call to be cutting my body in half. Peter doesn't want his bride in pieces."

No one was paying any attention to Katherine's step-sister, Sophia, or they might have wondered why a scowl darkened her face and why she was muttering into her teeth. "He wouldn't want the whole of you if he knew."

Katherine shook her finger at Lucy in mock severity. "Lud, girl, you've made proper breathing a chore. If this is the fashion among London bonton then 'tis nothing but pity I have for the poor souls. And at this moment 'tis sorrier I am for meself. I feel as bound about as a mummy in an Egyptian tomb."

Katherine, pale now as an early spring snowdrop, clenched her fists as her step-sister elbowed Lucy aside and snatched the wedding dress of pale blue bombazine, elegant in its simplicity, from her. Lucy had been studying the label on the box and now she announced proudly, "It came from London. In England. See, I am learning to read."

"More's the pity," snarled Sophia as she gave the child a vicious shove, "Irish wenches like you don't need to read. It makes you give yourself airs." Then she fingered the soft folds of the dress.

Like herself it had come from England, and that alone

made it superior to anything the dismal Irish had to offer. Suddenly her pudding face took on a cunning look. When the plot incubating in the dark recesses of her mind hatched, there was no knowing how she might benefit.

Katherine, seated before a low mirror, watched while her stepmother brushed out her long dark tresses, admonishing Lucy to pay careful attention so someday she could do a lady's hair. "See how I wind it into a low-slung bun behind, leaving a few curls free to dance around her face. You must always make it look as if those few strands escaped the bun of their own accord." She smiled wisely at the wide-eyed Lucy. "There's nothing like a curl dancing about a pretty face to catch a man's eye and set his fingers itching to touch it. Mind you, you won't often see hair as pretty as this, but a good lady's maid can manage a hairdo that'll do wonders for the most ordinary face."

Katherine, knowing her father's secret, had brushed aside his suggestion that Lucy should be her maid. The girl, pretty and smart too, must stay and help ease the old man's loneliness at losing his older daughter. Besides until Peter became heir to his father's property he had only his allowance and bank salary. Neither were sufficient in her mind to indulge in the extravagance of a lady's maid. She'd rather that money went to keep a riding horse for herself, and maybe a carriage. Katherine didn't mind economizing on things that held little importance to her if it meant getting those she truly wanted.

Anyway, she supposed Peter could unlace her corset tonight. He'd probably want to. Later, after the thrill of doing it wore off, the kitchen maid could lace her up when she felt obliged to wear the silly thing. Which wouldn't be often if she had her way.

Katherine realized with an unpleasant start that a queasy feeling was building fast in the pit of her stomach. It's the tightness of my corset, she told herself. Women are always fainting when they wear these silly things. Especially if there's an attractive pair of male arms conveniently close.

Well, there'll be no shortage of male arms today, she thought grimly, but 'tis not falling into any of them I'll be doing. There will be tongues clacking fast enough as it is. Especially if my waist shows signs of thickening too soon. Katherine was giving her shoulders a determined twitch to dispel the dull edge of fear . . . she was never sick, and she wouldn't be now. . . when she caught Sophia's weasel-eyes studying her corseted figure with speculative intent. Sophia didn't know her secret. No one did. Except Henrietta. So why the interest?

The scrutiny continued until Katherine snapped irritably, "What's the matter, Sophia? Is mine the first corseted figure you've ever seen?"

"No. But it promises to be the most interesting."

Before Katherine could shake off the feeling of impending doom and think of some witty reply, her stepmother bustled up with a silver buttonhook, saying briskly, "Here, Sophia. Button her shoes. Lucy, you help me with the dress. It's almost time for the ceremony."

Chapter Five
A Pricked Finger

The double wedding ceremony was over, the toasts had been drunk, the guests had left. Stephen and Henrietta had driven away in a green coach. Peter and Katherine were finally alone as man and wife in the privacy of their own bedroom.

Peter smiled a warm, relaxed, and very masculine smile. It set her heart pounding in great excited thumps as she turned to melt willingly into his arms. His hands working with urgent intent at the buttons closing the back of her dress, their soft warmth as they slipped it off, their lingering tenderness that was almost reverence as they stroked the creamy smoothness of her shoulders before hurrying to loosen the wretched corset strings, drenched her in an agony of desire. When his hands began caressing the white mounds of her softly rounded breasts she suddenly grew taut and pulled away from him.

The scissors? She'd carefully hidden them in her reticule. But where had she left it? A startled glance around the room showed no sign of it. Then she remembered. She'd dropped it out of sight, on the far side of the bed. Peter, assuming her sudden change was due to maidenly modesty, whispered as he carried her to the bed, "Don't worry, Princess. I'll try and make your first time easy." Then he strode to the dressing room to disrobe. When he came back his nakedness and his desire were covered loosely by a fine woollen dressing gown.

While her husband was gone, Katherine had moved quickly to take something from her reticule and hide it under her pillow. Now she was smiling up at him as she stretched her warm arms to bring his dark head closer to her own.

And then life and time blurred in a blinding surge of passion and desire.

When finally their lusts were satiated and she was cradled in the love and warmth of her husband's arms, Katherine forced herself to stay awake until the deep even breathing of the man beside her told her he was asleep. Cautiously she reached for the scissors she'd hidden under the pillow, jabbed them into her fore-finger, then carefully withdrew it so as not to leave a tell-tale smear on the white linen pillow slip. After squeezing her finger to make sure it bled enough (she wasn't sure how much "enough" should be, but better be safe than sorry), she smeared blood generously over her upper thighs and the sheets. Then, to be on the safe side, she wiped a little on Peter's legs too. But the finger still bled. Great Mother Mary! What if it wouldn't stop?

Frantically she reached for her reticule, found a handkerchief and wrapped it tightly around the finger, willing it to stop bleeding. And it did. Only now she had a bloody handkerchief to get rid of. Oh well, it could be easily hidden under the pillow until there was a chance to wash it out. A self-satisfied smile curved her lovely lips as she drifted off to sleep, confident her husband was all hers now. He would never suspect. Unless her baby strongly resembled its father. But that was a chasm Katherine hadn't yet reached.

When Peter finally awoke and pulled back the portières around the four-poster bed, sunlight was flooding the room. He yawned, stretched lazily, and turned to study

Katherine's face, which, relaxed in sleep, bore a look of childish innocence and complete trust. Overwhelmed, he could scarcely believe this beautiful woman was really his wife. His gaze was soft and filled with desire as his eyes rested longingly on her face.

Gently he raised a finger to trace the perfect bow of her lips, slightly parted now in sleep, caressed the slender line of her throat, the firm, well-rounded breasts, and then slid across the flat stomach and down until with a sort of reverence he touched the secret place below. Katherine murmured sleepily and then, suddenly conscious that there was a naked, hard-muscled body pressing against hers, reached up sensuous arms to pull him still closer. Her urgency matched his own.

How long they lay entwined in a lovers' embrace neither could have said, but when Peter finally got out of bed, pulled on his dressing gown and looked down at her slender nakedness, his eyes were suddenly full of compassion and self-condemnation.

He dropped down on the bed beside her and gathered her gently in his arms, murmuring, "Oh, my darling Princess, can you ever forgive me? I didn't mean to hurt you. Truly I didn't. It's just that, well . . ." He was interrupted by Katherine's soft laughter floating warm and sensuous in the quiet bedroom. "Oh, my love! It was because I wanted what you had to give as much as you wanted to give it. Anyway it didn't really hurt. Not for more than a second." She thought she shouldn't dismiss the matter too lightly or he might get suspicious.

While Peter was getting dressed she quickly retrieved the scissors and blood-stained handkerchief from under the pillow. The scissors she shoved to the very bottom of her reticule, the hanky she left near the top, so she wouldn't forget to take it out and wash it at the first opportunity.

Then, to her consternation, she noticed that in picking up the scissors she had somehow re-pricked her finger, for there was a drip of blood on it. Hurriedly she raised it to her mouth and sucked the drop away. But another persisted in taking its place. She had to do something. And quickly. Before Peter came back. But what? Then she thought of a simple little gold brooch she often wore. But a frantic search in her reticule failed to reveal it. Then she remembered. She had used it to pin an extra hanky under her dress.

By the time Peter returned fully clothed she was sitting on the edge of the bed in her shift, staring ruefully at a brooch in her hand and a spot of blood about to drop from her index finger. To the question in her husband's eyes she said simply, as a small child might, "I pricked my finger. It's bleeding "

"Well, Princess, let's get a handkerchief and wipe it away." He glanced around but not immediately seeing one, snatched up her reticule before she could protest. Frozen in timeless terror she watched helpless as he opened it, reached inside, and pulled out a handkerchief stained with dried blood. She forced a laugh. "Oh, dear. I forgot. This silly brooch is always pricking my finger. I don't know why I keep using it."

"I don't either." Peter spoke with an aura of authority as he took the brooch from her hand and tossed it carelessly aside. Then with his arm comfortably around her waist he picked up her finger and raised it to his lips, sucking the pricked spot until the bleeding stopped.

As the days passed Peter soared to new heights of happiness and Katherine was filled with the exquisite sweetness of one who is experiencing Heaven.

Chapter Six
Is God's Supply of Angels So Low?

When Peter returned to his duties in a Dublin bank Katherine threw her energy into learning to cook, manage a home, and entertain guests in a way that would make Peter proud of her. She supposed that was what would be expected of a bank manager's wife.

But she still found time to ride. Her father, Seamus O'Connor, had given her Jeremy, a well-bred sixteen-hand mahogany-bay gelding who had been her favourite horse ever since she had outgrown Boots, a sturdy Connemara pony with four white socks.

Jeremy, with black points, a tiny white snip between his nostrils, and the look of eagles in his eye, was a level-headed animal, equally at home between the shafts of a city phaeton or soaring over hedges to the ringing cries of tally-ho. Yet despite that, Katherine couldn't get a certain grey mare out of her mind.

Owning the grey had become an obsession. An obsession that dominated her thoughts the way lamps attract moths, singeing their wings, sometimes burning them to a crisp. For the time being she'd pretend to be satisfied with Jeremy, because Peter mustn't buy her another horse until she'd had time to carry out her plan to own the grey. And if she played her cards carefully, he wouldn't.

One evening Katherine, in a simple dress of sprigged white lawn and looking as demure as a sixteen-year-old alone for the first time with a suitor, smiled shyly at her husband. But the finger softly tracing teasing circles on the back of his hand sent a sensual message that brought a hot rush of desire. Dear God, how he loved this wife of his.

As his arm about her tightened, she raised her eyes to his, then dropped them as if overcome by a sudden rush of modesty. Her voice when she spoke was scarcely louder than the whispering of a soft summer breeze. "Darling, don't you think we ought to wait until we're settled in Grandon before you buy me a horse?"

Peter's well-marked brows lifted in surprise, the indulgent smile flickering around his mouth was quickly replaced by a look of settled resolve as he got up to lean against the mantel-piece the better to see her face. "But, Princess, I planned . . ."

Before he could finish speaking Katherine raised serious eyes to his. It was time to fire her clincher if she wanted to win this argument.

Clasping her hands primly in her lap she murmured shyly, "Peter, until the baby is born it might be wiser if I don't ride much. Besides, Jeremy goes so well in the phaeton I'll be safe driving him. Even in Dublin traffic."

Hearing the word "baby" Peter jumped like a shot rabbit. He reached her in two eager strides, swept her into his arms, and smothered her with kisses, murmuring, "Princess darling. You've made me the proudest man in Dublin."

Katherine smiled craftily against his collar. Peter lacked an eye for a horse. One grey mare would look much like any other to him. She could buy the mare and have it sent to her father's stables to be foaled out, saying it was to be a surprise birthday present for Peter . . . which of course he mustn't know about until she gave the word. It seemed like a very simple and sensible plan. All she had to do was find the mare, and buy her. It almost sounded too easy.

Peter's promotion had become official. He would be leaving Dublin soon to open the Provincial Bank of Ireland's new branch office in Grandon. But before moving there he was anxious to see the town and meet some of the people he would be dealing with.

He had hoped Katherine might go with him but she had said. "It's best you go on your own the first time. You'll meet more of the right people if you're not worried about your wife sitting bored and restless in lodgings smelling of peat and poverty."

"I'll miss you too, dear," she had whispered, clinging to him as if she would never let him go when it came time to say goodbye. Finally she pulled away, smiling bravely up at him through tear-misted eyes. "But 'tis only a few days you'll be gone. And while you're away 'tis thinking I'll be doing of your getting back." Tension sometimes made Katherine lapse into street Irish.

"That's my brave girl. We'll make it a second honeymoon." With those words and a hug so fierce Katherine wondered how there could be any breath left in her, he was gone.

Katherine had four days on her own. That ought to give her time to carry out her plan. Except she wasn't clear how to find the farm with the grey mare. She knew it was somewhere in the Wicklow hills. She supposed when she reached the general vicinity of the place there would be landmarks she would recognize. If she didn't, one could always stop and ask directions. Except now she suddenly realized she didn't know whose farm she ought to ask directions to.

"I know," she told herself, "I'll visit Henrietta this afternoon and casually bring up the occasion of our trip to see the mare, and then as if it is only idle curiosity ask if she remembers the name of the man. I'm sure I can do it without raising her suspicions. She's such a trusting soul."

The young brides had so much to talk about it was almost time to leave before Katherine managed to work in the question she had come to ask.

At first Henrietta had shaken her head. "I don't pay much attention to the names of labourers. Or tenants. They all sound so much alike. But wait, I do remember. When I heard Stephen call the woman Mrs. Tully I wondered if she could be related to your father's groom, but of course Tully is a common name and with the peasants all having such large families, there could be hundreds of Tullys. And none of them related."

Katherine nodded in agreement, and shortly afterwards kissed Henrietta warmly and took her leave.

That evening Katherine fed Jeremy an extra measure of grain and told Bridget, the maid, that as Peter would be gone for a few days, and she, Katherine, intended to visit a friend while he was away, it might be a good time for Bridget to go and see her family. "Especially as your mother is expecting her thirteenth child and can surely use some extra help. And Bridget, there's a couple of old shawls and a woollen skirt in this basket. The skirt won't fit your mother until after the baby comes "*and then the poor soul will be pregnant and swelling again within a three-month*" but the shawls will be useful. And before you leave go to the meat-safe and take out a slab of bacon and some butter and eggs, and oh yes, there's a loaf of barm brack. Take that too. I baked it before Peter left. It'll be stale before he gets back, so your family might as well have it."

"Oh ma'am, thank'ee ma'am. Sure'n 'tis a holy angel ye be. Jest like me Marm seys ye are." Having said that, Bridget, looking as if she was torn between the desire to hug her mistress and the knowledge she ought to curtsey, settled for the curtsey, then ran happily from the room.

Poor child. If I'm the best she can do for an angel then God's supply of angels must be so low He's scratching the bottom of the barrel. Katherine's face looked unusually grim. The skeleton fingers of remorse had reached out and grabbed her by the throat. *My sins are like the waves on a mighty ocean. Always more waiting to wash ashore.*

The next morning the sun was a scarlet orb hanging just above the horizon when Jeremy's iron-shod feet clattered down Sackville Street and over Carlisle bridge. The waters of the Liffy, reflecting back the sun's first light, ran red as blood. Involuntarily Katherine shivered, not certain if it was caused by the coolness of the day, or someone walking on her grave.

After leaving the city behind she gave Jeremy a free rein and the great mahogany-bay stretched into a stride that ate the miles. The twitter of birds practising their early dawn rehearsal had now changed to a full-throated morning chorus that rose around her in a blend of many voices.

Gradually the distant purple of far-off hills took on a green-tinged mistiness. Then that too changed until they became the emerald green of Ireland, pin-pricked on the less exposed slopes with splashes of gold and purple, the skeletal remnants of last year's more persistent stalks of gorse and heather. Becoming more frequent were great outcroppings of rock.

She travelled a country broken by wandering ravines and rocky hillsides with their tiny fields outlined in blackthorn hedges or free-standing stone fences. And now too the hovels, the only homes the peasants ever hoped to have, worsened, telling a grim story of poverty and hopelessness.

Remembering her step-sister's scathing remarks about the Irish, Katherine involuntarily tightened the reins, making Jeremy switch his tail in protest. "The peasants deserve to be poor. If they weren't so lazy they wouldn't need to live in filth and squalor. It's no wonder their English landlords have so little sympathy for them. How can anyone respect people who share their hovels with chickens and pigs, and breed like rats? It wouldn't take a whole lot of effort to put up a shed for their animals. Water, soap and elbow-grease would soon take care of the dirt. Don't make the excuse to me that their homes are dirty and damp, as well as cold, because the thatch is gone. It shouldn't take much skill to thatch a roof. Or dig peat to fuel their fires. A few pegs, a hammer (my goodness, they could use a stone for a hammer if need be, there's enough of them lying about), and they could repair broken boards and sagging doors if anyone had the will to do it. And if the women planted flowers around their door . . . "

Sophia's list of things the tenants might do, would do if the Irish had the gumption of the English . . . her tone implied . . . went on and on.

As much as Katherine hated to admit it, there was some truth to what Sophia said. But with one major exception. One *had* to know the facts.

The day a tenant put a new thatch on a roof, built a shelter for his animals, repaired a hedge, carted a few more stones off a rocky slope, planted another half-dozen hills of potatoes, or improved his holding in any way, his rent went up. And with rents and tithes already exorbitantly high, few tenants on poorer soil had any hope of ever rising above the abject poverty into which they had been born, and in which they would die.

Katherine wondered bitterly how much enthusiasm Sophia would have for cleanliness if her life-energy revolved around scraping together rent money to keep a roof, no matter how miserable, over her head. How much enthusiasm could she muster, and maintain, for trying to grow flowers when every green shoot was rooted up and eaten by a lean and searching pig? How long until she saw the futility of sweeping constantly accumulating dust from a dirt floor? How long could she listen to the hungry whimpering of a brood of listless children? The grumbling of a husband so emaciated there wasn't enough stamina or spirit left in him for a paying day's work, even if the opportunity presented itself, because there was little but potatoes (and often too few of them) to fill his or his family's distended bellies? And probably she'd have another child on the way. To live? Or to starve?

"Faith and Bejabbers! 'Tis wagering Oi be she'd be not one wit improved over yon Irish peasant women." Katherine had spoken aloud in the vernacular of the street Irish, with such vehemence Jeremy was startled, and he leaped as if stung by a hornet.

Now, as she calmed her startled mount, she looked about and realized she must have come further than she had thought. Some of the hovels began to look almost familiar. But there must be thousands of huts that look no better, and no worse, than these, she told herself. I'll stop soon and inquire if anyone knows the name Tully. If not, perhaps they've heard of the grey mare. There can't be many mares like her in these parts. The locals, with the keen eye for good horseflesh that's common to all Irishmen, would almost certainly know her.

Suddenly, and without any warning, she pulled Jeremy to a walk in a way that made the horse toss his head in protest. What was that up ahead? There appeared to be a commotion. A confrontation of some sort. Approaching slowly, she heard a harsh, raucous voice booming with self-assumed authority: "Yer out now. And yer stays out, hear? The thatch comes down termorrow. So quit yer snivelling. Wailing won't change me mind. Pay yer rent and ye stays. No rent and out ye go. Them's the landlord's rules. 'Tis naught to me whither ye finds work or starves in yon ditch."

A big burly agent, for such he was, looking as if he had a chunk of chilled steel for a heart, turned away from the figures huddled on the ground long enough to throw an evil grin totally devoid of humour in the general direction of Katherine, who was sitting on Jeremy, staring in stunned disbelief at the tableau being played out in front of her.

The object of the man's attention were two women. One, a young, tired-looking mother with two scrawny, wide-eyed children clinging to her skirts, embraced her off-spring in mute and terrible silence, as if despondency and exhaustion had withered the roots of her tongue. The other, an older woman with a sunken face, her match-stick arms clutching a body so thin and frail it looked as if the arms were all that held the skin on her bony skeleton, cowered on the ground moaning, in obvious despair. Standing well back and huddled together as if hoping to escape notice and therefore perhaps delay the time of their own eviction, were a handful of women and children. Katherine supposed they were neighbours.

She had heard about the cruel evictions and the uncaring attitude of agents, but this man's cold, naked brutality was stark and terribly real. She felt suddenly sick. Snakes were writhing and churning inside her stomach. Great Mother Mary! What if this were happening to her? Or her family?

The agent's dense black brows hooded snake-eyes whose thick lids added a look of depravity to a face already repugnant. He cast an anxious glance to where a storm cloud was hanging low on the western horizon, raised one eyebrow to suggest Katherine too had better pay it heed, then turned and viciously lashed a good-looking black mare into a headlong gallop.

Katherine, feeling as if she had turned to stone, dismounted stiffly and, after tying Jeremy to a post, approached the young mother. Little more than a child herself, the woman had a face torn with worry but dry-eyed, as if life had long ago dried up all her tears. Her two skinny toddlers, with no shoes and dirt-streaked faces, clung to the safety of their mother's threadbare skirt and stared wide-eyed at the well-dressed young woman approaching them. The pretty lady was smiling, and in the lives of these little waifs smiles were a novelty.

Katherine, trying desperately to keep smiling despite tears that persisted in misting her eyes, impulsively reached out her arms to encompass all three, whispering, "Look, I've brought you some sandwiches." She had carried them with her in case she might find no convenient pub to supply a meal.

As the children wolfed down the food, Katherine moved to comfort the older woman keening as if for the death of a loved one. Which indeed she was. Her son had been killed by a falling rock two weeks before, and without him the little family had no hope of ever paying rent. They were utterly, absolutely destitute. "But have you no relatives who could take you in?" asked Katherine gently of the old woman whose bleak and rheumy eyes showed a total lack of hope. The woman only shook her head, clutched a well-worn shawl tighter around her frail body, and wailed afresh.

The younger woman — she had been pretty once — spoke with such bitterness as Katherine had never heard. "There's no one. Those here-abouts can't help us. They can't take in extra mouths when they can't feed their own." As an after-thought she added, "Me only brither's in Canada," in a manner that suggested they had as little hope of getting to Canada as they had of going to the moon.

"You can't stay here. With no food. No shelter." Katherine's own voice seemed to have taken on a sudden wail.

The young woman shrugged her shoulders with the dejected air of one whom life had long ago beaten down and totally defeated. "Not much choice, ma'am. Others before us have starved in the ditches. We won't be the first. Nor the last. With spring coming perhaps there'll be roots to eat. Until the frosts come. Then . . ." she stopped speaking as if there was no need to continue.

An idea was forming unbidden in Katherine's brain. She had heard Stephen tell Peter that immigrant families were going to North America for as little as a few pounds. He said some of the more caring landlords were actually paying their tenants' passage to the New World just to get rid of them. This eased the landowner's conscience as well as freeing up his holdings so the land could be turned into more profitable sheep and cattle pastures. But Stephen had also told Peter that on some ships conditions were so terrible that many who left Ireland with visions of a better life in a new country died miserably in the holds of disease-ridden ships. *Well,* Katherine thought irreverently, as her fingers rummaged inside the tiny reticule she had fastened securely around her waist, *that's a chance people with no choice have to take.*

When she withdrew her hand it held the gold sovereigns she had carefully hoarded from a small yearly inheritance left her by her mother. She was honest enough not to buy a mare her husband didn't approve of with money he had given her. But now she supposed grimly the mare would have to wait. And then in a rush, as if afraid she might change her mind, she quickly thrust the money into the young woman's work-gnarled hand. "Here. Take this. It's enough, and more, to buy passage to Canada. When you get there I pray the Good Lord in Heaven will help you find your brother."

Before the startled woman could do more than shower her hand with kisses, or the children could resume licking their sandwich paper to make sure no crumb was being wasted, she turned abruptly and hurried to untie Jeremy. As she rode away cries of thanks and prayers for "the sweat angel lady's health and safety" followed her.

Drat it. What made me go and do that? Katherine thought angrily. *Now it will be months before I have money enough to buy the mare. By that time someone else might have her. Oh Damn! Damn! Damn!* Then she shrugged in a philosophical manner. *It isn't as if the poor souls didn't need help.* Then on a bitter note, *But there are thousands no better off. One person can't help them all.*

Even if I can't buy the mare now, since I've come this far there can't be any harm in going to see her. And having reached that decision Katherine set Jeremy into a brisk canter that soon brought her within sight of the cottage with the freshly thatched roof, and as before a woman with a clean apron came to the door to greet her. "Mare, ma'am? There be no mare here. Not now. She's gone a fortnight since. To a young lady from Dublin, ma'am. Like yerself, ma'am. Though t'wasn't seeing her I was. Me husband's brother, him that's a foine groom in Dublin, owned the precious creature and the young lady where he works had a fancy for the mare. Though she niver came to see the sweet animal." This was said as if it was a puzzle to the speaker that anyone would buy a mare they hadn't seen.

Katherine saw nothing puzzling about it. The young woman, whoever she was, had simply told the groom to find her a suitable horse, and he had done so. Well, so much for that. Thanking the woman, she turned Jeremy and rode away, feeling inexplicably as if she had been stabbed in the back.

Witnessing the horrors of an eviction had upset Katherine, and now anxious not to return the way she had come she swung Jeremy onto a likely-looking track that led through a stand of towering beech trees. It would no doubt join up with the main road a few miles further on.

Sun-stroked leaves danced and fluttered in the afternoon breeze, their tiny islands of light and shade dappling the darkness of austere old tree trunks. But the path, for it was little more, was liberally sprinkled with stones, so for safety's sake she held Jeremy to a walk. Sunk in morbid speculation about the fate of evicted tenants, she lost track of time and distance.

Finally a full bladder warned her she had better find some secluded spot to relieve herself.

There was a trail branching off just ahead. Maybe she should ride down that? But the gloomy overhang of trees, the bordering rocky boulders, high enough to conceal from sight those travelling it, be they man or beast, sent cold chills up her spine. Nor did she like the stone-strewn pathway . . . stones that lay like the whitening knucklebones of abandoned hope. Dangerous for a speeding horse. There was something dank and sinister about the place. Even evil. Jeremy sensed it too. He tossed his head and showed the whites of his eyes. She turned back.

As she did, a magnificent stag appeared in the road ahead. She pulled Jeremy to a stop, marvelling at the noble beauty of an animal so splendid it would have set the hand of a Synders or a Landseer reaching for a brush.

Then, as if acknowledging her presence (or inviting her to follow), he dipped his head in a bow, flicked his tail in a proud and autocratic manner, and disappeared among the trees. Katherine, hoping to see him again, moved slowly to where he had disappeared. Although peering carefully through an overhang of branches revealed no stag, she was pleased to see a tiny clearing, caressed by sunbeams and carpeted with grass.

What better place to stop and let Jeremy eat his fill, and rest a bit? She too felt tired and nearly exhausted, but there would be no food for her. She grimaced at the thought of the sandwiches she had given away. Then she shrugged. "Thy need was greater than mine."

The gelding's teeth were tearing hungrily at the grass when Katherine settled herself comfortably against a tree trunk, intending to stop for less than an hour. She noticed that when sitting she had a clear view of the trail just vacated, but unless a passer-by stooped low they could see no sign of her. Comforted by that thought and the warmth of the sun on her face, she closed her eyes.

When she opened them it was with a start. She had an uncomfortable, yet distinct, feeling that a dark and ominous shadow had crossed over her face, that two gruff and furtive voices had been whispering secrets too dangerous to be spoken aloud. "Whist lad, yon rope's brought justice today. Now oi hides the evidence and may the divil take his soul."

The words had sounded real enough, but they didn't make any sense to Katherine's sleep-clogged mind. But then dreams rarely make sense when one awakens. So of course it was a dream. It had to be. There was no one here. A quick peek out of her hideaway showed only a deserted road. But what about the heavy tramp of boots? Had she dreamed that too?

Even now she fancied she could hear footsteps fading into the distance. She supposed she had gotten too tired before she stopped and now her mind was playing tricks. She could hear Jeremy nibbling grass behind her in the desultory fashion of a horse with nothing better to do. That was real enough. It also meant his hunger was appeased and it was time to go.

As she was heaving her pregnant body to its feet, the sound of a breaking twig, the soft thunk of hooves on mossy soil, the jingle of a bridle chain, catapulted her upright. Chains? There were no chains on Jeremy's bridle!

Fear spun in her mind like a leaf caught in a white-water whirlpool, but she forced herself to move towards the sound. As she did she heard Jeremy's soft squeal, the squeal of a horse warning another not to come too close. The next moment she saw her bay gelding watching a tall horse half hidden in the trees, a horse which except for being black and having a feminine head, looked a dead ringer for Jeremy.

But the black's coat was dull, matted with dried lather. Her eyes were listless, her mouth bloody, there were deep whip welts on her flanks. Her head drooped. She sidestepped nervously, limping, when Katherine moved towards her. No wonder she limped. Her knees were scraped raw and already puffing up. They would need immediate attention if the swelling was not to become a permanent blemish.

Crooning softly as if the animal was a frightened child, Katherine was finally able to reach the bridle, to loosen it and the saddle girth. When she moved exploratory fingers softly over the mare's quivering body, the animal actually cringed in terror. "You poor dear," she murmured as she felt a maze of old and new welts criss-crossing each other. "My guess is you've had a rough run-in with a devil more fiendish than old Beelzebub himself. Wouldn't I just love to get my hands on him. I'd give him a taste of his own whip he wouldn't soon forget." From the grim set of her face, the anger blazing in her eyes, it was easy to believe she meant exactly what she said.

She petted the black until the mare quit trembling, then stooped to run her hand over the animal's front legs. When she straightened, a puzzled expression was fighting with the anger that suffused her face. What to the eye appeared as a barely discernible ruffling of the hair above the right fetlock, to the hand felt like a heavy welt. It might have been caused by a sharp blow from a whip handle. Or had it been caused by something else. . . ?

Katherine studied the mare with such concentration that furrows formed between her eyes. Then, as if neither perspicacity nor intuition were helping to answer the questions tumbling about in her mind, she reached for Jeremy's bridle. "Sorry Blackie, but I've got to go. I hope someone finds you and takes care of those knees before it's too late. You stay here and rest. There's lots to eat, and I'll stop at the first pub I see and tell them about you. Maybe they'll know who you belong to. Why you're running loose."

As Katherine rode from the little glade the sun was already dipping its great red belly into a black jagged horizon of storm clouds. They appeared to be moving up fast. Jeremy tossed his head impatiently but she held him to a gentle jog. Better to get wet than have him stumble and fall, as she supposed the black must have done. However, as soon as Jeremy reached a better road she let him settle into a rocking-chair canter.

Roiling clouds flung out stabbing shafts of lightning that pierced the deepening gloom. Katherine wasn't afraid of getting wet, but riding in a bad electrical storm frightened her, so it was with welcome relief that she swung onto a broad carriage road. The wind, risen now to a screeching fury, was lashing trees and everything in its path with sadistic frenzy. Katherine, crouching low in the saddle and with the wind behind her, never looked back as Jeremy stretched into his racing gallop.

Thunder marching steadily closer could scarcely be heard above the maniacal roar of the wind. But there was no doubt as to the ferocity of the approaching storm.

The young woman had no idea how far it was to shelter, or indeed if she might find any. She was completely and thoroughly lost. But Jeremy seemed to know where he was going. She had no choice but to trust his instinct.

Although the rain continued to pelt down, the main

storm veered off towards the sea almost as suddenly as it had come up. As the rain lessened and Katherine slowed her steaming horse to a walk, she realized with a surge of dismay that Jeremy was labouring now, his head low, and breathing hard. He seemed almost spent. She remembered guiltily that Jeremy was getting old. It wasn't fair to expect him to have the stamina of youth.

Her blue eyes suddenly lit up, their colour intensified and deepened by the dark smudges of fatigue beneath them. Her thoughts were back on the grey mare. There might still be a chance to buy her. If she did, perhaps the disturbing feeling that the mare was linked with her own destiny would go away. Just find her new owner, and negotiate a sale. If said quickly it sounded simple. There couldn't be that many grey horses in Dublin. She'd ask Patrick about it when next she saw him. He might already know the mare's whereabouts. Then something like a strangled wail escaped her lips.

Soon she wouldn't be seeing anyone in Dublin. Not for months. Maybe not for years? Grandon was to be her home.

While these thoughts percolated with slow resentment in Katherine's brain, Jeremy's head came up and, mincing a little, he half swung his head to look behind. Katherine turned to follow his eyes. To her utter amazement, there, a few yards from Jeremy's tail, was the bobbing head of a lame horse, its bridle chains catching the last vestige of a dying day. Holy Mother of God — the creature followed us! Oh, those poor battered knees! Well, one thing was sure. The animal mustn't go on following her. If it was to escape the knackers it needed rest. Its knees attended to.

Haggard from hunger and exhaustion herself, she gave a small cry, when a sharp bend in the road revealed the dim lights of what looked like a public house ahead.

Dismounting stiffly in the courtyard, she handed Jeremy's reins to a stable boy, saying, "Give him a double measure of grain and a good rubdown. The same for the black, please. But her knees need attention. Until a farrier recommends something better, apply alternate hot and cold compresses to help bring down the swelling. Can you manage that?"

"Yes ma'am, thankee ma'am. Sure and 'tis happy oi'll be doing it for ye." Then he added as if in after-thought. "Me fither's a farrier, perchance ye wishes to speak to him?"

"No thanks, boy. The black isn't my horse. I don't know who owns her. She just followed me here. Her owner must decide what should be done."

While speaking Katherine was feeling in her reticule for money, and realized with a sense of shock that there were only a couple of shillings and a few farthings left. "But of course I'll pay for what I've asked done. Here." And she offered him two shillings, not sure if he would consider that sufficient pay for a night's work with the mare.

Evidently he did, for he flashed her another smile, then murmured, "Me thinks Oi knows him who owned yon mare. And bejabbers 'tis better off oim thinking she be without the loikes of him."

Katherine, not noticing the boy had spoken of the owner in the past tense, turned and, dragging one leaden foot after the other, moved nervously toward the dingy entrance of what a sign above proclaimed to be Murphy's Pub.

Suddenly the thought grew in her mind like a festering boil that she might be safer riding Jeremy, even in the storm, which had stopped now, than entering this pub. Women of her station did not normally ride without a male escort. And certainly never at night. Yet here she was, not merely alone, but wet, bedraggled, and on the verge of collapse. Even worse, she had been followed by a horse with damaged knees and a suspicious welt on one leg. What would people think? On top of all that she had almost no money. Certainly not enough to pay for a night's lodging.

Despair like a convict's ball and chain dragged at her thoughts. She was tempted to crouch in the shadows and wait for Jeremy to eat, and then go on. But common sense told her that without food she could faint and tumble from the saddle. Where was the sense in that? She had done nothing wrong. Besides, she was cold and very, very hungry, and she didn't want this escapade to harm her unborn child.

A determined glint shone in her eyes as she pushed open the pub door, but her heart was hammering so furiously she shot a covert look around the room hoping no one else could hear it. To her surprise no one even looked up when she entered.

In the smoky haze cast by a small peat fire a few sputtering candles shed a miniscule yellow glow on little knots of roughly dressed men, talking in uneasy undertones . . . the way men do when there is trouble afoot.

Hoping to soak up some of the fire's meagre warmth, Katherine moved closer to it, and in doing so attracted attention to herself. The room suddenly became ominously silent. The men shot her quick, furtive glances as if wanting to see all there was to see without appearing to show any interest in her. She turned and rapped authoritatively on a well-scrubbed wooden table, hoping to attract the landlord's attention so she could order food.

Instead, a buxom woman with plump rosy cheeks and a motherly face came hurrying from the kitchen, wiping her hands as she walked on an large white apron that extended from neck to ankle.

"Oh, deary me. Yer ladyship's soaked. And 'tis not getting much drying from this poor excuse of a fire yer'll be doing." She spared a disdainful glance for the fire, pushed at it briefly with the toe of her heavy black boot, then hurried on. "Yer best come in the kitchen with me, ma'am. 'Tis toasty warm in there. After yer dries out and gets some vittles. . . Irish stew, fresh baked soda bread, and hot apple tart is what there is tonight,. . . into yer belly, ye'll be wanting a night's lodging Oi's no doubt."

Katherine shook her head with a forlorn little smile. "I can't afford a night's lodging. I have no money. I gave . . . I lost it," she added quickly, then wondered in some surprise why she hadn't told the woman the truth. "Oh but I have a few coins left," she hurried to explain, afraid the woman might think she couldn't pay for even a simple meal.

The woman, who had been bustling about helping Katherine off with her wet outer clothes and pulling a chair near the fire for her, stood back now with arms akimbo. "Yer Ladyship best know yer'll not be leaving Molly Malone's public house hungry. Nor tired. Money or no, there's food and lodging for yer tonight. Poor young leddy, and yer so heavy with child as shouldn't be out on such a night a-tall a-tall. Yer best stay in here with me. I don't want them louts out there a-staring at you over their pints. Whatever yer reason for being here wet and alone is naught concern of theirs. Or mine." She plunked a huge platter of steaming stew down in front of Katherine, with the sharp admonition, "Eat!"

As she sliced and buttered a generous piece of soda bread, thick and fragrant from the oven, Molly Malone looked towards the door with an air of nervous apprehension. Then she leaned forward and spoke in a low, almost conspiratorial voice. "The men are upset tonight. There's been an accident. Only there's them as are whispering maybe it weren't no accident. Brutus Hardstone, an evil man, an agent hated and feared in these parts more than the divil hisself, was thrown from his horse this afternoon and killed. Me, I ses 'tis no wonder he was killed. The marvel is it didn't happen sooner. Not when he rides like one demented, one hand on the reins, the other on the whip. But there's them as say his mare, too noble a beast for the likes of him to be abusin, would never stumble and fall. Unless someone set out to trip her." Her voice now was scarcely a whisper, as one talking to herself. "A cord secretly stretched across a narrow, dim-lit path has tripped more than one horse I'll wager. And when it's over, and the rope is gone, where's the evidence? Unless the rider is only stunned. In which case who's to tell the difference between a held stone smashing a man's skull or a stone on the road doing the same thing?" Then she sighed. "But if the authorities call it murder there'll be more evictions, more beatings, more burnings. So much cruelty gets heaped on the poor poverty-trodden peasants so landlords can go on living as if it was their duty to amuse themselves to death."

"But whist now! What be Oi thinking to burden a tired young leddy's ears with such troubles. If them as knows don't blab, the authorities may let it pass. Sure'n you just finish yer apple tart while I goes and puts a hot brick in your bed to warm it. And then yer can put yer poor wee tired head down for a good sleep before ye rides further."

Katherine thanked her and before long found herself in a bare little room containing nothing but a simple bed with heavy patchwork coverlets, and a wooden chair. But it was clean. In minutes she had drifted into the sleep of the utterly exhausted. Tomorrow would be time enough to tell her story. If she had to.

Katherine awoke to find cheery sunbeams frolicking in every corner of the room. A gentle breeze caressed the latticed window. Someone, perhaps Molly Malone herself, had recently left a ewer of hot water and a basin on the chair. There was soap and a linen towel beside it. Silently blessing the woman's kindness, Katherine climbed out of bed to enjoy a thorough sponge bath before getting dressed.

She went downstairs wondering what a new day might bring. Last night's crowds were gone. The pub was deserted save for three men in the uniform of the Royal Irish Constabulary. Were they travellers like herself? Or here to investigate a murder? Her heart felt as if it was in the grip of a boa constrictor, but she held her head high as she walked to a table in a small alcove. She hoped to eat, listen and observe, without herself being subjected to scrutiny.

Molly's smiling "Top-o-the-marnin to ye ma'am, 'tis a new person ye be looking this marning" was accompanied by a platter of hot scones and blackberry jam plus a serving of crisply fried bacon and one egg. Molly hesitated before going back to her kitchen, fidgeting with the cutlery as if she had something on her mind and wasn't sure of the best way to get it out. In the end she said nothing, but looked towards the three men picking fastidiously at their meal and left to return in a few minutes with a scalding cup of tea. "The stable lad'll bring yer horse when 'tis ready ye be to leave. With sunshine, yer'll be having a bonny ride to Dooblin. 'Tis not far."

It's almost as if she wants me out of here before the men decide to question me, Katherine thought with a smile as she pressed the last of her coins, along with a fine silk scarf, into the woman's hands, hoping that might be recompense enough for Molly's kindness.

She was glad the scarf wasn't the one Patrick had given her. That one had been a gift to his grandfather from a wealthy French aristocrat he had helped escape from a forced marriage. The countess had told the young Irishman the scarf had once belonged to the wife of a Chinese mandarin who claimed it would bring good luck to whoever wore it. She said it was a replica of a painting the 8th-century emperor Ming Huang had of the beautiful horses that were his special pride and joy. Horses that had been sent to him as a tribute from the most influential sheik in all of Central Asia. Years later, in the Mongol Period, another emperor commissioned Chao Meng-fu, acknowledged as a skilled painter as well as a sorcerer possessing great magical powers, to reproduce the earlier painting of the horses onto a fine silk scarf. The Mongolian emperor wanted it as a gift for his number-one wife so no demons would harm her.

Katherine didn't put a lot of stock in the scarf bringing its wearer good luck. It certainly hadn't done much for Patrick's family, but it was distinctive. And she liked it.

Now she shoved all thoughts of the scarf aside and tried to catch snatches of the men's conversation. "Sure'n 'tis seeing the mare meself I'd like to be doing. 'Tis a chance it weren't no accident she fell." The speaker wore the uniform of a corporal.

"Oh, blast ye and yer ferret nose, Mike. Me, I'm for pressing on. 'Tis too far we've got to ride, and a nasty job to do when we gets there, to waste moments lookin at a broken-kneed animal."

"'Tis agreeing Oi be with Donal, sir. Ye can't see murder mirrored in a beast's hide."

The man called Mike shrugged, but his smile hinted he wasn't one to be persuaded against his better judgement. Katherine tensed. Mike could be trouble.

Surreptitiously stuffing the last segment of buttered scone into her mouth, she moved quickly to a side door which she supposed led directly to the stable. She was right.

Mike wasn't the only one anxious to see the mare this morning. Would the welt on the black's fetlock feel any less damning after a night's rest? It didn't.

She straightened and began stroking the mare's velvety muzzle, realizing with a start the farrier was watching her closely. He was a kindly faced man. Probably Molly Malone's husband. As their eyes met, his, like a spaniel begging for a bone, seemed to be mirroring a plea. *Why, he wants me to forget anything I might have seen,* she thought, and gave her head an almost imperceptible nod. It wasn't as if the welt was noticeable . . . except to someone like the Corporal, who she suspected had a keen eye for a horse.

She mounted Jeremy in a whirl of indecision. It was really none of her affair. Yet if the man called Mike did notice something suspicious it would be his duty to investigate further. And then what?

A stench as from a cart-load of decaying bodies seemed to fill her nostrils. The memory of yesterday's eviction, helpless women and children left to starve by a louse in man's clothing "doing his duty," the cringing terror of the black, the damning spider-web of welts criss-crossing her whip-slashed body, were vivid in Katherine's mind.

Those words, "Yon rope done justice," floated in her memory like the phantom muttering of some abandoned soul . . . had she dreamed them? This morning she was sure she hadn't. The words, the tramp of heavy work boots, had been real. Too real. Those men had passed close to where she lay hidden. So if the authorities even smelled murder, investigations would certainly start. There would be floggings and torture. And then retaliations.

She shuddered at the thought of chain-reaction terror unleashed on innocent people. A terror she could perhaps prevent. If murder was suspected she would almost certainly be called upon to testify. Under oath what would she say? Would she perjure herself by denying any knowledge of the affair? Or would she speak out about her dream? And have to live forever with the horror of knowing she had heaped death and sorrow on people who, driven to distraction by unfair laws, were only trying to mete out the justice denied them by Westminster.

A frown of deep determination creased furrows in her forehead, but her eyes met the farrier's in a way that cemented a feeling of rapport between them.

For the sake of her own peace of mind, as well as for the Irish who might be incriminated, she would stay and try to prevent the Corporal (she didn't have a plan yet) from touching the mare's legs. As plan after plan whirled through her mind, only to be discarded, she talked to the farrier in what she hoped would seem a casual manner. "What are the chances of the mare's knees healing so she can become a useful horse again?"

"Not good. Unless she gets a year's rest. And then perhaps she might never be safe over jumps. But yes, a gentle ride for a lady, no doubt."

"Without rest, what would happen to the mare?"

"The knackers. Or an off chance she'll be sold next fair day in Dublin. Likely end up as a broken-down cabby's horse. 'Tis a pity to see such breeding go to waste. But there," and he shrugged helpless shoulders, "that's life. Be it horse or man."

While Katherine had been listening and asking questions, she had been skillfully extricating a pin from the folds of her riding habit, and now held it in her gloved hand in such a way that without any perceptible movement on her part she could jab the pin into Jeremy's wither. He'd have to play his part if her scheme was to succeed.

While Katherine sat patting the gelding's glossy neck, hoping he would understand what she intended to do was for a good cause, three uniformed men emerged from the inn. Two walked immediately to horses already saddled and waiting for them. The third, Mike, strolled casually towards the farrier, who was bent over rubbing a pungent ointment onto the open wounds on the black's knees. The Corporal's glance flicked impersonally over Katherine before fastening on the mare. "Nice animal," he said tersely to no one in particular, as he opened the black's mouth to determine her age, "Pity she's so badly blemished. Must have taken a hard fall."

Katherine watched like a cat at a mouse hole as his questing eyes ran up and down the mare's legs. She had become so strung up that her own nervousness fuelled the bay's. Jeremy began to fidget and hop like water droplets hitting a hot stove. But she made no effort to calm him. Instead, the moment Mike stooped to run his hand down the mare's leg, she jabbed a pin so viciously into her mount that he reared and lunged towards the black in surprised indignation. Mike straightened and jumped clear of the wildly flailing feet. He appeared to be about to leap forward to catch Jeremy's bridle when he realized his rider had him under control again. Now her voice rang out harsh and peremptory, but she hoped it also held a suitable squeak of fear. "You there. Get that mare away from me. Your ointment is frightening my horse. It stinks worse than dead fish." And wanting to give emphasis to her words, she slyly administered a second jab that set Jeremy rearing and lunging again.

The farrier touched his cap respectfully but she fancied she caught a conspiratorial wink as he led the mare away, muttering, "Sure'n 'tis sorry I be, ma'am, to be causing a fine young lady like yerself trouble. Whist then, 'tis just taking the mare to a far paddock I'll be doing."

Katherine quickly moved Jeremy in a way that blocked the man Mike from following the mare. If he asked her to step her horse aside she wasn't sure what she would do, but she was saved from having to make that decision because Mike seemed to have lost interest in the black in favour of the mahogany bay. He was watching Jeremy in a manner that made it difficult to say if he was studying the horse or the rider. Maybe both? Jeremy continued to cavort like a horse momentarily expecting a bomb to explode beneath him. His rider, despite being obviously pregnant, still sat a horse with "the prettiest seat in Dublin."

Although the Corporal's flint-hard eyes had been temporarily softened by his natural male appreciation for beautiful women and handsome horses, Katherine suspected he was the type who would never forget a face, or a horse. That knowledge made her uncomfortable.

But at the moment she had another, far more demanding concern — how to get the soldiers away from the inn before the Corporal's interest in the black resurfaced. Should she pretend to be frightened of riding alone and ask for their escort? She knew from their breakfast conversation they were heading towards Cork. How far would she have to ride with them before she could give them the slip and head back to Dublin? Whatever happened she mustn't arouse suspicion.

Then the matter was taken out of her hands.

An urgent shout split the morning silence. "The divil take ye man! Be ye coming er not?" The Corporal, touching his cap, nodded briefly to Katherine, then strode briskly to where his waiting companions were muttering they had wasted too much time.

It wasn't until their horses had clattered out of the courtyard and the sound of their iron-shod hooves had faded into the distance that Katherine turned and rode slowly towards Dublin. She knew instinctively the farrier would keep the black well away from the prying eyes of any travellers who might stop at the pub. In a day or so the welt should disappear. With just a bit of luck the secret she shared with a farrier (who to her surprise had spoken as an educated man) might never be known.

She debated how much to tell Peter about the black mare, which she suddenly realized she wanted. Apart from the damaged knees she was a good mare, as good as Jeremy, or better, and so similar in size and conformation they would make a good carriage pair. Peter had promised her a mare. Why not the black? She could be sent to one of his father's many holdings . . . the one near Grandon perhaps . . . to heal and rest. And breed?

Yet if she asked her husband for the black, was there any hope of ever owning the grey? If she told him she'd gone riding with the express purpose of buying the grey, even though she knew it was against his wishes, what then? She shuddered. Peter could be as grim and unbending as the Ten Commandments when standing by his principles. Oh dear, why did life have to be so complicated?

She was still worrying over how much, or how little, to tell her husband, when she reached home and handed Jeremy over to the stable boy.

Peter wouldn't be home until tomorrow. That would give her time to sleep on it.

When she let herself into the house she was startled to find the door wasn't locked. It was as if someone had been there ahead of her. *Oh dear, how could I have been so careless?* Yet she could almost remember locking it. Strange. A puzzled look flooded her face as she entered and took a quick look down the hallway. Nothing seemed out of place. And yet . . . ?

The sound of a heavy step behind her as she was shutting the door set her heart thumping in frightened bumps.

Thieves! Sweet Mother Mary! They're still in the house. Instinctively she snatched at the first thing her hand closed on and whirled about brandishing a stout shillelagh that had been in the stand beside the coat-tree. Brian Boru's wild and ancient battle cry exploded from her lips as, blinded by a mixture of terror and rage, she lunged viciously at the shadowy figure in front of her. But before the cane connected with its intended victim it was wrenched roughly from her hand and thrown to the floor. A deep masculine voice said sternly, "Is that the way you welcome your husband?"

Katherine's world was knocked askew. Her mind struggled against panic. He shouldn't be home yet. What had happened? Why was he looking at her in that hard, undefinable way? This man with animal watchfulness in the steely glint of his eyes wasn't her husband. Not the one she knew and, yes, loved. He was a stranger. Someone who looked overtired. And underfed.

She struggled to control the waves of panic cresting within her. Cold premonitory shivers chased up and down her spine. All she could think of was "He's found out the child I'm carrying isn't his."

"Where have you been?" The rough demand seemed to require an immediate response, and it brought Katherine's lowered eyes to his. But before she could reply he hurried on. "Can you imagine how I felt when I hurried home a day early to be with you, and found you gone? And Bridget too. And no one having any idea where either of you were. I've spent the last few hours lashing myself through the fire-pits of hell. Oh, Princess," it was almost a cry of despair, "I'd gone away, left you alone. If anyone had harmed you I'd have been fair fit to do murder. Although from the welcome you were about to give me I fancy I need not have worried much on that score." Now his voice sounded as if it might be fighting laughter.

A tiny giggle bubbled to her lips as her eyes flew to the shillelagh on the floor. It looked quite harmless now. Then with a small inarticulate cry she rushed into her husband's waiting arms and buried her head against the warmth of his chest. Her voice sounded muffled. "I didn't expect you back until tomorrow so I gave Bridget a few days off . . . to go help her mother. The poor soul's pregnant again. Soon enough Bridget won't be close enough to be popping in for visits. Left on my own, I decided to take a long ride and I must have gone further than I thought, for I got caught in a storm and stayed the night at a little public house a few miles from Dublin. Lud, but I'm glad you're back. You've no idea how scared I was at going into a place like that alone. Or how empty a bed is when there's no man to share it. Please don't ever go off and leave me again. Promise." The arms encircling her tightened into a fierce embrace, she smiled into the eyes probing hers, and they both knew hers would be a willing surrender.

Later, much later, after their passions had been surfeited, and after Katherine had fixed them a tasty meal of bacon and eggs and hot crumpets, she told Peter most, but not quite all, of what she had been doing while he was away. Peter had pulled a small settee close to a well-stoked fire. Now, with her head resting comfortably on his lap and his hand thoughtfully stroking her dark hair, she traced lazy sensuous butterfly circles on the strong planes of his face as she told him about the black mare. And how it might be for sale next market day.

And he agreed, yes, indeed it might be a good investment. Especially as (and this Katherine had been careful to point out) the black and Jeremy were so much of a size they would make an attractive pair of carriage horses. "For when the children are small and I'm not riding so much," she took pains to add.

His voice was low and caressing. "It's time you stopped riding Princess. Until after our baby is born. And that's an order." Katherine reached for his hand, and carefully opening the fingers kissed each one in turn. Peter, as if in a hurry to get back to more serious love-making, said briskly, "Then it's settled. I'll get word to Malone the mare's to come here until she can be sent to my father's for breeding and a year of pasture rest."

In the glow of firelight Katherine's delicately etched features were like a rare cameo as she drew the dark face down to her own. She hadn't told her husband of the welt on the mare's leg. That was a secret known only to herself and another woman's husband. And it had to be kept that way.

Chapter Seven
Ebony Angel and Turko

"What a splendid idea! A dinner party for our families before we leave Dublin. Let's ask Henrietta and Stephen too."

Then Peter's handsome face took on a thoughtful look. "I haven't seen my brother Albert since he got back from England. I wonder if a year of fostering at Sir Anthony Blockless' estate in Surrey will have given him English airs, and the conviction we Irish are a poor uneducated lot who deserve no better than we get?"

The next moment Peter hurried on, his voice anxious now. "But do you feel up to it, Princess? You mustn't go fussing over a splendid meal and tire yourself." Peter Moriarty's dark eyes were bright with concern as his fingers absently folded his monogrammed linen table napkin and slid it into its silver ring. Then he pushed his chair back from the breakfast table and crossed to gently kiss Katherine's upturned face.

"Of course I'll manage all right, silly. Bridget is getting better in the kitchen, and I'll have her sister come in to help with the cleaning and silver. Fanny can lay out the best china and crystal too. Perhaps she can even help Bridget serve.

"And darling, I can hardly wait to show our family Ebony Angel before she leaves for the country. She's such a sweet mare, so gentle and responsive. I'm almost sure her knees will heal so there'll hardly be any scars. The swellings went down a deal after we had them lanced. They are draining so much better now.

"As for Turko, he already thinks I couldn't manage without him." As she spoke Katherine stooped to pet a small Irish terrier whose doggy eyes shone with adoration.

"With Ireland in such a ferment these days I feel better when I have to be at the office all day knowing you've got Turko. He's not big, but by Jove, when his hackles are up he'd not back down from the British army." Having said that Peter gave his wife a warm hug, picked up his bowler hat, took a blackthorn cane from a stand near the door, and went out.

Katherine hummed happily as she sat down to study a dog-eared cookbook (it had been her mother's) and prepare a menu. For her first dinner party it was important that everything be exactly right. For the next two days the kitchen was awash in a gourmet array of mouth-watering sights and delicious smells.

The day came. The meal was a triumph. Peter carved the goose, roasted to a delicate golden brown, with the élan of an old pro. He smiled down the length of the table to where Katherine, flanked by his brother Albert and Stephen Cassidy, appeared to be listening intently to their animated conversation. But not so intently she couldn't flash him the whisper of a smile, which caused him to immediately raise one eyebrow in the suggestion of a shared secret.

The seating arrangement seemed perfect to Katherine. Mrs. O'Connor on Peter's right, motherly soul that she was, was busy impressing Henrietta on his left with the importance of getting a good supply of nappies on hand before the baby was born. "Because afterwards there's never enough time for extras."

Donal Moriarty and Seamus O'Connor, leaning across the table eagerly discussing business opportunities for their recently acquired shipping line, were in a private world of their own.

Katherine's step-sister was the misfit. Utterly bored, she jabbed viciously at a pickled onion, which promptly flew into the gravy boat. When not chewing noisily on the food she shovelled into a mouth that never completely closed, she aimed glances at her mother that suggested she was condemning that lady for having the audacity to bring her daughter to such a dismal country. If spoken to, Sophia acknowledged the speaker with a grunt, or a grimace-like attempt at a smile that wrinkled her face like mud drying in an empty puddle.

However, that changed abruptly when Albert turned his attention to her. Sophia became all smiles and sweetness. They both seemed caught up in the need to surrender all their secrets to one another as quickly as possible.

Albert, with good features and the shoulders of an athlete, might have been termed handsome except that his eyes held a dangerous glitter of self-interest. Now he appeared intent on impressing Sophia with an account of the year he had spent in England as the adoptive son of Lord and Lady Blockless. Apparently they shared the same poor opinion of Ireland.

Stephen became very quiet. In a few days he would be leaving his wife and unborn child. He'd only be away a year, but if the voyage to Australia was plagued by storms and bad luck it could be much longer. He wouldn't allow himself to think of that possibility.

He'd rented a pretty little cottage for Henrietta near where her sister lived on the outskirts of Skibbereen. When

Peter and Katherine were settled above the bank in Grandon they'd be close enough to see her often, so he hoped her days wouldn't feel too lonely. Stephen loved the sea but he loved his wife more. The thought of leaving her alone while he was half a world away, enjoying the life she couldn't share, troubled him. Yet Henrietta had repeatedly reassured her husband, "You worry too much, dear. Of course I'll miss you and I'll be counting the days until you get back. But I'll manage. Lots of wives do, you know."

Stephen allowed himself a small sigh. There was no doubt about it, Henrietta was made of good stuff. She'd always be there waiting for him.

His eyes rested momentarily on Katherine, beautiful and vivacious as ever despite approaching motherhood. Then they shifted to Peter, looking very much in control at the head of his own table. But Stephen, knowing how unbending his friend could be when riding a course he considered right and proper not only for himself but for all those associated with him, gave a hidden sigh. Most men would envy Peter, as women might envy Katherine, for indeed they made a striking couple. So why was it he had this feeling that his best friend's marriage would be plagued by heartache? Then he shrugged. Lots of marriages knew the full measure of heartache. Why worry about one more?

Now the meal was over. Everyone was declaring it delicious but they were so chock-a-block they couldn't manage another morsel. So Katherine suggested the ladies retire to the drawing room until the men had finished their cigars and brandy.

Mrs. O'Connor and the two young mothers-to-be chatted happily near the fire; Sophia, her eyes dark with disdain, her lips compressed into a thin line of brooding discontent, sat a little apart. Sometimes Mrs. O'Connor spared her a look that suggested she was puzzling how she had managed to produce such a difficult offspring. Surely the girl's vicious nature must have come from the father's side of the family.

Sophia, watching the door for Albert's return, fiddled with her hair,smoothed imagined wrinkles from a pale yellow gown, or picked her nose. Then, when no one was watching, she'd slyly wipe her finger on the heavy damask curtain behind her. Her mind was scheming how to wangle marriage to a younger son, then turn it to her own advantage.

Turko, convinced his mission in life was to stay close to his mistress, was asleep now with his head on the toe of Katherine's black buttoned boot. When the men, their smokes and drinks finished, came to join the ladies, the dog woke up long enough to wag his stub tail as Peter sat down beside Katherine and draped one arm over the back of the settee behind her. He did it without touching her, but in a manner that gave a clear message that this was his woman. And Katherine, sensing his love, smiled warmly up at him.

Then the conversation took an unexpected turn. Donal Moriarty fixed Katherine with a pale stare. "Just exactly when do you expect to make me a grandfather?" Before Katherine could reply Henrietta smiled coyly at the older man. "We had a double wedding, sir, so I fancy we'll both be birthing nine months from the wedding night. That's my reckoning. Give or take a few days for the vagaries of nature. Of course . . . ," and here she looked demurely at Stephen who was holding her hand as if he never intended to let it go, "of course there can't be a double christening. Ours will have to wait until Stephen can be there, but there'll be no need for Peter and Katherine to wait."

Sophia, antagonism spearing her eyes and a malicious smirk curling her lips, inched nearer to Henrietta. She spoke in a rasping voice that sounded like the croaking of a sick frog. "If it's a joint laying-in you two are planning, Henrietta, don't count on Katherine waiting for that either." Then, as if another thought had just occurred to her, she said slyly, "Isn't it strange that first-born babies rarely take nine months?"

Katherine felt as if a viper was intent on destroying her and her unborn child. It took a lot of effort to force her face into the semblance of a frozen smile and speak calmly. "What do you mean, Sophia?"

Her words weren't properly out when Turko, his hackles stiff, his teeth bared in an angry snarl, suddenly sprang up and hurled himself at Sophia.

If Peter hadn't instinctively lunged to grab the dog's collar as he flashed past and drag him, still growling and snarling, away from the frightened girl, it's hard to say what might have happened. When he was banished from the room everyone began talking at once.

What had come over the dog? He seemed to have been sleeping peacefully beside his mistress. Was he having a bad dream? Dogs do have dreams . . . The talk and speculation continued. All thought of anything Sophia said was forgotten. Perhaps no one except Katherine had really understood her vicious innuendoes.

Sophia sat cowering within the protective circle of Albert's arm, too frightened to speak. But Albert swung on his brother angrily. "That dog is a menace. You should have him destroyed."

"Nonsense!" There was an authoritative ring to Stephen's voice as he leapt to the dog's defence. "The animal was having a nightmare. He wouldn't have bitten her."

Hearing this Seamus O'Connor remarked dryly, "Begorrah. Of course 'twas a nightmare the poor wee beastie was having. I've had a few meself when I'm about to do some biting. Except I wake up too soon." The sour look he aimed at his step-daughter suggested any dog who'd bite her deserved a cherished life.

Katherine got up with the look of a hostess who has learned to deal effectively with household vagaries, saying quietly, "I must tell Bridget to put the kettle on the hob for tea." She needed to get out of the room. Quickly. Before anyone could hear the furious pounding of her heart. As soon as the door had closed behind her she dropped to her knees and scooped the little dog into her arms, hugging him until his body wagged the tail and his eyes danced with doggy delight.

She knew Turko's behaviour hadn't been a nightmare. The tension brought on by Sophia's remark had communicated itself to the dog sleeping with his head on her foot and he had instinctively sprung to her defence, and saved her from . . . . she didn't quite know what. Except her happy, ordered life had seemed perilously close to crashing. Obviously Sophia suspected. But she couldn't really know. Could she?

Katherine fought down a shivery feeling and forced herself to re-enter the room as if there was nothing more important on her mind than who would take both cream and sugar in their tea.

She looked around pertly, saying, "Bridget will be a few minutes readying the tea things, so who would like to come and see Ebony Angel?"

Everyone would except Peter and Albert. They elected to stay and catch up on brotherly news.

Seamus O'Connor's eyes narrowed thoughtfully as he ran his hands gently over a hide smooth now and glossy from much grooming. "I'd wager this mare was sired by Ireland's Choice, the stud who produced two of England's recent winners at the steeple chase. And if I'm right that makes her a half-sister to Patrick's grey. The one Sophia bought from him a few weeks back. Seems some gentleman refused her because she'd been serviced by an inferior stallion. Sophia got her for a fraction of her real value because Patrick needed the money to send his brother's family to America.

"Ireland's Choice is a great sire. Many of his offspring have been exceptional." O'Connor pushed back his cap with a thoughtful air before he continued. "If me auld eye for a horse hasn't deserted me both the black and the grey are worthy representatives, but I fancy the black, if her knees don't fail her, may prove the better of the two. It would be interesting to see them in a matched race."

Hearing Sophia was the owner of "her" grey Katherine had to lean heavily against the black's shoulder for support. Disturbing sensations exploded inside her. Sophia would never agree to sell to a step-sister she hated. That meant the grey mare was lost to her forever, so she had better beat down the feelings that persisted whenever she saw the mare. Feelings that the fates had linked her happiness to a horse she could never own.

Katherine tossed her head in a proud, determined fashion. She must rid her mind once and for all of that silly notion about the grey. For of course that's what it was. A silly notion.

If her father or Sophia didn't know it was Peter who had refused the offer of the mare there seemed no reason to tell them now. She shot Stephen a conspiratorial glance but neither he nor Henrietta seemed to have been paying any attention.

She sighed with a twinge of irritation, handed the lead shank to Ben the stable boy, slipped Ebony Angel a carrot, and then led her little group back towards the house.

As she did, Sophia sidled up to her, her voice low and deadly. "So it was Peter who refused Grey Lady . . . because she's carrying a scrub foal. And now you're sweating blood. If your child has red hair how will you explain *that* to Peter?" Her words were laced with malice.

Katherine, ignoring the knot twisting her stomach, spoke stonily in a voice cold with contempt. "Sophia, it's obvious you've never heard of Grace O'Malley, Ireland's Pirate Queen. Or know that she, Granuaile, was my mother's ancestor. Or that when she found a Nordic man near death from a shipwreck near Achill she nursed the red-haired stranger back to life and health. And love."

"So the O'Malley ancestor you're so proud of was a bastard?" Sophia spat out the words in a contemptuous fashion, as if they were red-hot coals that must be expelled quickly before they lost their power to harm.

"Sophia, you English have no idea how simple marriage and divorce was in Ireland under the old Brehon Law. When Grace no longer wanted her current marriage partner all she had to do was to tell him in front of her clansmen "I dismiss you" and that marriage was over. With no questions asked.

"However, her liaison with the Nordic man was no trial-marriage but a true love affair. When Granuaile's lover was ambushed and killed while hunting she immediately avenged his death by attacking Doona Castle in Blacksod

Bay, the stronghold of the MacMahons who had murdered him. After annihilating the entire clan she claimed their holdings for her own.

"So make no mistake about it, Sophia. I have that Pirate Queen's fighting blood in my veins. And you'd do well to remember it." Having said that she stalked away, her head high, her step proud.

But she didn't feel as confident as she had tried to sound. She and Peter would soon be leaving Dublin. In Grandon, where no one knew them, and there would be no Sophia with her adder tongue, Katherine hoped her secret would be safe.

Chapter Eight
Mothers-to-Be Meet

"It's obvious, Katherine. You miscalculated. You must have. I'm much bigger than you, and my baby isn't due for another two weeks. Yet you say yours should have come more than a fortnight ago. Do you suppose you weren't pregnant when you married Peter? Would that be possible?" Henrietta Cassidy's tone was speculative as she picked up a monogrammed silver sugar shell, measured a scant spoonful, and held it poised over a fine bone china tea cup, her eyebrows arching into another question. "Still cutting down on sugar? And no cream either?"

Katherine nodded, reached for the proffered cup, then settled herself more comfortably in the fine old Venetian settee that dominated her friend's drawing room. "Not a chance, Rietta. I was pregnant right enough." She patted her own swollen belly, then studied the way her friend's protruded with majestic dignity. The laugh that followed sounded as if all the fairy bells in Ireland were ringing a Hallelujah chorus. "The wee people are smiling on me, Rietta. It's those mischievous leprechauns. They are slowing my baby's birth to spite my step-sister for bad-mouthing everything Irish. Because for them that is blasphemy."

"Sophia's sly innuendoes about your pregnancy frighten me. I worry she has somehow learned your secret." Henrietta's friendly face wore a troubled frown as she absently flicked a crumb off the fine woollen dress that covered her swollen body with a sort of dignified venerability.

"Well, she doesn't know. How can she? I've never told anyone, but you. She's pretending she knows something, because . . . well, because she's always looking for some way to get back at me." Katherine's words were clipped and confident.

Suddenly she jerked bolt upright on the settee. Her tea slopped into the saucer, but she didn't notice. Her hand had flown to her half-open mouth; her eyes looked as if her brain had just had a frightening revelation.

"Rietta, do you remember that day? When we thought the bedroom door had come open on its own? Do you suppose . . .? What if she *was* listening? Maybe she really know."

Henrietta put her hand soothingly on her friend's arm. "Katherine, if she really knew she would have caused trouble for you before this. Isn't that her nature? Besides, I clearly remember you saying she'd gone in the dog-cart with her mother, to take a bowl of beef broth to an old tenant woman who was feeling poorly. She can't have been in the house."

"Oh but she could, Rietta. When I was riding that day I met my stepmother driving back alone. I didn't think much of it at the time. Sophia has always considered a dog-cart below her station in life so I supposed she had chosen to take a short cut and walk back rather than be seen riding in it. But what if she didn't go with her mother? What if she was in the house all the time?"

Katherine's disturbed frown was accompanied by a sad little wisp of a smile that flickered momentarily over the slender oval. Then, like a sprite shamming the wisdom of the ages, she arose to embrace her friend. "But no matter what she knows, Rietta, I don't think she can hurt me now.

Not really. What's a few weeks? Lots of babies come early. Actually mine is overdue. I expect that is giving Sophia second thoughts about raising dragons she can't see."

Henrietta didn't look so confident. "What if the child has red hair?"

Katherine's eyes sparkled with a laugh that didn't entirely match her feelings. "Pshaw, Rietta. Don't worry. I'll tell them the baby inherited it from Grace O'Malley's shipwrecked protégé. And if Sophia tries to harm my child she'll learn I'm as fierce and avenging as my famous ancestor. It wasn't for nought she earned the title 'The Dark Lady of Doona.'" Her voice ended on a clipped and threatening note.

Henrietta's troubled frown as she refilled their tea cups suggested she might be seeing more complications hidden below the apparently smooth surface of that plan than her friend was yet aware of.

She watched, undecided whether to voice those fears, as Katherine sat down again. Watched as the younger woman pulled up her skirts to run her hands absently over legs crawling with purple veins, veins bulging through the near-transparency of her skin like over-gorged worms. The gentle massaging seemed more ritual than from any hope of returning them to their pre-pregnancy contours.

Suddenly Katherine pushed down her skirts and looked slantwise at her friend. "I best be getting home or Peter will be worried. He clucks and scolds now like an old mother hen. Says my legs wouldn't be so swollen if I rested more. If he had his way I'd spend all day with my feet on a hassock."

Henrietta interjected, "Well, if you paid more heed to Peter your legs might not be so bad." But her friend hurried on.

"After today Peter says there's to be no more driving myself in the carriage. He made me agree to keep the horse to a walk on the rough spots before he'd let me come to see you this morning. It's all so annoying.

"If I'd married a peasant I'd be expected to hoe potatoes or turnips until my water gushed. And 'tis not leaving my bed beforehand my husband would be doing. We'd be sharing it with one or two wee spalpeens. That is, if we were lucky enough to have a bed," she added in a thoughtful fashion.

"Peter doesn't sleep with me now. Says he won't until after the baby comes. He's afraid his loving might hurt it. Or me. Claims he can't trust himself to share my bed. Faith, Henrietta! When a woman waddles like a duck and her belly balloons like an old brood mare can you imagine a man having any trouble in that regard? I can't, but Peter says I've never looked so beautiful to him." Katherine shook her head as if there was just no understanding the male of the species.

"Anyway, I wish the wee thing *would* hurry up and come out. Wee? It feels as big as a house! Anyway, it's time to get the whole messy business over and done with. I want my husband loving me again at nights. You've no idea how empty a bed is when there's no man in it."

Seeing the strained look on her friend's face Katherine clapped a hand to her mouth. "Oh, Henrietta! How could I have been so stupid! Please forgive me. Of course you know. Far better than I. But you're different. I wouldn't have let Peter sail off to the other side of the world leaving me alone for who knows how long. I'd have stowed away until it was too late for him to turn back and put me off. I'd work in the galley. Or help rig the sails. Do anything if it meant I could stay with him. I'm sure I'd find something a woman could do."

Henrietta's face was warm with understanding. She didn't bother to tell her friend that if she showed up on board a ship she'd cause a mutiny. When men are at sea for months without seeing women, just the sound of a female voice can cause trouble. Instead she said, "Of course I forgive you, dear. I knew when I married Stephen he'd be away a lot. But don't worry. We'll make up for lost time when he is home. Which might be in less than two months, if storms don't delay him.

"You mustn't fret about me being lonely. I have my sister and her family next door. And after our babies come you and I can compare notes again. But I am pleased we had this visit today. Send word as soon as your baby is born. I'll do the same with mine." *And I'll pray your child has dark hair and grey eyes like Peter.*

Katherine called for her carriage to be brought to the door and arose with some reluctance. "Are you sure you'll be all right, Rietta . . . ? With your husband half a world away you must promise to get word to Peter and me right away if you need help. We'll come. Day or night." And after a warm embrace the two young women parted.

Katherine climbed awkwardly into the carriage and tried to settle her swollen body comfortably before taking Jeremy's reins from the stable boy, Ben (who had accompanied her at Peter's insistence), then turned to wave to her friend. As she did a shiver skittered down her spine, for despite her outward bravado she was more frightened than anyone knew.

Only she knew the baby was weeks overdue. If it was big-boned, like its father, would she have the strength to force it out? Her bones were fine, her body slender. And she had another worry. What if the babe showed no resemblance to Peter?

Despite her O'Malley blood, she didn't know if Ireland's Corsair Queen's Nordic lover had red hair. Or even if he had sired an O'Malley child. That was a guess . . . something sung about by the bards of County Clare. And not denied by Granuaile herself.

There was a wild, impetuous streak hidden below the surface of Katherine's apparently mild exterior that made her a kindred spirit to the woman pirate who had defied tradition, and gained fame. And notoriety. They both lived by their own rules. But Katherine was the child of a different century.

Chapter Nine
A Difficult Delivery

The drive home, like her pregnancy, seemed to be lasting forever. And she was in a hurry to get them both over and done with. On a sudden impulse she slapped the reins on Jeremy's well-rounded rump in a way that sent the carriage jolting over some of Ireland's roughest roads. It sent her rocketing back and forth across the seat until the shy young stable lad pleaded, "M'lady. Please take care. Ye'll be doing yerself an injury if ye drives so reckless. The master wouldna like it."

For answer Katherine compressed her lips into a grim line and urged Jeremy into a rollicking gallop. She drove as if trying to outdistance her fears. The carriage bucked and bounced behind the racing horse until Katherine's swollen body seemed in danger of flying off into space. She told herself she had carried the child long enough. Now it was time to shake it out.

Suddenly the wild glitter in her eyes changed to a look of fear. Maybe she had gone too far. The warm wetness gushing out between her legs, soaking her clothes and the seat beneath, warned her the baby's birth was imminent.

Almost instantly her stomach cramped as a terrifying explosion starting somewhere deep inside set off body-wracking pains that swirled and grew like widening ripples in a lake. She gasped and grabbed wildly for the carriage hand rail. Moments later the frightened Ben, who had taken the reins from her, pulled Jeremy to a heaving stop in front of the bank, and was off and running, yelling at the top of his very good lungs. "Mr. Moriarty, Sir! Please come quick!"

Katherine, determined to maintain a dignified appearance so as not to start tongues wagging, began to climb awkwardly down from the carriage. But another pain swept over her. It was so bad she had to shut her eyes and put all her concentration on not blacking out. A moment later she felt the warmth and strength of Peter's arms around her, protecting her. They spoke a wordless language and for the moment she felt safe.

Weariness had drained every vestige of colour from her face, but she managed a weak little smile as she raised her arms to encircle his neck. He had never seen her look so stricken and his mutter of self- condemnation had a vicious edge. "I knew I shouldn't have let you go so far." The next moment he was ordering Bridget to run for the midwife and he was carrying Katherine up the stairs as easily as if she had been a doll.

Reaching the bedroom, he shut the door behind him with one foot, then gently laid his wife on the bed. His eyes were dark with worry, but his voice was low and reassuring, his hands caressing and very gentle as he removed her clothes and helped her into bed. "You know I love you, Princess, but if it's too bad this time I'll never ask you to bear me a second child."

The pains were coming harder. Closer together now. Katherine wanted to lash out at him. "You stupid man. You won't be having a first until there's a second." Instead she released one hand from his to stroke the furrows that were creasing his forehead, furrows that were giving a pinched look to a face almost as white and frightened as her own.

Before she could speak another pain wracked her body. She clamped her teeth to hold back the scream that was trying to escape and clung to Peter's hand in a way that made his knuckles crack. Katherine was determined she wouldn't scream. No matter how bad the pains, there'd be no sound from her to tell the idlers that hung around the town square what was going on. There'd be no lewd, lascivious winks, no sly nudges, no "So 'tis Moriarty's wife who's birthing today."

She was an O'Malley woman and Katherine had convinced herself no O'Malley would scream in childbirth. What might be acceptable for other women wasn't acceptable for an O'Malley. "But darling," Peter protested, wiping away the sweat beads of agony that clustered on her face, "if it helps, open your mouth as wide as you can and scream until it crisps the termites in the beams. No one will think the less of you." But Katherine only clung to him and clamped her teeth harder.

At that moment footsteps were heard rushing up the stairs, and the midwife closely followed by a wide-eyed Bridget burst into the room. In moments Peter was banished from the bedroom, told he had done his part and now he best get back to his banking business until he was called.

Although he would gladly have stayed and given his wife the support of his love and strength, he knew the mores of society forbade a husband from attending a birth. Unless you were a peasant. They often delivered their own children. Some, he knew, valued their wives less than they did their cows. A cow's progeny would pay the rent. A woman's meant another mouth to feed when there was already too little to go around.

After what seemed a lifetime of waiting to Peter, the harried midwife rushed downstairs, wiping her hands on a bloodied apron as she ran. Her voice was brittle. "Things aren't going well. Fetch the doctor, and be quick about it. Drive like all the fiends in hell are after you. And while you're at it, do a bit of praying. Pray as you've never done before. Pray for your wife. Pray that the doctor isn't out on another call. But no matter where he is, don't come back without him. And hurry, man. Hurry!"

Before the woman had finished speaking Peter was out the door and running with every inch of his body. He would ride. On horseback he could go by way of the boreen, jump the creek, and save precious minutes.

He never stopped to consider he wasn't an accomplished rider, that he'd be riding Ebony Angel, a mare whose damaged knees might not have healed enough to make it safe to ask her to jump. On top of that he'd be leading Jeremy, because Jeremy would get the doctor back faster than the brown cob the man normally rode.

Seconds later Peter was crouched low in the saddle, a whipping black mane framing his face as Ebony and the bay, with nostrils flaring, ears laid flat, raced each other through the night, their hoof-beats blurring into a thunderous drumroll. He had never ridden at such speed before.

The sky crackled with stars. A sombre crescent moon, intent on hoarding its meagre light, did little to lighten the path for the horses. But just as they neared the brook a few vagrant moonbeams escaped earthward to dance and sparkle briefly over the rippling surface of the water.

Peter, a man with no experience rating jumpers, simply whistled in Ebony's ear, shut his eyes, and clung to her mane as they neared the stream. He mustn't fail now. If he did Katherine would die. And he would have murdered her just as surely as if he had held a pistol to her head.

Almost before Peter realized it the mare rose like a swallow and then the stream was behind her. She was running neck and neck with Jeremy again, matching him stride for stride. He pushed back a sob of relief. If Katherine and the child lived he had her horses to thank.

In a few more moments, in answer to his thunderous shout, a light came on in the doctor's house, and while the man dragged on his clothes and snatched up his bag Peter let the horses blow. There was a fast return trip ahead for the gelding. He knew he ought to ride slower on the mare so as not to compound the injury the ride might have done her. But when both men were mounted Ebony had her own idea about that.

She fought for her head so violently she threatened to unseat her rider until he gave her a free rein to catch up with Jeremy. Despite the fears for Katherine's life that gnawed and tore at his mind he sensed a thrill when Ebony, running flat out now, sailed effortlessly over the stream. This time he hadn't clung to her mane. The doctor spared him a quick sideways glance, "You've got a fine pair of animals."

Peter watched the doctor rush up the stairs, three at a time, then turned reluctantly back to where the horses were standing with their heads hanging low, their sides heaving. Great swirls of grimy sweat lathered their normally glossy hides.

Impatiently he called the stable boy awake. "Ben, walk them cool, then give them a thorough rubdown; pay special attention to the mare's legs. After they're dry offer them sips of water spread over the next hour. When they've drunk their fill they can have a double ration of grain." *They deserve it. And more,* he thought as he hurried wearily towards the bank foyer, his walk a blend of run and stumble.

Worry tore at his brain. His stomach was tight. If only he knew what was going on. If only he could do something, anything, to help. The silence was intense. And terrifying. The darkness, relieved only by the tiny yellow light of a guttering candle, seemed threatening. Maybe he should light a lamp, but somehow the gloom of the night seemed more in keeping with the gloom in his heart.

His eyes grew bleary . . . He felt completely wiped out, done in with a weariness he had never known before. His mind was trapped in an agony of worry and remorse. Remorse that he, nine months ago, in pleasure, had been responsible for causing his wife such pain now as no human should be expected to endure. It was that remorse which was twisting his mind into a tormented knot, driving him to pace relentlessly around the foyer. Turko padding anxiously at his heels, whining each time a half-strangled moan escaped his master's throat.

Except for Bridget's occasional quick footsteps as she trotted to and from the kitchen for more hot water and cloths, and sometimes a low worried voice as the bedroom door opened and shut, the place was wrapped in eerie silence. If only Katherine would scream, he'd know she was still alive. But there was nothing. Just a silence that tore at his nerves the way a wolf tears at a freshly killed carcass.

Peter desperately wanted to rush upstairs, demand to know what was going on. She was his wife, his beloved. She was bearing his baby. Why wasn't it his right to be with her, to comfort her? If she was dying he wanted to gather her into his arms and by osmosis let his life flow into her.

Twice he strode towards the stairs, grim lines of determination fighting those of worry and despair on his haggard face. But each time when his foot touched the first step he stopped, ran his hand through tousled hair, and turned back.

What if his presence distracted the doctor and the midwife? What if he got in their way? They were both competent people with years of professional experience and now they were doing everything humanly possible to save the life of his wife and child. So he did the only thing left to do. He prayed.

He knelt and prayed, oblivious to the frenzied fingers clutching at, and sometimes pulling out, strands of his own hair. Nor did he realize a little dog, sensing something dreadful was happening to the people he loved, was licking his face with long urgent strokes. For Turko's doggy mind told him if he licked hard enough and long enough, he could take away their troubles. Nor did Peter hear the heavy tread of tired feet slowly descending the stairs. Or Turko's soft whine of recognition.

He heard nothing until he felt a hand on his shoulder and heard a voice saying as if through a mist of fatigue, "Your wife gave birth to a son. It's a miracle how she did it, but the child is alive. A fine baby. Far too big for a woman her size to deliver. She's had a terrible ordeal." Then as if speaking to himself, "In all my years of practice I've never seen her equal. All those hours of body-tearing pains and she never screamed. Not once. A few stricken moans, a half-strangled whimper when the agony was too much for human flesh to bear, but never a proper scream escaped her lips.

"Your wife is a remarkable woman. But she's badly torn and the tearing will take weeks to heel. She might not deny you her bed, but I'm warning you to not enter her until I give you permission. If you do it could cause irreparable damage. Given proper care now I think in time she might be able to manage another child.

"In the meantime, this one's a right lusty spalpeen who'll need a wet nurse until Katherine gets her strength back. I know of one with enough milk for triplets so I'll stop on my way home and arrange for her to come.

"By the way, your stable boy needn't see me home. I'll call a cab. My old bones are too tired to enjoy another of your wild rides. Although I must say if I'd been slower getting here, it might be sadder news I'd be giving you.

"Now get upstairs, son, and get acquainted with your child. And congratulate your courageous little wife. She did a fine job." With that he patted Peter affectionately on the shoulder and watched the younger man bound effortlessly up the stairs.

For Katherine the hours in childbirth were a blinding blaze of agony, an agony such as she had never imagined possible, but an agony of which mercifully she would soon remember little. Now, too tired to open her eyes and see her baby, she drifted into a troubled sleep. When she finally roused enough to realize she could have the luxury of a breath without the searing pains of childbirth, she half opened one eye. Peter's anxious face was hovering over hers, his hand warm against her cheek. "Ah, my darling Princess. 'Tis a blessed sight ye are for me eyes, for 'tis a cursing and despising meself I've been doing for causing ye such pain." His lips brushed tenderly against her face as he spoke. She only stared up at him as if she had nothing to spare. Not even a smile.

Then the midwife, her wisps of grizzled hair hanging like a fringe below a cap that had been pushed askew and was no longer quite clean, bustled up. "Here, Dearie. It's time you saw your child. He's a bonnie babe and in no time you'll forget all the pain and tearing his coming caused." Katherine opened both eyes and half raised her head. Then she let it fall back with a low moan. The baby's hair was the colour of a well-worn copper pot.

She looked desperately, almost pleadingly towards Peter, but he was gaping at the infant with an indefinable expression on his face.

Katherine screwed her eyes shut. Her heart hammered like an out-of-time piston. She didn't have the strength to face a man as uncompromising as the Ten Commandments where his principles where concerned. But he had been smiling. Hadn't he? She was afraid to look.

Then she heard a deep and very masculine voice goo-gooing baby-talk to the infant. It sounded so incredibly silly she allowed herself the luxury of a tired little smile. A moment later he was stroking her hair, brushing back the sweat-drenched tendrils that clung wetly to her forehead, their darkness making a face already drained of all colour look startlingly white against the pillows. She raised her hand to close around his as if needing its strength to restore her own. An exquisite feeling of security surrounded her as she heard him murmuring softly in her ear. "I'm so terribly proud of my Katherine aroon. You've given me a fine big son. Now I want you to rest and grow strong. I must send word to your father, and mine."

The next few days were black blurs of pain for Katherine. Sometimes she vaguely sensed Peter was beside her, holding her, murmuring words of encouragement and love. Sometimes a different man seemed to be taking his place. That must be the doctor. When she moaned, which was often, Mrs. O'Clarety, the midwife, and Bridget hovered around her like anxious wraiths.

Sometimes she almost wished they would all go away and leave her to die in peace. Instead they spooned nourishing broth between her lips whenever she opened her eyes, changed the bloody cloths between her legs so gently that sometimes it almost didn't hurt, sponged her fevered body with such regularity she'd think, They *must be trying to wash away my wickedness. But they'll not succeed. I'm too full of it. They'd better spend their time doing something useful.*

Then Katherine would squeeze her eyes tight so no one could see the tears of self-pity she was too weak to prevent and Mrs. O'Clarety would whisper to Bridget, "If you pull the drapes closer perhaps she'll sleep now." And sometimes Katherine did.

When three weeks had passed and the frightening pallor began to leave Katherine's face, she was able to sit up and spoon-feed herself, even hold the baby in her arms for a few moments, and sometimes even help to bathe him. It was when she took off his tiny clothes for the first time that she first saw the dagger-shaped birthmark on his chest. She gave a startled scream. "Oh!" *Well, at least it isn't on his face.*

The next day, the doctor agreed that the grandfathers, who had set out for Grandon at first word of the birth, could now see their grandchild and his mother. "But only for a few minutes. The mother has had a terrible ordeal. It's a miracle she and the child both live."

And so it was that Katherine opened her eyes from a tangled sleep one day, half of her still seeming shrouded in dreams, to find her father's arms around her. The bristly chin whiskers brushing her face were giving her what as a child she had called his monkey kiss.

"Sure'en 'tis a foine big grandson you've made me auld heart happy with, Macushla. But 'tweren't no call to do it on such a grand scale. I'd been roit happy if ye let the babe do his growing on the outside of ye." Katherine clung to her father, too weak to stop the tears of happiness that trickled down her face before stopping to sparkle a while on the old man's whiskers.

When he gently drew away from her she realized there were others in the room. Peter's eyes were sending her messages of love. His father was studying the new babe as one might study a horse he was about to buy. "Big enough for two months," he rasped grudgingly, "but with his red hair and round face, Oi can't be saying as how he takes after aither side."

At that moment Sophia stepped from behind a screen and shot a malicious look at Katherine, but when she spoke it was to Peter and the grandfathers. "Why not ask the mother about the baby's looks? I'd like to hear what she has to say about that. Go ahead, Peter. Ask her."

Katherine, caught off guard by her step-sister's venom, felt her heart beating like the wings of a trapped hummingbird. She stared straight ahead with the rigid, unfocused eyes of someone seeing the erection of her own gallows and the execution that was soon to follow, but was almost too tired to care.

For a moment the only sound in the room was the muted ticking of the marble clock on the mantel-piece. The grandfathers glanced momentarily at Sophia as if she had said something so outrageous, so stupid it didn't warrant a reply. But ripples of anger slid across Peter's darkening face as he whirled on Sophia, gripping her shoulders with rock-hard fingers that drove into her flesh and made her cower.

"You've the mind of a slut." And with that he gave her a shove that sent her stumbling from the room.

At that moment a log burning in the grate settled, hissing noisily as it released a shower of sparks. *It's like a good old Irish benediction*, thought the doctor, who had been watching from the shadows to make sure his patient's strength was not over-taxed. Now he quickly ordered everyone from the room.

When Peter stooped to give his wife a lingering kiss, murmuring, "Sorry Mavourneen. I hope I didn't upset you," gratitude shone in her eyes like midnight stars; she clung to him, whispering, "Darling Peter. I love you so very much. You're far kinder to me than I deserve." The soft look he threw her said he didn't agree at all with her last remark.

Katherine knew her step-sister's reasoning power disintegrated the moment her mind seized upon an idea, yet now when the new mother slept peace covered her face like a fine mantle of newly fallen snow.

However, eventually all snow must melt. And when it does it turns into raging rivers that roil towards the sea, sometimes leaving havoc and heartbreak in their wake.

Chapter Ten
Could Happiness Last?

Sometimes when Katherine sat with Peter's arms around her in the privacy of their own apartment, watching and laughing as little Andrew grew into a sturdy child with a shock of wavy red hair, greenish-brown eyes, the spirited independence of his mother, and no outward resemblance to his father, a puzzled frown would flit across Peter's face. But the memory of his wedding night quickly erased any doubts that might have been forming.

Peter was sharing her bed again. Earlier than the doctor thought wise, but Katherine had insisted. At first she had winced and clung to him in near tears when he entered her, even though he tried to be careful. Now he could tell she was enjoying their lovemaking and anxious to get another baby started. In fact she seemed obsessed with the need to have another child.

Katherine hadn't ridden since Andrew's birth — the doctor had sternly forbidden it — but she enjoyed driving Jeremy in the phaeton with Andrew's basket on the seat beside her. She had become a familiar sight on the roads around Grandon. She often stopped at some poor bothan to offer a freshly cooked barm brack, or soda bread, to the hungry peasants who called the hovel home.

Sometimes she drove out to see Henrietta and her twin boys, James and John . . . boys born two weeks after Andrew "with no trouble at all." But then they were so tiny Katherine felt a wave of smugness sweep over her as she saw them beside her own husky son. The two together didn't match Andrew's birth weight.

Now neither the crook in her baby's little finger, the one the doctor said might never be quite straight, nor the dagger-shaped birthmark that had so startled her when she first saw it on his chest seemed of any importance.

Stephen, arriving home sooner than Henrietta had expected, brought his wife and their two sons to see Katherine and Peter. And of course Andrew.

When all three babies had been properly admired, the two young women drew apart to compare notes on motherhood, leaving the men to talk of more masculine concerns.

Peter was anxious to know what his friend thought of the *Queen O'Malley* after a long sea voyage in her.

"She's a queen, and no mistake," Stephen enthused. "I'm not denying I had me doubts at first whether iron vessels could be any improvement over the wooden ones. But when the *Great Britain* hung on the rocks in Dundrum Bay for months, blasted by the fiercest storms the Irish Sea could throw at her, yet still in good condition when she got off the rocks, I had to do an about-think. Wooden ships, even vessels like the *Suffolk*, are no match for iron ships.

"What makes the *Suffolk* so special?' Peter's question hinted at a hidden motive.

Stephen took a deep breath and leaned forward before replying. "Well, the *Suffolk* and her sister ships were built of good solid oak, keels were seven lengths of oak with a depth and width of 18 inches, ribs were over a foot wide and a good foot apart. Plus the boats had the added protection of external planking four inches thick near their keel, decreasing to two inches near the upper deck."

"Are you telling me that ships like the *Suffolk*, solidly built throughout to withstand gunfire or storms, are going to be outdated? Obsolete? It seems a pity. Why, those old ships carried 70 tons of iron and 270 tons of shingle in their holds just to give them stability in battle or in a bad blow."

"That's right, Peter. In my opinion the wooden brigantines and privateers that made Cork City one of the richest ports in Europe in the seventeen-hundreds have had their day. I'm sold on iron ships. I'm sold on the new screw propellers too. You know the ones I mean?"

"Are you speaking of those patented by that Englishman, Francis Pettit Smith?"

"Yes. But . . . ," and here Stephen sighed as if honesty made him make the concession, "when a wooden ship is fitted with those new steam-driven propellers, as well as sails, it's possible to reach America in less than three weeks."

"I'm glad to hear your opinion of steam-versus-sail, Stephen, and how you rate iron ships to wooden ones. It certainly agrees with what Andrew Hennessey would have said about them, but then he built the first steamboat in Ireland so naturally wouldn't be saying anything against them. Anyway, a new client who approached the bank last week for a substantial loan shares your opinion about the superiority of steel. He predicts a great future for the shipbuilding industry here in the south. At the moment he's considering setting up either in Cork or in Grandon. Cork has the advantage of being known as one of the richest ports in Europe, thanks to both its ship-building industry and the slaughter houses that ship thousands of Irish cattle each year to European markets. However, Grandon, on Bantry Bay, has one of the best natural harbours in the world."

Stephen slapped his friend enthusiastically on the back. "Either site he settles on, your client has the right idea, old man. If I had money to invest I'd be fancying finding it a spot building the new ships. Changes are coming. It's inevitable. There'll be fewer sailing ships with auxiliary steam, more steamships with auxiliary sail. And when expertise in building motors and utilizing their power improves, the next step will be all steam . . . There's an exciting future for steam right enough."

Peter's dark brows lifted into a question, a wicked glitter dancing momentarily in his eyes. "What about the midshipmen's uniforms? Will they become as outdated as the ships the lads serve on? Or will the Admiralty vote to keep the coats with three brass buttons on their sleeves? I'm told they were put there to discourage young midshipmen from wiping runny noses on their sleeve.

Stephen grimaced. "A filthy habit that. It earned the lads the nickname 'snotties.'"

But before Stephen could say anything more Peter shifted uneasily in his chair, his long legs stretching unconsciously towards the glowing warmth of the fireplace. Steepling his fingers, he stared at them absently, his mind searching for the exact right words.

"The future for iron ships powered by steam sounds brighter than the future for the Irish people. I can't see anything good in that crystal ball unless the level of manufacturing in this country can be raised substantially. Failing that, what solution is there? Except emigration." Peter's voice was worried.

"The country has too much rocky, unproductive land, especially around Grandon and further west, to support so many mouths. There isn't enough fertile land to divide among today's exploding population. Six sons can't eke out a living for six families on a fraction of the land their father farmed and still saw his brood go hungry.

"As I see it, the only solution, apart from emigration, is for Ireland to follow in England's steps and encourage more manufacturing. The drawback is Ireland has no coal, no source of cheap fuel. But if Irish exports weren't taxed so unfairly by the British I still think we could compete." As Peter finished speaking worry furrowed his forehead. His mouth was grim, his eyes brooding.

"Promoting industry has always been your forte, Peter, hasn't it?" Stephen's face was an oval of concern as he absently tapped the bowl of an unlit pipe against a cupped palm.

"Exactly. That's why I'm going out on a limb. Only last week I made a substantial loan to clients eager to start a creamery in Grandon. With so many dairy cows in the area it's an idea that should float. There's no reason why Ireland can't produce butter and cheese equal to Danish products, and they should command similarly good prices in our shops. As they should in England and on the continent. Oh I know, a creamery isn't going to solve Ireland's problems, but it is a step. How do you eat an elephant if not one bite at a time?"

After the Cassidys had left, Katherine snuggled close to Peter. "I don't know how they can seem so happy. Stephen will soon be sailing off to the other side of the world again. Henrietta will be left alone with nothing but her children and her worries for Stephen's safe return. Praying there'll be another safe voyage charted up on the company books. What sort of life is that? It wouldn't suit me. Nobody's luck can last forever."

Peter smiled affectionately as he reached to pull his wife into the warm circle of his arms, his face bending until it gently brushed against the soft sweetness of her hair. "Well, I expect Stephen and Henrietta have learned to make the most of the best, the least of the worst. Life for all of us is made up of circumstances over which we often have no control. Except our own reactions to them."

Katherine tilted her face for her husband's kiss then pulled away. "I must check on Andrew. Did you notice how he waved his rattle when he discovered it made the other babies laugh? I'm sure they'll become great friends."

As Katherine left the room, her lips were compressed into a troubled line. "Am I making the most of the best? Peter and I are happy now, but what if . . . ?" She shuddered, crossed herself, then wondered why. She wasn't a Catholic.

Chapter Eleven
Turko and the Enemy's "Flag"

"You've done it again, m'lady. Another strapping son ter make yer husband proud. Though Oi must say 'tis not him who plants the seed as has much to do with yer accomplishment. His part is done in nought but pleasure. We women," and here Mrs. O'Clarety's kindly face took on a sour look, "we're them as does the work. And there's little enough of pleasure in any of it."

The midwife stopped long enough to wring out a cloth from the basin of tepid water dominating a bedside table before speaking again. When she did it was as if she was crooning comfort to an exhausted child, a crooning that seemed in keeping with the gentleness of the hands sponging Katherine Moriarty's sweat-drenched body.

"Yer too fine a frame for easy birthen, m'lady. With three sons me advice is leave birthen to women better built for it. There's them as can do it with no trouble a-tall a-tall. For you 'tis near a miracle."

Katherine's white face on the pillow, her dark hair cascading around it like an ebony halo, looked hauntingly lovely to the man who stooped to kiss her before taking his third son from the midwife presenting it to him as proudly as if she herself had been responsible for its existence. Which in part she had been, for while Katherine's second and third sons had been normal size at birth, forcing them out into the world had not been easy. The doctor said it was partly her build. Partly due to the scar tissue from her first delivery.

Peter Moriarty looked down at the infant in his arms and smiled. The tiny red-faced bundle of humanity squirming his annoyance at the world had the same dark hair and blue eyes as his two-year-old brother, William Peter. People often said how much young Billy looked like his father, whereas when they saw five-year-old Andrew they shook their heads. Some wondered.

Katherine's eyes were closed, her face etched with the lines of exhaustion. She was caught in the daze of a dreadful weariness. Peter, sensing her need to rest quietly, handed the baby back to the midwife and tiptoed from the room. The agony, the ordeal his wife had endured, tore at his soul. No man had the right to expect so much of a woman. But she had determination and courage. And a lot of heart. He smiled wryly to himself. Those were the qualities she once told him one looked for in a horse.

Katherine took longer to recover from this confinement. Longer before she wanted Peter sharing her bed. Longer before she could enjoy his love-making. The doctor had warned Peter there might never be another child. Indeed it would be better for Katherine's health if there were not. But with three sons Peter was content.

Old Seamus O'Connor, hearing his third grandson was named Michael Seamus, immediately added a codicil to his will. The other grandfather, Donal Moriarty, grumbled, "'Tis strange Andrew Donal doesn't look more like a Moriarty." But young William Peter's looks had seemed to please him and Billy had soon gained a special place in the old man's heart.

Hearing this Katherine had smiled confidently to herself. Her two younger sons seemed assured of sponsorship for whatever they wished to do in life. She had long ago made up her mind the inheritance from her mother, small though it was, must be saved for Andrew's education. She had too proud and independent a spirit to expect her husband to educate another man's son. Even though he was unaware of it. However, she'd have to find a way to make Peter think it was just a woman's whim and not become suspicious about why she was so anxious to do it.

Andrew, going on six now, was attending the National School in Grandon. It was a mixed school that taught no frills but concentrated on the three R's. It wasn't free but, as it was church-related, parents paid as much (or as little) as their circumstances would permit.

After National School those able to afford more education must go to the grammar school in Cork. Or Dublin. Cork was closer, but if Andrew attended school in Dublin he could stay with her father, or Peter's. In any case, that decision didn't have to be made for a few years yet. "In the meantime enjoy every minute you have them with you," Katherine told herself.

Andrew, a lively, thoughtful youngster, was adored by his younger brothers.

The Moriarty boys never had to *look* for trouble. Trouble had a way of finding them.

It was a fine spring morning. The sun shone, the birds sang. The sidewalk seemed the ideal place to play marbles. Andrew, teaching Billy and Michael the finer points of scoring with the pretty glass alleys his father had given him for Christmas, remembered to step aside and speak politely to the priest who strolled past, then turned to watch.

If the boys hadn't been so intent on their game they might have wondered why the "man of the cloth" had stopped at the corner, apparently to watch them play. Did a priest have nothing better to do on such a fine day than lounge at the corner, mouthing words of encouragement whenever one of the lads made a good shot? The Moriarty boys weren't members of his flock. They were Protestants.

And had the boys looked, they might have wondered why the good Father was beckoning with a hand-behind-his-back wave. Why not wave openly if he wanted to attract attention?

So the boys, intent on their game of marbles, had no warning that disaster in the shape of a policeman was about to strike. They didn't know the upholder of the law was racing towards them like an avenging angel until his body leaned into the turn. What they saw then was a red-faced police officer bearing down on them, his arms outstretched, his legs pumping furiously, his breath like a blast out of hell.

"Begorrah! Oi've got ye now, ye young rapscalions. An tis runnen ye in Oi'll be doing."

Terror shot into Andrew's throat when he saw hands as big as grain-scoops reaching for his collar. "Run, Billy! Run!" he screamed. Dodging the avalanche of fury descending on him, he snatched up Michael and made a wild grab for Billy's hand to help propel him faster. There seemed little hope the boys could outrun the law. But why did they need to? They had only been playing marbles.

Suddenly a blur of tan flashed past the boys and planted itself squarely in front of the policeman. Turko's growls, exploding from deep in his throat, sounded like an about-to-erupt volcano. His hackles were stiff, his eyes were blazing. The lips drawn back in a vicious snarl exposed a full mouth of razor-sharp teeth. The little dog was quivering in anger and leaning forward as if straining against an invisible leash holding him momentarily in check.

The hefty policeman, seeing his path blocked by a small Irish Terrier, promptly booted the animal out of his way. That was a mistake. Turko, exploding with rage, flew at his assailant and sank his teeth firmly into the seat of the man's pants. The man was much too big for the dog to flip and kill as he would a rat. So Turko braced his feet and hung on with all the tenacity for which his breed was famous.

Suddenly there was the violent sound of tearing cloth, followed by a high screeching wail. "Ochon! Ochon! The cailleach's got me!"

The policeman slammed to a halt, his hands trying frantically to cover the flabby expanse of ballooning buttocks protruding like neglected yeast dough, dough that having overflowed its original accommodation was in a rush to spread into more commodious quarters.

It reminded Mrs. Lee-Jones, the young woman crossing the intersection, of the slabs of freshly killed sowbelly hanging in her husband's shop. She fought back a naughty giggle at the sight of such an unusual exhibit.

The constable, his face the colour of a flaming sunset, jammed his bare bottom up against the weathered picket fence, then quickly thought better of it and lurched ahead, cursing savagely under his breath. The boards felt cold as Arctic ice. Worse, they were generously studded with splinters that jabbed at his naked buttocks like the tines of a meat fork in the hands of a wronged wife.

Mrs. Lee-Jones watched the officer's futile attempts to pull together the rent through which vagrant breezes, having no modesty at all, were playing hide-and-seek. She appeared to be controlling an outburst of laughter with considerable difficulty.

The policemen, feeling it important to maintain some

semblance of the dignity he felt his uniform demanded, had drawn himself somewhat stiffly up to attention, but his voice sounded squeaky. "Marnin to ye, ma'am." Then, by way of apology for not touching his cap, he said tersely, "Yon cailleach's got me. Sure'n that animal's more devil than dog."

The woman's eyebrows arched upwards but she maintained a straight face with remarkable aplomb as she watched Turko trotting home with a chunk of cloth dangling from his mouth. He looked as pleased with himself as if he had single-handedly captured an enemy stronghold and was carrying away their flag to prove it.

She spoke briskly, her eyes fixed on the policeman again. "Officer, if ye don't mind me sayen so, ye best whip off yer jacket and get yer bottom covered dacent like. I don't expect ye be wanting the Temperance Society ladies inspecting yer privates, comparing them to what they've got back home, because at this moment they'd get a right good view of everything you've got down there. And the ladies *are* headed this way."

The officer's face blanched. He looked as if he had been sentenced to a flogging, but he did as he was told. Clutching the coat tightly around his bare buttocks, he turned and ran. The flapping of the empty sleeves appeared to be propelling him to even greater speed.

Katherine and Peter were puzzled when their sons arrived home, too breathless to speak. It was Michael who managed to blurt out between sobs, "A policeman tried to catch us. He was going to throw us in jail."

Ignoring his parents' gasped "whatever for?" he gulped half hysterically as a worse thought surfaced. "What if he sent us to Australia on Uncle Stephen's ship? And we had to work in chain gangs until we died? Then we'd never see you and Mamma, ever again." That thought brought a fresh outburst of tears.

Peter quickly scooped the boy up and cradled him in his arms, soothing him, "Oh, Michael. We'd never let anything like that happen to you." Katherine felt a momentary stab of terror. What if Peter couldn't prevent it?

"Well," said Billy, having regained his breath and standing now with his feet apart, hands on his hips in a Napoleonic stance. "It almost happened. It would have. Except for Andrew, and Turko. Andrew helped us run real fast. Turko bit the policeman and made him stop chasing us." Billy flashed a smile around the room that said the affair was over, he'd had his say, and now it could be forgotten.

But Katherine turned to Andrew with a frown. "What were you children doing to make a policemen come after you?"

Andrew, nervously shifting from one foot to the other, raised troubled eyes to hers. "Nothing bad, Mamma. We were playing marbles with the alleys Dadda gave me. A priest kept telling us how well we played, so if the priest didn't see anything wrong with it, why did the policemen?" His face was puzzled. So was Katherine's as she turned towards her husband.

Peter stroked his chin thoughtfully, then a look of sudden understanding crept into his face. "I wonder if there isn't an old bylaw on the books that forbids playing marbles on the sidewalks. If Father O'Turke knew about it he may have seen it as a chance to get back at me. Yesterday I turned down his request for a loan to buy new silver chalices. I said I thought the church should be thinking more about feeding the poor of the parish than adding silver chalices. It sounds to me as if the good Father was beckoning up the policeman, making sure our boys would still be playing marbles when he got there." Peter's normally pleasant face took on an abrasive look.

At that moment Bridget entered the room. "Sir, ma'am, Mrs. Lee-Jones to see you. Shall I show her in?"

"Certainly, Bridget." Then, to her husband, "We work together on the Women's Guild."

A woman whose face suggested she had a love of laughter in her heart entered the room.

Turko, proudly carrying the "enemy flag" edged in ahead of her. After looking around as if to verify that everyone present realized he had done something of merit, he deposited the chunk of cloth in Katherine's lap. She picked up the dirty square between thumb and forefinger, held it aloft for a moment with a look that said she regretted the need to contaminate even two fingers with so foul an object, then quickly dropped it onto the floor.

Mrs. Lee-Jones was having trouble controlling her laughter, but her story verified what the boys had said. Suddenly Peter was conscious of a great fullness in his chest. A deep-rooted surge of pride in his boys, and in his dog, almost overwhelmed him. To hide his emotions he reached for Michael and buried his face in the dark hair which, no matter how often it was brushed, still managed to look like a pony's shaggy mane.

After Mrs. Lee-Jones had left, Peter's smile encompassed the room. "Don't any of you worry about this. I'll take a stroll and have a friendly chat with Anthony Black. As chief of the Royal Irish Constabulary I think he'll see the foolishness of keeping such a law on the books. But until it's revoked you boys are not to play marbles on the sidewalks. Understood?" Three heads nodded in unison.

Chapter Twelve
An Aborted Dog Fight

Most mornings Peter took his sons with him to swim in Bantry Bay. They had learned quickly to become good swimmers. Perhaps that was because his method of teaching a boy to swim was unorthodox. He'd toss the lad off the pier, then jump in after him . . . just in case the youngster didn't resurface. Peter maintained children learned to swim faster as toddlers, because toddlers have no fear of water. It had worked with his brood. In no time at all they were frolicking and sliding in and out of the water as easily as seals on a rocky coastline.

One morning when they were walking back along the sand after a swim, a powerfully built stranger in a morning coat and top hat strolled towards them, imperiously twirling a heavy gold-studded cane. Closer inspection showed he had a cruel mouth, a predatory nose that looked as if it had been stuck on hot and had run, and small, crafty eyes scowling at the world from under craggy brows as if the universe was his to do with as he pleased. But the Irish Terrier straining on its leash beside him was a magnificent-looking animal. It made Turko, standing beside Andrew with a look of doggy curiosity on his face, seem a midget.

"Good morning, sir," Peter said politely. "That's a fine looking dog you have."

"Quite so, my man," the stranger said with a cold, condescending air. "The best fighting terrier in Ireland." Whereupon he slyly unsnapped the leash and shoved the dog towards Turko. The animal, needing no other encouragement, sprang at Turko with a vicious snarl. Peter let out a startled shout, but before he could intervene the big terrier was reaching for Turko's jugular. And Turko, never one to back away from a scrap, was reaching for his.

Andrew, screaming "You get away from my dog," was fiercely kicking the bigger animal with his bare feet. The only effect that had was that a dagger-shaped birthmark on his chest turned a vivid red, making it more noticeable than usual.

With each dog's teeth firmly embedded in the other's throat it looked like a fight to the death. As Peter watched, the big dog's eyes began to glaze over. Immediately the stranger, his face twisted into a horrendous scowl, began cursing savagely and beating Turko with his heavy cane.

Peter shouted, "Stop it. You'll kill the dog." He roughly shoved the man aside, snatched up both dogs by their collars, strode out into the water, and held their heads under until, half-drowned and gasping for breath, they released their death grips. Then he tossed the big terrier towards its master, saying curtly, "I suggest you keep your animal leashed, sir. Obviously he isn't the fighter you think he is." Then he turned to the boys who had been staring opened-mouthed. "Andrew, you and your brothers get dressed, and take Turko home. I'll be along in a few minutes."

Andrew shot a hostile glare at the man, whose steely eyes were sweeping him with a look that said nothing they saw would ever be forgotten, but stored away until it could be hauled out and used to his own advantage. And today the birthmark on Andrew's chest had caught his attention.

"No, your Lordship," said Peter coldly a few minutes later, "I'll not accept your offer. Turko is not for sale. Not even to Ireland's Chief Justice. There are things we Irish value more than money." With that he swung on his heel and walked after his sons. No voice of caution stirred within to warn him he'd just made an enemy of the most powerful, the most vindictive man in all of Ireland.

Chapter Thirteen
A Tea That Failed

Concentration worked a furrow between Katherine's eyes as she turned the pages of a dog-eared cookbook.

"Which 'at-home' this week, Princess?" Peter asked idly as he looked up from his morning paper.

"This is for the women whose husbands, or fathers, have a title or a profession. Those who consider themselves so superior, so elite they'd feel insulted, contaminated even, if asked to drink tea socially with the wives of the tradespeople they deal with every day. It's disgusting. But because I'm the bank manager's wife I'm expected to entertain both classes . . . but at two separate 'at-homes.'"

"I know, Princess. It's a stupid system. But there it is. Some of the bank's best customers are tradespeople."

"And some of their wives are my best friends." stormed Katherine. "So why can't I invite whoever I please? Whenever I please. Oh I know, I know. It's all for the good of the dear old bank. And my dear old husband," she added with a sly twinkle as her normal good nature returned. "I'd entertain Mrs. Devil herself if it meant helping you to get a promotion. Not that I'm in a hurry to leave Grandon. I like it here."

"That's my girl," Peter said softly as he pulled her to him. He kissed her warmly before saying, "Oh, by the by, the Earl of Grandon asked me to send you his wife's regrets. She can't be at your 'at-home' this week. She had to go rather unexpectedly to visit a sick relative in Northern Ireland."

It didn't bother Katherine that she was expected to have the wives of bank customers in for tea every month on her "at-home" days. What still irked was the need for two separate teas — one for the upper crust, one for the lower. The importance of that was something she had learned the hard way. She could giggle about it now. At the time she had been too furious to feel the mortification she supposed such a social blunder ought to have caused her.

The doctor and Peter had both insisted Katherine must have no "at-homes" until she felt completely recovered from her three difficult pregnancies. Consequently, Michael was almost two before she had her first "at-home" tea. And then, because her husband's advancement could be influenced by those they knew socially, she had gone to a lot of trouble to make a good first impression on the wives of the bank's best customers.

Yet despite her careful planning and the days spent preparing for it, her first "at-home" was a disaster. It came perilously close to blighting her husband's career. Maybe their marriage. And it might have done so . . . except for an unexpected visitor.

It had started out nicely enough. The invitations, engraved with the date and time of the "at-home," had been distributed at her husband's discretion. However, without his knowledge, she had invited Mrs. Lee-Jones. Mrs. Lee-Jones had become a good friend to Katherine, and her son Brian was Andrew's best friend. Her husband owned a thriving drapery establishment catering to the carriage trade, as well as several smaller shops. He was one of Grandon's highly respected citizens, one of the bank's most valued customers.

There was no snobbery in Katherine. A poor man worthy of respect was better than a corrupt and perverted king in her eyes. Sycophants who grovelled to impress those they hoped would help them up the social ladder were insufferable bores. How could such people have any effect on her life, or the lives of those she loved? The repercussions triggered by inviting women from different stations in life to meet as social equals in her drawing room had never entered her head.

Still, Katherine might have carried off the faux pas successfully if it hadn't been for Lady Enid Highips from over towards Killenlough.

Sir Percy Highips had acquired his holdings and his title for services rendered to the British in some relatively minor Irish skirmish. A skirmish that was soon quelled and quickly forgotten except by those who forfeited their property, or those who had gained from it. Sir Percy was in the latter category. Being a mild-mannered man, he did his best to get along with everybody, and he usually succeeded. But not so his wife. Lady Enid remembered her own humble beginnings and was determined no one else should.

When Lady Highips first swept up to Katherine on the afternoon of her "at-home," the younger woman's mouth opened, then closed without a sound. She had to gulp twice to strangle a giggle before she could murmur a polite "How-do-you-do, your ladyship. So glad you could come today."

The woman had sagging breasts, darting eyes, flabby jowls, and a sallow complexion. Her mouth, compressed and haughty, looked as if it might have been stuck on as an afterthought below a massive nose. It was a face to frighten a baby.

Her body was like a sprawling wilderness rising out of the mists of a dazzling Paris creation that oscillated when she moved like the rainbow-hued caparison draping a

Rajah's elephant. Her hat had recently had a remarkable encounter with a flower shop. The brown hair haphazardly frizzling out below it looked as if it had been stuck on with glue. Her presence dominated Katherine's drawing room in a blinding clash of colour and poor taste.

Ignoring Katherine as someone of small importance, Her Ladyship quickly glanced around the drawing room, and spotted Lady Bingham from Mullagatoony Castle. Having done so, she quickly brushed past Katherine, almost trampled Mrs. Anthony Black, wife of Grandon's well-liked Chief of the Royal Irish Constabulary, and completely ignored Canon O'Hara's wife and daughter Marjorie in her drive to zoom in on the titled lady. She was like a falcon sighting prey, diving to get it in her talons.

"My dear Lady Bingham, I cawn't tell you how happy I am to see you here today. I always say it is so rewarding when one can have a stimulating conversation with someone in one's own class."

Lady Bingham's brows arched in a curious fashion and her mouth twitched a little as she replied coolly, "Really, Lady Enid? Then I fear you often feel quite unrewarded. You've met Mrs. Black, of course." Mrs. Black was acknowledged by the coolest of nods. As was Mrs. O'Hara, a meek little woman who had been staring absently off into space as she perched on the high-backed sofa rather like a sparrow contemplating flight.

Obviously annoyed to find the chair beside Lady Bingham already occupied, Lady Enid squeezed herself into a fine old armchair of carved walnut. Wheezing from the effort, she looked around with magisterial dignity. Realizing she was sitting next to Marjorie O'Hara, the Canon's pretty daughter, Lady Enid managed the briefest of smiles. As if her smiles were something to be dispensed with miserly caution. Marjorie didn't return the smile. The girl seemed to have lost her normal sunny nature.

Then the self-styled lady raised a jewel-studded lorgnette and studied the furnishings with a distinct air of disapproval. "Why my dear Mrs. Moriarty, this place looks positively dowdy. Cawn't the bank do better for you?"

Katherine bristled but managed to keep her voice cool and impersonal. Her eyes swept over the huge stone fireplace, the mahogany bookcase taking up most of one wall, the Chippendale mirror in ornate rococo style, the high mullioned windows, the coffered ceiling, the good, but no longer new furniture . . . furniture that seemed to give the room an air of timeless tranquillity. "It's really very comfortable and we like it. Don't you agree it has a lovely antique look? You know, like a grand old dowager down on her luck?" Lady Enid didn't answer. She had never had occasion to know a grand old dowager, down on her luck or otherwise.

At that moment Bridget announced Mrs. Lee-Jones and Katherine, smiling, rose to greet her friend. Lady Bingham looked mildly surprised when she saw the newcomer. Mrs. Black's eyes sparkled, as if she was suddenly anticipating an interesting afternoon after all. Mrs. O'Hara and her daughter appeared too intent on their own thoughts to pay any heed to what was going on.

But Lady Enid's face turned purple. She began spluttering like a cat that has just been hauled scratching and clawing out of a barrel of dirty rainwater. As she faced Katherine, the pudgy hands gripping a gold-studded walking cane were white-knuckled. Her face grew twisted and contorted as she fought for words. When they came they burst from her like flames exploding through a burning thatch.

"How dare you insult me like this? I've never been so humiliated in my entire life. Mrs. Moriarty, the disrespect you've shown me is reprehensible. Surely you must know better than to allow a commoner into your home while I, a titled lady, am your guest? And you don't need to think you can get away with it."

Lady Highips was pounding the floor with her walking stick as she spoke, hammering home each word with deadly venom. Then, without any warning, her cane was raised abruptly and pointed at Katherine as if it was the sword of Moses calling down the wrath of God. And if God knew what was good for Him, He'd send it fast.

Meanwhile the noise, reaching the bank below, startled the clerk in the teller's cage. Thinking that a portion of the ceiling was about to fall on him, he accidentally knocked the money he had been counting onto the floor, then had to scramble to retrieve it. A customer saw him drop down and, sure he must have been shot, made a wild dash for the door. He didn't want to be accused of murder.

Back upstairs Katherine's drawing room had suddenly grown deathly quiet. Sweat dripping off Lady Enid's three generous chins could actually be heard plopping onto the floor.

Katherine stood rooted in stunned amazement, her tongue withered at the root.

Lady Enid drew herself up the way she imagined a grand duchess might, and swept from the room. In reality her exit made Katherine think of a rutting walrus. But her departing words floated back with menacing clarity. "You've not heard the last of this."

Lady Bingham, followed by Mrs. Black and the O'Hara ladies, rose quickly, saying, "We'd better go too, Mrs. Moriarty. We'd be happy to get to know you better. But some other day." Then Lady Bingham patted Katherine's arm in a comforting gesture. "Don't worry, dear. We all know what the woman is like." With that they were gone and Katherine was alone with Mrs. Lee-Jones.

Or was she? Mrs. Lee-Jones too had vanished. That good lady, having immediately sensed what she had walked into, had discreetly disappeared down the hall. Now she was in the kitchen enjoying a cup of tea with Bridget. Katherine prowled the drawing room like a caged panther. She was furious.

Furious for committing the faux pas and ruining a tea she had so hoped would go off well. And furious with Lady Highip . . . . who did the old hag think she was anyway? But she was more furious at the snobbery of a class system that put insufferable people on a pedestal because they had a title.

Later, when she poured her woes into Peter's sympathetic ear, he looked serious. "It's a rotten system, I agree. But it happens to be the system, and unfortunately we aren't in a position to ignore it. That woman's husband could, I suppose, go to the board of governors and stir up trouble for me. But I don't think Highips will go that far. Not if he gets his head out from under her heel long enough to have a proper thought of his own.

"Unfortunately they've got a title and more money than breeding and sometimes that's what talks. On his own Highips is a fairly decent chap. But I'm not sure how much influence he has over his wife. Anyway, I'll have a quiet talk with him. He'll understand you didn't invite Mrs. Lee-Jones here with any idea of humiliating her ladyship. But from now on, Princess, you must have two at-home days. And it might be a good idea if you dropped a little note of apology to Lady Enid. To smooth her ruffled feathers."

Katherine exploded like torched gunpowder. "Never! I'll never apologize! I'd rather pluck the old hen and throw her out for the crows to peck at."

Peter's face was a sombre study in concentration. This could prove a sticky business after all. He'd better handle it carefully. When his wife considered herself in the right she could be as inflexible as tempered steel. He was still pondering the matter when Bridget knocked at the drawing-room door in breathless haste, her eyes bright with excitement.

"Sir, ma'am, there's a gentleman downstairs as sends up his card. Says if it's convenient he'd like to pay his respects. And ye should see his coach. Baint nothing like it been seen before in Grandon, I'll warrant."

While Bridget was rushing back down the stairs Katherine quickly glanced at the card, then moved towards the beautifully framed rococo mirror. After smoothing the folds of a blue dress that matched her eyes and fitted her to perfection, she reached to nervously push a stray curl back into place. Lord Millhaven? Somehow the name had a vaguely familiar ring. Wasn't that the court dandy whose name had often been linked with that of the Prince of Wales when that scion of England's hope had indulged in his sometimes nefarious escapades? Yes, that must be where she'd heard it.

Meanwhile Peter, who had moved to a window looking down onto the town square, let out a gasp of surprise. "Now why is a man with a carriage like *that* visiting *us*?" Katherine hurried to his side. The coach was indeed a magnificent conveyance. Emerald green, with heavy gold trim. A coachman, a footman and a postilion, in matching uniforms as resplendent as the noon-day sun, were controlling the restive six-in-hand with easy expertise. The horses were jet black. And beautiful.

A crowd of dogs and small boys had followed the coach up the street. Now that it had pulled into the square and stopped, adults too flocked to look and gape and speculate, jostling each other for space like bees around honey.

Certainly nothing that grand had ever been seen in Grandon before. Lady Highip, passing in her coach, rapped smartly for the driver to stop, then waved an imperious hand at a small boy. "Who owns that carriage?" she demanded in a harsh voice. "And what's it stopped there for?"

"Don't roightly know who owns 'er ma'am, but 'tis someone moighty fancy that's fer darn sure. Reckon he's a friend of the Moriartys."

As the Highip carriage moved away Lady Enid chewed her underlip in vexation. What wouldn't she give to have such a conveyance stop at HER door. Envy tempered with regret jittered up her spine. Perhaps she had been too hasty in berating Mrs. Moriarty. The woman, or her husband, obviously knew someone of importance. And Lady Enid had a theory that if one hoped to advance one's own cause, important people should be cultivated. With assiduity.

Yes, I'll do it. I'll write her an apology as soon as I get home. Blame it on the curse we women have. And I'll include an invitation to a dinner party. If I invite other important people they can hardly refuse. Let me see. There's Lord and Lady Bingham, Dr. and Mrs. Butler (they're already friends of the

Moriartys) and there's Lord Dunraughton. I doubt they've met him. He's been roaming around America a lot since he lost his wife. And that must be almost six years ago. . . . Suddenly Highips' wife ordered the driver to whip up the horses. She was in a hurry now to get home and set her plan in motion.

Meanwhile Lord Millhaven had acknowledged Peter with a brief nod, but his hooded eyes had studied Katherine carefully as he gallantly bowed and lifted her hand to his lips. A few moments later, seated in the drawing room, he said, "You're the living image of your mother right enough. Just sad I am I can't call you me daughter."

In response to Katherine's startled gasp, the puzzled frown on her husband's face, he hurried on. "You don't know me, Katherine . . . I may call you that, mayn't I?. . . but I once knew your mother. You could say I was a rejected suitor." His smile was glum, as if he was looking back on a lifetime of blunders. "Threw me over for your father. But I like to think I might have had a chance if I hadn't been deemed an Englishman.

"When I told her my father had died and I, now the fifth Earl of Millhaven, would have to return to England to take my rightful place as head of the Millhaven estates, she drew away like a frightened doe, saying she couldn't marry me if it meant living in England. She returned my ring and refused to see me again. Not even when I went to say good-bye.

"Hardest thing I ever did . . . to go without seeing her again, but at the time I believed she would come to see that living with me in England might not be so bad. Instead, when I next returned to Ireland it was to find her married to another." His voice was ragged, edged with tenderness and sorrow.

He prowled back and forth, his face muscles twitching, his eyes staring straight ahead, but seeing only the past.

Finally he half smiled, causing his face to crease in a way that hinted there was still a devil lurking somewhere in this man. "I'm not proud of the years I spent disgracing the family name. After your mother rejected me I tried to drown myself in drink and wild living . . . until I finally met a woman who spent her life trying to make me forget your mother. I never did, of course, but eventually one has to accept that life doesn't fulfill all our desires. So I picked up the left-overs and tried to build on them."

Katherine's eyes were as big as barrels as she sat in stunned silence, staring at a man who until today she had barely known existed. A man with what had once been copper-red hair, now generously sprinkled with grey, a wide but deeply furrowed brow, a nose not quite straight, and a determined chin. Despite his age he bore a subtle look of virility, a certain harshness that both intrigued and repelled her. And made her feel that somewhere, somehow she might have met him before. But that of course was impossible.

Finally, a slight cough from her husband reminded her she ought to pull the bell and have Bridget bring up tea. When it arrived she was struck with an impish desire to giggle. Lord Millhaven, cohort of royalty and lion of English society, was eating what Grandon's gentry had walked away from an hour earlier. In fact from the way that nobleman was stuffing his mouth with buttered barm brack and tiny tea cakes, he was finding it quite a pleasant undertaking.

He was speaking to Peter. "As Bank Manager here you must have a good idea what the real conditions are among the tenant farmers. As you probably know, our English

Parliament under Lord John Russell is of the opinion Britain mustn't offer free help to Ireland's indigent or it will demoralize the country. They feel if a man can eat without working, he won't work. Even talk of creating employment through a program of public works has the opposition yowling. They claim any such plan would interfere with private enterprise and have a long-term negative effect. And tell me, why is it the tenant farmers are so poor? Years ago when I was in Ireland most of them could provide a reasonable living for their families."

Peter allowed himself a sad smile. "Well, your Lordship, if I could answer all those questions I wouldn't be a bank manager in Grandon. I'd be sitting up there beside God.

"You asked about outright relief. Human nature being what it is, there'll always be a few who'll ask for dole even if work is available, but by and large I don't think so. Dole is no more than subsistence living. When a man is healthy and can better himself by working, he'll work. But conditions are such now that tenants on the poorer farms are unable to even subsist, and if we have another bad potato year the number of hungry can only increase."

"But why?" asked Lord Millhaven, leaning forward with a puzzled look, "Why is it when Ireland produces cattle, hogs, and sheep for export — corn too — the people still starve?"

Peter sighed heavily. "That's the crux of the problem. Tenants must sell whatever few animals and grains they are able to raise on their holdings to pay the rent and taxes. Keep a roof, albeit a poor one, over their heads. If they paid smaller rents and fewer taxes to your government they wouldn't be so dependent on the potato crop. There is no shortage of food in Ireland. There is a shortage of money to buy it."

"In that case maybe the idea of creating public works isn't all bad. But I don't understand why a crop failure in Ireland should be so much worse than a similar failure in England."

"That is something I can answer," Peter remarked. "In England you have more industry, factories where young men leaving the land, or older ones for that matter, can get work. Ireland has little in the way of industry. And what we produce is subject to heavy English taxes. On top of that Ireland has an ever growing population. Farms that once provided for one family are divided and shared now between many."

"If the landlords didn't demand such high rent would the tenants' lot improve?"

"Only to a degree. I tell you, sir, it's a terrible problem we're facing. It doesn't seem reasonable to expect a landlord to bankrupt himself by lowering rents, when if he had no tenants, he could put cattle or sheep on the land and get substantially better returns for himself. But then what would the people presently on the land do?"

"Emigration?" asked Lord Millhaven.

"That is certainly one solution. There are landlords now paying the passage so their tenants can go to America and the land owners can then turn their holdings into pasture with a clear conscience. Unfortunately, not all emigrants are lucky enough to have their passage paid. Nor will all who emigrate survive the sea voyage . . . I'm told conditions on some vessels are worse than those on the slavers you Britons oppose with such self-righteous fervour. However, those who survive the trip can usually better themselves in the new world, and then many of them send back money so their relatives can emigrate."

Lord Millhaven grunted irritably, "Doesn't sound like much of a solution. Don't imagine the poor devils fancy leaving their country. For many it would be forever."

"You're exactly right, sir. When an Irish emigrant leaves, family and friends hold a wake. For them he's as good as dead."

Lord Millhaven looked at Katherine, who had been listening with rapt attention, then turned back towards Peter. "I've always claimed Ireland had the most beautiful scenery in the world, the loveliest women, and the finest horses. While I haven't taken time recently to inspect your horses, I can certainly vouch that Grandon is tops when it comes to scenery and women. Now, if you good people will excuse me I'd better get on my way. I have to be in Cork by nightfall. Thank you, sir, for your assessment of the Irish situation. I'll take what you've said back to Westminster. But don't hold your breath. Most members are a stubborn, stiff-necked lot who don't take kindly to outside advice. As for you, Katherine my dear, if you're like your mother I don't fancy any amount of persuading could induce you to come to England, but if you do you'll find a warm welcome awaiting you at Millhaven. Before I leave would you grant the whim of an old man who would have liked to have had you for his daughter? May I kiss you?"

He opened his arms and with a small, inarticulate sound Katherine moved into them.

When the door closed behind him Peter put his hand firmly on his wife's shoulder, and together they watched as Lord Millhaven started towards his coach, then stopped and turned back when he saw the Moriarty boys playing near the bank entrance.

He appeared interested in what Andrew had in his

hand. Katherine grimaced. Andrew was forever rescuing things like frogs, that didn't need rescuing, or injured birds, that did. "He's having quite a conversation," Peter muttered almost resentfully. "Wonder what he finds so interesting about our boys?"

"He's an old man with little left but memories of wasted years, and dreams of what might have been. Our boys, grandchildren of the woman he loved and lost, are stepping stones leading him back to all that was best in his life."

As Katherine finished speaking Lord Millhaven moved towards his coach, then turned to look up at the window and, seeing their faces, took off his plumed hat and gave it a jaunty flourish, reminding Peter of the way a General signals victory. A moment later he was gone in a whirr of wheels and a blaze of gold and green. The horses raced through a gaping crowd that respectfully sprang back, curtseying and doffing their caps as if to royalty.

Peter scarcely noticed. He had just realized his oldest son had the same colour hair as their departing guest. Then he shrugged inwardly. Lots of people had red hair.

The dust from the coach hadn't properly settled when three excited boys, with flushed faces and unruly hair, burst in upon their parents.

"Guess what!" shouted Michael. "That man has a crook in his finger. Just like Andrew. Only his is worse. He says the leprechauns made it crooked because long ago he spied on a wee green man when he was hammering the sole on a fairy queen's shoe. He says because Andrew's finger only has a very small crook, perhaps his leprechaun was working on an elf's shoe. Or the shoe of a very young fairy."^

Andrew, looking superior and far wiser than his younger brother, put his hand in his pocket and pulled out something to show his parents. He knew there were no such things as leprechauns. The man was just fooling. But he hadn't been fooling when he opened Andrew's fingers, then closed them around ten gold sovereigns, saying, "I stole them from a leprechaun's pot of gold. I think he'd like you to have them. To help make up for giving you a wee crook in your finger." And then when he saw Billy and Michael carefully studying their hands, hoping they might discover they too had a crooked finger, he had laughed and taken Billy's hand and closed it on five gold sovereigns. He closed Michael's on three.

"Leprechaun indeed," Katherine scoffed to Peter. "More like Dr. Butler's forceps. It's lucky the lad doesn't have worse than a crooked finger for all the pulling and straining that went into his birthing."

Peter looked at her absently. "Just the same, Princess, it was kind of Lord Millhaven to be so generous, though I expect a penny to folks like us means more than a sovereign does to him." Then he stood up and spoke brusquely, "Tomorrow I'll have the boys open savings accounts. With Ireland in such a turmoil one never knows what the future will hold for any of us."

The day's events had shaken Katherine more than she realized. Suddenly her eyes misted, her lips quivered, and she cried. Not for herself, but for a lonely old man who might have been her father, and now had nothing but his memories. Finally she looked up at Peter and managed a tremulous smile. Their hands met and knit together. They had each other.

Later that evening Peter ran his hands gently over the delicate slope of his wife's shoulders as she sat on the bed with her legs curled around herself like a cozy kitten. She was so deep in thought his touch startled her.

"Still thinking about Lord Millhaven's leprechauns?" he quizzed.

"Oh, in a sort of way," she murmured, "but I expect lonely old men with loads of money like to wallow in nostalgia. And why shouldn't they? They can afford to indulge their whims. No matter how fanciful if it makes them happy."

Then, as if having said that the matter was settled to her satisfaction, she raised her arms and encircled Peter's neck, drawing his face close to her own. "When your father dies you'll inherit most of his property, won't you? Isn't that the way it is when you're the older son?"

"Theoretically that is so, but not necessarilly. Except for titles that have hereditary rank. They *must* go to the oldest male heir. Those given without hereditary rank die with the bearer."

Remembering Lady Highip's threat earlier in the day, a frown creased her forehead. "Are you trying to tell me as gently as possible that you may not inherit your father's wealth? That if for some reason you lost your job we could end up paupers?"

"Of course not. I could find other work." Despising himself for alarming her he said quietly, "As regards inheriting from my father anything is possible. Your step-sister, my sister-in-law, appears to be devoting her life to ingratiating herself with my father. You can be sure she isn't doing it for our benefit."

Then he laughed a warm and very masculine laugh, "We'll make out. Don't worry your pretty head about it." A moment later his searching, arousing hands tugged at her nightgown, caressed her waist and hips, moved down to her thighs and back again in a way that mesmerized her mind, set every inch of her body on fire. She clung to him, felt his hard strength, and a feeling of infinite sweetness swept over her, for no matter how often he made love to her it was always a wonderful, electrifying experience of touch and feeling. His slow deliberate hands, moving possessively and unhurried, were as sensual and intimate as a lover's kiss. She was caught up in wave after wave of passion that left no room for thoughts of her step-sister.

Much later when Peter was sleeping, one arm keeping her snuggled comfortably against his warmth, her mind ranged. She was fiercely proud of her boys, all brought into the world under extreme duress but all with perfect bodies and sound minds. Perfect except for Andrew's little finger, left hand, and a red mark on his chest. A mark that when she had first seen it had brought a startled scream to her lips. It had looked so like the hilt of a dagger plunged into his heart. Now of course she knew it was only a birthmark. Lots of people had them. Besides, what had looked like a blotch of fresh blood at birth had now faded to the dun of weathered brick.

Peter's long body curled around hers stirred, and unconsciously he drew her closer. Katherine's fingers moved lovingly as she gently stroked the hand that even in sleep felt possessive and exciting as it rested lightly just below her breasts. This was the way they usually went to sleep, even when sleep hadn't been prefaced by a passionate coupling. *It's as if we're sharing our love through osmosis,* she thought as she wiggled a little closer to the man she loved.

Katherine suddenly realized it had been years since she'd given Patrick Tully a passing thought. That affair had been the grope and fumble variety, when speed to get her skirts pulled up, his fly unbuttoned, and the act over with had seemed the over-riding concerns. She knew now that what had been between them was brought on by a man's need and her resentment. Resentment over what she thought was an arranged marriage.

She had known Peter when she was still a little girl, and had worked at not liking him, even though he tried to be kind.

Anger had roiled her mind whenever she thought of marriage. Why was it Irish parents couldn't credit their off-spring with enough sense to choose their own life-mates? Why was she being treated like a mare who must be taken to a carefully selected stud, so her offspring would have all the proper qualities?

Katherine's lips curved into a delicious smile as she felt Peter's leg wind itself a little closer to hers. Well, her off-spring did have all the proper qualities. Obviously her father had been smarter than she thought.

Katherine wondered briefly what would have happened if Patrick hadn't made her pregnant. Would she have risen up in outright revolt and refused to marry Peter? And if that had happened, then what? Her father had been an indulgent parent, lavishing her with love and affection — spoiling her, some said — but where customs and mores were concerned he could be rock hard. Would he have locked her in her room until she had, as he would say, "come to her senses"? If he had would she have escaped and gone off with the first man who looked even remotely respectable? A man who might have used her, then thrown her aside like a worn glove.

Suddenly a burst of understanding like an unexpected ray of sunshine grabbed at her mind, enveloped her, giving her the illusionary warmth of peace and tranquillity. She realized now that if she hadn't been pregnant she'd probably have run away. So it was her first-born who had brought her to Peter and to such happiness that she sometimes wondered how long it could last.

Chapter Fourteen
Meet Canon O'Hara and Kerry Cattle

Attending church had never been a high priority for Katherine. She felt closer to God when sitting on a boulder at Saint Finbarr's rocky Stations of the Cross, or riding some lonely mountain pass, than when worshipping in a richly vaulted man-made cathedral. Fleeting glimpses of Bantry Bay shimmering in the distance, a gem-stone mirroring the greens and golds and browns of Ireland, gave more lift to her soul than elaborately carved arches reaching heavenward. The finest stained-glass windows couldn't equal the glory of twilight's red and gold streamers flaring and dipping across the dome of Heaven as they mingled and blended with the deeper shades of purple and indigo. The sun's salute to a dying day. Man's architecture, no matter how impressive, couldn't stir her as did God's handiwork.

Her mind rebelled at the hypocrisy of a religion that had tradespeople and servants climbing steep and narrow stairs to the church's half balcony to sit on rough-hewn benches, whereas those they served sat in comfortable pews in the sanctuary below. The church's "upper crust," in their magnanimity, allowed the "working class" to worship the same God . . . but not while sitting alongside their superiors.

Nevertheless, accompanied by Peter and their three boys, Katherine now faithfully attended the Church of Ireland service every Sunday morning. At her suggestion they sat in a back pew. There were several reasons for this. All perfectly valid ones, she thought.

Sitting beneath the balcony her boys would not be squirming around in an attempt to catch the eye of one of their friends above (Peter and Katherine never stopped their sons from having friends among the working class). If Billy and Michael began slyly punching each other she could frown a warning without anyone seeing. Nor would anyone notice when she handed out the paper twists of raisins she invariably took to church for when frowning might not be enough.

She could hardly wait until the monotonous droning of Canon O'Hara's sermons put the two younger boys to sleep. Andrew was old enough now to sit bolt upright, staring at the pulpit in a way that depicted total concentration. In reality he was, in all probability, seeing himself on Whiddy Island, shooting quail with his father. Despite his youth he was becoming a crack shot.

Katherine kept a surreptitious eye on her husband too. If his lids drooped, his chin tipped forward, and his mouth started to gape a little she knew a snore, which at home would seem little more than a pleasantly relaxed sigh, would soon be reverberating through the hallowed confines of the church like rocks bouncing down a tin roof.

Other husbands might snore in church, and many did. Hers wasn't allowed that privilege.

The moment his eyes closed and he started to nod he got a sly poke in the ribs that brought his head jerking upright, a tiny, unreadable smile tugging at his mouth and a hand reaching for hers. The fingers curling warmly around her own held a message that they would always be best friends. That was another reason why she liked a back pew.

When Katherine considered the men in her life were behaving with proper decorum, she relieved the monotony of Canon O'Hara's sermons by watching people in the pews ahead.

There was Mrs. Butler, looking lovely in a burgundy wool dress. She was alone this morning so the doctor must be out on a call. Or perhaps he'd had a late-night emergency and was catching up on sleep. Katherine had grown to know Mrs. Butler quite well. They were good friends.

Her eyes flitted to Lady Enid, looking immensely pleased with herself in a brilliant red dress and heavy gold chains that clanked when she moved like a gaoler's keys. She had the self-satisfied air of one who, having once found life recalcitrant, had finally succeeded in pounding it into submission. Her ample buttocks overflowed the seat in a way that reminded Katherine of a tired old dray horse trying to sit on the cart pole.

Sir Percy, perched on the edge of the pew, looked remarkably like a bull-frog on a lily pad hoping someone would say "Boo" so he could spring up and disappear. Even his face looked like a frog. But Katherine decided she liked him better than his wife. At least he seemed sincere.

Lady Enid's gushy note of apology, plus a warm invitation to a dinner party, had arrived minutes after Lord Millhaven's carriage had swirled away. Katherine had acknowledged the apology with a cool "Thank you" and replied "Perhaps some other time" to the dinner invitation. Peter had insisted she not refuse completely. Sir Percy was a valued bank customer. And his wife had apologized. Profusely.

Katherine's gaze flew swiftly over a flower garden of hats. It took one's mind off the monotony of the service to speculate which head-pieces had recently received a fresh infusion of flowers or perhaps just a single ostrich feather.

Her eyes stopped on Mrs. O'Hara. She and her daughter Marjorie, with young Jamie O'Hara jammed firmly between them . . . as if they were afraid he might suddenly leap up and try to escape . . . always sat directly below the pulpit. Katherine felt vaguely sorry for them. *They can't even yawn without the Canon seeing. If they did they'd probably get a long lecture when he gets them home about the evils of committing something so sacrilegious in the hallowed sanctuary of his church.*

Marjorie, nearing thirty, had a bland and pretty face, a face lacking in character, but she had an hour-glass figure that caused men to turn their heads for another look. Yet Marjorie usually appeared calm and serene, as if unruffled by any awareness of the message her body was sending to the male animal. Katherine wondered idly why she had never married. She must have had offers.

Today Katherine sensed a subtle difference in Marjorie. Almost as if she had suddenly learned she had a woman's body and didn't like it. Perhaps she had a secret lover? If so it certainly wasn't making her happy. *I suppose she's scared witless her father will find out and beat her* Katherine mused.

Then her gaze shifted to twelve year old Jamie and her eyes darkened. She'd heard the gossip about him. "Such a trial to his parents. Not quite right in the head you know. It was such a difficult pregnancy that the Canon sent his wife to the south of France for her health. And she didn't come back until after the child was born. Marjorie went with her of course. What a dear, kind man the Canon is. So considerate of others. Imagine, denying himself the favors of his wife, the company of his daughter, for all that time?"

Then the speakers would sigh, think of their own husbands, and frown.

Jamie had the look of a scared rabbit when his parents where near. *It's as if he expects them to overhear his thoughts and punish him for them,* Katherine thought. *Or perhaps he's trying to insulate himself in a vacuum where no feelings can enter, and nothing can harm him.*

Whatever the boy's problems she felt sorry for him, so Peter sometimes had him over to help Ben in the stable. Jamie loved horses, and they responded well to him. He liked helping in the garden too.

Katherine felt convinced there was nothing wrong with the boy that a liberal dose of understanding, sprinkled with love and encouragement, couldn't cure. One day she decided to speak to Marjorie about it, and then wished she hadn't.

All the colour had drained from Marjorie's face, and a goaded look took possession of her eyes. Cold anger hardened her usually pleasant expression as she whirled on Katherine, hissing, "Mind your own business. The boy's a troublemaker. I wish he'd never been born." Then, pivoting, she had rushed headlong from the room.

That evening when Katherine snorted out her disgust to Peter, he had stroked her hair and said quietly, "If the Canon didn't spend so much time dwelling on the things the world is doing wrong, perhaps he could see what's wrong in his own household."

Now Katherine's eyes swept higher, to where Canon O'Hara was thumping the pulpit, waving his arms, exhorting God to send down a shot of righteous wrath to straighten out his erring congregation. She stifled a yawn.

In her opinion the Canon's version of godliness seemed excessively concerned with the value of a virtuous woman, punishing prostitutes—stoning if necessary—and putting away adulterous wives. Why didn't he give the husbands a blast now and then? It didn't seem fair. No woman fell without a shove from a man.

Idly Katherine speculated on what the Canon would say if he knew she was a fallen woman. For she supposed she was. She'd got herself pregnant out of wedlock and by another man. That must constitute fallen. Not that she'd give a big black damn what the Canon might think or say. Peter was different.

She hoped now that they loved each other so very much he would forgive her for having once allowed her body to become contaminated by another man. Surely he would see it could have done no lasting harm, for together hadn't they made two near-perfect children? That thought comforted her and she raised her eyes to where Canon O'Hara seemed to be finally winding down.

His wife was such a frail, insipid little woman she didn't look as if she could stand up to a mouse. And the Canon was no mouse. He was a tall, muscular, overbearing man who looked better suited to a plough than a pulpit. His face was handsome in an empty sort of way. As if when God handed out looks he had forgotten to add character. Katherine got the distinct feeling he would be a hard man to live with, never giving nor caring past his own immediate needs.

A sudden irreverent thought popped into her head. But try as she would she couldn't picture meek little Mrs. O'Hara indulging in intimacy with her big demanding hunk of a husband in their conjugal bed.

Although no one knew it except his wife and his daughter, Canon O'Hara rarely shared his wife's bed now, and then only if other opportunities had been slow to present themselves. Of course such opportunities could only be seized when incognito. However, long ago he had learned to gratify himself reasonably well by fantasizing about the pretty matrons in his parish while playing with his "puddings." More recently he had discovered another means of gratification.

In the pulpit he preached hell-fire sermons against the evils of elicit couplings, while his cold and calculating eyes bore into the faces upturned towards him. Strange he hadn't detected even one guilty twitch this morning. That could only mean he must take pains to inject more of the wrath of God, more fire and brimstone, into his sermons. The evils were there. It was up to him to root them out

Canon O'Hara sighed as he ran his tongue around his dry lips in a sensual fashion. His sermon had incited his own body to such a fever pitch it was burning for the very things he had condemned. His slitted eyes glazed with ill-concealed lust as they followed his wife and daughter down the aisle and out of the church. They followed other women too.

Katherine shook herself angrily. You're imagining things. The Canon is a good man. Only last week she'd seen him walking with his daughter. Only they hadn't been walking. Not when she first saw them. It had looked like . . . Oh God!

The meaning of what she had seen slammed into her with the full force of a killer hurricane. She looked so suddenly thrown off balance that Peter murmured softly, "Are you feeling all right, Princess?" She nodded, telling herself, *I'm letting my imagination run away again. And I'd better stop it. Henrietta is always telling me it will get me into trouble if I don't learn to curb it.*

Actually I didn't see anything. Not really. Just a father embracing his daughter. What's wrong with that? I hug my boys all the time.

Yet a nagging doubt persisted. Marjorie had looked frightened when she left the church, her face dark with hostility and fear, but when Katherine asked Peter if he'd noticed anything different about the girl he replied, "She looked the same as she always does to me."

Hearing that Katherine felt as if she had stepped out into full sunlight. It was only her imagination playing tricks again.

As Peter's family strolled homeward they went by way of the Catholic church where little knots of country folk were visiting outside after the service. The bonneted women huddled in close conversation. Their menfolk lounged a little apart, sometimes gesticulating towards the children clustered shyly on the outskirts like spindly trees around a thicker copse.

Suddenly Billy looked up at his father. "How many cows do you want for me, Dadda?"

"Cows? I don't want any cows!"

Billy's face dropped. "You mean you'd only get a few chickens? Or maybe a pig for me?"

"Why, Billy, whatever makes you ask such a silly thing? You're worth more to your Mamma and me than all the cows in Ireland."

Billy looked slightly mollified. But only for a moment. "But Dadda, country folk get cows and other animals for their children. It happens all the time. I hear men every market day saying things like, 'Begorrah, Joe, 'tis a sight ye are for me auld eyes. I've been a'mean'en to tell ye if ye still fancies me Tilly for yer Donal ye'll have to up yer offer. One cow baint enough for sech a foine lass. Not when ole man Currier over Schull way be offering a milker and two young pigs. Course his boy is a mite strong for the drink in me, mind. Not the worker yer Donal is aither. So meself oi'd be favouren agreeen to asken a wee less from ye. If ye can see yer way to offering meybe a young hog, a pair of layers and the cow we could make a deal. Keepin in mind me Tilly is a foine lass, with her mither's knack of makin a meal out of nothen. There'll be some cookin pots and kitchen needs, en two foine wool blankets. Wove 'em herself, her did. And moighty proud of them she be. And ifen the tatters don't fail I ken send enough for a twelve-month.'

"When the man called Joe looked doubtful, Tilly's father scratched the back of his leg, rubbed his hands together, then spoke slowly. 'Oi could maybe add a cockerel and a layer ifen that's what it takes to close the deal.' After that the men shook hands, slapped each other on the back and walked away."

Peter laughed at his son's mimicry of dealings he had so often heard himself. Tilly and Donal might not meet until their wedding day. But the marriage would probably work out. As far as Peter knew, such unions usually did.

Hearing that Katherine had snorted, "Maybe that's because the woman has to make it work. What other alternative does she have?"

Peter had no easy answer to that question.

Billy smiled and seemed satisfied when told children from well-to-do families weren't bargained for. Not like peasant youngsters.

But Katherine's ordinarily sunny face took on a look of deep thoughtfulness. Times were changing. Slowly.

Perhaps by the time her sons were young men they could choose their wives without any parental influence. She looked at Peter and a soft smile curved her lips. Her marriage had been arranged.

Before they reached home Peter's eyes had scanned the sky. "Looks like a perfect afternoon for a picnic. We could have it on Whiddy Island." At the mention of Whiddy Island Andrew's feet began dancing like a restive thoroughbred anticipating a gallop. "Oh Dadda! Can you and I shoot quail?"

"I don't see any objection to that, son. If your mother doesn't mind being left alone with your brothers, that is."

Katherine didn't. It always pleased her when her eldest son and Peter shared a father-son relationship.

Katherine leaned back on the seat watching her husband in languid fascination. Even in shirt sleeves he was an imposing figure. Tall, wide shoulders, narrow hips, powerful legs and a square-jawed, aristocratic face that bespoke integrity and strength. It was a kind and generous face creased with lines of laughter. Yet there were times when it turned hard and grey and unfeeling as a granite wall. Those were the times Katherine didn't want to think about. Instead she watched his muscles rippling beneath his shirt, the concentration on his face as he showed Andrew how to row so as not to "catch a crab."

She smiled at the look of rapt attention on the faces of the two younger boys too, and idly let her hand ruffle the soft hair under Turko's jaw.

There were only two guns propped up on the picnic hamper today. She'd stay and read to Billy and Michael, keep them amused, while the "men" went shooting.

They all agreed, Bridget's sausage rolls were the best ever. So were the raspberry tarts. When everyone claimed they couldn't eat another bite, Billy asked if he could give the last sausage roll to Turko. Having done so he rolled onto his back, clasped his hands behind his head, and looked for faces in the clouds. Katherine brushed the crumbs from her lap and put the remnants of their picnic lunch back in the hamper. Peter and Andrew were already heading off with their guns. Turko capered beside them.

Michael was searching for spiders. Or maybe today it would be beetles. He was always bringing her crawly things to admire. Peter said they should encourage him because he had the makings of a great naturalist. But secretly Katherine wished he could be a great naturalist without the necessity of keeping bugs and spiders and ants, and sometimes mice, boxed up in his room. She had learned to her despair that insects and rodents have a way of escaping from even the tightest box.

So when Michael came running up now with his face flushed as much from excitement as exertion, she steeled herself to admire yet another of his finds.

"Look, Mamma. I found a really long one this time." And having said that he proudly dumped a brown, wriggling worm into her lap. It was so big and repulsive. Katherine involuntarily shrank back with a startled gasp and brushed it off. Michael said almost apologetically as he stooped to retrieve his find, "It's only a worm, Mamma. Not a snake."

"Of course it isn't a snake." Billy, who had been alternating reading with cloud-watching, spoke in an older brother voice. "There are no snakes in Ireland, Michael. St. Patrick drove them all out."

"Good thing. I doubt I could bring myself to pet a snake." Katherine shuddered inwardly and warily extended one finger. She wouldn't disappoint the boy. She'd touch that slimy elongated invertebrate if it killed her.

When Michael considered his worm had been properly admired he carefully wrapped it in a linen serviette and tucked it into a corner of the picnic hamper. It should be safe in there.

While her son was wandering around looking for insects, Katherine kept a cautious eye on a herd of cattle grazing in the distance. At first they had looked peaceful enough and she dismissed them as harmless. Now she wasn't so sure. They were milling in a restless, uneasy fashion, flinging their heads high and tossing their horns as if something was worrying them.

Katherine felt a stirring of fear. Fending off belligerent animals wasn't something she had done before. But if it came to that she'd better have something to hit them with.

The rocky island supported few trees. But there might be sticks along the shore, thrown up by the tide. The boys raced away as eager as puppies and came back just as proudly, each carrying a small stick. She had hoped for something more like her father's blackthorn shillelagh. But she didn't dare risk letting the boys go too far in their search.

Katherine's fear of cows had begun when one knocked her down as a child. It had grown with each passing year. Now it took a tumultuous leap. The stick clutched in her hand was so old and brittle it wouldn't out-live a tap, certainly not a proper wallop. And why weren't Peter and Andrew back?

She watched the cows break rank and hump off at a stiff canter, their backs rising and falling, their tails high, their angry bellows mingling with the thud of many hooves.

"Quick! Billy! Michael! Help me carry the hamper and pillows. Get everything back into the boat so we can leave the minute your father and brother get here." A goading urgency lashed her like a rising wind.

"Now, you boys stay right here in the boat. And don't move. I'm going back up the cliff."

She picked up a couple of hand-sized rocks as she ran, scarcely realizing neither they, the stick, nor indeed she herself, would be much of a deterrent. If the cows were out for blood it would take more to fend them off than a frightened woman, a brittle stick, and a couple of rocks that would doubtless be hurled so recklessly they wouldn't come close to the racing cows.

A second later when her head burst above the cliff she froze. Sweet Mother Mary! Save them! The prayer came out on a ragged gasp of breath. It seemed that nothing short of divine intervention, a thunderbolt, or the ground opening under their feet could stop the stampeding herd . . . a herd coming flat out at an angle that would block the hunters' escape route to their boat. The red-eyed Kerry bull leading the charge had sweeping horns, an evil look, and an explosive snort. A devil in a black hide.

The terrified scream erupting in her throat died when a small dog spun around and faced the cattle, snarling as if prepared to swallow the bull with one gulp. Half crouching now with his head low to the ground, his teeth bared, his feet braced, his hackles stiff, Turko looked so formidable the bull planted his feet and jolted to a stop.

There was a wild mad glint in the herd sire's eyes, snorts

exploded from his nostrils like dust from a blasted stump. His wicked horns hooked and slashed at a little dog whose teeth threatened and taunted as he danced away, always just out of reach of the vicious thrust of the deadly horns.

The heifers, for such they were, had drawn up behind their leader in a mixture of astonishment and panic, as if they hadn't quite reached a decision whether to turn and high-tail it out of there to safety, or wait in the hope there might be still more exciting developments.

Katherine had the good sense to turn and run, knowing her son and husband were close behind her. When she and Andrew were in the boat, Peter turned, raised fingers to his lips, and gave a piercing whistle. In moments Turko came streaking down the cliff with an avalanche of hair and horns crashing down behind him. Peter pushed off with the oars, while Katherine and Andrew pulled the swimming dog into the boat. They didn't even scold when he shook water over their clothes.

"Well," said Peter with an almost sheepish grin as he watched the cattle mill out into the water, "I've heard stories about wild Kerry cattle, but that's the first time I've seen them in action. And I don't want another such encounter."

"Look, Dadda. The bull's swimming out after us. What if he catches us and upsets the boat?" Michael's words, begun as a high-pitched squeak, ended in a way that suggested he had a mission in life that would take more than a Kerry bull to change. "I won't let him drown my worm. I'll take it with me." And having said that Michael leaned forward, retrieved his napkin-wrapped worm from the picnic hamper, and stuffed it inside his shirt. Then he sat back looking as if swimming from Whiddy to Grandon was as commonplace as eating.

"Turko, do be quiet." Andrew, still gulping mouthfuls of air, pulled a quivering little dog into his arms, a dog who had been standing with his front paws over the stern of the boat as if on the point of launching his body after the barks that were flying like arrows from his mouth.

The bull, now the dog was no longer taunting him, turned and swam back to where his heifers waited near the shore.

"Wow! That was close." Billy's eyes were a mixture of concern and relief. "Would he really have killed us?"

"Possibly. He certainly appeared to have something like that on his mind," Peter's tone was dry, almost whimsical, "but don't forget we were the trespassers. We were on his territory. However, we had our guns. I'd have killed him before allowing him to hurt anyone. But I'm glad I didn't have to. It would have been a last resort. One doesn't normally go around shooting other people's cattle."

"You've shot on Whiddy before, haven't you?" Katherine was curious as to why today the Kerry cattle had acted so differently.

"Yes." Peter stopped as if considering a possibility he hadn't thought of before. "Turko no doubt saved us when he held the cattle back, but I expect it was him they were really after. Some cattle instinctively hate dogs. Especially strange dogs. Maybe today the wind was right to get his scent." Having said that he turned to his son half apologetically. "I'm sorry the shoot was a failure. Not a bird sighted, not a shot fired."

"It wasn't a total failure. I learned enough to leave Turko home the next time we go to Whiddy." And having said that Andrew buried his face in the neck hairs of the little dog asleep in his arms.

Peter Moriarty smiled at his son with a satisfied air as he rested the oars, pulled out a well-used pipe, and tapped it into a cupped hand in a way that filled the silence with a comfortable, civilized sound. Not until the pipe was refilled and drawing to his complete satisfaction did he pick up the oars and send the boat scudding towards port.

Chapter Fifteen
A Flogging, a Death, and a Shared Secret

"When you ride today, don't go past the barracks." The words crackled with authority. They hinted of revulsion too.

Katherine stared at the man who had bounded up the stairs like a shot-at stag. Her face was a mixture of astonishment and perversity. "Why not? I always take that road. It's the best way to get out of Grandon."

Peter's face was taut, his voice clipped, his mouth grim. He had the look of someone carrying a full load of disgust. "Well, you won't like it today. Not unless you care to join those who flock to a flogging as if it was a circus."

Katherine's face blanched, her knees sagged, icy dread sluiced through her veins, her voice was a barely audible squeak. "A flogging! Is it someone you know?" Her face was etched in horror.

"No. It's some poor fellow from a farm too small and rocky to feed his family. So he tried poaching. And got caught."

Her tongue felt thick and lifeless, her eyes narrowed in a frozen face as her mind took in the full import of a flogging. What if the man died? Many did. What if it was happening to someone she knew? Her husband? A son? Her body tensed and vibrated like a band of tempered steel. It was as if it was she who awaited the next blow.

Peter's attempt to smile was a failure, smiles seemed inappropriate. Instead he said gently, "It happens all the time, you know. Our judges believe if they make an example of those caught it will discourage others from risking a similar offence. Floggings are filthy and degrading, both for those who suffer and those who are forced to perpetrate. Yet people come to watch, and the authorities encourage it. To instill more fear into them I suppose. Eventually floggings will be done away with. But it won't be in our lifetime." Having said that, Peter turned with a heavy tread and went slowly back down to his office.

Katherine felt a sense of terrible vulnerability . . . as if some shadowy, ominous presence was closing in on her. After quickly pulling the heavy drapes she refused to go near a window. She didn't want to see crowds in their Sunday best flocking to the flogging like vultures honing in on a kill.

She knew sounds coming from the barracks could scarcely travel so far, but she still had to fight a terrible urge to crawl back into bed, cower under the covers and block her ears to the terrifying whistle and snap of the cat-o'-nine-tails as it did its deadly work. She didn't want to hear the agonized screams wrenched from a man whose quivering back was slowly and persistently being reduced to a mass of pulpy sinews and splattered blood.

But she couldn't just sit and think about the terrible agony being inflicted on some poor helpless peasant. She had to do something to help take her mind off the flogging. Maybe a flurry of baking, a full day in the kitchen, would help keep her mind from dwelling on the horrors of British justice. Tomorrow she would take everything she baked to the poor wretch's family.

But tomorrow the flogging would be wiped from her mind.

"Why isn't the wheel on the pony cart fixed? I told you last week one rim was loose and needed resetting." Katherine, tapping her foot angrily, made a sweeping gesture of annoyance. Her eyes snapped. Now the food she had baked for the family of yesterday's victim of British justice would have to wait for another day.

Ben, the young stable boy, stood cap in hand, tugging nervously at his shock of brown hair. "'Tis sorry I am to disappoint ye, ma'am, but the wheelwright's been sick. He couldn't get to it before today."

"Hasn't he an apprentice who can take off a tire, heat it red hot, pound it back onto the wooden frame, and dunk the whole into a tub of water? Gracious me, I could almost do that myself. It isn't a job needing a whole lot of skill."

"No ma'am, I don't 'spect it is. Unless you're dead." The lad's head was lowered a little and a forlorn expression filled his face.

"Dead! What do you mean dead? Who's dead?" The questions shot out.

"The apprentice, ma'am. Died four days ago from typhus. That's why oi couldn't get the wheel fixed for ye. Not with the wheelwright too sick to work hisself."

Katherine's face looked drained as she paused to let this information sink in. Then she put her hand kindly on the stable boy's shoulder. "Don't fret, Ben. Twasn't your fault. I expect tomorrow will be soon enough. Now if you'll saddle Ebony I'll give her the gallop she missed yesterday."

"Yes, ma'am. Roight away, ma'am." And the stable lad hurried away as if an angel had just smiled on him.

The cruelty of yesterday's flogging was too vivid a gash across Katherine's mind for her to ride past the barracks. She'd take the rocky trail that wound around the bay. If she followed it long enough it would take her out of town.

Ebony tossed her head, impatient for a free rein. When they had left the town behind and a stretch of sandy shore loomed ahead, the mare launched into a gallop that flared her nostrils, put a wild, excited glint in her dark eyes. The wind rushing past stung tears from Katherine's eyes, tears that vanished on the wind and took with them her earlier ill humour and yesterday's dark memory.

She laughed, revelling in the mare's speed, her sculptured sleekness, her controlled power and grace. Then knowing it was reckless to ride so fast, she began to pull rein. She could get killed (her mother had) and then what would become of her boys? A shadow seemed to pass over her like the phantom whispering of an abandoned soul.

A moment later the mare, who rarely shied, snorted and swerved so violently Katherine was catapulted out of the saddle.

Sand cushioned what could have been a bad fall. She was still fighting to control a mixture of nausea and vertigo, trying to get herself re-oriented, the sand out of her mouth and eyes, when an angry voice cut across her brain.

"Damn you to hell! Why did you come here? I was almost ready to do it. And now . . ." the voice trailed into a helpless sob.

"Do what? Why shouldn't I ride this way if I choose? Who are you anyway? And what do you mean by scaring my horse? I might have been killed." Katherine spat out the words along with a quantity of sand as she angrily brushed more grit from her face and eyes.

A moment later she gave a low horrified gasp. "Marjorie O'Hara! What are *you* doing here?"

"I came here to kill myself. And now you've spoiled it." The words were as clipped and naked as the stark black lettering on a "no trespassing" notice.

Katherine swallowed hard, groping for words that refused to come.

Marjorie was moaning as if caught in a terrible daze, but it was no ordinary moan. It was the strangled wail of a distraught soul. When she spoke again her words came out flat, devoid of any feeling.

"Now I'll never get enough courage to drown myself. I thought I could, and I did try. Honestly I did. But I'm such a coward I couldn't make myself walk out into the water. And now that you're here it's too late." Her voice throbbed with anguish.

It sounded as if the girl was making excuses to herself for having failed an all-important assignment. An assignment she hadn't wanted to commit to in the first place. Her body shook, her words ended in a long-drawn-out wail that dissolved into muffled sobs when she pulled the wet hem of her heavy skirts up over her face, as if trying to blot out some terrible memory.

Katherine's heart drummed against her ribs. Marjorie's confession had filled her with a mixture of astonishment and panic.

Get a grip on yourself, or 'tis small comfort you'll be to the girl, Katherine told herself sternly as she reached to take the wailing woman into her arms and pull the skirt from her face. "It can't be that bad, Marjorie. Nothing ever is after you talk about it."

But tears continued to tumble down ashen cheeks as if a floodgate had ruptured. Body-wrenching moans shattered the afternoon silence.

Katherine was thoroughly frightened. She had no idea how to comfort the girl.

Instinct told her that for the sake of propriety Marjorie's intention shouldn't become public knowledge. Yet at this moment that's what it seemed in imminent danger of becoming.

Ebony had vanished. Katherine knew her riderless mare returning to Grandon would trigger an immediate search. A search which under the circumstances it seemed essential she prevent.

Raising three fingers to her mouth she gave a sharp whistle followed by a soft, "Ebony, come Ebony," without any real hope of being answered. Almost immediately a black head shoved out from beyond the outcrop that had hidden Marjorie. And the mare nickered.

With the immediate need for concocting some trumped-up story to provide suitable cover for Marjorie gone, Katherine concentrated on comforting the distraught woman. But with so little success she began to wonder if it might have been better if the mare had gone home. At least that would have brought help, and she wouldn't be in this mess alone.

Marjorie was crying with such hysterical abandon, Katherine was scared something would snap. Attempts to comfort the Canon's daughter only triggered more frightening outbursts of despair. Vaguely Katherine remembered hearing that a hard slap sometimes works where kindness won't. *Well, Be-Jesus,* she thought irreverently, *if 'tis slappin will do it, 'tis slappin she'll get.* Grimacing in concentration she hauled off and landed a head-jolting smack on Marjorie's face with such force she feared for a moment she might have broken her own wrist.

Perhaps the blow broke the rhythm of Marjorie's sobs or perhaps she was afraid of getting more of the same. Whatever the reason she began making a conscious effort to control her crying.

When the wails had subsided to convulsive sobs and Marjorie had made a half-hearted attempt to mop up the flow of tears, Katherine spoke sternly. "First you scare my horse and almost kill me. Then you drown me in tears"—she looked ruefully at her sodden riding habit—"so now you better tell me what's troubling you. It can't be so bad you have to kill yourself."

"It is. It's worse. I'm pregnant," squeaked Marjorie with a look that suggested she was about to let go another torrent of tears.

Katherine, fearing she was going into hysterics again, shook her roughly by the shoulders. "Now you listen to me! You're not the first girl who put the act before the ring and got herself pregnant. And you won't be the last."

Katherine said this with a sternness she was far from feeling. It was one thing for a girl to get pregnant out of wedlock. But it was quite another if that girl happened to be the daughter of Canon O'Hara, the Church of Ireland's over-zealous watchdog. A man at his most thunderous best when righteously denouncing the sins of the flesh from his pulpit. Why, if the man found out his own daughter was among the fallen he'd probably beat her to a pulp.

Then an even darker thought surfaced. Perhaps he already knew. Her mind twisted in contempt. If he had learned Marjorie's guilty secret it was probably his idea that she drown herself. He could then suitably grieve over the tragic and, of course, accidental drowning of his daughter, while secretly thanking God from sparing him a scandal. Her death would be a face-saver. He would never have to admit to having sired the worst of all evils. A wanton woman.

Having convinced herself that such was the case Katherine was determined to do whatever she could to help the girl. But first she had to get her talking about it.

When a girl gets pregnant there is always a man hiding somewhere in the bushes. Marjorie appeared a biddable little thing, too conscious of social mores to overstep them. She was not the type to become involved with someone unsuitable to her rank. So what was the problem?

"Why not tell the man and get married?" she urged gently.

"I can't. He has a wife." It was no more than a blubbered whisper.

Sweet Mother Mary! This was worse than Katherine thought. But Marjorie's next words stunned her speechless.

"It's my father," she whimpered tonelessly. "He's been taking me since I was sixteen. Says it's my duty. That I owe it to him. My mother isn't well, so he says I must do this for her too." Marjorie huddled into herself looking as defenceless as a blind kitten.

"And your mother?" gritted Katherine. "What does she say?" Her face was the essence of revulsion, her hands were clenching and unclenching as if imagining themselves around the Canon's thick throat.

"She says I must submit. And pray no one finds out. Or it will ruin my father. And I must never allow that to happen."

Katherine had a sudden violent urge to vomit. But her mind was scrambling, searching for straws.

"You're a pretty woman, Marjorie. Haven't any local men wanted to court you?" She hoped there might be a likely husband lurking in the shadows. Someone who knowingly, or otherwise, would help the girl out of the mess she was in.

Marjorie's voice was thick with unshed misery. "There was. Once. But he was a Catholic. When my father found out he flew into a terrible rage and told him if he dared show his face around me again he'd have us both flogged."

"Did you never see the man again?" Katherine asked, telling herself if the fellow gave up so easily he probably wasn't that great a bargain.

"Yes. He came to say goodbye. He said there was no future for him in Ireland. He was going to a country where a man's religion wasn't held against him. When he got to America and could afford a wife he'd send for me. He's a barrister now, you know." She ended on a note of pride.

"Do you know where he is?" Katherine was beginning to see some glimmer of hope for the girl.

"Not really. But he left me an address."

"Well, what are we waiting for," Katherine said briskly. "Write to him. Tomorrow. Or better yet, tonight. The sooner you're packed off to America the better."

"But I can't go. I won't marry a Catholic. It's not my religion." Marjorie's voice verged on panic again.

Katherine's face hardened. "Your father's a Protestant. Do you like what he has done to you? Is that the religion you want to live by? Don't be stupid. God doesn't give one cold damn about religion. It's Christianity he's concerned with. And if your father has one drop of that then I'm a turnip.

"Now you listen to me. You go home and say nothing to anybody. Just look as normal as you can. Tomorrow pack whatever you can carry and hide it in the garden. When it's dark I'll be there to take you to a friend who needs a young woman to help with her growing family while her husband is away. You'll be safe with her until you hear from your barrister friend."

But she thought uneasily, *I hope he doesn't share my husband's scruples. This man won't be getting just a tarnished bride. He'll be getting the child of incest.*

Aloud she said, "It's getting late, Marjorie. There's a storm brewing. It'll be quicker if you ride double with me."

But Marjorie shook her head. There was a stubborn set to her jaw. "No. I'm frightened of horses. Anyway it's not far. I'll take the short cut along the cliffs. I often go that way."

"But it'll soon be dark," Katherine protested, conscious of an uneasy feeling in the pit of her stomach. She wouldn't risk walking that trail after dark. Even in daylight it was no place for a person with fear of heights. Tonight there was a slice of a moon but it was reeling drunkenly as it rushed in and out of racing clouds.

Obviously Marjorie knew the short cut so well it held little concern for her. She managed a weepy smile, hugged Katherine for being such an angel, then hurried off, her head lowered into the buffeting wind.

Katherine mounted Ebony, her mind awash with questions. Questions that left her with only nebulous answers, like storm-lashed waves sweeping shoreward and then retreating back out to sea. She must see Henrietta tomorrow. And she better pray her friend hadn't already found a suitable young woman companion, and that she wouldn't think Katherine's scheme too nefarious to share. If she did . . . what then?

That question, and others, drifted unanswered into the teeth of the approaching gale. What if the young barrister had given up on Marjorie, and had found himself another wife? What if when he learned the truth he said, "Thanks, but no thanks. I want a virgin."

The whole affair was really none of Katherine's business. What if meddling got *her* into trouble? She was no angel despite what Marjorie, or anyone else, said. Her wings were black as ebony. What if Peter . . . ? What should she tell him . . .? What if . . .? What if. . . . ? Oh dear. Why did life have to be so complicated?

And why was that storm coming up so fast? Far-off stabs of lightning had been splitting the sky, playing a friendly game of hide-and-seek with the approaching darkness for some time. Now it was as if all the ravening hounds of hell had suddenly broken loose. Jagged chains of fire were shafting clouds that roiled and surged and billowed as they raced before the fighting pack.

A flame of fear grabbed at Katherine's mind. She should never have allowed Marjorie to go home alone. Not in a storm like this. But it was too late now. The woman was no child. And she wasn't a fool. She could easily find shelter in the leeward side of a rock. The storm would be over as quickly as it started. Its kind always were.

Katherine urged Ebony into a canter that filled her ears with the roar of the wind and the thud of galloping hooves. She didn't hear the screams gibbering ghoulishly on the wind before fading into silence. Had she done so she might have assumed they were the shrieking voice of the storm.

Sometime later, when Peter came bounding up the stairs saying he had an evening meeting and might be late, Katherine managed to look serene and unruffled as she stood to kiss him goodbye. That meant the evening was hers. She could plan tomorrow's strategy. But first she'd put her feet up and relax a while. Her shoulder, hurt in her fall, ached abominably.

"Mrs. Moriarty, ma'am. You've got to wake up. There's been a terrible accident."

Katherine's mind struggled back from the blurred oblivion of sleep to realize Bridget was shaking her shoulder and pouring out words that smashed into her brain with the full force of a killer hurricane. Her first shock of disbelief turned into the dread certainty that it was all too true.

For a moment her own life threatened to come crashing down around her. Then she got a grip on herself. "Tell the doctor's lad to wait. I'll go with him." Her eyes were dark and frightened. She didn't want to be out alone tonight. There was too much evil on the prowl.

When the buggy drew up outside the doctor's house, Mrs. Butler came running down the steps to clasp her in her arms exclaiming, "It's all just too dreadful. And no one seems to know quite what happened." In answer to the unspoken question in Katherine's eyes she hurried on.

"Canon O'Hara is dead. Fell off a cliff near Deadman's Point and broke his neck. His wife was found wandering around like a drugged dog. She either can't or won't speak. No one can find Jamie. He seems to have vanished. Marjorie is badly bruised, either from a fall or from a terrible beating—the doctor won't say which—and is haemorrhaging so badly she's like to die. When they first brought her in she asked for you. Since then she says nothing."

The furious hammering of Katherine's heart was loud in her own ears as she moved slowly towards the man watching her. The doctor's tall figure was bowed as though a great weight rested on his shoulders. His face was grim but his voice was gentle when he took her by both hands and drew her towards a comfortable chair beside the fire. Then he nodded briefly at his wife and she left the room.

"Now my dear, anything you say to me in this room will be strictly our secret. And I would like the same assurance from you. In an attempt to do what is best for my patient, and her mother, I'm going to break professional etiquette and tell you things I hope no one else will ever know." Katherine nodded mutely.

The doctor studied his interlaced fingers thoughtfully before speaking, and when he did it was with a great deal of care, as if he wanted to be certain he said only what was relevant to the case. "Did you know Marjorie was pregnant?" Seeing Katherine's miserable nod he continued. "Then you know the name of the man?"

She gave an even more miserable nod. "Canon O'Hara." The whisper had the dead sound of dry sand inching across a dreary street.

The doctor's mouth tightened as if to say *that figures.* Aloud he said, "Do you think he knew?"

"She didn't say. But I think so. When I found her she was intending to drown herself. What puzzles me is why anyone scared witless of water would choose to kill herself by drowning. With all her clothes on. Even if she, or somebody else, wanted it to look like an accident, wouldn't it seem more realistic to drown while swimming?"

A frown darkened the angular planes of the doctor's face. "When she left, did you think she was still suicidal?"

"Of course not. I wouldn't have left her if I had. She seemed quite cheered by the prospects of being a live-in companion to a friend of mine. And there is a young man in America. A Catholic. I tried to convince her being Catholic isn't the worst thing in the world. But with her upbringing I'm not sure she believed me." Her words ended on a wry note.

"Very well, I'll tell you what I know. It's a sordid story. Her mother came to me two weeks ago begging, offering a substantial bribe, if I would give her the name of a Dublin doctor who did abortions. Naturally I thought it was she who wanted it so I told her to my knowledge she would have no trouble delivering a healthy child. Anyway, no doctor worthy of his profession will consider an abortion unless the mother's life is in danger. I offered to examine her in the event there was something I wasn't aware of, but she grew flustered and insisted she didn't need an examination. There was absolutely no doubt about the pregnancy.

"When she dragged herself out of my office she had the look of an old woman stricken with the futility of existence. As she left I fancied I heard 'There's more than a mother's life in danger,' but it was such a weak little whisper, barely above the threshold of sound, that I dismissed it as having no relevance.

"Immediately after the storm tonight I got word there had been a bad accident. Canon O'Hara had fallen off a cliff and broken his neck. His daughter had fallen a little further on . . . where the cliffs aren't so steep. She was badly bruised and haemorrhaging but had no broken bones. The baby is dead. Marjorie is very weak from loss of blood. She'll be sore all over for a while, but she'll live. The Canon's walking cane, a vicious-looking weapon, was found somewhere between where he fell off the cliff and where Marjorie fell. It had blood on it.

"Her mother was found wandering along the cliff above where they found the Canon's body, clutching her coat around herself and wailing like a lost banshee. Since then she hasn't spoken. Marjorie isn't speaking either. Except to ask for you.

"No one will ever know exactly what happened . . . unless the mother or daughter talk, and frankly I hope they don't. If what you and I suspect becomes public knowledge, Marjorie and her mother might as well have died with the Canon. If it is accepted as an accident then the women have some chance of living a normal life. And surely they deserve that after the hell they've been put through. The Canon has paid his debt. Now, having said that, would you like to see Marjorie?"

Katherine nodded mutely. This was the most terrifying night she had ever known. And it wasn't over yet.

Marjorie's eyes searching Katherine's were dark and pleading; words burst from her lips like the fiery flow of lava. "Everything I told you today was a complete lie. And you've got to believe that. I was angry when my father wouldn't buy me a new frock so I did it to get back at him. Of course I'm not pregnant. I never was. I'm ashamed for having told you such a silly thing. And I don't want to go to your friend's home. I want to take my mother far, far away from here. I never, ever want to see Grandon again. We'll go to my mother's widowed sister in Belfast."

As Marjorie made her startling confession Katherine shot a quick glance at Dr. Butler, who nodded imperceptibly and dropped her the suspicion of a wink.

Katherine stooped to give the face that was the colour of death a reassuring kiss. "Marjorie. Of course I believe you. I never breathed a word of your other story to anyone, and I never will. So you can forget everything that happened this afternoon." Having said that, she looked half apologetically towards the doctor and discovered an approving look on his face. "Now the doctor and I both want you to put all your energy into getting strong again."

"Thank you both for being so understanding. I don't deserve such good friends." Marjorie's finely tapered fingers seemed obsessed with twisting and retwisting the white linen bed sheet into a long tormented tangle. Her haunted eyes flickered miserably over faces filled with compassion before she spoke again, and when she did it was as if the words had been dragged up from the bottom of a deep and putrid well with great difficulty. "I've thought it all out while I've been lying here. Jamie can't come with us. I don't ever want to see him again." Hearing the startled gasps this bit of information produced she moaned pitifully, "I'm sure I've made the right decision." Then as if she had used up all her strength she fainted.

Dr. Butler's eyes met Katherine's as if he was despising himself for being such a fool; his voice was rimmed with emotion. "Well, perhaps she has. I've known for a long time the boy wasn't wanted. Now I know the reason. That woman lying there is his mother. The dead Canon is his father."

For a leaping moment Katherine feared she might be going to vomit, then she got a grip on herself. There was a shocked and frozen look on her face as she whispered almost inaudibly, "Poor little unwanted boy. What's to become of him?"

Instead of replying the doctor said, "I'm going to give her something to make her sleep. She's got a long, hard recovery ahead. Both mentally and physically."

When Katherine was back in Dr. Butler's office he turned and, putting both hands on her shoulders, looked down into her eyes. "Mrs. Moriarty, you've had a wretched time tonight. I'm sorry for inflicting it on you, but between us I think perhaps we will have given back life and self-respect to two women who deserve a lot more happiness than has been their lot these last few years. As for Jamie, I'll see him in the morning. I know a childless couple who need a young lad around the place. He'll get more love and understanding there than has ever been his lot." Then he smiled as if suddenly realizing he had everything reasonably well under control. "Did anyone ever tell you you're an angel?"

Katherine smiled sadly. "No doctor. Well, maybe . . . an ebony one."

"Well, I've a mind to do a bit of angelling myself. Who's to say what caused Canon O'Hara to fall off the cliff? Did he throw himself? Was he shoved? Was it an act of God? A bolt of lightning? If his wife and daughter know they aren't saying. And better they don't. A hint dropped to my groom about the dangers of a lightning strike will be all it takes to head off any ugly rumours." He grinned at Katherine like a small boy with a shared secret. "By the way, earlier today your husband told me you had a box of baking you hadn't been able to deliver, so I picked it up and took it to the poor chap and his family when I was out that way this afternoon."

To the grim question in Katherine's troubled eyes he answered tersely. "He'll live." Then, more quietly, "I'll have my groom drive you home. You've had a long day."

But for Katherine the day wasn't over yet.

As she ran up the bank steps intending to go in by the back entry, she heard one of the horses whinny. *I better take a quick look at them, just to make sure they're all right.* As she flung open the stable door both horses greeted her with low, anxious nickers. It was so dark inside she couldn't see a thing, so she lit a lantern—there was something about those whinnies that started bubbles of apprehension percolating within her.

She moved into the warmth of the stable, holding the light high, then gave an indrawn hiss of breath that sounded shockingly loud in the stillness of the night. Her foot had touched something soft. Startled, she lowered the lantern and found herself staring into the sleep-befuddled face of Jamie O'Hara.

"Jamie! What are you doing here?" The words exploded from her like a cracking whip.

"I'm sorry, ma'am. I didn't mean any harm." Then he began to cry, but there was a fighting line to his mouth. "I'm never going back. Never. They don't want me. All I do is cause trouble. My parents and Marjorie had a big fight and I hid behind the curtains and heard everything. Marjorie isn't my sister. She's my mother. She said she hates me and she hates father because he's going to give her another baby. It will be my brother. Or sister. She was crying and carrying on something awful. Said she was going to kill it." Jamie started to cry again but when Katherine's arms closed around him he sniffed violently and made a manful effort to control his voice. "When my father shouted at her 'Go ahead, you Jezebel. Do it. And yourself too,' she hurled a heavy vase at him and ran out of the house.

"Soon as he got the blood wiped off his face he began bellowing, 'Where's my walking cane? I'll teach that harlot respect for her father.'

"My mother, only she isn't my mother, grabbed him and tried to stop him, screaming, scratching his face and yelling, 'You fiend. If you so much as lay a finger on her again I swear I'll . . . .'

"It was then my father hit her so hard she went flying across the room and crashed up against the fireplace. I was sure she must be dead. I knew if anyone found me hiding behind the curtains they'd think I killed her, so I ran away and hid in some bushes until it got so cold that I crept in here. You won't send me back, will you?"

The eyes pleading with her were frightened, the mouth quivering.

"No Jamie. I won't send you back. Right now I'm going to give you a big bowl of hot soup. After you've eaten it I'm going to put you to bed so you can have a good sleep. Tomorrow I'm going to take you to Dr. Butler's house because he knows a couple who want a boy just like you. A place where you'll have a good home and will never feel frightened, or unwanted, again. But Jamie, I want you to promise you'll never talk about any of this to anyone. Except the doctor," she added as an afterthought.

Jamie smiled contentedly as he watched her extinguish the lantern, then hand in

hand they walked towards a new life for Jamie.

Chapter Sixteen
Meet Tim Watson

A solitary rider on a black mare moved slowly down a rocky trail dotted with tiny puddles mirroring the sun. In the distance a river uncoiled itself and slithered like a python towards the sea. Nearer, small patchwork plots of land tied the hillsides together with freestone fences and blackthorn hedges. Here and there single threads of peat smoke rose from bleak stone hovels, then plummeted earthward like the battle flags of a defeated nation. To the north a few sheep filtered upward towards the Caha mountains. Away to the south, but not quite visible, lay Bantry Bay.

Katherine sighed and stopped. It didn't seem possible Ireland could be facing another year of potato failure. Not when every tiny dwelling appeared to be flanked by lush green potato plants, voluptuous vines that seemed to promise the end of famine.

Yet Peter had been unusually worried at breakfast when he told her the dreaded virus was already showing up in some counties. Or perhaps it was a different strain this year. Potatoes that looked sound when dug turned rotten almost overnight. Nor did cooking help prolong the tubers' life. When dropped into cooking pots they developed so foul a smell they weren't edible.

Katherine slowly dismounted and, looping Ebony's reins over one arm, led her to a boulder alongside the trail. Her eyes were dark and brooding as she sat lost in thought, her elbows on her knees, her chin supported by loosely cupped hands.

She loved Ireland. Yet how could she love a country trapped in the stench of misery, the heart-wrenching odour of hunger and hopelessness?

There were soup kitchens for Grandon's poor and she helped with them. But what of tenants on more distant holdings? Those too weak to walk the distance? Would they be left to die and rot along the roadsides?

An eagle from some remote and craggy aerie drifted silently across her line of vision, but she was too lost in thought to notice that not all eagles had yet disappeared from Ireland. Nor did she notice when Ebony pricked up her ears and looked towards a rider approaching from the rocky pasture above.

The rider was almost upon her when the sound of a metal-shod hoof clinking on stone catapulted her to her feet. She spun around.

A man who looked as if he was no stranger to sun and wind and outdoor living was staring at her, almost apologetically. Square-jawed, with prominent cheekbones, he was not exactly handsome, but his was a face that suggested integrity and strength of character.

Katherine usually rode astride. Riding alone as she often did she felt safer astride than on the conventional side saddle ladies were expected to use. She had little patience with woman who martyred themselves to decorum, whether it was wearing torturous steel-boned corsets that distorted their bodies to fashion's dictate, or rode small, and to her mind, uncomfortable side saddles. She wore a split riding habit that hung like a skirt when mounted astride.

"My apologies, ma'am, for startling you. I saw your saddle and mistook you for a man." His lips twitched into an approving grin. "Not often a lady in this country has the sense to ride astride. Or maybe courage would be a better word. It's never easy to break with tradition. Where I've been women ride a horse and handle a gun, just like their menfolk.

"Really." Katherine's voice was cool and distant. She had no desire to continue this conversation, even though she did feel a vague stirring of interest.

His eyes, which she noticed were grey and very direct, swung in an arc to encompass a panorama expanding and spreading like ripples from a tossed pebble. "Magnificent scenery." He seemed to be speaking to himself. "Few places have better. But I hate the country. It stinks of discontent, oppression, and injustice. I can't wait to leave again."

Here his face took on the look of a man caught in the glow of nostalgia. His voice was low and pensive. "Picture it. Mountains looming like dark and jagged storm clouds on the far horizon, changing when the sun climbs above an eastern foothill into brilliant white-domed minarets that rise lonely and aloof from battlements roofed in sun-stroked snow.

"Summer breezes rippling prairie grass, giving it the boundless look of ocean waves stretching to eternity. Grass where herds of buffalo, elk, and antelope, too, are the ships that ply back and forth. A land where sprawling wastelands broken by lonely buttes and straggling ravines give man and beast protection from the winter storms that periodically blast the land. Blizzards that can come charging in like the whip-lashed cavalry of Genghis Khan, driving before them swirling, drifting, tumbling snow pellets that blind the eye, sting the flesh, and goad animals to drift stupidly before them, some to their death.

"Green-black forests breaking in wave after wave of shadowed darkness. Wooded grandeur that knows no end.

"I tell you, ma'am, it's a vast and lonely land, one of the most desolate and forbidding regions on earth. A land where winter snows shroud the landscape like the death of hope. In summer it's mosquitoes—mosquitoes fighting over whether to suck their victim dry on the spot or save some blood for a midnight snack."

Katherine had been listening in silent fascination but now she laughed in a disapproving manner. "You mean you actually *like* a place like that?"

"Yes, ma'am. I do. You would too if you were there. It's a rugged, harsh, explosive land that gets in your blood and binds you to it. Challenges with thrown gauntlets you can't refuse. Imagine snow-covered hills, scoured and polished by a chinook, scintillating in the moonlight, flaunting their diamonds in the face of the moon goddess. Imagine skies of deep midnight-blue sparkling with stars so big and brilliant you feel you could reach out and pull one down. Or the aurora borealis—rainbow lights that curtsy and sway across the northern dome of heaven like stately dancers gliding and dipping to their own ethereal music. A land where the howl of a wolf pack quivering the darkness, long drawn out and hauntingly plaintiff, blood chilling in its loneliness, is a tremulous reminder of life's miracles, mysteries, and sorrows.

"It is a savage, long-maned land waiting for men, and women, with hopes and dreams and courage to tame it into one of the best regions on earth." The man spoke with the quiet air of one who knows whereof he speaks. His face glowed with the light of a vision only his eyes could see.

Katherine suddenly realized she had been holding her breath. Now she spoke more cynically than she intended. "If you like the place so well why are you in Ireland?"

"Unfortunately I inherited some property and have to come back periodically to see to it. By the way, I'm Tim Watson." He smiled at her so engagingly that Katherine extended her hand murmuring, "And I'm Mrs. Moriarty." His hand clasp was warm and strong.

He's the sort of man who has a lot of himself to give, Katherine thought rather irreverently. Then she noticed her companion was frowning at her in an uncomplimentary manner. "Moriarty? Would you be related to the Albert Moriarty who recently acquired property in the area?"

"My husband has a brother Albert. I wasn't aware he had property in this vicinity. My husband and I don't see much of them," she added as if by way of explanation. Then she rose, brushed the dust from her skirts, and half smiled. A moment later she spoke decisively, and for some reason which she couldn't have explained to herself, rather irritably. "You've made your land sound strangely captivating but I fancy there'd be a lifetime of struggles and heartaches for immigrants landing there with little but the clothes on their backs. And there'd be nothing resembling happiness for any of them."

"Mrs. Moriarty, life for most of humanity is largely made up of struggles and heartache." A dark gloom had descended on his face. "Happiness, if one is lucky enough to find it, is a fleeting thing to be grasped and clung to . . . each precious moment savoured to its fullest, for too often happiness has gone before we knew we had it. But then, that's a dour note to end our conversation on. When I saw you sitting so still on the rock I was concerned you might have fallen and been hurt. It's not often folks ride as far as this high pasture of mine."

"You mean this property is yours? I'm sorry. I didn't know. I didn't mean to trespass." Katherine felt vaguely flustered at having trespassed on this man's land. For there seemed something about him she wasn't sure she liked.

"Not at all, Mrs. Moriarty. 'Tis pleased I'd be to have you ride this way any time."

"Thank you," she replied somewhat stiffly. "But it's not likely to happen again. I don't often ride this far."

His smile was enigmatic. "Well, as it seems we are both heading in the same direction, may I have the pleasure of your company?"

Tim Watson sat his horse, a magnificent liver-chestnut stallion, with the easy grace of a born horseman. Man and beast moved as one. And his saddle was a monster thing such as Katherine had never seen before. He saw her looking at it in astonishment and smiled. "It's a Western stock saddle. More comfortable than your typical English pad. And not so easy to fall out of.

"The high back is called a cantle, the long-stemmed mushroom in front is the horn, or pommel. That's what cowboys take a dally around, which means taking a quick twist around it with their rope in a way that makes the rope secure without it being fastened. When a wild steer or bronco gets to fighting its guts out on the noose end of a lasso, a man might suddenly find himself sailing through the air, riding a saddle with a broken cinch. Unless he can give the rope a quick flick and let it come loose."

"You mean you actually catch wild animals by throwing a rope at them?" Katherine's blue eyes danced with sudden interest.

"Not always, but I am getting better at it. Do you want me to give you a demonstration?" The little devil dancing around the corner of his grey eyes made Katherine think it was time to put this man in his place. Now her voice was crisp with hauteur. "Not necessarily. What would you use for this 'demonstration'?"

As if sensing what had been on her mind, he grinned. "Don't worry, Mrs. Moriarty. Someday I might try roping myself a pretty woman. But not if she carries another man's brand." Then he sobered abruptly. "Not all men can read another's brand. Doesn't your husband worry when you ride in lonely areas alone?"

"Of course not. He trusts me."

Tim Watson's well-tanned face turned a deeper brick red.

"Please forgive me, Mrs. Moriarty. I didn't mean what you're thinking. You're a lady and may not realize that all men, underneath their civilized veneer, their facade of respectability, are savage animals at heart. There are so-called gentlemen, as well as peasants, who if they saw an opportunity to indulge their lusts would make no effort to curb their carnal savagery."

There was something stern and lonely in his eyes but his voice was so sincere Katherine couldn't be offended. Neither could she quite manage to raise her eyes to the grey ones watching her. Her long lashes drooped and lay dark against the delicate tones of her cheeks as she thoughtfully patted Ebony's satin-smooth neck.

As if sensing what was on her mind he spoke again. "You ride a splendid mare, ma'am, but don't trust her speed too much."

An indignant protest trembled on her lips but he silenced her with a sweeping gesture. "I'm talking to you like an older brother. Please take it as such." The suggestion of a smile hovered at his eyes but his words were low and serious. "If you persist in riding alone I'll show you a spot on this trail that someday might save your virtue. Perhaps your life."

Katherine gasped at the pure audacity of this man. On the other hand his words rang with sincerity, the wisdom of experience. One who has seen much of life, and not always liked what he saw. So why not go with him? It could do no harm.

Ebony fell into step beside the chestnut, and for a while neither rider spoke.

"It's not much further. Just around this bend. See that tree?"

Katherine nodded as a gnarled old beech growing close to the trail came into view. A lower branch, bleached with age, and as thick as a man's leg, overhung the trail.

"Ride under it and don't duck your head unless I tell you to. There, just as I thought. You easily pass below the branch. Now watch what would happen to me." And having said that Tim Watson walked his horse up to the branch and stopped just as it seemed certain the limb would catch him under the chin and drag him out of the saddle. "You can picture what would happen if a man slammed into it at a neck-or-nothing gallop?"

Katherine laughed and it sounded like the tinkle of a silver teaspoon in a china cup. "I think you said it aptly. Neck or nothing. But you could have swung your horse out and missed the branch. Or ducked and gone under it."

He nodded in automatic agreement. "Precisely. But how many horses, startled at discovering they're on the edge of a gaping chasm, won't crowd back towards the tree. Not many unless they happen to have lost their natural fear of the place. And yes, it would be possible to duck under it, but horses coming around the bend, running flat out, are on it almost before the rider has time to sense his danger. Especially if his eyes are glazed with lust. And there's another thing you should know. An hour before sunset the sun's angle blinds the rider to the branch."

Katherine felt a sudden feeling of gratitude trickling through her, not that the branch would ever serve her any purpose. Still, it didn't hurt to know where it was.

A few minutes later the horses reached a fork in the road. He smiled at her in an impersonal fashion. "Grandon lies that way. I go this." Almost instantly the chestnut stallion had plunged down a steep dip and was out of sight.

A reflective smile briefly touched her lips as Ebony galloped towards Grandon. *I fancy there's more to Mr. Tim Watson than meets the eye. But I don't expect I'll ever know what it is. Peter will be interested to hear Albert has acquired property in Cork County. Does that mean he's living here? And Sophia? I wish I'd asked Mr. Watson more about them. I got the feeling Albert isn't his favourite neighbour.*

A bleak feeling settled over her, a shiver skittered along her spine. Her blue eyes held a disturbed look. It might have been better had she never met Tim Watson.

Chapter Seventeen
"Please Sir, I Forgot to Wash My Feet"

"Dadda, could I go to grammar school in Cork? Dublin is so far away." The wistful look on Andrew's face tore at Katherine's heart. A troubled feeling was forming a disorganized ball in her chest as she looked anxiously towards her husband. But speculating on another person's thoughts, the decisions they might make, seemed a pointless exercise. So she gave it up and waited.

Peter took the pipe from his mouth, examined it with exasperating care, then stroked his chin, his mind lost in deliberation. Finally a half smile, both affectionate and indulgent, curved his mouth. "I expect it could be arranged. Your mother and I had thought you'd be taking your schooling in Dublin, and staying with Grandfather O'Connor. We imagined you'd prefer that to a boarding school."

With arms folded across his chest and legs apart, Andrew's stance suggested here was a matter deserving careful consideration. Watching the face above its well-tanned column of neck Katherine felt a tug of pride. Her oldest son was handsome in a boyish sort of way. His coppery hair complemented a cleanly chiselled face burnished by that special mixture of sun, wind, and youth. His brownish-green eyes sparkled with an eagerness to meet life's challenges and come out the victor.

When Andrew spoke it was slowly. He was choosing his words with great care, as if he was anxious not to be misunderstood. "If you don't think Grandfather O'Connor would mind, I'd prefer the boarding school in Cork. Living in a dormitory I'd make more friends than if I lived with Grandfather. And Dadda, you've always told us it's those we know, not what we know, that often most affects our lives." He stopped a moment, then flashed his parents a persuasive smile. "Besides, Cork isn't as far as Dublin. You'll be able to come up for award-days and things like that." He didn't add that his friend Brian Lee-Jones would be at Cork grammar school. And Brian's father, having expanded his drapery business to the meat and grocery trade, would frequently be in Cork on business. That meant an opportunity for both boys to get food hampers from home. Another important consideration was he had been invited to travel back and forth between Cork and Grandon in the Lee-Jones carriage whenever there were school breaks.

When the first letter from Andrew arrived Katherine was in a dither of excitement. Her eyes raced over the questions about how things were at home to what she really wanted to know. Then she devoured every sentence, savouring it like a gourmet morsel.

"Brian Lee-Jones and I share a dormitory with four other boys. Anthony Armstrong is tall and skinny. He comes from near Balleylicky. He says our Daddas must know each other because his father does banking in Grandon. Billy Mooney is from a town across the Caha mountains called Kenmare. It's in Kerry. He reminds me of a fat, friendly puppy. Only he talks a lot, especially about his town. I think he's bragging but he says every word is true. If it is, then Kenmare is an interesting place. You might like to hear about it.

"Before 1782, Kenmare was called Nideen. Nideen belonged to an English army surgeon who had come over with Cromwell's troops and stayed when he talked a beautiful but wily Fitzmaurice heiress into marrying him. Billy says the heiress was artful because Cromwell had confiscated the Fitzmaurice land and given it to the doctor for his help subduing the troublesome Irish. By marrying the doctor the heiress was able to keep her family's land for her children.

"At that time no one considered Nideen of much value. It was too hard to reach. Carriages had to depend on ropes, levers, and stout shoulders to push, pull, and pry them over precipitous trails. Mooney, B, (all the masters call us by our surname and an initial) says the scenery around Kenmare is so spectacular that when a Scottish engineer, Alexander Nimmo, saw it he built a proper road between Cork and Kerry. There's now a tunnel on the road that's known as the tunnel of echoes. Mooney says everyone ought to sing in it at least once in their life just to hear the echoes rolling and tumbling into the distance. Maybe some day we could ride through that tunnel, Mamma, and then see the suspension bridge at Kenmare. It's the first suspension bridge in Ireland.

"Billy also says there's a spot in the Cahas where there's a spectacular view of Killarney Lakes on one side and Bantry Bay on the other. I'd like to see that too.

"Now, for fear you'll be wondering if Billy Mooney's love of Kerry hasn't coloured my thinking to the detriment of Grandon, which it never will, I better tell you about the other boys.

"Charles Roach and Peewee Smith come from Passage West where their fathers work for the shipbuilder, Michael O'Brian. He and the Hennessy brothers launched the first steamer to be built in Ireland right here at Passage West in 1815. It was the harbour ferry between Cork and Cove for many years because its top speed was 6.5 knots an hour, which sounds impressive for a twelve horsepower engine. But Roach claims Cork's steamship, *Sirius*, of the St. George Steam Packet Company, was even more famous because in 1838 she was the first vessel to cross the Atlantic to America by continuous steam. So you see, I'm learning things besides school work.

"Both Peewee and Charles live close to Cork so it's easy for their parents to send up food hampers. And when any of us get a food hamper we all share. Brian's father has business in Cork next week so his mother is sending up a roast chicken. Mamma, would you have time to make an apple tart, with lots of cinnamon and sugar on top? And maybe some of those special biscuits? They could come with Brian's hamper.

"It's nice having the Cassidy twins here but they're on another floor so we don't see much of each other. But I have met one of their roommates. His name is Harry Feakes. His parents must be very rich because he lives in London, goes home for all the school breaks, and says he only came here because Irish girls are prettier than English girls. He brags he's going to marry Rosie Cassidy when she grows up. And he's only seen her once. I don't like him.

"Tell Billy and Michael to pay attention to everything Mr. Whitebottom is trying to teach them. If they don't want their knuckles rapped they better learn to hold their slate pencil without a crook in their index finger. I didn't. To my sorrow.

"I was doing a Euclid assignment when without any warning the headmaster's ruler came down on my knuckles so hard I thought he'd broken them. The pain was so bad I was tempted to jump up and let him have one straight between the eyes. But I remembered just in time this wasn't a Church School. To hit a headmaster here means instant expulsion. And you know I don't want to bring disgrace on you, Dadda, nor ruin my chances for any further education, so I jammed my arms against my sides and kept them there.

"However, I think you'll agree it was totally unfair of him to hit me without any explanation other than 'Moriarty, A, that is not the way to hold a pen.'

"When I replied, 'Please Sir, I've never been shown any other way,' his face went fiery red. 'Moriarty, A,' he roared, 'go to my office.' When I got there I had to lower my pants and lean over the punishment barrel while he swished a number of canes through the air, testing them. When he found one that suited him he proceeded to use it on my bare buttocks until he got out of breath.

"Don't worry Mamma. All the boys get caned. Friday is 'Doomsday,' when everyone gets punished for whatever offences they committed during the week. And when something as minor as hanging your cap on the wrong peg calls for a caning, you can imagine it is the rare boy whose name isn't on the Doomsday list. Christopher Jones—his home is in Wales, but he stays with an uncle in Cork during the school year—says he's sure he holds the record for the most canings. That's a record no one wants to challenge. Everyone likes Chris.

"I think most of the masters like me because I'm a conscientious student, here to get an education. Whereas there are boys, especially sons of wealthy parents, who horse around a lot.

"Well, dear parents and brothers, the lights-out bell has

gone. That means everyone is to be in bed with their candle out when the headmaster makes his evening check, or there'll be reason for more canings. And that is something none of us needs more of right now.

Your loving son, Andrew."

A surge of pride swept through Katherine as she carefully folded the letter and put it aside. Peter would want to read it as soon as he came in, for he shared her pride in their eldest. She rarely remembered now that Andrew wasn't really her husband's son.

Back at the Cork grammar school Doomsday Friday had come and gone. Punishment had been meted out.

Now it was Saturday evening and an air of jubilation existed in Andrew's dormitory. None of the boys had, as yet, got their names on next week's Doomsday list. And more important, three food hampers had appeared earlier in the day. Hampers that had been hurriedly stashed under beds and were now about to be brought out. Tonight there would be feasting.

But not until the heavy tread of the headmaster making his final round had faded into the distance.

When it was deemed safe, six boys furtively crept out of bed and lit a single candle. To make sure none of its meagre light could escape under the door to betray them, Andrew jammed his school blazer against the crack.

With that done Anthony announced hungrily, "I says we lay out the food and let the feasting begin. Billy me lad, your bed is central. Best we spread pickles, roast chicken, sardines, and smoked herrings on it. The tarts and such-like can be on Andrew's bed. All except the cake Billy's mam sent."

Peewee Smith's eyes glazed with anticipation as they surveyed a cake heaped high with frothy white frosting. His pudgy body quivered like an eager poodle as his tongue edged out to alert his lips to the sensuous, glutinous pleasure soon to be theirs. "I vote for polishing off the cake right after the chicken and smoked herring, so let's leave it on Billy's bed."

"Great idea," Andrew agreed. "The other sweets can stay under my bed until we're ready for them." He gave the hamper a push like a man in a hurry to hide the evidence. He had been struck by a vague feeling of apprehension. As if things were going almost too well. And it couldn't last.

The headmaster had made his rounds, but there was always the chance one of the other masters might stroll by. Andrew moved quickly to the window, fiddled with the drapes, then turned away, satisfied no light would show through them.

The dormitory was awash in smells to delight the olfactory senses of a monarch. The roasted chicken glowing in its delicately crisped and golden skin was being ravaged by six hungry youths tearing off chunks as savagely as a pack of starving wolves. After it was reduced to a scrawny carcass their attention turned to the herring, but at this moment no one felt hungry for herring. Billy's cake looked too tempting.

Billy raised a knife dramatically over the cake like a zealot preparing to plunge the sacrificial dagger into the heart of the very thing he loves the most. But while the knife was still high above its intended victim, Anthony hissed, "Footsteps! Quick! The candle! Hide the evidence." Like one stunned by unexpected circumstances Billy's knife-arm froze in mid-air, then slowly dropped to his side.

Footsteps were indeed coming down the corridor, and they sounded louder than the march of doom.

The next moment the room was plunged in darkness, and six boys, feigning cherubic innocence seemed peacefully asleep in their beds, quilts pulled up to their chins. The immediate sound of deep breathing was further enhanced by a few stentorian snores that rippled the air waves and threatened to quiver the curtains. No one heard Billy Mooney's gasp of dismay.

When the headmaster flung open the door and peered inside he was greeted by such a salvo of snores, he started to quietly back away. Obviously he had been mistaken. A headmaster's intuition isn't always right.

Then his nose started to twitch and wrinkle like an Irish wolfhound identifying a scent. There were so many exotic smells bombarding him he scowled fiercely when he thought of the greasy mutton and half-cold potato he'd been served for his supper.

A dormitory reeking with the mingled aroma of many foods vibrated with the sound of heavy breathing and whopping snores. The headmaster, lamp held high, strode into the room sniffing audibly. Immediately the volume and pitch of the snores increased. Especially from the bed where Billy Mooney lay huddled amid the squashed, mangled and odoriferous remains of a chicken carcass, a quantity of pickles, smoked herring, open tins of sardines, and a sticky goo that moments before had been a beautifully iced cake. He felt like a broody hen caught hatching a clutch of crocodile eggs.

The headmaster, head outstretched, lips curling to expose an expanse of yellow and decaying teeth, his generous nose twitching like a stallion smelling a likely filly, stopped beside the bed where Billy Mooney was manfully striving to break the world snoring record.

"Mooney, B!" the headmaster's roar was like the thunder of many guns. It rocked the building and sent the sparrows sleeping under its eaves darting off in alarm. "What is that I smell?"

The answer, when it came, sounded small and very pinched. "Please sir, I forgot to wash my feet."

A big hand flashed. Quilts were yanked back. A boy cowered. And for a fleeting moment a pair of steel-cold eyes almost twinkled.

Then came the dreadful voice of doom. "To my office. Immediately. All of you."

Chapter Eighteen
A Narrow Escape

Andrew burst into his father's office, his eyes sparkling as if he had just been handed a maharaja's jewels. "Dadda, guess what? Anthony Armstrong has promised me the use of his bicycle this weekend. He has to go to a cousin's wedding in Killarney, so he says I might as well make use of his machine."

"That's very nice, son," murmured his father absently. "Are you sure you know how to ride it?"

"Yes, it's quite easy really, once you get the hang of it." Seeing Billy's envious eyes he gave his brother's shoulder an affectionate pat. "You can ride it too, Billy." Then, as if overwhelmed at his own magnanimity, he quickly added, "When I say so,"

"What about me?" wailed Michael. "Don't I get to ride it?"

"Not this time. You aren't big enough to reach the pedals. But I'll give you a ride on the handlebars."

Katherine smiled at her sons. They got along well. Most of the time.

But why would anyone want to ride an ugly contraption that needed constant pedalling when you could ride a horse? She shook her head. The vagaries of the young were completely beyond her comprehension. But Andrew had taken pains to fill her in on the history of the bicycle.

Anthony Armstrong's machine sounded as if it was a vast improvement over the "dandy horses" that showed up in the 1818 era. Those machines, designed by Baron de

Saverbrun and modified by Dennis Johnson of Long Acres, were so costly none but the wealthiest society dandies could afford to ride one. Hence the name dandy horses.

However, by 1840 Kirkpatrick MacMillan of Dumfries, Scotland, had made a bicycle so improved over the first design that he got himself arrested for furious driving. And that, of course, skyrocketed the bicycle into immediate popularity.

Katherine, leaving to attend a meeting of the local women's group, smiled happily to herself. Her two older boys, taking turns riding the borrowed bicycle up and down the hill road near the bank, were meeting her values and expectations. Michael, playing nearby, was waiting for a ride on the handlebars. All three looked happy. If only everyone in Ireland could be so happy.

Today she had to chair a meeting to try and come up with some plan whereby women such as herself could help the growing problem of the overcrowding plaguing Ireland's poorhouses. The situation in Grandon looked hopeless. Peter predicted it could only get worse.

The soup kitchens, staffed by volunteers, were doing what they could, but it wasn't enough. Not when so many were starving. Her eyes grew pensive, her mouth resentful.

If only the government would put a stop to the exportation of all Irish foodstuff, and make it available to the poor at prices they could pay, at least until the potato disease had run its course, there would be no famine in Ireland. The country produced much more food than was consumed locally. But it was the export of Irish produce that put money into government coffers, into the pockets of the already rich English landlords, and it was of small concern to them if millions of Irish peasants starved to death. The country was over-populated. Why worry if some died? With the birth rate so high there would always be more to replace them.

Katherine knew Peter was having sleepless nights. He had gone against his better judgement and made several shaky bank loans that could put his job on the line if they weren't repaid. Mrs. Lee-Jones declared her husband was walking holes in the carpet because of the decline in his business. Others told similar stories.

Now Katherine was walking home. The meeting had adjourned, with the general consensus being the women were already doing everything they could. Some murmured that the immensity of the potato failure may have been magnified. Human nature has a tendency to make the most of the worst. Crops around Grandon looked healthy.

When Katherine got within sight of the bank her heart did a flip-flop, her steps quickened. It was unusual to see such a crowd in the town square . . . when it wasn't market day. Tension tugged at her mind. Was something wrong?

Little knots of people huddled together talking in anxious undertones, as people do when there's been a tragedy. As she rushed up the bank steps a beady-eyed old woman screeched, "Kilt entirely! Kilt by e's own brother 'e was. Oi seen it with me own two eyes. Dead as a shot rabbit 'e was."

The old crone was hopping about excitedly, flapping her scrawny arms like a feisty rooster trying to fly on a broken wing. Her hands, swollen and gnarled and dirty, clutched at empty air in their eagerness to impress the world with what she knew.

Katherine grabbed her roughly by the shoulder and shook her. "What are you screeching about? Who's dead? What happened?" But the woman shrank back, suddenly too frightened to speak.

A man moved out of the crowd, doffed his hat respectfully and began speaking. "Beggen yer pardon, ma'am, we don't rightly know anyone is dead, but there has been an accident. Old Mother Magarity here claims she saw it all, heard the older boy shouting, "You've got to stop. You've had more than your fair turn." When the younger lad laughed and pedalled right on by, the other braced himself to grab the handlebars the next time the bicycle flew past him. He stopped the bicycle quick enough, but his brother was catapulted off over the handlebars and skidded along the ground. When the policemen carried him into the bank he hung limp as a dead fish, bleeding a lot too, but your husband sent for the doctor. He arrived a few minutes ago." Seeing Katherine's stricken face he said kindly, "I expect the lad was just knocked out. It takes a lot to do a young un in."

As Katherine hitched up her skirts and raced up the stairs she met Dr. Butler at the top. "The lad's going to be all right. Just a dislocated shoulder and a few nasty scrapes and bruises, but if the look on your husband's face means anything your eldest son may soon be in worse shape. I've never seen Peter in such a rage."

Inside she felt terrified, but her face was hard and resolute as she raced towards Andrew's room. Hearing the whistling thud of belt leather striking bare flesh with such force it jolted a muffled grunt from her son's clamped lips added fresh fuel to her anger. Billy wasn't dead. It had been an accident. She knew that. Andrew would never intentionally hurt his brother.

She wrenched the bedroom door open and sprang for Peter's upraised arm, yanking it down, spinning him around. "How dare you thresh my son!" Her voice was low and deadly.

Peter, startled by her attack and more than a little ashamed at allowing his temper to get the better of him, muttered half apologetically, "He's my son too, you know."

"No he's not! He's mine!"

The moment the words where out, her hands flew to her mouth as if to somehow drag them back. But it was too late. She shrank away from Peter, wide-eyed and terrified, cowering as if expecting him to use the doubled belt on her.

Instead he said coldly, "We are both upset. I suggest we speak of this when we've had time to calm down and behave in a rational manner." With that he turned and strode out of the room, his back as stiff and unrelenting as an iron bar.

Katherine forced herself to hide the terrible fear she felt from Andrew, who was looking as if his world had flown apart too. As indeed she supposed it had. But when he started speaking she realized, with something like a stab of relief, that he had as yet no idea of the full import her words might have on their lives.

"I'm sorry, Mamma. I didn't mean to hurt Billy. It's just he wouldn't give the bike back and kept taunting me that I couldn't make him. So I had to show him. Didn't I?"

"I suppose so, son." She was too worried right now to think of anything more logical to say.

Katherine huddled near the fireplace, her arms hugging her body as if trying to stop her resolution from seeping away. She'd be eternally sorry for deceiving her husband, but she had given him two fine sons who were the image of himself. She hoped her husband would realize that that counted for more than a premarital transgression.

She was so wrapped in misery that she failed to hear Peter enter the room until he said coldly, "Can we talk now?"

She spun around to see her husband standing with folded arms, his shoulders bowed as though under a heavy weight. There were haggard lines around his mouth, a great sorrow in his eyes.

She forced her backbone ramrod straight. "Peter, I'm sorry I . . . ," she began miserably, but he interrupted her.

"I'm sorry too. Sorry because somehow I've made you think I don't love Andrew as much as I do the boys who carry my Moriarty looks. Andrew is more your son than mine in that respect, and he's yours because it was you who worked a miracle and delivered him alive. All I could do was wait and pray. But he isn't solely yours, just as he isn't solely mine. He is ours. And together we must do what we think is best for him.

"This afternoon I was angry and thought he needed to be punished for hurting his brother. Now after speaking to both boys I realize I was too hasty in my judgement. Billy was perhaps more at fault. He broke his word by not stopping as agreed upon. The boys realize now they should both have behaved better. They are friends again. What about us, Mavourneen? Can we be friends again?" His voice was husky with emotion.

Her startled shock of disbelief at Peter's irrational interpretation of "he's not yours, he's mine" momentarily knocked her off balance. She had to work to get her mind and throat unscrambled, control the furious hammering of her heart.

Peter's eyes had locked with hers and held them captive while he spoke, but now they held such tenderness a surge of relief washed over her. She moved into his waiting arms and raised her face. He bent his head and claimed her lips.

Her day of reckoning had not yet come. Perhaps it never would.

Chapter Nineteen
Lady Highips' Dinner Party

To Lady Highips' pinched mind it was important that she be an acknowledged friend of all the right people. People whose rightness would rub off on her and give her some vestige of prestige among those "to the manor born," a foothold her husband's money and title had so far failed to provide.

Today that good lady looked as pleased with herself as if she had been granted a tête-à-tête with a king and come away with his crown. Her dinner party promised to be a huge success.

Getting Lord Fitzdemon, Ireland's chief justice, to her table was a streak of pure luck, for when not in England one might suppose he'd spend most of his time in Dublin.

But as good fortune would have it (good fortune from Lady Enid's point of view, quite the opposite for the hapless victims who would suffer from his interpretation of British law), he was in the locale dispensing justice. And because Sir Highips, at his wife's insistence, had brought a suit against a carriage maker for faulty workmanship, he had met the man.

Sir Percy secretly knew the fault wasn't with the carriage maker, but with his own wife. She was constantly ordering the horses whipped up, no matter how rough the roads. Nevertheless he had done as his wife had ordered. Although it took some inveigling (something Sir Percy didn't approve of, nor did he like stooping to), the chief justice had accepted his wife's invitation to dine.

Lady Enid had sensed a subtle snub in Mrs. Peter Moriarty's cool, impeccably proper acceptance of her ladyship's invitation. But now she smiled cagily. When that woman found herself seated between Lord Fitzdemon and Lord Bingham, she couldn't fail to be impressed with the Highipses' circle of friends. Mrs. Moriarty was, after all, only a banker's wife. However, in the event two titles weren't enough, Lady Enid had ordered that Lord Dunraughton be seated across the table from her.

Lord Dunraughton was a man who wore his weathered good looks with such complete unconcern it gave him an air of mystery and intrigue that set Lady Highips' curiosity twitching. He most certainly would impress Mrs. Moriarty.

And impressing that lady was, after all, her prime reason for this dinner. For Lady Enid was plagued with a burning desire to meet the owner of the magnificent equipage she had once seen outside the Moriarty residence. Rumour had it the man was connected to British royalty. And Lady Enid was convinced that if she could just once entertain a scion of the House of Hanover her social standing would be secure. She knew no better way to get her foot in the door of the royal palace than through the Moriartys.

Apart from Lady Bingham, who would sit at her hostess's immediate left, the other guests, Peter Moriarty, Dr. and Mrs. Butler, and Mr. and Mrs. Albert Moriarty would be scattered rather haphazardly at her husband's end of the table. Her spouse was apt to get tongue-tied in the presence of beautiful women, but she knew he felt comfortable enough talking to the doctor's wife. As for Sophia Moriarty . . . well, no one, no matter how generous with compliments, could call that woman beautiful.

As Lady Highips surveyed her guests, seated now at a magnificent dining table resplendent in silver and crystal accoutrements, she became more convinced than ever there must be more to Katherine Moriarty than appeared on the surface. She felt certain that lady and the handsome, enigmatical Lord Dunraughton were previously acquainted. So why had neither admitted it? Were they secret lovers?

The thought of herself indulging in such an impropriety with the gentleman in question set the shafts of hair sprouting from a mole on her chin quivering with illicit desire. It took a conscious effort to drag her thoughts back to the question puzzling her.

When Lord Dunraughton had entered the Highips' drawing room Katherine had been standing with her back to him, in deep conversation with Lord and Lady Bingham about the young mares she intended to put in the coming sale for two- and three-year-olds. Lord Bingham was her mentor in such matters, as well as pasturing her young stock with his own. Katherine was anxious to learn if he thought the sale would attract the English buyers. Without them the prices would be poor and she might be well advised to hold her stock over for a future sale.

Then Lady Enid's honeyed voice cut in on their conversation. "Mrs. Moriarty, have you had the pleasure of meeting Lord Dunraughton?"

Katherine was turning to face her hostess, murmuring, "No, I haven't had the pleasure," when she looked up. Her eyes snapped to attention, her mouth gaped. She tried to speak but choked and lost her breath. Coughing and spluttering, she seemed in danger of strangling. The frantic appeal her eyes shot to where Peter had been standing moments before went unanswered. Peter wasn't there. He had stepped out to see Sir Percy's new dairy bull.

The next moment the man referred to as Lord Dunraughton had one hand firmly around her waist, and was thumping her vigorously on the back with the other, saying gently, "There, there. You'll be all right in a moment," but thinking *My God, this woman doesn't wear a corset.* Aloud he said, "It's just a catch in the breath. But a beastly feeling while it lasts. I know. I've had it happen myself."

When the horrible choking sensation was gone, and her eyes had stopped watering, Katherine looked up at the man standing beside her and murmured politely, "I'm pleased to make your acquaintance, Lord Dunraughton. But I'm sorry I made such an unladylike scene. I hope you'll forgive me, and forget it ever happened." Her words were iced in frosty hauteur. *Sotto voce* she hissed, "Tim Watson, it was all your fault. Sneaking up on me like that. Why didn't you tell me you were Lord Dunraughton?"

Drawing her hand through his arm he drew her a little apart. "There is nothing to forgive. And I won't forget. One rarely does, you know. Not when the experience was enjoyable. Haven't you noticed how the memories of our bad experiences tend to slide into oblivion, while we rarely forget those that are pleasant? Which is all to the good, of course. Otherwise our lives would be burdened with more sorrow than a human can bear."

"I can't imagine what you found so enjoyable about thumping a choking woman on the back." She shot him a hostile glare.

His grin was impish. "It renewed my faith."

To her sharp, "Don't be ridiculous. How could it do that?" he replied with a slow, provocative smile.

"Very easily, Mrs. Moriarty. I discovered you're not a woman to dissemble. Every inch of you is real. You haven't tortured your body into a steel cage for the sake of fashion. I admire you for that."

Looking as if her sense of propriety had been offended, she was about to swing on her heel and march away, when his hand on her arm tightened. "Please. I didn't mean to offend you. Can't we be friends?" He smiled and she felt something gentle wash over her.

Katherine shot her dinner partner, Lord Fitzdemon, a quick glance from under long dark lashes, and decided she didn't like the man. He had thin cruel lips, a bulbous nose, spreading as if it might once have been broken, ice-cold eyes, and a general air of supreme confidence in himself, coupled with total disdain for his fellow man. She shivered.

He was speaking to her now in a smooth, slimy voice that made her think of snake oil. "I understand your husband has listed two young mares in the sale next week. Have you considered entering the dam in the race that's to be run just before the sale? Seeing how the parents perform can be an incentive for buyers to dig deeper into their purse."

"No, I hadn't thought of it. In fact, I wasn't aware there was to be such a race, but I can see the logic of it. Except Ebony hasn't had any training. I just ride the trails around Grandon."

"I'm surprised your husband can find the time to leave the bank and ride with you."

"Oh, he doesn't ride with me. I ride alone."

"My dear Mrs. Moriarty, are you telling me a woman like yourself rides alone?" His eyes had taken on a wolfish glitter. "Surely you must realize how dangerous that could be. Your Irish peasants have less scruples than the wild animals they live like." His tone was smug, vindictive, and so full of self-righteousness that Katherine bristled.

"Lord Fitzdemon, it's a pity you're so busy meting out British justice that you haven't bothered to learn anything about those you sentence. If you had, you might know Irish peasants merit their reputation for kindness and hospitality. Even at the poorest hovel no one is turned from the door without some token of welcome. It may only be a mug of brackish water, but it is offered in friendship and generosity.

"May I also remind you Ireland is not England . . . where I'm told there *are* places where no woman would dare to ride alone. Here I feel completely safe roaming the most desolate mountain trails."

The chief justice of Ireland allowed himself a deprecatory shrug as he gave her a censuring scowl. "It's obvious you know nothing about the true nature of the Irish peasants. Haven't you heard of their burnings, stabbings, murders, mutilations, uprisings? I have to deal with them every month."

A feeling of recklessness overwhelmed Katherine as she glared at her companion. "Certainly I've heard of them. And I've heard of floggings so cruel that if they don't kill the man outright they leave him scarred for life. And his only crime might be poaching a salmon or a pheasant to feed a hungry family. I've also seen families evicted and left to starve. Do you call that British justice?" Katherine voice was scathing.

"And furthermore," she raced on, "do you consider the Devon Royal Commission set up to study the problems of land ownership fair? It isn't. Nor was it intended to be. Not when those sitting on it are all landowners. Of course their findings would be against the tenants.

"How do you think Irish tenants feel knowing their families were dispossessed of land that had been rightfully theirs since Cuchulain fought and killed Ferdiad? Or Queen Maeve battled for ownership of the famous brown bull of Cuailgne? Is it realistic to expect the conquered to feel kindly towards those who now totally control their lives?

"I believe the Earl of Clare, the Tory lord chancellor, is reported to have said when speaking of the English landlords that 'from the first they have felt hemmed in by the indigene, Irish whose families have peopled their country for centuries, and are now brooding with smouldering indignation over what they see as British injustice.' So why in the name of common sense doesn't Westminster soften the harshness of their anti-Irish laws and restore Irish lands to their rightful owners?"

"Madam," said Lord Fitzdemon, making an attempt to hide the fury Katherine's outburst had invoked in him, "I don't make the laws. I carry them out."

Lord Dunraughton had been watching Katherine with interest, but now an uneasy frown creased his forehead. She was a spitfire, a fiery champion of Ireland's rights and he liked that about her. But perhaps she had gone too far. Fitzdemon would be a dangerous enemy.

When Dunraughton's voice broke the stilted silence that followed Fitzdemon's last remark it was low, direct, and forceful. "She's right you know, your Lordship. There would be no trouble in Ireland if you English had stayed home.

"In a country more densely populated than China, where three quarters of the labouring class have only haphazard employment, having a small plot of land where they can grow their own potatoes means the difference between life and death. Without potatoes they have no hope of surviving. With them they may live in squalor, but they won't starve."

"Yes," snarled Lord Fitzdemon with an evil leer, "they live to produce still more litters of filthy brats who grow up to further compound the problem of not enough land."

Lord Dunraughton looked as if he was seeing a situation for which there was no solution. When he spoke there was something hard and cold in his grey eyes, and his voice was brittle. "In view of Ireland's exploding population, with land rents already eighty to one hundred percent higher than in England, and British laws always so detrimental to the manufacture of Irish goods, can you tell me, your Lordship, what you think the future holds for the poor of Ireland?"

Lord Fitzdemon fingered one corner of his moustache before he spoke. "Well, there is conacre, a system whereby those too poor to rent land can offer to hire a small holding. As you know it isn't exactly a lease, more a licence to occupy. Some, if luck is with them, can succeed and in time move up to a better lease. Others . . . ?" He waved his hand and shrugged. "The British army always has an opening for Irish soldiers. They make great fighting men. I have to admit their stamina, courage, daring, love of excitement, and complete disregard for danger has won more battles for English commanders than that country's own soldiers ever have."

"Yes," interjected Lady Bingham, who had been listening with avid attention to the exchange of words. "It was largely the Irish boys who broke Napoleon's power in the Peninsula and again at Waterloo. They helped carry the British flag to India too, as well as many other far-flung places around the globe. When my husband was in the India Service he said, 'Give me a regiment of Irish lads to command and I'll hand you the earth.' And what did they get for risking their lives to bring England fame and glory? One shilling a day."

Now Mrs. Butler leaned forward, speaking with every inch of her body. "If Ireland is to survive, changes in our laws are imperative. Yet laws alone won't solve the problem of Ireland's exploding birth rate. My husband tells me in the last sixty years it has increased by one hundred and seventy-two percent.

"He believes girls of sixteen and boys of seventeen or eighteen wouldn't be rushing into marriage if their home conditions weren't so bad. If only there was some chance for more of them to find jobs, go into service, . . . anything that would raise them above the terrible squalor they were born into. Their parents' hovels are so small, often with neither bed nor blankets, that huddling together of the sexes at night becomes a necessity."

Now Dr Butler was speaking forcefully. "It's my opinion the Act of Union of 1801 compounded Ireland's troubles. Its object was not, as so many believed, to help Ireland, but to bring her more abjectly under the British boot. As for free trade, all that did was make Ireland a dumping ground for British surplus, which of course, in view of the higher taxes in Ireland, caused what little industry we had in this country to collapse."

Sophia Moriarty had been stuffing her face with the exotic creations of Lady Enid's French chef, but now having reached repletion she sat back with a contented sigh. Looking squarely at Lord Fitzdemon she shouted in the voice of a drill sergeant, "Well, I entirely agree with you, my Lord. The Irish peasants are a dismal lot and deserve no better than they get. Poor is no excuse for filth." Her nose wrinkled in studied distaste. "My husband's tenants see nothing wrong with allowing a pig to share their hut. For all I know they sleep with it. In fact I expect they do. Most don't own a bed, just a filthy rag of a blanket on the floor. Sometimes not even that. So why wouldn't they sleep with their pig? It would help keep them warm." She gave a high cackling laugh as if she had said something quite clever. "And of course there's always the creature's dung outside the door, which the chickens scratch in until there's as much inside the hut as out."

Lord Fitzdemon's ice-cold eyes were on Sophia's face and they were insulting in their appraisal. But it was Lord Dunraughton who spoke and his words were clipped with bitterness.

"And I suppose, Mrs. Moriarty, your husband has never waived a tenant's rent so the family might perhaps better themselves with a proper blanket? Or a shelter for the pig? As I expect you must know, such an improvement would benefit yourselves."

To Sophia's startled eyebrows, Lord Dunraughton continued. "If the pig should die, leaving the tenant with nothing to sell to pay the rent, I expect your husband would have no qualms about evicting him. In which case any and all improvements the man made as a tenant become yours. Nor would you, I expect, consider helping the brighter lads to write their names and learn to read. Have you any idea how helpful literacy can be? Not only to those who stay in

Ireland, but to those who emigrate in search of better things?"

Sophia tossed her head and snorted grudgingly, as if she could spare nothing, not even a moment of compassion. "Of course not. What the tenants do, or what happens to them, is no concern of mine."

"It might soon become a very real concern." Dr. Butler spoke with a lowering look of gloom so out of character with his normal cheerful nature that it sent shivers of apprehension racing up Katherine's spine.

Up until a moment ago he had been deep in conversation with Lord Bingham, the two Moriarty brothers, and Sir Percy about the merits of more lime on the soils around Grandon, the value of manure as fertilizer for potatoes, and the possibility of establishing a more lucrative dairy trade with the continent.

Lady Enid had offered little to the table conversation, her energies alternated between glaring at the servants making the many removes, and ogling Lord Fitzdemon.

When she suggested the ladies retire to the drawing room while the men enjoyed cigars and brandy, Katherine realized with a start she had no idea what she had eaten, which of course was a pity because Lady Enid had spared no expense. The French chef alone would have cost her more than if she had waived all her tenants' rents for a year. Did that mean Lady Enid's dinner party was a success? Katherine supposed it must have been. So why did she have this uncomfortable feeling about it?

However, the rest of the evening passed pleasantly enough, with the talk mostly revolved around the coming sale of young stock, and whether there were enough sires and dams in the area to make it feasible to have a pre-sale race.

Peter objected when Katherine said if Ebony raced she ought to ride her. Whereupon Lord Bingham promptly said one of his stable lads could ride Ebony. He had ridden in other races and was really quite an experienced jockey.

Anyway, if one believed Lord Fitzdemon, no other horse stood a chance against his black stallion, so it was just a matter of deciding the placing of the also-rans. Sophia's mare, Grey Lady, the mare Katherine had once wanted so badly, would be running. If Ebony could beat her Katherine would be happy. But Ebony had not been in training. All the other horses had.

Lord Bingham had three mares entered, Squire Gordon two, Highips one, Albert Moriarty had entered Grey Lady, and there was one other.

"What about you, Dunraughton?" Lord Fitzdemon's voice held an open sneer. "Aren't you entering your chestnut stallion? I hear he's worth a king's ransom."

"That depends on the king and who's doing the ransoming." Dunraughton's voice was dry and completely non-committal. "But no, I'm not running Khemsahib. I don't need a race to tell me the qualities I'm looking for in a horse. However, I do plan to be at your sale." Then he spoke to Lord Bingham. "If it's convenient for you I'd like to stop in tomorrow to have a look at the young stock you're consigning. Mrs. Moriarty's too."

A moment later, having said his thanks to the Highips', he was gone. Katherine hadn't seen the loneliness in his eyes as he had looked briefly in her direction. Sophia and Lady Enid had.

Chapter Twenty
A Rigged Race?

Katherine knew if Ebony was to race she must be trained systematically. Sometimes she rode along the sandy shore when the tide was out. Sometimes she rode towards the Caha mountains, where there was room for a long gallop. Twice she rode to Beech Cliff and galloped Ebony under the overhanging branch. To her surprise she had discovered a tiny clearing not far beyond the gnarled old tree. It was a twin to the secluded spot where she had rested the day she had first seen Ebony.

As memories came flooding back her body stiffened and she shivered. But she forced back the sense of foreboding, reminding herself that finding this place must surely be a good omen. The other had brought her Ebony, hadn't it? And now on the very eve of something that promised to be important for both of them, they had stumbled upon this one.

The day of the race dawned clear and sunny. Peter and Katherine drove out to the race tracks in a hired carriage, a carriage Peter said he had trouble getting because so many English buyers had been ahead of him hiring transportation to the race and sale site.

Lord Bingham's stable boy, Owen, had ridden Ebony twice and seemed to have a feeling for the sensitive nature of the mare. Katherine's hopes were high.

Peter in top hat and morning coat looked extremely handsome as he tucked her hand under his arm and guided her towards the saddling area, stopping often to exchange a few words with the many who greeted him as an old friend.

Katherine felt a surge of pride. She hadn't realized how well liked Peter was. She supposed as bank manager he knew and understood their problems and had at times been able to help them overcome their financial ones. She also knew Peter was very worried about what the potato failure was doing to the economy, as well as to the lives of the peasants. That was partly why she hoped for good prices from the sale. It would be money they could put aside to help pay for their boys' education.

As they neared the saddling area and Peter was stopped by yet another man, he nodded for her to go on ahead. He would catch up.

Katherine smiled at Ebony's soft nicker of recognition as she reached to pat the glossy muzzle before speaking quietly to the jockey. "Good. I see you remembered what I said about not carrying a whip. She will give you her heart without it. But she'll fall apart if one touches her. Especially with a rider she doesn't know."

Katherine noted with a certain amount of pleasure that Grey Lady looked fit and ready. She was standing quietly as if conserving her energy for the race ahead. Not so a huge black stallion that had come flying into the ring in a savage burst of fury. He reared and screamed hatred like an old grizzly in a leg trap as a whip slashed wickedly against his powerful neck muscles. His eyes blazed dangerously.

He was a hard-muscled creature with lightning-fast reflexes, an evil temper, deadly heels, a powerful bite . . . and a complete lack of discrimination. If he saw an opportunity to wreak vengeance on the human race, one individual was as good as another.

When his eyes honed in on Katherine petting Ebony he reared explosively and lunged towards her, his two handlers dangling from his halter like corpses kicking on the end of a noose.

Katherine was hypnotized by the powerful crocodile jaws bristling with dirty yellow teeth zooming in on her. She heard hoarse shouting, but her feet refused to move.

Suddenly a blurred figure flashed past, the stallion's head was yanked around. Someone else dragged her to safety.

For a moment she sagged, limp with fright, against the muscled body of her rescuer, then disengaging herself she half turned to smile shakily into a face still drained of colour. "Princess. That brute could have killed you." Peter's words were soft against her hair. "I must find Dunraughton and thank him. I couldn't have reached you in time if he hadn't leaped in and turned the stallion aside. He's a good man. I hope he wasn't hurt." Peter's voice was brisk now and to the point.

But his need to go looking for the man was saved when a moment later Katherine found herself looking into Tim Watson's very direct grey eyes. "You gave me quite a turn, ma'am. I was afraid the stallion was going to savage you. A brute like that has no place as a breeder. If he were mine he'd go to the knackers."

"Perhaps, Lord Dunraughton, the fault is not all his. The best disposition can be spoiled by a vicious owner. And if I'm not mistaken that animal knows all there is to know about vicious owners." Katherine's eyes held his.

"You're right of course, Mrs. Moriarty, but some dispositions take more to spoil than others." His smile was enigmatic as he turned away, saying, "I fancy the race is about to start. I'll be watching your mare. She'll give a good account of herself if Fitzdemon's stallion doesn't throw her off."

It took three men to hold down the Fitzdemon entry and get him to the starting line, but once the horses were off and running his rider seemed to have him under control, perhaps because the animal had leaped into an early lead and there was no other horse to challenge him. Grey Lady and Ebony were running easily side by side, gradually edging ahead of the rest of the field, but Lord Bingham's brown mare and Squire Gordon's roan looked to be running with lots in reserve. It was still an open race for all but the black stallion. Katherine supposed he already had it in the bag.

Suddenly her voice was sharp with excitement. "Look at that! Bingham's mare is creeping up on Grey Lady. And look at Ebony run. She's stretching into her ground-eating stride. Look! Look at her go! She's moving up on the stallion!" Katherine was shouting ecstatically, her hands wildly pummelling Peter's arm. He was smiling at her in complete understanding. The field was strung out now behind the two blacks.

At that moment Katherine heard Tim Watson's quiet voice behind her. His face was lined with concern. "Your mare is running a great race, but it might be better if she doesn't pass the stallion. Fitzdemon has an unscrupulous jockey, with orders to win whatever the cost."

"And if he doesn't?" Katherine was flushed with the scent of victory.

"Then I suggest your husband lock you up somewhere safe and keep you out of Fitzdemon's sight. The man's a devil when crossed," muttered Lord Dunraughton, speaking more to himself than to Katherine.

Neither she nor Peter heard his words. Peter was watching his wife's excited face, thinking how very beautiful she was. She was watching Ebony inch ahead, her nose even now with the stallion's withers. He was running open-mouthed and labouring, while the mare seemed to be nicely getting into her stride. The crowd was wild with excitement. Every Irishman loves a good horse, a good race. Few liked Lord Fitzdemon, or his French horse. Still, a race was a race.

Suddenly a great gasp went up from the crowd, followed by an angry roar. Katherine clutched Peter's arm in open-mouthed horror. Then she was screaming. "He can't do that. He's whipping Ebony. Hitting her in the face. Not letting her pass."

She was one hundred and fifteen pounds of unadulterated fury, wanting to leap up and grab Lord Fitzdemon *and* his jockey and shake them both until their teeth flew out. And she'd ask no outside assistance doing it.

But Peter laid a calming hand on her arm. "It's not the race that's important, it's the bidding at the auction. Prospective buyers seeing what happened will bid accordingly. In fact, Ebony coming in second under those circumstances may be to your benefit. Everyone will be paying special attention to her progeny. Come now. There's time for a cup of tea in the church pavilion before the auction starts. Will you join us, Lord Dunraughton?"

"I haven't time for tea. I've got to go to Ebony, see she's properly cooled out," protested Katherine, pulling away from the arm resting lightly around her waist.

A dark frown swept across Dunraughton's weathered face. His eyes glittered like polished steel as he looked at Katherine. "If you would trust me to do it, ma'am, I'd be happy to take care of your mare."

In a low aside he whispered to Peter, "Don't let her out of your sight. And whatever you do keep her away from Fitzdemon. He's the type who would murder his parents, then expect clemency because he's an orphan. If the bidding goes against him today he could be out for blood. And he won't be particular whose it is." Then he gave a brittle laugh. "I don't expect you'll be meeting him in a church pavilion."

Peter's arm tightened protectively around Katherine's slender waist. As he drew her away her eyes dwelt for a moment on the retreating form of a man who was suddenly taking on some importance in her life. She allowed herself a tight smile. Her mind was a jumble of emotions where Tim Watson was concerned.

Never having attended an auction before, Katherine found the biding hard to follow. But when her mares, lots eight and nine, were brought out even she could tell there was an aura of excitement in the air, and Peter had whispered, "What did I tell you? Buyers have been sitting on their hands waiting for them."

Even the auctioneer seemed to be momentarily thrown off balance by the speed of the bids. When the gavel finally fell on the two-year-old, Peter whispered to her, "She fetched twice the price you hoped for," but Katherine scarcely heard. She was watching wide-eyed as the bids rose on the three-year-old. As the price spiralled upwards bidders began reluctantly shaking their heads, jammed their hands in their pockets, and craned their necks to see who was still bidding.

When it had come down to two Katherine followed the general direction of gaze and gave a horrified gasp. Lord

Fitzdemon! She started to jump up to protest but Peter pulled her down, whispering, "Owners are not allowed to bid an animal back. I'm terribly sorry, but it is an auction, so no matter who buys her there isn't a thing we can do about it." Seeing her stricken face he murmured gently, "He'll probably put the mare to stud and she'll have a good enough life. It's not as if she was a stallion a man rides every day."

A moment later the gavel came down and the auctioneer called, "Sold to . . . ," but neither Peter nor Katherine caught the buyer's name, nor could they see who the auctioneer was looking at. Except it didn't appear to be Ireland's chief justice. Katherine sighed and her heart seemed to give an enormous jerk of relief.

When the selling was over Peter and Katherine eased themselves through the crowds of well-wishers so she could give her fillies a farewell pat. On the way Lord Bingham came up to them beaming. "Great sale, wasn't it. And your two topped them all. Expect everyone is pleased. Except Lord Fitzdemon—no one seemed inclined to offer what his were worth. And it serves him right. I've never seen such poor sportsmanship. The man should be horsewhipped out of the country. But he's chief justice so we'll say nothing, and he knows it. But watch out for him. Especially you, Katherine. He's the sort to carry a grudge."

As they neared the horse area Peter heard his wife's sharp intake of breath and felt her fingers dig into his arm. Lord Dunraughton was standing near the black fillies, their lead ropes in his hand, giving instructions to a man who appeared to be his groom. Her heart gave a joyous little jerk. There was no one, she suddenly realized, she would rather see get her fillies than Tim Watson. There was something gentle and vaguely intimate in his eyes as he smiled. "I really only intended to buy one, but I couldn't let that swine get a good filly. Not after what he did to your mare. Anyway," as if he was making excuses to himself, "they are such a well-matched pair it seemed a shame to split them."

"Oh Lord Dunraughton! How can I ever thank you for what you did?" And with an impulsive little cry she threw her arms around his neck and kissed him on the cheek.

"Will you still thank me if I tell you I'll be taking them to Canada next month?" His voice sounded flat and totally devoid of feeling but his eyes watching her were smouldering with poorly concealed interest.

For a moment Katherine felt as if her feet had been jerked out from under her, then she managed a fragile smile. "Well, if they can take Ireland I don't expect Canada will defeat them. But please don't let the Indians get them."

Tim Watson smiled his slow lazy smile. "I'll do my best in that regards ma'am, but few Indians would treat either a horse, or a prisoner, worse than your own chief justice." Having said that he turned to Peter. "You'll be interested to know I plan to mate the fillies with Khemsahib before I leave. The colonies are sadly in need of better horseflesh. With luck these two will be the foundation stock that start a fine new line."

"But is there much demand in the territories for horses such as you have here?" Peter's tone was questioning.

"Surprisingly there is, and it's growing. John Rowland, chief factor at a place called Fort Edmonton, a huge grizzly of a man, has such a passion for horse racing that he's had a two-mile race track built, where animals are tested for speed and endurance. And by the way, if you plan to breed Ebony again I'd be proud to have her go to Khemsahib. I'm leaving him with my sister, Evelyn Watson, until I return the next time."

Katherine demurred. "I'm afraid the breeding fee to a horse as fine as Khemsahib might be too rich for my purse." But he smiled at her.

"Let's just say there would be no fee. I'd like to leave you something in return for the pleasure I've had in knowing you."

Startled, she looked up and saw sadness in his eyes. Seeing this imposing figure, tall, wide-shouldered, his presence radiating power and authority, looking so like a little boy who has just lost his mother, she had to force back the feeling she should take him in her arms and try to comfort him. Instead she said primly, and because she could think of nothing better to say, rather inanely, "I've enjoyed knowing you too." Then there were quick handclasps and Peter was ushering her away.

Just as they reached their rented carriage a rider came thundering past, his face as mean and ugly as the great black brute he rode. This had not been a good day for Ireland's chief justice. And by God, somebody was going to pay. Katherine levelled a vicious glare in his direction. He didn't see her.

Chapter Twenty-One
Berry Picking Gone Wrong

It was a perfect day for blackberrying. Sun-dappled trees bordered a trail better suited to wandering sheep or a saddle horse than a jaunting cart. Andrew's face was a study in concentration as he drove the pony between dovetailed hills, hills now shadow-flecked under a deep blue sky dotted with clouds floating in and out of fanciful configurations. Long-fingered rock fences, generously interlaced with thorny blackberry bushes, wove in and out among the high-knuckled hills.

Katherine smiled at her charges. Henrietta's twins, James and John, were basking in their official capacity as guides to the berry pickers. They were equally proud of having been first to fill their containers with the luscious blue-black fruit. The other children had chosen to fill their stomachs first.

Rosie Cassidy, two months younger than Billy, had been racing with that young man to see who could eat the most berries. If the winner was judged on the degree of staining around mouth and teeth, it was a dead-heat finish.

Andrew, looking quite grown up, sat in the front of the jaunting cart and drove the Cassidy pony, Peanuts, so named because the twins said his dun colour and fat little body reminded them of peanuts. Michael had chosen to stay with Henrietta's fourth child, Harold. They shared an affinity for collecting bugs and whatever other insects they could lure into their nets.

"Mamma, I think we should turn back. This trail is getting too narrow. There isn't room now for two vehicles to pass." Andrew sounded worried as his eyes took in the narrow trail feeling its way around corkscrew curves hugged by rock fences and massive trees.

Katherine grimaced as she realized with a jerk that Andrew was right. There was no place the jaunting cart could pull out to pass an oncoming cart. But now John was speaking with easy unconcern. "The best blackberry patch is only a little further on. And Andrew, you don't need to worry about meeting another cart. Not here. This road is scarcely ever used., except by shepherds. Or sometimes a rider."

"Talk of the devil," James spoke with mock solemnity. "There's a rider coming up behind us."

Katherine recognized the horse. It was Grey Lady. But who was the rider? It wasn't Sophia. Nor Albert. Her brows drew together in a puzzled frown, then smoothed out as recognition took over. She knew that rider, even though she hadn't seen him since her marriage.

"Why Patrick, what a pleasant surprise. Fancy seeing you in this lonely part of the country."

Patrick Tully's ruddy face glowed with pleasure. "Sure'en 'tis pleased I am to have taken this short cut this morning, ma'am." As he was speaking his eyes swept over the five children in the jaunting car, then returned to her with a questioning look.

Katherine laughed. "Only Andrew and Billy are mine, Patrick. The other three are Cassidy children. But I do have another son. He's more for bugs and beetles than for berry picking. But tell me about yourself. What are you doing here?"

"Well, ma'am, I work for your husband's brother and at the moment I'm taking Grey Lady to a stud, and this trail offers a bit of a short cut."

"Are you married, Patrick? Do you have a family?" She was pleased that the sight of the man who had taken her virginity all those years ago, and fathered her first-born, brought none of the old stirrings. She could talk to him as casually now as one talks to any acquaintance.

Patrick shook his head. "No ma'am. This country has too many mouths to feed without me adding to it. Not that I'd have minded were I squire of me own land. But a labourer's chances are too uncertain the way Ireland is now. So I've decided to emigrate. I'll be sailing next month from Cove. Lord Dunraughton says I'll easily get work in Montreal, or anywhere in the New World. So it's roight glad I am to have chanced on you this marnin."

"I'm pleased we met too, Patrick. And I do wish you every success in Canada. It sounds like a fascinating country."

"Thank you for your good wishes, ma'am. And glad I am to have made the acquaintance of your two foine sons. His eyes flicked over their faces and stopped with a jolt on the shock of hair the colour of polished copper that had escaped the confines of Andrew's cap. There was an indefinable look on the rider's face as he moved away. Katherine didn't notice it.

Her ears had caught the thud of galloping hooves, the rattle of carriage chains, the clanging and jolting of wheels protesting a rock-strewn trail. Her face blanched. In moments the carriage would be careening around the curve ahead, giving the driver no time to stop his racing horses before they crashed into the jaunting car. There was no room for either vehicle to pull out and get off the trail.

"Quick, children!" she screamed. "Climb up on the rocks. Get well back from the road. Andrew, you too," she commanded.

"No, Mamma. I'll stay with Peanuts. You've always told me a horseman's first concern should be for his horse."

Before Katherine could argue a heavy coach drawn by a pair of well-muscled bays came whirling into sight. But the driver paid no more attention to the pony and cart than if he'd seen a crouching rabbit.

Katherine jumped in front of the cart, screaming as she did for Andrew to leave the pony and jump to safety among the rocks. Her wildly waving arms were like the terrified flapping of a grounded eagle. Fear flooded her mind. Then without being quite aware of how it happened, a blur of white streaked across her vision.

Patrick had spurred Grey Lady into the path of the near horse, intending to grab its head and use every muscle in his powerful body to drag it to a halt. Instead, the animal shied away so violently it sent its mate crashing into the trees where it fell in a tangle of flailing hooves and broken harness.

The carriage had a crazy forward list. A broken front wheel made it difficult for the vehicle's only occupant to open the door and force his way out. When he did his face was livid. Sweat beads of temper stood out on his forehead as he rammed his body towards where Patrick was helping the driver control the terrified team, as if intending to slash him across the face with his heavy silver-mounted cane.

When he looked up, saw Katherine standing numb and half stunned, he stopped as if he had suddenly come up with a far better plan. He turned and beckoned imperiously to four horsemen in Royal Irish Constabulary uniforms who had galloped into sight and were now pulling their horses to a stop a few feet behind the damaged coach.

"Put that man in irons. Take him to the garrison and tomorrow morning he's to be flogged for interfering with Irish justice. He came damn near killing me. A thousand lashes . . . if he lives that long."

Katherine flew at Lord Fitzdemon like a fighting bantam. "You can't do that, your Lordship. He didn't mean you any harm. He was only trying to stop your carriage before it smashed into the jaunting car and killed the pony as well as my son and myself. If anyone is at fault it's you for allowing your coachman to drive in such a reckless fashion on these narrow roads. It's you who should be flogged." Her eyes were black with fury, and her hands clenched and unclenched as if hoping for permission to tear the man apart.

"My dear Mrs. Moriarty, you seem to forget that in these parts I *am* the law. I not only can have that peasant flogged, I intend to see a thorough job done of it. Unless of course you have it in your noble heart to save your friend. Or is he your lover?" The weasel smile he threw at her was dripping with cruelty. His eyes, laced with animal cunning, swept over Andrew (who was standing squarely in front of Peanuts so the frightened pony couldn't bolt), then back to where Patrick was still trying to quiet the terrified team. A wildly slashing hoof had ripped open Patrick's shirt, exposing a well-muscled chest on which a birthmark shaped like a dagger's hilt was clearly visible.

"What do you mean?" The words were the barely audible whisper of a victimized woman. Inside Katherine was splitting apart with fury, andher mind hovered close to the panic button, but instinct warned her if she was to somehow save Patrick's life she had to keep her wits about her and not let anger negate her woman's wiles.

She already knew what this man wanted. It was what his type always wanted. But how it was to be taken might be open to negotiation. She held her chastity like a clenched fist, but it was a fist that when forced open must hold a dagger.

He twirled his cane with sadistic vigour. "I want you, my dear. I've always had a fancy for spirited women. It makes the taking of them so much more . . . interesting." His eyes were calculating slits of cruelty. *You're a beast and a cad*, she mouthed at him silently as he continued.

"The world sees your spirit and your beauty. I intend to explore your, shall we say, your hidden charms." His laugh was evil.

"And if I refuse?"

"Then you'll watch your friend cower and scream as his flesh is being ripped from his bones. Somehow I don't fancy you have the stomach for that." He ran his tongue around his lips in an erotic fashion as if already savouring the horrors of a flogging.

While he had been speaking two uniformed men had put manacles on Patrick and were taking him away. He appeared too stunned to comprehend that by this time tomorrow he would be a mass of torn and rotting flesh.

Katherine's mind was leapfrogging. She had it in her power to save Patrick's life, the life of the man who had fathered her firstborn, at the cost of a few hours' discomfort to herself, and the loss of her chastity. A chastity she had already lost. Lost long ago . . . to the very man whose life was now at risk because he had saved her life and the life of their son.

Surely it was better to agree to Fitzdemon's terms than be forced to endure the horrors of witnessing a flogging, and living the rest of her life with it emblazoned on her memory, knowing she could have prevented it.

The memory of something her governess had once said came rushing back. "If you are given an unpleasant task, don't waste time grumbling and complaining, but do it with good grace and get it over with."

Katherine didn't trust Fitzdemon. She hated him and everything he stood for. But he seemed to have won this round. Yet before she carried out her part of whatever bargain they struck she must make certain he carried out his.

She levelled a cold and haughty stare at Fitzdemon, but her lips smiled. "Very well, your Lordship. I'll spend an evening in your company in exchange for a signed pardon. You write and send it immediately, and it must unequivocally release Patrick Tully from any blame in connection with your accident. And it is to be effective from the time of writing.

"Furthermore, as I assume there is something of the sportsman in you, as there is supposed to be in every Englishman, I'll make you a sporting proposition. Tomorrow I'll meet you one hour before sunset [she named a spot] on my black mare and I'll race you for my chastity. If your stallion can beat my mare before we reach the straight-of-way on the other side of Beech Cliff corner I'm yours for the evening. But if my mare outruns your stallion the deal is off. And Patrick Tully still goes free. Agreed?"

The evil leer twisting Lord Fitzdemon's mouth vanished. The lust-glazed eyes that had been insolently stripping her naked, looked momentarily startled. One white, impeccably manicured hand thoughtfully fingered his moustache. He seemed on the verge of refusing her challenge when

Katherine spoke again, her words ringed in scorn.

"Surely, Lord Fitzdemon, you aren't afraid? You said your stallion was unbeatable." Katherine forced her face to look demure and completely innocent as she murmured, "Or were you bragging?"

When Lord Fitzdemon finally inclined his head to agree to her terms she realized their conversation had almost certainly been overheard by the two men sitting patiently on their horses awaiting further orders.

I suppose the whole country will hear about this, she thought bitterly. But perhaps if he hadn't felt the need to save face in front of them he wouldn't have agreed. *At least the children are out of earshot.* Whatever the outcome of tomorrow it was important she not have to explain her part in it to Peter. If he knew he'd want to rush out and kill Lord Fitzdemon, which could have dangerous repercussions for her husband. One didn't kill the Lord Chief Justice of Ireland with impunity. A dreadful fear enveloped her.

Luckily Peter was in Dublin trying to convince Robert Murray, chairman of the Provincial Bank of Ireland, he was wrong in claiming the devastation caused by the failure of the potato crop was being grossly exaggerated. So Peter wouldn't know what his wife was about to do. She hoped he'd never find out.

Suddenly Lord Fitzdemon threw back his head and laughed an evil laugh. "You strike a hard bargain, my dear, for which I shall claim extra pleasure when I win the race. As of course I will."

Katherine inclined her head, her face frozen in the semblance of a smile. "Then write the pardon, your Lordship, and send it with one of your men. I want Patrick Tully released immediately."

Lord Fitzdemon, looking as if he had more bile than blood in his veins, began to scrawl something imperiously on a slip of paper, which he handed to an officer whose friendly face seemed to be telling Katherine he was a gentleman even though he had the misfortune to work for a blackguard. Her secret would be safe with him. And he would see the message got delivered promptly.

He had no sooner set spurs to his horse and galloped away then Lord Fitzdemon beckoned to the remaining officer. "You there. I need your horse. You can stay and help mend the wheel." With that Lord Fitzdemon was gone and Katherine was left alone with a young man who was looking at her with troubled eyes.

"Begging your pardon, ma'am, but 'tis worried I am for you. His Lordship is the devil's tutor." His voice was clipped and anxious as he began removing his revolver. "Here, ma'am. You best have this. The man's a monster, with no respect for women."

But Katherine shook her head. "Thank you for your offer. But I can't take your gun. It would only get you into trouble. You'd get flogged. Then I'd have to do it all again to try and save you." Her smile was grim, her voice little more than a frightened whisper. Then it strengthened as determination flooded back into her. "I truly believe my mare is faster than his stallion, so nothing's going to happen to me. And if it does . . . ." She shrugged. She wasn't about to tell anyone her real plan.

As they spoke the coachman looked up and beckoned from where he had been wiring up the broken wheel. The carriage was ready to inch past the pony cart and proceed on its journey. The young officer touched his hat and was moving away when she stopped him with a low whisper.

"Please. Ask your friend not to tell Patrick Tully what made Fitzdemon release him. It's best he never knows."

The man inclined his head in understanding, but she hadn't forbidden him to tell someone else. She was a brave woman, but no woman should be left to face Lord Fitzdemon alone under these circumstances. He must reach the barracks and find a horse.

Katherine was thankful the children didn't ask a lot of questions. Only Andrew looked anxious when she returned to the jaunting car saying, with a cheerfulness she didn't feel, "Time to turn around and head for home. You have to be in Cork for school tomorrow."

"What about you, Mamma? Will you and Michael stay with Aunt Henrietta until Dadda comes home?"

"I expect Michael will want to stay, but I must get back to Grandon today."

"But Mamma? I thought you intended to stay with Aunt Henrietta too." Andrew's voice was troubled.

"I did, but something unexpected has come up that I must attend to. But don't worry, dear." She tousled his copper hair and tried to smile even though her mind was shrivelled by misgivings that bordered on panic. "I'll be back in a few days and maybe next weekend you and I can ride through the tunnel of echoes. Or visit Saint Finbarr's Stations of the Cross." As she said it Katherine's eyes hardened, her fingers clenched.

Would she ever be back? So much depended on the outcome of tomorrow. If her plan aborted she could end up dead, or in a penal colony in Australia. But she mustn't let herself think about those possibilities, or she would lose the courage to carry out the plan fermenting in her brain.

Chapter Twenty-Two
A Race Until Death

The sun exploding above the horizon was flinging fiery ribbons of flame across the dome of heaven. "Red sky in the morning, sailors' warning," Bridget chanted tonelessly as she rattled the stove grates.

Katherine scowled as she crawled out of bed, hurriedly pushed back the tendrils of dark hair clinging around her face, and stared at her reflection in the mirror above the washstand. *What will I look like when this day is over? Will I ever look the same again?* There was a grim twist to her mouth as she wound her hair into a tight bun, jabbing in more hairpins than were normally required to keep it in place.

Today nothing must go wrong. She had a race to run. A race she *must* win. It seemed imperative that she stay positive. She'd look after the mare herself this morning.

But when Katherine opened the stable door and stepped inside it was as if she'd been hit on the head with a board. Waves of worry sluiced through her. Jeremy, nickering, had touched Ebony's nose, and the mare had responded by lifting her tail and making water. Her vulva winked.

"Oh no-o-o!" Katherine's drawn-out wail sounded as if it had come from a barrel lined with corrugated iron. "Ebony! You can't be! You just can't be in heat! Not today of all days! Oh, Ebony!"

Apprehension swept through Katherine like a school of darting minnows. Estrus sometimes stops mares from reaching their peak performance. Would that happen with

Ebony? If it did there was absolutely nothing she could do about it. It was too late to back out now. So she'd better try to think positive, or hope that a mare in heat might throw the stallion off his race too.

Then another grisly thought stabbed her mind. If the stallion got free of his rider he'd immediately savage the mare, and kill Katherine in his lust-crazed frenzy to breed Ebony before anyone could stop him. Katherine squared her shoulders and slammed the door shut on that thought too. *I'll take a twist of black pepper in my pocket and throw it in the stallion's face if he attacks Ebony. The pepper might work where no amount of whipping would.*

It was afternoon, and Katherine was riding slowly towards the designated spot. She wanted to feed and rest the mare before Lord Fitzdemon arrived. She carried a ham sandwich for herself.

Before she reached her destination the sky, near cloudless earlier, showed a piping of murkiness edging the far horizon. Katherine watched it creep slowly higher with a growing sense of unease, then reached to touch the stiletto hidden in her boot, her face twitching with revulsion. Could she use it on a fellow human? Only if . . . . Her face suddenly looked cold, resolute, and very desperate.

Now that the afternoon was well advanced she walked to where Ebony was nibbling grass, patted the black's neck, tightened the girth and then mounted, nudging the mare to where she could peer anxiously down a trail that wound around hills like wrinkles on a giant's face. Lord Fitzdemon was late.

Her lips compressed into a hard line, her fingers nervously rearranged a scarf that needed no rearranging. It was the scarf Patrick had given her long ago. She had worn it today hoping the luck an old Chinese Mandarin had claimed for it would rub off on her. Today the luck of the Irish might not be enough.

The worry knot in her stomach hardened into a block of granite when she saw Lord Fitzdemon. The man was bringing his grooms, his carriage, *and* an armed bodyguard. Why hadn't he come alone? *Does the bastard think I've planned an ambush?*

A rush of anger swept across her face as she glowered at the entourage.

Lord Fitzdemon's weasel eyes watching her from folds of flaccid flesh held a sensuous glitter as he inclined his head in a brief greeting. She levelled a vicious glare at him. "Do you make a habit of having your bodyguard attend your assignations? Perhaps to bear witness to your sexual prowess, your Lordship?" Her voice was scathing.

For a moment he flinched as if she had cut him with a whip. Then he recovered and said tersely, "As soon as I'm mounted, the grooms and carriage will withdraw. As will the troops after their captain has fired the starting shot."

Katherine allowed herself a tight and spiteful smile. "Are you sure, your Lordship, it wouldn't be better if they stayed? If they are watching perhaps you'll be too ashamed to attempt to win by whipping my horse and frightening her."

Lord Fitzdemon's voice retreated into a snarl, his beady eyes glared at her with animal venom. "There'll be no one staying to watch. Tonight you'll be mine. And there'll be no escape."

Katherine tossed her head with an arrogance she was far from feeling. "Don't forget, your Lordship. You have to catch me first. Or the deal is off."

He leered darkly and she felt something evil wash over her.

Then he stalked to where two grooms were controlling a restive horse and slashed at it wickedly with his whip until he appeared to consider the creature sufficiently subdued to mount.

No one saw the white horse on a high ridge where one could look eagles in the eye. But if the glint of sun on glass meant anything it wasn't eagles its rider was watching.

Only the young captain saw a second horseman moving stealthily through trees bordering an old beech that clung perilously close to the trail ahead. And seeing it his spirits lifted.

Finally, obeying a curt nod from Fitzdemon, the captain stepped forward, revolver in hand. A speculative gleam had crept into his eyes as he watched the plunging stallion try to rid himself of a hated rider. But now the powerful horse seemed to have been beaten into submission. The captain raised the revolver to fire the starting shot when, without any warning, the stallion reared again in a final attempt to dislodge his rider. When the gun went off Ebony exploded into her racing stride and had a half-length lead before a whack between the ears brought the stallion down and running.

Sensing what had happened, Katherine felt some of the tension leave her body. If she could keep this lead Fitzdemon wouldn't be able to whip Ebony and frighten her into breaking stride. As she leaned forward to whisper encouragement in her mare's ears the Mandarin's scarf at her neck slipped and fell.

The big black was running with every muscle in his powerful body. Fitzdemon, his face masked in fury, was slashing the creature unmercifully with his heavy whip.

The beech tree corner was coming up fast. So was a dark storm cloud. In moments the sun, which was blinding both horsemen to a limb that could garrotte a rider as effectively as the neck cords in a Spanish torture chamber, would be blotted out. Fitzdemon would see the branch and swing out to avoid it.

"Sweet Mother Mary," breathed Katherine, "please let the sun shine for just one more minute."

But just as Ebony galloped below the branch the sun was swallowed up by the growing cloud. Katherine's secret weapon had become a gnarled old limb. Dear God! This race wasn't over yet, and now for her it might never end. Ireland's chief justice would see to that.

She scarcely heard the man's savage curse when he saw his danger. Spurring and slashing he yanked the stallion sideways to avoid the branch, but in doing so the big animal lost his footing and skidded to the very edge of a crumbling cliff that would bring death to anything that went over it. For a moment it seemed the cliff was about to claim two more victims Then the stumbling animal made a heroic effort and got his feet back onto firm ground again.

Now that Fitzdemon's immediate danger was past, the terror that had blanched his face turned to maniacal rage. The woman was widening the gap between them. But he'd make her pay. By God, how he'd make her pay! The stallion too. The brute had almost killed him. His whip rose and fell with merciless rhythm, as if the strength in his arm alone must propel the straining animal.

Great gasps of breath ballooned Fitzdemon's cheeks; his face took on the red and bloated look of a boiled but rotting lobster. His eyes, shooting venom at the world, seemed ready to jump from their sockets to search out more victims for his anger. Sweat beads of fury trickled off his nose. A terrible rage ripped through him as he mind-blasted the woman who had tricked him, the captain who had fired the starting shot, the stallion who . . . .

The whip-hand, raised to administer yet another slashing blow to a lathered and blood-flecked animal, dropped. The whip fell from nerveless fingers.

Meanwhile fear enveloped Katherine in a black and terrible shroud. It wouldn't matter if Ebony won the physical race. Her plan had failed. And Ireland's vindictive chief justice would spend the rest of his life making sure she and all those she loved paid dearly for it. Her hands sweat blood. She touched the hidden stiletto, her face grim with a terrible determination.

Her horror-numbed mind failed to register the shriek that split the air, catapulting off the rocks to echo and re-echo into the distance in ever diminishing repetition until it was lost in the thud of galloping hooves.

She risked a backward glance, a glance that said there was a riderless horse behind her. Which of course was impossible. Fitzdemon must be hidden by the stallion's whipping mane.

She fingered the twist of pepper in her pocket. Would it repress a man as well as his horse?

Katherine didn't see a rope whistle snake-like through the air, didn't hear the ring of iron-shod hooves on the rocks above her. She didn't hear a thud, or the grunt of a horse struggling to get up. She did hear a shout, a sort of victory whoop. Was Fitzdemon so sure of success? Icy dread sluiced through her.

She looked down at her boot again, the boot that hid the stiletto. There was white desperation on her face. Any minute now she'd have to steel herself to use it. Plunge it deep. First into her assailant. Then into herself? Could she do it? She had to. There was no other way to protect those she loved from terrible reprisals.

When Katherine realized she could no longer hear the pounding hooves of a following horse, she risked another backward glance and was startled to see Fitzdemon standing beside his fallen black. Only the man hadn't looked like Fitzdemon. He looked like . . . . But that was impossible. Sweet Mother in heaven! She must be hallucinating.

At that moment she was too tired to make sense of anything. Except Ebony seemed to have won her race.

Now that the adrenaline surge was gone Katherine was left with a terrible weariness. She slipped from the saddle too weak to control the violent shudders threatening to tear her body apart, and huddled beside a large rock, her face hidden in her hands.

She didn't know that the black stallion was tied up like a trussed hog. Or that a tall figure, broad of shoulder and narrow of hip, with strong arms and powerful back muscles, was looking down at him with a satisfied air, his thumbs hooked contemplatively into his tooled leather belt. Then one hand moved to the neck of a liver-chestnut stallion. "Begorrah, Khemsahib. We did it. Best throw of me entire life. Now let's find out what happened to his rider."

Moments before, a man in the uniform of the Royal Irish Constabulary had galloped into sight, and having bent briefly over the fallen figure of Lord Fitzdemon, he straightened and whistled between his teeth. "B'Jasus! Dead as a turnip. Now won't that be making the divils in hell happy."

Tim Watson hurried towards the officer, a puzzled expression on his face. The captain grimaced. "I fancy we best be getting Dr. Butler to confirm it, though I can almost say meself what caused it. His Lordship has had blackouts before. Dublin doctors warned him if he didn't control his temper, apoplexy would do him in. And now 'tis happy I am to see it's happened. Before he harmed the little lady."

Then he straightened and smiled sparingly. "I'll have the carriage brought up for his body. The grooms can take the stallion. Me, I'd be for putting a bullet in his brain. Although one never knows. Kindness sometimes does wonders. And the poor animal has had little enough of that in his life. You're mighty fancy with a rope, sir, catching his feet like that." The Captain's face was wreathed in admiration. "Do you suppose I could learn the trick?"

"My throw today was pure luck," Watson grinned. Something deep inside him had been writhing in angry torment ever since hearing the message the young captain had ridden hard to bring him the night before. The thought of Fitzdemon possessing a woman, a woman he had no right to think about as he did, had set his blood at such a boil he knew there had been more involved than luck.

And now when he looked towards the small figure huddled beside a rock like a sack of potatoes carelessly tossed from a passing cart, his face became granite hard. He quickly remounted and nudged his mount into a gallop. His eyes were dark with determination, but there was something else too.

A moment later he felt bathed in a warm protective glow, a driving need to protect the woman he cradled gently against his shoulder, silently willing his own strength to give her the courage she needed to put this horrible nightmare behind her. It wasn't until the convulsive shuddering stopped that he spoke. "You've nothing to be frightened of now, Mrs. Moriarty. Fitzdemon is dead. A brain haemorrhage, apoplexy, brought on by his own violent temper. Not you, nor any one, can be blamed for his death."

To the unspoken question in her eyes he murmured, "The young captain was worried for your safety. When I heard about the race, the price you'd be forced to pay if you lost, I came here to kill the fiend . . . if the tree didn't do it for me.

Katherine shivered convulsively and raised her eyes to his. "I'm glad you didn't. You would have been hunted down and brutally flogged before they allowed you the oblivion of hanging."

Watson shrugged laconically. "But first they'd have to find me. I have many friends."

She suddenly felt very vulnerable. This man stripped her of all need to dissemble. Some strange stirring within her insisted she be completely honest with him, for Tim Watson deserved that much. If he condemned her for what had happened all those years ago, did it really matter?

She twisted her fingers into a nervous knot before speaking in a voice that was the whisper of dead leaves drifting down a lonely lane.

"Fitzdemon was going to have Patrick Tully flogged to death. When all he had done was save me and his son . . . our son . . . from being run down by Fitzdemon's carriage. And he was going to force me to watch."

At the words "our son" a tremor swept through the man beside her, a dark, inscrutable look flooded his eyes.

She was speaking now as if to herself and it was important she be very honest. "If I wanted my marriage to last I had no choice but to agree to Lord Fitzdemon's demands. It wasn't just that I couldn't allow an innocent man to be flogged. I'm hiding a mistake. A mistake my husband must never know about."

Then, without quite knowing why, she told him things only Henrietta had heard. Katherine shuddered as if trapped in unbearable remorse when she began speaking. Then she raised her eyes and continued bravely. "You see, my husband puts great importance on women coming to their marriage bed a virgin. I didn't, but he thinks I did." Her words ended on a tortured moan. The next moment she took a determined breath and continued, for Katherine Moriarty wasn't one to avoid the rough spots in her life. "He believes one illicit mating puts a blemish on all that woman's other children. I don't understand how, but Peter . . . perhaps other men believe it too. So I've *got* to keep my secret from him. Had I refused Lord Fitzdemon after he stumbled on my secret yesterday he would have done more than flog a man to death. He'd have gone to Peter asking if he had ever wondered why my eldest son and the man who was once my father's groom had identical birth marks and the same red hair."

Her delicately sculptured face held unbearable remorse, her tapered fingers were absently interlacing themselves, when she suddenly looked staggered at what she had just done. "I've never told anyone . . . except my girlfriend . . . what I've told you. And I don't know why I wanted to tell you something I've hidden all these years. Except . . . except it seemed important you know the truth about me." She looked at him with a sad little smile that pulverized his heart.

The strong hand that had closed firmly over her slender fingers gave them an understanding squeeze. His arm around her shoulder tightened. On his face was the weathered look of a man who has been taught by experience to ride with a tight rein on his emotions. "Your secret is safe with me, little lady. And I think none the less of you for what you've told me." The words seemed to give her courage. They had come from a man who had experienced years of rugged living.

Without either of them realizing it the sun had long since set. The rider on the white horse, seen only by the eagles, had reluctantly put away the glass and moved down off the ridge. Night had stolen over the land, bringing with it a darkness intensified by the deep gloom of a starless sky. The wind was rising to a screaming crescendo and the first drops of rain were already splattering on the rocks when Katherine spoke with startled urgency. "It's late. I must go home."

"You're not riding home tonight. Not in a storm. I won't allow it. You'll come home with me. It's only a few miles if we go across the hills. Come, I'll help you mount."

They drew apart but their eyes met and held, his dark and unfathomable, hers troubled and questioning.

There was hidden authority in his voice as he continued, "I'll send a messenger to let your husband know you're safe. I'll take you home in the morning."

At her tired protest, "I can't. People would talk. Ebony is sure-footed. She'll find the way," his expression hardened.

"You'll not go. I won't allow it. You and your mare have both had a long and stressful day. You'll come with me. Don't fret about your reputation. You'll be perfectly safe. My sister lives with me."

Katherine couldn't find the energy to protest any longer. When Tim Watson helped her into the saddle she said with a listless little sigh, "There will be no need to send a messenger. My husband won't be back from Dublin until the end of the week."

The wind howling with insane fury at the blackness of the night, the injustices of the world, soon whipped the pins out of Katherine's hair. Numbly, for she was battling total exhaustion, she followed Tim Watson as he picked up the trail across the rock-strewn hills. The stygian dark of a starless night hid the face of a man fighting to control forbidden feelings.

Chapter Twenty-Three
Tragedy Strikes . . .

It started like any ordinary day. The sun shone, dogs chased cats, mothers scolded children. Katherine smiled. After shopping with Andrew in Cork for a new school blazer they were to meet Peter, returning from a week in Dublin, for a late tea before going on to Grandon.

Mother and son were moving in companionable silence down one of Cork's main thoroughfares when they were startled by a sudden commotion. A yapping dog had terrified a heavy dray horse into rearing and falling backwards in the shafts, smashing the cart and contents as it fell. This so frightened a nearby team of matched greys hitched to a splendid brougham that they broke away from the barefoot boy who had been left to mind them, and were now racing driverless down the street towards two stiff-backed nursemaids. The women, wheeling babies in their prams, were exchanging gossip as they strolled, completely oblivious of the destruction bearing down on them.

Katherine screamed a warning, but it was Andrew who catapulted into action. He flung himself towards the onrushing greys, made a far-reaching grab for their heads, but was only able to reach the bridle of the near horse. Katherine recognized the animal immediately as Grey Lady. He managed to partially slow Lady, only to further frighten the other horse, which was running now in a mindless panic.

The terrified gelding was dragging the carriage and his mate in a circle around the boy clinging leech-like to Grey

Lady's bridle, while Andrew tried desperately to reach the cross reins that controlled the pair.

At that moment the younger nursemaid, an Irish lass with more courage than good sense, shoved her perambulator through the open door of a nearby shop, snatched the ever present umbrella from the pram, and sprang forward frantically waving the opened brolly in the gelding's face. All hell broke loose.

In seconds both animals were down in a tangle of broken harness, threshing hooves, and a splintered carriage pole. Katherine, her body terribly twisted, had been hurled violently against a brick wall. Andrew, lying under the carriage in a pool of his own blood, had a great gash on his head. There was shock and disbelief in the eyes of the men who rushed to help. Their kindly faces were frozen in horror as they dragged the mangled body of the boy from the blood-soaked ground. They had to get him out from under the still rocking carriage quickly. Perhaps it was already too late.

There was a vacant look in Katherine's eyes when the men went to help her. She couldn't scream. Her screams were frozen at their source. Only the thin pitiful moan of a soul in mortal agony escaped her lips as they lifted her.

It looked as if there had been a double tragedy.

A doctor elbowing his way through the gathering crowd spoke brusquely. "Carry them to my surgery. Three doors down. I'll examine the lad first. He looks beyond human help, but I'll do what I can."

The doctor was cutting off Andrew's torn shirt when a breathless man rushed in, his face scratched and streaked with dust, his shirt ripped, his cap gone. "How is he, doctor? Will he live?" The doctor, without looking up, shook his head, then seeing the man's stricken face asked gently, "Are you his father?"

There was an agonized silence before Patrick Tully was able to answer. Then, as if he had just made the hardest decision of his entire life he said numbly, "I sired him."

"Well, sir, it was a brave thing your lad did. In all probability he'll not regain consciousness. But you can take some comfort in that. He'll not be suffering unbearable pain before death gives a merciful release."

At that moment a harsh, authoritative voice was heard demanding, "My son! Where is he? I want to see my son."

When Peter Moriarty rushed abrasively into the surgery the doctor looked up with distaste. It was as if his sense of propriety had been offended. Peter, ignoring his son and the surgeon, jolted to a stop, his eyes sweeping Patrick. When he spoke his voice was iced with contempt. "What are *you* doing here?" Before Patrick could reply the doctor grunted almost angrily, "To be with his dying son, of course."

"That's not his son. He's my . . . " the sentence ended in a horrible squeak. Peter's eyes were riveted on Patrick, registering the likeness so obvious even in death between the boy he had called his son and the labourer standing before him. A labourer whose shoulders sagged now as if under an unbearable weight. His face twitched convulsively as he strove to control a soul-shattering grief.

In that instant everything Peter held dear in life came crashing down around him. It was as if a violent storm had blasted his heart. It raged on inside him, ravaging his mind, fusing his intelligence, allowing a devilish plan to grow and coalesce in his brain. His gaze flickered ruthlessly over the labourer gently massaging Andrew's limp hands now, as if by doing so he could bring life back into them.

Unreasoning fury hardened Peter's voice. "If he's your son, then take him! And you can bury him too." His eyes harsh and unyielding, he strode from the room in a towering rage. *If my wife has the good sense to die along with her bastard brat there'll be no need to expose the shame she's heaped on me, or the harm she's done to my sons.* Moriarty believed that only then could he maintain his respectability, and not become the butt of coarse jokes or the ribald pity frequently aimed at cuckolded husbands.

However, the doctor, his dark eyes granite-hard and his mouth unsmiling, called him back in a hostile voice. "Sir, the woman, your wife I presume, will likely be in a coma for some time. But unless the blow to her head has caused permanent brain damage I find no reason why she shouldn't make a complete recovery."

When the doctor wiped his hands on a white linen towel and turned away, Peter realized with an unpleasant jolt that if he wanted to save face he had to backtrack. And he'd better do it fast. It was too late to erase his angry denial of his son, but by God, he'd lay a smoke screen to camouflage it.

A grim-faced Moriarty stood apart, a solitary figure that had the look of a derelict count whose sagging body had to keep a long-standing appointment with the devil. As he watched his sons Billy and Michael kneel in tearful silence beside an open grave he knew he ought to go to them. Take them in his arms, try to comfort them, and show some of the sorrow he ought to feel for the death of their brother. But he couldn't.

He refused to think of his wife's firstborn as the boy he had been tricked into believing was of his seed. Instead he stood in stony silence while a plain wooden casket was lowered to its final resting place in the cemetery adjoining Grandon's parish church.

If anyone wondered about the lightness of the casket they might have put it down to the slimness of the body it held. Billy and Michael, still stunned by their brother's death, didn't question their father when he told them Andrew was so mutilated it was best they didn't see him in death, but remember the face they had loved in life.

However, there were those in Grandon who secretly questioned why no one had seen the body, why the funeral had taken place so early in the morning, and why Katherine Moriarty was with the nursing nuns at the convent instead of in her own home. "Her not being a Catholic a'tall a'tall."

Still others countered, "The nuns are dedicated women. They'll give the poor creature the best possible care. She's always been a good friend of Mother Superior."

"From what I be hearen she'll not be knowen what sort of nursen she be getting."

"The Butlers' maid told my Minnie the doctor says she just needs more time. Poor soul."

"And 'er husband ba'nt hisself since the accident. 'E's too much of the drink taken. Drown'en 'es sorrow 'e is in the bottle. Not like es self a'tall a'tall."

Sometimes Katherine screamed, momentarily coming bolt upright in bed, her body drenched in icy sweat, her eyes laced with fear. Then she would slip into merciful oblivion again. Other times she struggled briefly into consciousness. But when she did the terrible torment in her eyes caused the nuns to quickly cross themselves, relieved when she lapsed again into the unconsciousness that offered her peace from whatever terrible things were troubling her.

Dr. Butler was puzzled. He said it was as if she had lost the will to live. Her injuries weren't life-threatening. The doctor at the accident believed she had been conscious when her husband had spoken to her. But he hadn't heard what was said. He hadn't considered that any of his business. Nor did he mention what he had learned about Andrew. That was a professional secret he would carry to his grave.

Katherine had been conscious, had heard every damning word Peter had hurled at her that awful day. Too weak to speak, unable to defend herself, she had had no choice but to listen. She heard herself condemned as a conniving, deceitful whore by the man she loved. The man she thought loved her. Instead he had snarled at her. "I hope you have the good grace to die quickly and join your bastard son in hell." She supposed he wanted to be free to marry a virgin who would give him sons to carry on the proud Moriarty line—sons that were not tainted by peasant blood.

Each time Katherine struggled back to reality, shock and disbelief turned to awful certainty. Her son was dead. Her husband wished she was.

His incriminating words echoed and re-echoed in the pit of her soul as though they had been shouted into a tin barrel. They fought for dominance in her mind like lurid bursts of lightning stabbing the blackness of a midnight sky. Sometimes her eyes were glassy with anguish as she clasped her arms around herself, trying to contain forever her memories of happier times. Sometimes terrible shudders tore through her. There was no peace in her world. Even the bedclothes lay heavily, like the weight of a dreadful remorse. She was obsessed with the awful certainty that her destiny, the destiny of those she loved, had been linked to that of a mare who, like herself, had once been mated to a scrub.

Why, oh why hadn't she listened to that foreboding years ago? If she had told Peter then that she too carried the seed of one he would have deemed a scrub, seed that would (he believed) contaminate every child she bore him, none of this would have happened. And Andrew would be alive today.

She never stopped to tell herself *but there would be no Billy and no Michael.* Instead she would slip back into blissful oblivion.

Weeks later when Katherine was having longer spells of lucidity, her husband, at Dr. Butler's insistence, came to see her. The moment he had Katherine alone he turned on her. "Why did you never tell me Andrew was not my son?" His voice was low and deadly, his fingers white-knuckled as they fondled the handle of his cane as if in anticipation of using it on her.

Katherine looked at him as if nothing really mattered any more and said numbly, "Because I was afraid. I didn't want you to think your own sons were inferior because of a terrible mistake I made when I was young and thoughtless. I'd never have done it, Peter, if I'd realized how important it is to men that their brides be virgins. When I found out it seemed best to make you believe I was the virgin you expected me to be. It was really quite simple." She gave a harsh laugh devoid of all traces of humour.

A great bitterness ringed her voice. "How is it gentlemen consider it sport to deflower peasant girls? Do you think your seed brings improvement to all their future offspring? And you are doing them a favour?" She shot Peter a look that chilled the self-righteousness in his soul, but before he could tell her she was wrong to think he had seduced peasant girls, she had called for one of the nuns to show him out. So Katherine never knew she had been his only love. He had never wanted anyone else. But now he had lost her. And he didn't really care. He was too busy trying to hate her.

She had deceived him. Degraded his sons. Denied them their heritage—the right to his uncontaminated seed. The grim look on his face as he left the convent would have driven thoughts of unfaithfulness out of a whore's mind.

Dry, tearing sobs of self-pity wracked his body and threatened to rip it apart until his fingers closed on the bottle of Irish whiskey in his pocket. Peter hadn't been a drinking man, but now his escape from reality was to get very, very drunk.

When Dr. Butler said Katherine was fit to return home, she shut herself in Andrew's bedroom, huddled on his bed, and cried herself into a state of near exhaustion. If Peter had come to her then and they had talked as two rational adults, perhaps their lives would have been different.

Instead she crept down to the kitchen and found a bottle of Bridget's cooking brandy. She needed something to dull the terrible ache in her heart. Stop the relentless churning of her mind. Shut out the problems for which there seemed no solution.

Meanwhile, Sophia, like a scrawny old hen cannibalizing an injured coop-mate, was pecking furiously at Katherine's reputation.

"Albert, you've got to tell Peter what his wife was up to when he was in Dublin. Visiting Henrietta indeed! If the slut wasn't having an affair with Patrick Tully why did she agree to race the chief justice? To save a peasant from a flogging? That's a likely story." There was deep scorn in Sophia's voice. "Or maybe she rather fancied being bedded by his Lordship. They say the man was a demon in bed." Sophia licked her lips with an eroticism that suggested she was anticipating what being a demon in bed might mean.

"How do I know any of this is true?" Albert protested weakly as he worked back the cuticle on his left forefinger. "I've always thought Katherine had eyes for no one but my brother."

Sophia looked at him pityingly, as if wondering why he couldn't develop a mean streak as vicious as her own. "She's probably been bedding Dunraughton too. They were huddled together when the carriage came for Fitzdemon's body. Don't tell me I'm mistaken. I know what I saw. And if you want proof, here's her scarf."

"Where did you find that?" Albert gulped as if trying to swallow his Adam's apple.

Sophia's voice was thick with the malicious spite of one intent on ruining another's reputation. "At the race site. What's more, do you have any idea where she spent the night?"

To her husband's bored look she replied with a viciousness that chilled the blood. "In Lord Dunraughton's bed."

Albert only shrugged and brushed a persistent fly off his nose. Where his sister-in-law chose to spend her nights was no concern of his. In fact, he was chilled by the hatred emanating from his wife and was asking himself why he had married a woman whose mind rarely struggled out of the gutter.

Now she was rushing on, eager to spill all the dirt she knew as quickly as possible. "Young Andrew's death was no accident. It was God's judgement on Katherine for attempting to pass a byblow off as Peter's son. And her pretending to be so virtuous!"

Malice had spread cold tentacles of hate throughout Sophia's mind. There was so much depravity in her heart even the devil would have shuddered at the way her tongue sullied reputations. "I hear she and Peter haven't slept together since the funeral. The entire town is speculating about them. But if your brother hadn't been so blind I could have put him straight about her long ago." Sophia managed a self-righteous sigh before adding, "And now Tully's gone."

In response to Albert's startled look, Sophia nodded. "Yes, Tully's gone. He disappeared right after Andrew was killed. Rumour has it he was last seen carrying a bundle of blankets to a horse doctor in Cove. Claimed he needed to spend time with some friend there before leaving for Upper Canada. But you don't need to worry. Lord Fitzdemon's groom has agreed to work for us. With the chief justice dead the fellow was looking for employment."

Hearing this, Albert's shoulders drooped as if under a great weight. His face looked bleak. "I don't like the man. If he worked for the chief justice he's a blackguard too. He'll abuse the horses. Rape the servants. You should have consulted me before you engaged him."

Sophia looked as if she had swallowed a quart of vinegar, but her voice was smug. "Don't take on so, Albert. You didn't object when I got your father to change his will."

Albert sank back sighing. It had become easier to agree with his wife than it was to oppose her.

Chapter Twenty-Four
. . . *And Strikes Again*

If Peter Moriarty hadn't been so macho, so full of old-fashioned virtue where women were concerned, hadn't been courting insensibility through recourse to whiskey, he would have reasoned that his wife had given him two fine sons so like himself that they could have been peas in a pod. So what lasting harm had her youthful indiscretion done? Instead, his tormented mind was convinced Katherine had betrayed him. She had never really loved him, but had been using him. It was all pretence. Stephen and Henrietta tried to talk sense into him and would have succeeded if Albert hadn't shown up immediately following their visit. He had come to obediently retell the tales Sophia had concocted. And with no one to deny them, Peter, in his drink befuddled state, supposed they were true.

Dr. Butler, hearing what was happening to his friends, growled angrily to his wife. "After all those 'thou shalt not' commandments it's too bad God didn't add an eleventh—'Thou shalt show compassion and forgiveness to those who transgress against you.' For I fear human minds often create mountains out of ant hills."

As for Katherine, she had gone to her late father's home in Dublin. He had died of a heart attack the day after hearing about Andrew's accident. And now she was going through his things, trying to straighten out his affairs, which were in worse shape than she had imagined, due to the loss of one of his ships a few months before. The *Pirate*

Queen had capsized in a violent storm while rounding Cape Horn.

Under different circumstances she would have wanted Peter by her side to comfort and counsel her, but now she was glad he wasn't there. She couldn't bear to think of the terrible despair she had brought on her husband. And in truth she was almost afraid that in his drunken state he might do her bodily harm. She sighed. At least Billy and Michael, grieving for their beloved older brother, were at school in Cork where none of the darkness in their parents' lives would affect them. Yet.

Had she had any inkling of the damage Sophia was doing to her reputation Katherine would have raced back to Grandon and tried to set the records straight. Instead, the business of settling her father's estate was filling her days and her mind. Since her stepmother's death a few years earlier she was the only one left to do it, and this seemed as good a time as any to get it done.

The potato famine was worsening. Some landlords were bankrupting themselves to help their starving tenants. Others were self-righteously demanding their rents. Evictions were common. People with no shelter and no food were dying in the ditches and roadsides. Starvation stalked the land. Anger rumbled and grew like dark and swirling storm clouds. Typhus galloped with ominous tread. Often there were not enough living to bury the dead.

Peter was incurring the ire of his superiors for making too many unsecured loans. His days were full of the appeals of the destitute. His nights were full of loneliness and anger. The number of empty bottles beside his bed grew.

When Katherine felt she had done all she could to straighten her father's affairs she decided to take some of the smaller items that had belonged to Sophia's mother to her, and then continue on to Grandon to try and somehow patch up her failing marriage.

After a long and tiring trip that ended with a jolting cart ride over rocky roads, she realized that the men moving in furtive groups of threes and fours were heading towards Albert's home.

She felt no fear. She had always been a friend of the poor; she was their "angel lady."

She knew that since the famine had worsened and evictions had increased, frustrated peasants were resorting to more and more retaliatory burnings and landlord attacks, if for nothing else than to work off their anger and hatred on the class they saw as responsible for their troubles.

She supposed Albert's home must be their target tonight. Certainly Sophia had no friends among the working class. Nor did her husband. He was a weakling who couldn't say boo to the fleas on his wife's nightgown.

Katherine noticed her driver looking around nervously as if seeking a place to hide. "Begorrah ma'am," he muttered into his teeth, "'tis no place for yer ladyship here tonight Oi's thinking. Looken like a burn'ens planned to me auld eyes. And 'tis not fancying Oi am to be part of it. Best we turn round and skedaddle."

"Nonsense. They're not out to do us harm." Katherine's words rang with more confidence than she felt. "If you're afraid let me off with the things I've brought for the lady of the house, and then you can leave. I'll make my own way to Grandon."

"B'Jasus, ma'am, 'tis a hate'en meself for leaven ye Oi

be, but Oi's a wife and five gosoons to feed. If Oi gets meself kilt entirely, who's to keep them from starvation?"

"You're quite right, driver. Just drop these boxes off and go on your way. I'll be all right." Katherine gave him the glimmer of a smile as she reached in her reticule to pay him.

That done, she stood beside the boxes he had unloaded onto the front steps of what had once been an impressive white house. Now, because of lack of paint and general maintenance, it had the run-down look of a derelict out-house. Obviously Albert's purpose in coming here had not been to improve the property. Katherine's lips set in a grim line. *He's dragging every last farthing from his tenants without giving a cold damn that they're facing starvation. After he's turned the fields into grazing for sheep he'll go back to Dublin bragging he's accomplished something for Ireland.*

Her eyes were almost savage as she turned to where Sophia was standing in the doorway glaring at her. *A female dragon,* Katherine thought bitterly, *who thinks only of herself.*

But Katherine hadn't come here to start a war so she said briskly, "In going through my father's affairs I came across these things of your mother's." She indicated the boxes at her feet. "I thought you should have them."

"Why didn't you leave them in Dublin? I don't want them here." Sophia spat out the words contemptuously. "We're already packed. Most of our boxes are on their way to Dublin. Now we'll have to hire another carrier." Sophia glared at her step-sister.

For a moment Katherine stood speechless. When she spoke it was in a voice iced in frost. "I wasn't aware you were leaving so soon. Does that mean you've raped the land, evicted the tenants? Well, I can't stop that. But there are the boxes. They're yours. What you do with them is no concern of mine. But if those men are as angry as they look you'll not be having to decide. I fancy they'll soon be torching them along with your house."

For the first time Sophia seemed to see the men crowding into her driveway and a look of terrible fear covered her face. She rushed into the house, to reappear a moment later gripping a heavy riding crop in one hand and stuffing a pistol into the pocket of her riding habit with the other. Glaring at Katherine, she raced around the corner of the house and disappeared.

When Peter heard Katherine was on the way to Grandon via Albert's home he felt a sudden rush of elation. Then gloom settled over him again. Was she coming to say she was leaving? And if she was, did he care? In his saner moments he knew he had hurt her dreadfully, but she deserved to be hurt. She had deceived him. Pretended to be a virgin. Made him think Andrew was his son.

Yet there had been times when she had hinted he was not, as if she wanted to tell him something he was too deaf to hear. Sophia too had often implied it. He had put that down to her spiteful nature. He had been too blind to believe anything but his own heart. And in his heart he had loved Katherine. Perhaps he always would. Now his mind was a torment of whirling doubts, making it hard to sort out the difference between love and hate.

He had loved Andrew. Been proud of him as only a real father has the right to be. The boy had been everything a father could desire, as were his other sons. So why was he upset? Was he wrong in believing a woman's body could be permanently tainted from having once harboured an influx of inferior seed?

His mind churned in black anger as he thought of a peasant stealing his wife's virginity, his seed contaminating her body. Yet, if he was to be completely honest, had it done him, Peter Moriarty, any lasting harm? Maybe, though he couldn't understand how, and would have hated to admit it if he had, Patrick's seed had actually improved on his own. Perhaps it was only his macho image that had been damaged. He sighed and took a long swig from the bottle constantly within reach now.

The rumour of a peasant uprising targeting his brother's home jolted Peter out of a half-drunken daze as effectively as if a boulder had landed between his eyes.

Good God! He knew that Katherine planned to stop at Albert and Sophia's on her way back to Grandon, so she might be involved. He snatched the pistol from his desk and jammed it into his pocket without bothering to check it. If he hadn't been so befuddled by drink he would have remembered the teller had taken it out the evening before for target practice and neglected to refill its empty chamber.

After another quick pull on the ever-present bottle he mounted a hired horse and spurred away like a Quixote seeking windmills. He was in too drunken a state to consider he ought to have alerted the police. But it didn't matter. Someone had already done it.

As Peter neared his brother's property, his drink-fogged brain told him he must avoid the crush of men armed with rusty blunderbusses, pikes, and pitchforks that crowded the road. He had to somehow get ahead of them, reach the house before they did, if he was to save his wife.

Pulling the horse off the trail he tied it to a tree, climbed over a free-stone fence crumbling into disarray, and cautiously worked his way through the holly bushes and beech trees hiding the buildings from his sight. It couldn't be much further now.

A terrified scream, the sound of a struggle, the sickening thud of a hard fist striking soft flesh, a coarse voice snarling, "Give 'er another one, mate. Give 'er another one. But don't kill the slut before I've had me poke at 'er," jolted Peter into a run. His pistol, drawn and cocked now, was held in front of him like a shield.

Half crouching to avoid low-hanging branches he failed to see the protruding root until his foot caught on it. He fell headlong, striking his head against a tree. In flinging up his arm in an instinctive but futile attempt to regain his balance, the gun flew through the bushes and got caught on a branch.

There was the sound of a sudden explosion followed almost immediately by another shot. And moments later the thud of a galloping horse faded into the distance. But Peter neither heard nor saw any of this, as he lay unmoving under a tree, his eyes glazed, his neck twisted.

Meanwhile Katherine, seeing flaming torches moving forward with steady and obvious intent, shivered for the outcome of this night. She must stop them. But how? While her mind was quickly thinking of plans and then as quickly discarding them as unworkable, Sophia, crouching low in the saddle, came racing past on Grey Lady. She was whipping the animal in a frenzied attempt to make her trample those leading the mob.

Suddenly, from the direction of the stable Katherine heard a shot ring out, followed quickly by another. As if those shots had been the signal for all hell to break loose, answering spurts of flame from rebel guns now began stabbing the semi-darkness.

At first only the occasional tinkling of breaking glass was heard as warning shots were sent into the air. But when Sophia fired recklessly into the crowd a retaliatory shot struck Grey Lady. The mare reared and fell, screaming in agony as a stray ball lodged near her heart. Her rider's leg was firmly pinned beneath her. For once in her life Sophia was speechless. Unable to move, too frightened to give vent to the imprecations incubating inside her, she cowered in abject terror.

The moment the mare fell Katherine felt a surge of reserve energy flood through her. Now she knew what she must do. She sprang to stand beside the fallen grey, and with hands upraised like a Moses holding back the sea, she called, "Men, I beg you come no further. Disperse. Go to your homes. Quickly. Don't bring reprisals on innocent families already suffering more than they can bear."

At first this was met by surly snarls. "She's one of them. We best be kill'en her too." But these were soon drowned out by other voices. "Yer roight, ma'am. Begorrah, 'tis off to me home Oi's going," or "B'Jasus, yer'll not be hurting yon lady. Oi'll no be allowing it. That's her as brung food to me family when Oi wasn't fit for nuthin after me floggin." There was a look of iron-jawed determination on another man's face as he took his stance beside Katherine. "Go home, lads. Irishmen don't make war on women." But he scowled darkly when his eyes fell on Sophia's face, as if perhaps there were times when making an exception to that rule might be desirable.

At his words the urge for revenge no longer seemed so important. The men began to silently disappear. Singly and in pairs they vanished like dark wraiths into the growing gloom. Moments later, when a dozen cavalrymen galloped into the courtyard, the place appeared deserted except for Katherine trying to release Sophia's trapped foot to the accompaniment of that woman's screams and curses.

The English officer in charge looked the type who might eat small children for Sunday breakfast, but he quickly ordered his men to lift the dead mare off Sophia's foot. Then he turned to Katherine with cool composure. "Now, ma'am, tell us who did this and we'll make him sorry his mother ever birthed him."

A feeling of revulsion overwhelmed her. "It was an accident. My step-sister was intending to gallop through a crowd when a gun went off by mistake and killed the mare."

"It was no mistake!" Sophia screamed. "It was a peasant uprising. That bullet was meant for me. If my husband had been here they'd have killed him too. They hate us. Same as they hate Lupe Blackadder, our agent who deals with them." At the words "Lupe Blackadder" her mouth dropped into a look of surprise. "Where is he? He was at the stable when I left." Then her face turned into a mask of black fury. "The coward. He must have run off and left me to face the rabble on my own. I'd be dead now if you soldiers hadn't come."

Deep-rooted hatred made it impossible for Sophia to acknowledge that it was Katherine, not the soldiers, who had saved her life.

A moment later the sound of a horse whinnying from the general area of the stable drifted in on the evening air. Two soldiers trotted off to investigate. Katherine, as if pulled by a force stronger than her own will, followed.

At the sight of her dazed, dishevelled husband, Katherine's heart leaped with a mixture of apprehension and a longing to be once again safe within the shelter of his love. But he shouldn't be here. And why was he staring at that large thing on the ground with the vacant expression of a man just awakened from a nightmare?

The premonition gripping her mind in vice-like jaws turned to sickening horror when the glow from the soldier's torch flicked its snake-tongues of light and darkness over the macabre face of Lupe Blackadder. The face of Albert's agent was more evil in the slackness of death than when its scowl put fear and hatred into the hearts of the peasants he bullied and threatened.

The soldier, long accustomed to the sight of death, looked impersonally at the body in the circle of light, noting only briefly the horrible death mask stamped with the look of savage, licentious cruelty that had been his trademark in life. His tongue hung sideways out of his mouth, his eyes protruded as if preparing to dart off into space, his neck twisted at an inhuman angle. His fly was open.

Katherine had risked one quick look, then with an gasp she had turned to look away when she heard, "B'Jasus! Here's another."

The soldier's torch was throwing its distorting light on a second body, a body with blood and brains still oozing from a gaping hole in its head. Contemptuously the man poked at the corpse with his foot, exposing an unbuttoned fly, a shrivelled penis. "That fellow used to be Fitzdemon's groom. Evidently his Lordship taught him whoring well, for he died ready enough to get on with it. Now where's the woman?"

He looked briefly towards Katherine and quickly dismissed that thought. She wasn't the type. And yet . . . ?

A strangled cry rose in Peter's throat when he saw his wife. She would have run to him but his tight nod was warning *stay back.* What was the real message? The momentary tenderness in his eyes that had seemed to be reaching for her soul was replaced almost instantly by a look as cold and impersonal as granite. The mouth compressed into a grim line, stern and non-committal, seemed to be holding her at arm's length.

"Well, sir. Looks as if you caught them in the act." The soldier's face was twisted into a lewd grin. "Come along, Mr. Moriarty. You can tell the judge about it and if you're lucky he may not sentence you to hang."

Anger coupled with a terrible fear sliced through Katherine, gouging her vitals like a twisting knife blade. "Take your hands off my husband," she stormed. "He didn't kill those men. Why should he? Anyway, he never carries a gun." she added limply.

"Doesn't carry a gun, you say. Now that's an interesting statement, m'lady, seeing as how I just found this pistol dangling from a tree. Where he threw it no doubt after the deed was done, hoping it wouldn't be found. For a murderer though, I must say, sir, you did a mighty poor job of hiding the weapon. You shouldn't have left it hanging there plain as plain for anyone to see. Pointing away from the bodies too, so no use saying it just happened to land there and went off of its own accord and killed two men. It is your gun, isn't it?" The soldier's voice was cold now, and terribly impersonal.

Peter mechanically reached out one hand and took the single barrel pistol, looked at it briefly, and then nodded. "Yes, I was carrying it. It was in my hand when I was running towards the sound of voices. When I tripped I must have struck my head on yonder tree and blacked out. For I remember nothing until I saw torches." He was gingerly feeling a growing lump on his head as he spoke.

"If as you say, Officer, you found the gun hanging in those holly bushes, then it must have flown out of my hand when I tripped. But as it was facing in the opposite direction how could it have killed even one man, let alone two? It's a single shot." There was a relieved expression on his face as he finished speaking.

"Well, if you didn't come here planning to kill someone, why did you come? And why did you have a gun? Your wife just said you never carry a weapon." The captain who had just ridden up to rejoin the others spoke in an icy voice.

"To protect my wife. I knew she planned to stop here on her way back to Grandon. Naturally when I heard rumours a rabble intended to attack my brother's place tonight I came to make sure she didn't get hurt."

Looking into his eyes, hearing his simple statement, Katherine suddenly wanted to explode with joy. Her husband still loved her. As soon as these boorish men realized they were making a terrible mistake, he would take her into his arms. Then everything in this world would be right again.

"Handcuff him. Take him away. Let him tell his story to the judge. He might believe him. I don't."

Katherine rushed to Peter and clung to his hand with such a look of grief and love and despair in her eyes that Peter gave her an encouraging smile. "Don't fret, Mavourneen. The judge will realize it was all a mistake. Go back to Grandon and wait for me there. I'll be with you soon." Then he was led away.

But when he looked back, it was as if his wife was melting in front of his eyes.

Chapter Twenty-Five
Stephen's Secret

"Whurrah, Whurrah. 'Tis a sad day for Oirland when the loikes of Peter Moriarty gets sentenced to ten years hard labour on t'other side of the world for a crime Oi suspects even the judge doesn't believe he committed. Sure'n 'tis beyond me understanden how two can die from one bullet." The speaker pushed up a cloth cap stained by years of sweat and toil, and unconsciously ran his hand through a thatch of dark hair, as if trying to fathom the workings of British justice.

"Oi's 'erd as how not many convicts gets sent to Australia now. But those who do might be better having a quick death on the Irish gallows. Thems as don't die in the stinking hold of a prison ship face death on a chain gang. If overwork don't do them in there's the floggings. Few men survive a thousand lashes. And there's some as kills themselves. Oi tells ye 'tis a turrible system when humans be driven into taking their own lives to escape suffering more than mortal flesh can bear. And 'tis all done to frighten the rest of us into living honest." This speaker, a tradesman in a coarse grey homespun suit, had a despondent air of greyness about him, as if life had become one long fight with grim reality.

A well-dressed gentleman with ego enough to flood a dry riverbed idly fingered a gold watch chain that seemed to be trying to hold in his protruding belly, then announced in a voice that brooked no argument, "The judge must have known what he was doing. He has a certain height of education."

An older man rubbed his gnarled fingers as if to straighten them, then spoke dryly. "That judge may have a certain height of education, but he's got a *terrible* depth of ignorance."

Another vigorously scratched the reddish-brown hair sprouting on his chest, rumpling it into giving off a rustling sound—a sort of subtle murmur suggesting there might still be room for hope. "Life in a felon colony doesn't always mean the end. Oi claims as long as there's breath there's hope. Peter Moriarty isn't one to give up aisy-like. Meybe he'll escape. Although faith be to God, Oi hears that's hard done in a vast, rugged country plagued by blistering winds that shriek across the land, clawing away hope, sucking up moisture, destroying life. A place stark and savage and desolate, overrun by poisonous snakes, giant lizards, deadly spiders, and natives who kill a white man on principle. Oi's herd there's them that prefers felon's fetters and the bite of the gaoler's whip to paying sech a price for freedom." Then the man's face brightened and his words took on a more cheerful tone. "Meybe with Mr. Moriarty's eddecation he'll get an aisy office job and soon get handed a big land tract in the outback where a man can live like an English lord and get wealthy raising sheep. With convicts to do the work. Oi hears how there's them that does it."

Having said this he pulled an old dudeen from a deep pocket and stuffed tobacco into its bowl with great care before striking a light on the seat of his pants. Only when the pipe was drawing to his complete satisfaction did he glance around at the little knot of men surrounding him, but the common pattern of misery on their faces said none of them shared his optimism.

No one paid much attention to a man, big of frame but sparse on flesh, who stood on the outskirts shifting uneasily from foot to foot as if some hidden weight had become too heavy to bear. He kept his hands jammed firmly into his baggy pockets, as if allowing them out might permit them to betray the terrible secret that burned into his mind like a red, hot brand.

Jud Malone had been a decent, hard-working labourer back when he could get enough work to properly care for his family. Now the system had ground him down until survival—for himself, and for his family—had become the dominating obsession of his life. And b'Jasus, although he had let his twelve-year-old daughter go into service at the big house so the pittance she earned could be hoarded to help buy passage to America, he was fiercely protective of her. She was his only daughter. He'd kill anyone who violated her body.

Suddenly his teeth ground together in a mixture of anger and remorse. His mind flew back to the night Grandon's respected bank manager had been accused of a double murder.

Some deep-rooted instinct had made Jud Malone leave the crowd intent on torching the home of Albert Moriarty, and walk towards the Moriarty stables. That was when he stumbled on a scene that fired his brain with madness.

A man Jud recognized as the estate supervisor had his fly open, exposing a gorged and swollen organ. He was astraddle his daughter, trying to jam it between her clamped legs. One huge hairy hand was over her mouth to stifle any screams, but he could have dispensed with that precaution for it seemed the child had mercifully blacked out. The other hand was roughly pummelling the girl's softly rounded breasts in a mindless orgy of sexual debauchery. A second man, Lord Fitzdemon's erstwhile groom, watched with gloating anticipation as he lovingly fingered his own penis, a weapon already cocked and throbbing to explode.

In a blind rage Jud had levelled his gun and pulled the trigger. Twice. And ended the lives of two filthy jackals. Jackals who deserved worse than the quick death they got. He should have cut off their balls and sliced open their hearts before sending them to oblivion. But there hadn't been time.

His daughter was in a dead faint. He had to get her to safety. Picking her up he crept stealthily off into the blackness until he stumbled on the dead supervisor's grazing horse. Hoisting the girl up, he rode quickly down a little-used path, then he loosed the animal, slapped it on the rump, and sent it galloping away. No one had seen him leave. No one knew what he had done. In a few weeks he and his family would be on a boat for America and safety.

Now hearing Peter Moriarty was accused of murder, the innate honesty that was part of Jud Malone's make-up set his nerve ends screaming.

Fiercely he told himself he must smother any thought of disclosing what had really happened. Peter Moriarty was a man of some importance. He must have friends in high places. Let them intervene. He, Jud Malone, was a peasant with few friends. And certainly none in high places. If his part in the murders became known he would be flogged insensible, then revived for his own hanging. He shuddered. With grim lips and troubled eyes he drifted away. For him the matter was closed.

Katherine's ashen face was locked in frozen disbelief. Her indrawn hiss of breath sounded harsh as grim reality, the stalking spectre of black despair, covered her mind in hopelessness. "It isn't true," she moaned. "It can't be." Yet the lines of sorrow etched around Stephen's haggard mouth and the dreadful pain in his eyes told her it was. Her husband hadn't been acquitted as everyone expected him to be. He had been sentenced to ten years (few prisoners got less) in a penal colony half a world away.

Katherine was caught up in a rushing avalanche of anger. "I know he didn't do it. Someone else shot those men. There were two distinct shots. And what about the horse I heard galloping into the distance? Why wouldn't the judge listen to me?" She pounded a fist into her open palm as if determined to drive home the truth.

"No judge will believe a woman's testimony, especially not when the accused is her husband. What he hears is that a man with an empty gun he admits to have been carrying is found at the scene of the crime. Peter says he has no recollection of anything that happened. Yet there are two men dead, and no clues found to indicate anyone else had been there. So to uphold his reputation as a hanging judge the magistrate had to sentence someone. He can't afford to lose face with his superiors."

Stephen was unconsciously cracking the joints of his fingers as if that might somehow lessen his anger. "Your husband has become the victim of the farce we call justice. But the judge must have had some doubts. Otherwise he'd have ordered Peter hanged." Stephen's voice was musing as if he was grabbing at crumbs and hoping to make a meal out of them.

Then he straightened. "Keep your hopes up, Katherine. Peter is a survivor. My hunch is that within a few years this will all seem a horrible nightmare." The words trailed thoughtfully into the distance before he spoke again. "You can take some comfort from knowing I've pulled strings. It's the *Queen O'Malley* Peter will be sailing in. Not one of those awful stink holes that pass as prison ships. And the doctor on board is a good friend of mine."

Having said that he gave her arm an encouraging pat, picked up his hat, and left like a man with a daring piece of strategy to attend to.

Katherine made a heroic effort to get control of herself. Her boys had lost a father. She mustn't fall apart before their eyes. Blowing her nose violently she supposed it was a crumb of comfort to know Stephen would be transporting her husband to the penal colony. There were captains who cared nothing about the human cargo dying daily of typhus or cholera in the overcrowded holds of their filthy ships, or of the bodies carelessly dumped overboard in the blackness of a starless night. Perhaps the dead man's name might be recorded. If so, word of his death might eventually reach relatives back home. Or it might not.

Peter almost wished he had been sentenced to hang. Wasn't a quick death to be preferred to a lifetime of living hell? Like all Irishmen he despised cowards. But surely it wasn't unmanly to fear floggings by sadistic gaolers who gloated at the sound of tortured screams, the sight of mangled flesh and mutilated bodies? Floggings that destroyed manhood and turned brave men into gibbering idiots.

As he and other prisoners were herded on board, Peter was in such deep despair at seeing the land of his birth for the last time and leaving his loved ones forever that he scarcely heard Stephen's hastily whispered, "Take heart. I have a plan."

The *Queen O'Malley* had been at sea for over a month, but Peter had seen nothing of the ship's captain. He sensed Stephen had been fighting night and day to keep his ship afloat and on course, for the cabin boy who brought the convicts' food said that the storm had been one of the worst in living memory.

Peter knew little about ships. Only that in a violent gale a seaman would have to be constantly switching a sailing ship's auxiliary motor off and on. Off to stop the wild racing of a propeller pitched high out of the water one moment, on again when it was plunged back into the wallowing depths of a trough. The masts and sails, he supposed, would need continual repair. Indeed, Peter would not have been surprised had the vessel broken up in so violent a storm.

The convicts clung to their bunks, the only anchor left to them in their uprooted lives, most too sick to care if they lived or died.

Peter, rather to his own surprise, proved to be a good sailor. The pitching and diving of the ship as it battled through the storm made him think bitterly of his own life. He had been plummeted from the crest of having everything a man could wish for, to the depths of despair. And his ship was still plunging. Would its shivering timbers split apart as it wallowed through the depth of this trough? Or would they withstand the pounding of life's waves and rise above adversity? If the farce of his trial was any indication, his luck had run out.

Despite his gloom Peter was determined to stay fit and healthy. He had never shied away from hard work, and by

God if it was work the gaolers wanted he'd show them how an Irishman could work. He almost looked forward to being bone tired. It might help him forget.

So he was startled the day the ship's doctor came to him and said in a carrying voice. "You've got a pallor I don't like. Best I get you to the isolation ward. Can't be having an outbreak of typhus, now can we?"

Peter was about to protest that he'd rarely felt better when the doctor dropped him a sly wink. Outside the hold the doctor wagged a finger at him, warning him to silence. "The Captain wants to see ye."

In the confines of the captain's cabin Stephen embraced his old friend, then stood him off at arm's length, saying, "Begorrah, you're looking a sight for me tired eyes. I was worrying about you cooped up down there with all those around you seasick. It was a rough go we've just had.

"Now listen lad. Tonight you die."

In response to Peter's startled look, a sly grin appeared on Stephen's face. "But only on the doctor's books. The tarpaulin-wrapped corpse heaved overboard tonight won't be yours, but a dummy made of empty grain sacks. As for you, you'll spend the rest of this voyage in my cabin, where no one enters without my permission. When we dock in Australia I'll spread the word you died at sea from typhus and I'll make sure the same story gets back to Ireland.

"I'm sorry about that, lad. But I didn't dare risk telling even Henrietta that I had a plan to save you. And you mustn't write, above all not to Katherine. Someone might get suspicious and start investigating.

"Now listen closely to what I'm about to say. As soon as the *Queen O'Malley* can be restocked and made ready for sea again she'll be taking gold seekers from the Australian gold fields to California. There's always some who want to move on in search of greener fields or bigger nuggets.

"You'll make them think you're heading for the gold fields too, and that your name is Peter Hillary. When I get back home again, which with luck could be in a little over a year, Katherine will know you're alive. Not as a felon, but panning gold as a free man in California. In time it should be safe for you to write to her care of my shipping office. By then the authorities will have forgotten you ever existed. And you can pick up Katherine's letters at this address, which I will give her on my return. It's near the docks in a place called Los Angeles."

Peter gripped his friend's hand and wrung it hard. What Stephen was suggesting seemed too good to be true. It was the promise of freedom, a right he hadn't properly valued until it was taken from him. A chance to resume a normal life. Perhaps even with the woman he loved, for the day Katherine had come to say goodbye he realized he loved her as fiercely as ever. And now he hoped he'd be able to prove it to her.

It never occurred to him that Katherine might not want to leave Ireland to pioneer a remote land of hardship and tribulation. He refused to listen to the small voice warning it might not turn out exactly as Stephen expected.

A well-stocked bookshelf helped shorten the tedious days of enforced confinement in the captain's cabin, and in the evenings he and Stephen picked up the thread of their old friendship.

When the *Queen O'Malley* pulled up anchor and sailed for Los Angeles, the name of Peter Hillary was among those on the passenger list. And for that gentleman the voyage was a pleasant enough experience. The days passed quickly listening and talking to fellow passengers heading for the gold fields. Peter was anxious to know all there was to know about prospecting, and about the country soon to become his home. At night, standing at the rail watching a sky pinpricked by stars that looked like winking nuggets, he wondered what his chances were of finding the motherlode in some remote California gulch, or even finding a stream that offered pay dirt.

When not listening and learning, Peter spent much of his time sitting on a big coil of rope, puffing on his pipe and thoughtfully watching the white-caps churning in the wake of the ship fade and eventually disappear. Without his realizing it, the waves were relentlessly carrying Peter Moriarty into oblivion.

In Los Angeles Peter Hillary delayed his departure for the gold fields until the *Queen O'Malley* could be refitted and Stephen had left for home. His days were busy arranging for the necessary prospecting equipment and grubstake. His evenings were spent with Stephen. But as days lengthened into weeks and still the *Queen O'Malley* wasn't ready to sail, Stephen's patience was stretched thin as fine paper. He grew gloomy and worried, as if he had been given a private blueprint for disaster.

Refitting the ship was taking too long. The delayed departure would expose the ship to severe winter storms.

When the *Queen O'Malley* was finally ready to pull up anchor, the two men embraced as good friends who never expect to see each other again. Peter brushed sudden moisture from his eyes but Stephen managed an encouraging smile. "Don't worry, lad. The minute I step onto Auld

Ireland's sod I'll let Katherine know you're a free man, alive and well. Begorrah, you'll maybe have struck it rich by the time she gets the message. But remember. No trying to contact her until she writes to you. It will be safer that way."

Another hard handclasp. Another final farewell wave. Peter Hillary watched through misted eyes as the *Queen O'Malley* sailed from his life, taking with her his only link with those who had known Peter Moriarty. He stood bowed and desolate, a man completely alone in an alien and hostile land. When the ship carrying away his past slowly slipped below the horizon a mantle of gloom enveloped him. It was as if he was seeing his own death. Then he squared his shoulders, took a deep breath, and turned to go. There was a lifetime of living to be faced, and Peter Hillary had best get on with it.

Chapter Twenty-Six
A Letter Edged in Black

The days and years ahead loomed like an endless grey blur on Katherine's horizon. Henrietta had asked her to share her home, and for her friend's sake she tried not to mope. But it wasn't easy. Then one morning she had what appeared to be a splendid idea. "Why didn't I think of it sooner? I'll write to Lord Millhaven. He ought to have enough influence with somebody to get Peter pardoned."

That thought lifted her spirits considerably. She picked up a quill, then chewed on it reflectively before dipping the tip in the ink pot and starting to write. Finally, having finished the letter to her complete satisfaction, she sanded it and inserted it into an envelope she addressed with a considerable flourish. An odd little smile hovered briefly around her mouth as she inserted a small golden key into the centre drawer of Henrietta's ornately carved escritoire. A moment later she brought out a silver teaspoon, her fingers stroking its delicately etched crest as if needing to make certain its engravings were sharp enough to be used as a seal.

"What do you think, Henrietta? Could I use this spoon's crest as my seal? It would mean more to Lord Millhaven than the imprint of my wedding ring. The ring means nothing to him. Whereas this . . . ." Her voice drifted into silence.

Henrietta ran her finger experimentally over the spoon. "Is that the spoon his Lordship gave your mother before he left Ireland? It must be. There can't be another like it. Those couchant hunting dogs below a bounding stag make it so distinctive. The holly leaves too."

Katherine nodded absently. "Millhaven told my mother the spoon was to remind her that if she ever needed help he'd come to her. No matter what. Do you suppose that might include me too?"

A moment later Katherine was holding a lighted taper to a bar of red sealing wax. As soon as a blob of hot wax fell onto the envelope's flap she blew out the taper, pressed the spoon's crest firmly into the softened wax, then held up the envelope for her friend to inspect. "There! That's done. If I send it immediately I should hear back within a week, maybe sooner. With that seal on the envelope Lord Millhaven can't help but notice it." She absently dropped the spoon into a little-used inner pocket of her cloak, picked up the letter, and turned to leave the room.

Henrietta was tempted to point out that Lord Millhaven might be out of the country. He travelled a lot. Or he could be sick. He was an old man. He might even be dead. If he was she didn't suppose there was any reason for Katherine to be notified. But it was so pleasant to have Katherine on such a high that she bit her tongue and said nothing.

As the days stretched to a week Katherine began to haunt the garden gate watching for the postman, but when the weeks stretched into months and still no letter from Lord Millhaven, it was Katherine's face that looked haunted. She tried to make excuses. "He's been away. He'll write the minute he gets home and finds my letter waiting. Or he's arranging for Peter's pardon before he writes. Such things take time."

She never once stopped to think that perhaps Lord Millhaven didn't get her letter. For such was indeed the case. It had arrived while he was in Scotland. And it, together with other mail, had been left on a hall table for his attention when he returned. But when that happened her letter wasn't there. It had been knocked from the table by the careless dusting of a new maid and had fallen unnoticed behind the panelling.

Despondency settled over Katherine like a shroud. Henrietta, in near desperation at how to draw her friend out of her apathy, brought home books on sheep. "Katherine, it's time you started studying these. You ought to learn about the wee beasties. There might come a day when Peter gets awarded a big chunk of land for good behaviour. When that happens he'll stock it with sheep. So you best learn something now about the breeds best suited to the country. No more moping. You're not the only wife who has to live without her husband, nor will you be the last."

Henrietta spoke with a brisk cheerfulness she was far from feeling. Her lips were set in a grim line. Somehow she was missing Stephen more than ever on this trip. She supposed it must be because she knew he would be away longer. Two years or more. California was a long way from his regular sailing route.

Yet for reasons she didn't understand he had seemed eager to go there, even when she had protested. She was beginning to wish her husband had a shore job where he could come home every night. Perhaps she'd suggest it to him. There must be lots of office jobs he could get in the shipping office. Yes, she'd do it. And having made that decision she started humming softly to herself as she filled the kettle and put it on the hob for tea.

Some months later, when two envelopes bearing Australian stamps arrived at Henrietta's house, Katherine grabbed the one addressed to her and tore it open with eagerness in her heart. It must be a letter from Peter. But it wasn't Peter's writing, and that bothered her. As her eyes flew down the page her face hardened in disbelief. Then, as the full meaning of the words hit her, she gave an almost inaudible moan. A moan that strangled in her throat. "He's dead," she muttered stupidly, as if in a trance. "He's dead. He died of typhus, at sea. So why does Stephen write, 'When I get back and tell you the details you'll understand why his dying wasn't as bad as it seems to you as you read this'?" Numbly she supposed Stephen must be trying, in some oblique way, to tell her Peter was better off dead than suffering the horrors of ten years in a penal colony. Reluctantly she told herself she mustn't wish her husband back to a life like that.

Her hatred of English judges who handed down verdicts with little attention to evidence would go with her to her grave, but for the sake of her boys she must try to live a normal life. She must be strong for them, for they had loved Peter dearly and with the optimism of youth expected to be re-united with their father after he had served his sentence and they had finished school. Now all their lives would be changed.

Chapter Twenty-Seven
More Than A Ship Is Lost

"Top of the marnin to ye, ma'am. Begorrah if it isn't yer roses that's a sight for me auld eyes this foine day." The elderly man doffed his cap to Katherine, returned the pipe to the mouth that looked empty without it, and smiled as he moved on down the street.

Katherine watched him for a moment before going back to thinning carrots. She had left this row until they were big enough to go into the thick soups that were Henrietta's specialty.

Somewhat to her own surprise Katherine had discovered she had an affinity for growing things. Gardening was filling more and more of her time. With the beautiful, spirited Ebony gone to stud at the Tim Watson estate, she no longer rode much, so time often hung heavy.

The click of the gate latch brought her head up for a moment. But it was only the postman, and she wasn't expecting any letters. She rarely got letters now, except from her sons. And she'd heard from them yesterday. *I'll finish thinning the carrots before I go in,* she told herself. *Then this job will be done and I'll help Henrietta clean them.* She brushed impatiently at an insect tickling her face, with no inkling the postman had brought letters that would change her life.

With the carrots on the scullery bench, Katherine pulled off her soil-stained gloves and called to Henrietta. When there was no reply she moved towards the small parlour, conscious of a vague stirring of unease. A moment later alarm raced from the top of her head to the soles of her feet, leaving her nerves tight, her mind trapped in fear.

Henrietta, her face a death mask, was staring at a letter in her hand with unseeing eyes.

With a small, inarticulate cry of compassion, Katherine sprang to her friend and flung her arms around the rigid body, pressing it close to her own. Henrietta cried as if that was the catalyst needed for a deluge of tears. The floodgates broke on a lifetime of loneliness that now stretched to eternity.

Somehow, between Henrietta's anguished sobs, Katherine pieced together that the *Queen O'Malley* had gone down, taking with her all hands.

There had been a hurricane off the Florida coast. No ship exposed to the brunt of its fury had survived. Numbly Katherine supposed there were other widows weeping today. But at this moment that was no comfort to her friend or to her.

She realized with a jolt she was now penniless. Then she felt overwhelmed with guilt that she could think of something as pecuniary as money when a friend's life had just been devastated. Katherine had been counting more than she liked to admit on the money Stephen would have brought her. Money she had insisted Peter take and which he hadn't lived to need. Money she had hoped would buy his freedom, or at least preferred treatment.

On top of that the income from her father's share in the *Queen O'Malley* was gone now too. It was an inheritance that would never have made her rich, but with careful management she had hoped it would educate her sons. Now she was destitute except for the small yearly allowance from her mother's estate, but that wouldn't keep the boys in shoes.

Struggling with the fog swirling in her brain she tried to determine how to go about getting enough money to keep her boys in grammar school. And then college. Peter had paid for a full year's schooling before he was arrested. But that year was long up.

Since then she had used what was left from the sale of Ebony's fillies . . . the sale before her life had been plunged into an abyss that was steadily growing deeper and darker. An abyss from which there now seemed little hope of escape.

There wouldn't be any horses to sell for a year, maybe two. The English and European buyers wanted only mature animals because they considered it important for young stock to grow and develop in a country that had the climate and the soil to produce the best horses in the world.

But at the moment, when Katherine needed money so desperately, she would have settled for something less than the best.

When Henrietta finally came to grips with reality, she announced, "I'll leave Ireland. There's nothing for me here any more. I'll go to England. I have a maiden aunt at Reigate who needs a live-in companion. She has a big house, Brackenfell. It has fine brick stables with rooms for grooms above, and spacious grounds and gardens. It's a beautiful place. The children can have dogs and ponies. And it's only twenty miles from London. Faith, now I've made the decision I can hardly wait to pack up and go. But 'tis missing you, my dearest friend, I'll be doing." She reached to embrace Katherine before adding in a hopeful voice, "Why don't you come with me?"

But Katherine shook her head sadly. "No. Ireland is my home, my heritage. I'll not be leaving. Faith, I couldn't if I wanted to—I've scarcely the money for a trip to Dublin. And I must go there to beg my father-in-law for help so the boys can finish their schooling."

Her mind crawled at the thought of such an abject act. But if she had to grovel then, by the Lord Harry, she'd grovel. Billy and Michael must have an education. That had become the driving goal of her life. Almost an obsession. She and Peter had dreamed of a college education for their sons. Now it was up to her to see they got it.

If it hadn't been for Sophia's treachery, flattering the old man at every opportunity, stroking his ego while maliciously maligning Peter and his wife, Peter, as the older son, would have inherited the bulk of his father's wealth. That was an unwritten Irish law to stop the dividing of property among so many sons that none had enough to live on.

Peter was dead, but shouldn't his sons benefit from some part of what might have been his? Surely the old man wouldn't deny his own grandsons the right of an education.

Nevertheless, for her visit to Donal Moriarty Katherine dressed with great care, in a simple gown that hid her from neck to ankle and only subtly hinted there might be a woman's body inside, for she was in truth a little afraid of her crotchety old father-in-law.

He was the sort of man it was easy to imagine carried a grudge against life. He had a bullet head, bare as a cannonball except for a lingering fringe of white, which he coaxed to grow long so the hairs could be combed across the shiny dome of his scalp. The lines scored across his prominent forehead had a look of brooding discontent. His eyebrows, once fiercely black but now salt and pepper, grew in wild profusion and stuck out like the hairy legs of a tarantula. His hooded eyes never ceased darting about as if hoping to locate a hidden investment opportunity. Or perhaps they hoped to ferret out some secret, unpious activity among the ungodly. Wearily she supposed she would be classified ungodly in her father-in-law's eyes. He had never acted as if he completely approved of her, although he had treated her kindly enough until Sophia had gone to work on him.

The Moriarty butler, dignified and aloof as always, gave her a compassionate smile as if somehow sorry for what he was doing, and ushered her into the old man's presence. Katherine moved across the room quickly to plant a dutiful daughter-in-law kiss lightly on his grizzled cheek. Then she came right to the point.

"Mr. Moriarty, sir, I've come to appeal to you for help. I need money to educate Peter's sons. The sinking of the *Queen O'Malley* wiped out whatever small inheritance I might have enjoyed from my father's estate. I'm penniless now, apart from a very small inheritance from my mother and whatever the foals from my black mare bring when they are sold. But there will be no money coming in from them for another year, maybe longer. And when it does come there will be expenses to pay to the man who provides for them."

The old man gave a disgruntled snort. "Young woman, you're a slut." The words came out cold and hard and iced with contempt. "You not only tricked my son into marrying a fallen woman, you tricked him into believing your bastard son was his own. 'Tis not one penny of my money you'll be seeing. I'll see you starving in the gutter first. For ought I know the other boys are bastards too. There'd be many a chance for it with you riding the way you did. I told Peter it wasn't seemly, that he was a fool to allow it."

"My husband trusted me," Katherine said coldly as her eyes, hard now as tempered steel, locked with his.

"More fool that he was," muttered Moriarty, the first to drop his eyes. Having done so it seemed important to him that he spit contemptuously out of the side of his mouth without appearing to care if it landed in the spittoon or on Katherine's shoes. The elaborate silver spittoon must have cost more money than it took to keep a boy in school for a year.

Inwardly Katherine was a seething volcano, threatening momentarily to erupt, but she struggled to keep her voice cool and reasonable.

"Sir, I admit it was a terrible mistake to marry Peter and make him believe Andrew was his son. It's something I'll regret as long as I live, but God knows apart from that I've been a good wife to Peter and gave him two of the finest sons a man could hope for. I'm not asking you for a red farthing for myself, but I am asking you, for your son's sake, to provide schooling for his boys, your grandsons, so they can develop into the sort of men you would be proud to have bear your name. For whether you like it or not it's your blood that runs in their veins and it's your name they will bring honour too. Or the reverse.

"Billy has his heart set on being a doctor. Michael wants to go into banking like his father. They are both doing well in grammar school, but if they are to continue there and later go to Trinity College your money will have to do it. I haven't any."

When she stopped speaking the scowl on Donal Moriarty's face chilled the hope right out of her heart. But she held her head high—her chin was as firm and white as finely chiselled ivory, and above it her mouth was a taut gash, startling in the pallor of her face. She said nothing. There was nothing more to say. She had said it all. The next move was his.

The curve of his cheekbone was harsh, his jaw line unyielding, his fingers unconsciously tapping his furrowed forehead as if warning his brain of trouble ahead. When he spoke his voice had retreated into a snarl. Yet he seemed to be feeling along a wall like a man groping in the dark for the right door to open.

"Young woman, I never give money away." There was a cunning look in his eyes now that frightened Katherine, for it made her think of a wily old wolf, as mean as it was dangerous. "But I do negotiate. You're asking me to support your sons until they're through school and college. Now that, as you well realize, is a considerable undertaking. Not that I can't afford it, mind you," he added hastily as if his ability to do so might have been brought into question, "but I'll expect something from you in return. You'll give up all rights to see your sons. Nor will you attempt to write to them. From this day forward you'll have no part in their lives. In return I'll see they have a comfortable home. They will have a suitable amount of pocket money, not much mind you, for too much money can spoil a boy quicker than too little. After grammar school I'll pay their college tuition. You need have no fear. They will be as well cared for as if their father was in charge, but if I ever hear you contacted them, or tried to, the deal is off. Understood?"

The words were flat and final, and hearing them Katherine's world crumbled.

The room grew hot and airless, blackness pressed in on her. It was unthinkable to never see her boys again, yet it was impossible for her to educate them. And without an education would they be above the labourers whose evicted families were dying by the thousands in Ireland's ditches? That was not the life she and Peter had dreamed of for their children. Would he forgive her if she allowed it to happen? When it was within her power to prevent it?

Yet not to see her sons, not to be allowed to explain to them it was part of their grandfather's terms that she must agree to never see or write to them again, was unthinkable. Their world had already been shattered by the loss of a brother, followed by their father's trial and death. If she vanished from their lives now, as she was being asked to do, with no explanation of any sort as to why, or why they must be uprooted and thrust into a strange life in a strange city, what would it do to them?

Huddled on the chair, her face buried in her hands, she tried to think.

There was a white ring of suffering around a mouth hard set with anger when she raised her head. "You're a fiend, sir, to expect a mother to agree to such terms. I'd see you in hell before I'd agree to them." Then she rose and drew herself to her full height, inwardly a seething mass of doubts and fears, but outwardly she appeared cool, composed, and very determined. She had the courage to do what needed to be done. And courage was something the man watching her admired, be it in a horse or a woman.

But his words were harsh and spiteful when he ground out, "Brave words me gel, but words don't eddecate sons."

"No, but money will," she spat back at him, "and I'll sell my soul to the devil to get it."

A tiny wave that might have been admiration passed swiftly over the old man's face. "Won't do you no good, gel. With the boys' father dead and a mother unable to support them, as you've just admitted, I'll claim legal guardianship. I'll not be able to prevent you from seeing the boys before I take them away from Cork, but by the Lord Harry I'll see to it that any letters you write go into the dustbin before they see them. Nor will you be allowed to visit them, until they're grown and out of my care."

Katherine sank back onto the chair, her mind in a turmoil. Could she make her sons understand she wasn't deserting them? All she wanted was for them to get the education she wasn't able to provide. Gradually a tiny glimmer, a shaft of hope filtered through her gloom. She hadn't promised not to try to keep in contact with them. She'd find some way to have her letters reach them.

The old man might rant and rave and do all in his power to prevent it, but what if he never found out? The wily old fox might find himself outsmarted by the vixen. She no longer felt like a woman trying to climb impossible mountains.

Donal Moriarty, idly fingering an envelope he had silently withdrawn from a desk drawer, looked at his daughter-in-law with morbid satisfaction when she raised her head and glared at him. "It seems you've given me no choice in the matter. But," and here she waved a finger fiercely under his nose, "if I ever hear the boys are not being properly cared for I'll protest your right of guardianship." With that and with head held high she turned to go, but he stopped her with a peremptory gesture. "Here, gel. This was to go to your husband. After I died. I've cut him out of my will with nothing except this five pound note. To buy mourning. It's no use to him now, but you need it. You're not wearing widow's weeds. Get yourself something decent in black."

He had moved towards her as he spoke and jammed the envelope into her reticule. She was about to snatch it out and hurl it at his feet when some inner instinct made her hesitate. A penny meant more to her now than a hundred pounds would to this old miser.

She spoke stiffly through frozen lips, the words coated in cold contempt. "I'm overwhelmed by your generosity, father-in-law, but 'tis not buying mourning for your son I'll be doing. The grief I have is no shallow, nebulous thing I must continually proclaim to the world by wearing widow's garb. My grief is in my heart, a hidden memory of shared happiness such as few are privileged to know. That is something I'll treasure and remember long after widow's weeds are tatters."

There was something sad and very lonely in her eyes but her back was rigid as she walked from the room.

Donal Moriarty watched her go with something close to approval on his grizzled old face. He admired spunk in a woman, and by God that gel had spunk. Maybe his older son hadn't chosen so badly after all. Suddenly he looked forward to getting to know his grandsons better.

Maybe he'd even consider making them his heirs. Recently he'd become disenchanted with Albert and his conniving wife. He was beginning to see that woman's flattery for what it was. And his younger son was a weakling. The old man had little patience with weaklings, especially in the male of the species.

Before leaving Dublin Katherine intended to visit her parents' graves. But first she needed to fortify herself with a stiff drink of Irish whiskey. *Just for a little comfort until this business is settled,* she told herself. It had been a long stressful day. And it wasn't over yet.

Leaving the alehouse with her purchase tucked inside her reticule, she almost stumbled over two old hags, derelicts of the human race begging for alms in a near drunken stupor, their toothless grins making more hideous faces already suppurating with pox. Their pale and rheumy eyes were sunk into skeleton holes of despair.

Quickly Katherine drew out a few coins and handed them to the women, who clutched her skirt and raised it to their lips as if it was an angel's robe. Katherine shuddered. She hoped they wouldn't give her fleas. As she hurried down the street their ribald cackling followed her like an ominous warning of things to come.

Despite the decay that age and wanton living had stamped on their faces, she supposed the women had once been pretty. Girls used by men to satisfy male lusts until their beauty was gone, then kicked aside. Now drink, bringing with it a mind-numbing oblivion to the horrors of living, was all that life had left for them.

A mantle of despair settled over Katherine like an imprisoning fog. Tears spilled down her cheeks as she thought how alone she had become. What if she ended up like those women? If she did, would anyone care? For a moment she was tempted to throw her bottle of whiskey away. Instead she took a long swallow before entering the grave-yard.

Kneeling on the damp earth her mind raced backward. These graves held all that was left of her parents. Her father, who had tried hard to be both mother and father to the child of a woman he had adored, always there for her with comforting words and gentle hands when tears needed drying or bruises mended. Hands whose fingers were strong and kind and straight. No crooked fingers there. Not like Andrew's or Lord Millhaven's.

Sweet Mother of Jesus! What am I thinking? That man isn't my father. Unbidden, the ugly snout of doubt had poked its head from the dark recesses of her mind. And she didn't like it.

Her mother, the beautiful lady full of laughter who had brought joy to her family, had died almost before Katherine could properly remember her.

Was Katherine more her mother's daughter than she had ever imagined? She would never know. And she didn't want to. Seamus O'Connor was her father. He'd always been there for her. Lord Millhaven, blast his soul, hadn't bothered to answer her letter. He could go to hell. If he wasn't there already.

Katherine suddenly found herself glad that Lucy, her father's servant, had two young sons who were small images of Seamus O'Connor. Regardless of who had fathered her, the O'Connor blood would be carried on to generations yet to come.

Suddenly it didn't seem such a travesty that the sons she could no longer support should grow up in the care of their grandfather.

Nevertheless, when she stopped in Cork to tell Billy and Michael what the future held for them she felt as if her heart had been torn out, thrown on the ground, and trampled on by elephants. But they had comforted her. "Don't worry about us, Mamma. We'll find a way to get letters to you. And you can send yours to Aunt Lucy. Perhaps we'll be allowed to visit her sometimes. We might even be able to meet you there."

Katherine couldn't know that Lucy was sickening with the dreaded typhus.

Chapter Twenty-Eight
Death Stalks

Henrietta's farewell advice to Katherine was "Now that your boys are in Dublin why don't you move back to Grandon? You have friends there."

But Katherine couldn't face living among friends from happier times. She didn't need that constant reminder of what she had lost. What she needed was some remote corner where she could live out her days away from sympathetic eyes and wagging tongues. But she did make a trip to Grandon. It was as if there was a need to say goodbye to her past so she could make a complete break with it.

She had no intention of living there, nor did she want to be recognized by former friends. So she took pains to wear the coarse dress of a peasant woman and partially conceal her face in an old shawl.

Confident no one would recognize her, she walked slowly past the bank where she and Peter had been so happy, then across the square to where she had shopped. Why were so many of the smaller shops closed and shuttered? She went into one that was still open and asked for a spool of thread, then was surprised when the skinny clerk lounging listlessly behind the counter shot her a look that said it was foolish to waste money on thread. It was food she should be thinking of.

Outside again she stepped respectfully aside to let yet another funeral procession pass. And as had been the case with the others, this one was followed by only two or three mourners. A man near her, respectfully holding his cap to his chest, crossed himself, muttering bitterly to no one in particular. "Soon them as dies will have no one left to do the burying."

Head down and hurrying now, she headed for the church and Andrew's grave. Crouched beside it she wondered what life would have held for this son had he lived. Certainly there would have been no education for him courtesy of her father-in-law. She sighed and arose to leave as a funeral procession turned in at the gates. For a moment she stood watching, wondering if it might be anyone she knew. Then she gasped in horror.

The bottom of the coffin dropped open and the body inside plummeted into the grave below. Immediately the coffin bearers snapped the bottom closed and walked quickly away. Business was brisk. There was no time to lose.

Katherine had heard Grandon had become a town so devastated by famine and death that the Golleen relief committee had devised what they thought was an ingenious invention—a hinged-bottom coffin, held closed with hooks and eyes.

Now she had seen it. It had not been just idle talk.

Numbly she walked away from her past and into the unknown.

Chapter Twenty-Nine
Famine, Disease, Death

Katherine wasn't one to go lightly into defeat. Thoughtfully, she assessed her options. There weren't many for a penniless widow in a country where the starving were dying in ditches like flies around poisoned sugar. She had hoped to find employment as a governess but no legitimate openings had shown up in that field. A landowner near Ballydehob had written that his children needed a governess, but his prerequisites sounded suspiciously vague, as though he was more interested in a governess's body than in her qualifications and capabilities as a teacher.

Nevertheless, Ballydehob wasn't far. Katherine decided she'd better go there and size up the situation. *I could be mistaken. I'll cope with a wife's snubs, or the servants shunning me because I'm not exactly one of them, yet in their eyes not quite the master-class either. But I won't be pinched and pawed by a husband or son waiting to trap me in a secluded corner. For the sake of my sons I'd have become the mistress of the first wealthy patron who fancied me, but now that need is gone I'll be no man's tallywoman. By the Lord Harry I'm respectable and I intend to stay that way.*

Katherine walked briskly up the driveway leading to a garish white house standing stark and alone without so much as a flower to soften its nakedness. Her nose wrinkled in distaste. The place reeked of discord.

"No, Mrs. Moriarty. Y'er not needed here. Position's filled." A sour-faced woman who looked as if she expected the worst from life and had never been disappointed was about to slam the door in Katherine's face, when a man suddenly materialized behind her. He had a dissolute mouth, wandering hands, and lewd eyes. When no other options were available he looked the sort that got their highs from mentally stripping pretty women naked and violating them. Mrs. Moriarty was still a pretty woman.

His smile slid into an oily leer when he suggested, "Why don't you step inside, madam so we can get better acquainted. There might be a sudden vacancy."

Katherine, standing on her dignity, replied with icy hauteur. "There'll be no need. I'm not interested."

While hurrying to get away from the cloying odour of iniquity and hate that seemed to cling about the place like an evil shroud, she saw what looked like a small funeral procession approaching. Except it couldn't be. What she had taken for pallbearers were men carrying a rough board mounded with straw. There was no corpse.

Puzzled, Katherine stepped to one side and watched. As the mourners straggled past her gloved hand flew to her mouth to stifle a startled gasp. A dead man's face was staring out at her through a gap in the straw.

Sweet Mother of Jesus! There have been so many deaths people are shrouding their dead in straw. But at least in Ballydehob they're still attempting to bury them. In Macroom starving dogs and street cats fight rats for the corpses.

She buried her face in her hands, her eyes burning with resentment. It seemed incomprehensible. Ireland, the land that was her home, her heritage, the land of her ancestors, had become a country no longer able to bury its dead or feed its starving. It was a country trapped in desperation.

Her mind was gripped in the tightening vice of futility. Why, why, why?

Why, when a quarter of the population starved for lack of money to buy the food Ireland produced, was food still being continually shipped out of the country? Only the potato crops had failed.

And why, while Erin's poor starved, did Charles Trevelyan, Westminster's chief representative in Ireland, piously read his Bible, twiddle his thumbs, and vote against providing free food or make-work programs? Did he fear by doing so he might demoralize the dying? Trevelyan, with all the fervour of a devout evangelical Christian, maintained that if indigent peasants were given free food they would become lazy and lie around waiting for handouts. Nor was he in favour of government relief in the form of work programs. That would mean unfair competition to private enterprise. And that, of course, would never do. It would harm those with money and resources at their disposal.

Consequently, he made sure that the few work programs agreed upon were so widely scattered that emaciated indigents often died of hunger and exhaustion trying to reach them. Those that got to the work sites built wharves having no purpose, roads leading nowhere, and stone walls where walls were not needed, for wages so slow in being paid that men died of hunger waiting for them.

Ironically Trevelyan had lost no time in ordering troops to ruthlessly beat back starving peasants trying to seize Irish food destined for export. After that he decided that having had such a stressful summer coping with the Irish problems, he needed and deserved a long holiday. So he took his family to southern France to lie about, read the Bible, enjoy the warmth of the sun, and treat themselves to that country's finest wines and gourmet foods.

Katherine's eyes were dark with despondency, her face was etched with lines of exhaustion and despair. She was about to reach for the bottle that so often brought her blissful oblivion now when her shoulders squared like a trapped whale rising above the murky waters of its prison. She drew herself up to her full height and hurled the bottle of whiskey into the ditch. Some poor starving wretch would find it, and perhaps die more peacefully.

As for Katherine Moriarty, she would go and scrub the tiny bothan that had become her home. She had scoured the place before she moved in, because it had been infested with fleas, but she'd do it again. One couldn't be too careful about fleas when typhus was killing so many.

Suddenly she shuddered as if the bony fingers of death had already reached out and marked her wrist—the wrist she'd scratched when first scrubbing out the cabin.

Leaving the public conveyance, she stopped to buy food before starting the long walk home. She could no longer afford the luxury of a hired cart. A scrawny women with the sad eyes of a starving hound watched her stow a week's supply of staples into her basket. There was such longing in the woman's eyes that impulsively Katherine handed her a coin. "Take it. It's not much but it will feed your family for a few days." Then she hurried away before she could regret the generosity she could ill afford.

But not before the woman had kissed her hand, exclaiming, "Sure'n 'tis heaven's own angel ye be, ma'am."

Chapter Thirty
A Little Dog Her Only Friend

Black-leafed trees swaying and fluttering in the evening breeze cast fidgety silhouettes against a lowering sky. The woman walked quickly. She must hurry if she was to reach the safety of her bothan before the storm broke. Lightning was already spider-webbing the sky with vivid flashes of fire. Thunder marched steadily closer on ominous tread, and the wind had risen to a screaming crescendo. Great pools of swirling blackness were momentarily dashed aside by each new blaze of light, after which the returning blackness seemed more intense.

Buffeted and breathless, Katherine let herself into the cabin with a sigh of relief and reached for a candle. Its tiny yellow light did little but cast sinister pools of advancing and retreating shadows as the candle flickered and threatened to go out.

Thunder-goaded rain cascaded from low-hung clouds as if the floodgates of heaven were weeping for a country trapped in hopelessness. The continuous play of lightning on the cabin walls made the candle useless. Defeated, it guttered and went out.

Katherine had put the basket of food away and prepared for bed. But now to her dismay she discovered the cabin roof was little better than a sieve. The bed was already soaked and no matter how many pans she put under the drips, they were never enough.

Wrapped in a warm cloak with her feet tucked under it, she huddled on a low stool to wait out the storm. The wind slammed against the craggy mountainside and whistled down the valleys. Lightning turned the dome of heaven into a great inverted volcano with streaks of red hot lava spewing from its crater, and thunder roared as if trying to scare the wickedness out of the world. It was the worst storm Katherine had ever experienced.

She awoke, cramped and cold and utterly miserable, but the sun was shining. Opening the door to survey the ravages of the storm, she was greeted by a low experimental "whuff" from an emaciated terrier so like Turko it might have been his son . . . except Turko had been dead for years.

This dog, on its haunches now, his head cocked on one side, eyes watching to see the results of its whuff, was little more than a pup. When nothing happened his head shifted to the other side, but he continued to study her from bright intelligent eyes. His laughing mouth displayed an array of white teeth and a red lolling tongue. A short tail thumped the ground in a hopeful fashion. Suddenly he whined eagerly and the tail thumped harder, as if the woman had passed inspection and he was in a hurry to tell her so.

At Katherine's soft "Ye poor wee creature. Sure'n 'tis starving ye be," he bounded to her side and wiggled in doggy adoration when she rumpled the hair on his neck and ran her hand over ribs struggling to escape their skin. "Come, little friend. We'll share what there is."

She smiled softly as she watched the little animal gulp down half a loaf of bread soaked in milk, then lick the floor to make certain he hadn't missed a crumb. Having satisfied himself in that regard he sank down beside her, gave a comfortable yawn, and went to sleep with his head on her foot.

"Whist then, little doggy, ye are so like me auld Turko 'tis certain I am the leprechauns sent you. Perhaps you'll bring me luck. Lead me to a pot of gold. Faith though, just having your company will be luck enough. I wasn't liking the thought of living alone. But what will I call you?" She studied the reddish coat thoughtfully for a moment. "I know. Since you found me, I'll call you Macha. After the wild fairy steed of Macha that came to Cuchulain on Slieve Gullion, when he was champion of the Red Branch Knighthood, to carry him to still greater glory."

Suddenly a troubled frown darkened Katherine's face. "Not that I expect there's much glory waiting for me. I better write to Tim Watson's sister. Or we'll both be starving."

With a hungry dog to feed it seemed important now to sell one of her young geldings before the little money she had left was gone. It would mean taking a loss on the animal, but she couldn't wait for the European buyers. She'd write Miss Watson today and mail it when she went to the village. She needed to buy meat for the stew she intended making for the family next door. The husband, Paddy O'Rourke, a Conacre man, hadn't had steady work for months.

A week ago O'Rourke's tiny plot of potatoes, although the vines still appeared lush and healthy, had developed the peculiar stink that warned the dread disease had struck. Now the leaves were pockmarked with black lesions, and underneath the white fungus was already spreading its spores to the tubers beneath the soil.

With their sole source of food gone what hope did this family, and thousands like them, have of surviving until the next potato harvest? Six of their eight children had already died of typhus.

Katherine had felt listless for days. Now her eyes had tired blue smudges beneath them even though she seemed to have slept well. This morning she had felt too exhausted to walk to the village, so she'd been glad to give ten-year-old Mickey O'Rourke a coin to run her errands. Now her mouth quivered as she saw the letter he had brought from Michael. (The one from Miss Watson could wait. She'd open it later.) As she read tears blurred her eyes.

"Dearest Mamma. Grandfather gave me this money for my birthday, but I want you to have it. I don't need it. Grandfather is kind. And Billy and I are happy.

"It would be nice if we could see you, but Billy has a new friend he thinks will deliver your letters to us, so Grandfather won't know about them. We got the letter you sent to Aunt Lucy, but now she's dead the house has been sold. So don't send any more letters to that address because if Grandfather finds out we are writing to each other he'll be terribly angry. Billy sends his love and he'll be writing soon. But he is very busy what with being captain of the soccer team and playing cricket too. And we're both learning tennis. Grandfather says next year he'll teach us golf, and bridge. He believes it's as important for gentlemen to know things like that as it is to know Euclid and Latin. Life here at school is different from what it was in Cork, but I think I like it better. It would be almost perfect if you could come and visit us. Your loving son, Michael."

Katherine folded the letter carefully and placed it close to her heart before unwrapping the little package that had come with it. Seeing two gold sovereigns winking back at her she suddenly looked as if she had lost her equilibrium. It wasn't right for her sons to be so worried about her that they sent her their birthday money. Nor was it right for her to go on writing to them, knowing that if her letters were discovered, it could cause her boys irreparable harm. If the old man refused to help them, then what would happen to them?

Enveloped in gloom she sat lost in thought, trying to make the hardest decision of her life while knowing all the time what it eventually had to be.

Katherine swallowed, but it did nothing to ease the hurting lump in her throat. Reaching for the second letter, she slit it open. As her eyes flew down the page the harsh cruelty of the written words jumped out to stab at her heart and wring a horrified cry from her mouth.

"I'm sorry, Mrs. Moriarty, but both your geldings are dead. They were struck by lightning along with two of Tim's in the storm last week. And your mare aborted a seven-month foal the next day."

Katherine's face was numb with shock. Slowly her fingers reached for the two gold sovereigns and fingered them as one in a trance. Michael's sovereigns were all that were left of the life that had been hers. She was a woman alone, without money, and nothing to sell. Except Ebony. Ebony?

With great reluctance she immediately wrote a letter to Tim Watson's sister asking if she would buy the black mare, but Miss Watson wrote a cold and condescending reply. "Any decision to buy or not to buy must be made by my brother, Lord Dunraughton."

And he's in America. The mare and I could both be dead before word comes back from him.

Katherine viciously crumpled the letter and tossed it onto the small peat fire that only burned now when she needed to boil water for tea.

"Ma'am, 'tis hate'n to bother ye Oi am, but young Mickey and meself is off for a work camp near Cork and 'tis wondering Oi am if ye'll look in sometimes on me Martha and the wee spalpeen. Me wife's milk's gone and the child is mewling and sickly for want of nourishment. If Mickey and meself gets work Oi hopes to have money to send them for food. And even save a bit for passage to America."

Paddy O'Rourke's skinny face looked trapped, hungry, and disillusioned, but his eyes held a glimmer of hope. Dully Katherine wondered if without money to buy food he and the boy had the stamina to reach Cork. They had existed on nothing but greens and a few turnips for weeks. A feeling of necessity overwhelmed her. She opened her reticule and handed them a coin. It was sadly inadequate, but it was the best she could do.

In the days that followed she took food to Martha O'Rourke, a woman no older than herself who had once been pretty but was now so emaciated and sick she had neither the strength nor the will to comfort the baby that cried continually. When the child died it was Katherine's arms that cradled it.

Martha's feverish eyes had held a mute appeal and a terrible sadness, but there were no tears left to shed when Katherine wrapped the tiny body in one of her own shawls. But when she came back from digging a shallow grave in the rocky ground and picked up the tiny cadaver to bury it Martha let out a long-drawn-out wail. "'Tis unconsecrated ground. And yer not of the faith to pray me babe out of purgatory. Wurrah wurrah. 'Tis a priest Oi's needen."

"Well, there is no priest. So it's either me or the rats. Take your choice." The words sounded harsh and brittle and totally devoid of pity, for Katherine was near exhaustion herself. But then she said more gently, "Don't fret, Martha. I'll say a prayer over the babe and I'm sure it won't matter a whit what religion it comes from or where the burial takes place, for I fancy it's Christianity God is interested in, not creeds or denominations."

Two mornings later Martha O'Rourke was dead. When Katherine saw three big rats scamper out from under the mound of rags covering the body, horror and revulsion raced up her spine. It took all her will power to make herself pull back the rags, for instinct told her the rats had already begun their revolting work.

Katherine's head ached continually, her body was either burning with fever or wracked with cold, but she was determined to somehow hack out a grave and drag the woman into it. She had to. There was no one else, only the rats.

Breath was rasping in her throat as she straightened her aching back. Leaning on the shovel, she looked listlessly from hands blistered and raw and swollen to the corpse she had wrapped in one of her own blankets and dragged to the graveside. Macha would keep the rats away from it as she worked.

The rodents wiped their whiskers with cheeky insolence and watched the dog from cold, calculating eyes. When he rushed at them they squeaked disdainfully, flicked their tails, and disappeared down their holes. But Macha had been too quick for one. After a flip that broke its neck he dropped it proudly at Katherine's feet. At her shuddered "Take the horrid thing away," he had given her a pitying look, then carried the rat off and eaten it. His teeth crunching on bones with such obvious enjoyment made Katherine vomit. She vomited easily these days.

Just a few more shovelfuls now and the hole would be deep enough. Wearily she ran one hand over her back and wondered if it would ever again be completely free of pain.

She smoothed the wrinkles out of the blood-stained wrappings that were supposed to be protecting her blistered palms, squared her shoulders, put one foot on the spade, and forced it to bite into the ground again.

"Father in heaven, in thy mercy welcome this woman into heaven and re-unite her with her children. And please let them never be hungry again. Amen."

Katherine supposed that wasn't the sort of funeral Canon O'Hara would have approved of, but at the moment it was the best she could manage.

The next day she didn't get out of bed. Macha ate the food she couldn't force down, then whined anxiously and tried to lick her face.

Katherine knew she was coming down with the dreaded killer, typhus. It was the fleas. There had been fleas in the cottage before she moved in and she had often found one on her clothing after returning from the O'Rourke hovel.

"But faith, little doggy, I was so conscientious about keeping myself clean. When did the vermin bite me? It takes more than one bite, you know." Macho wagged his short tail, his eyes aglow with love for the woman he adored.

Within a week, two at the most, Katherine supposed she'd be like her neighbours. Dead.

With no one to bury me I'll be left to rot. Or be eaten by rats. At that thought her mind recoiled in horror and she turned her face to the wall as if unable to face the dread reality of it.

Her mouth grew hard and taut. *My sons must never know their mother wasn't properly buried. I must write to Donal Moriarty today, in a disguised hand. Tell him Peter's wife died of typhus and was buried in a small country cemetery.* With so many dying there would be nothing unusual in that. Her boys would grieve, but they were young. They'd get over it.

Having done that, her mind felt better. But she wasn't about to wait for death to creep up and trap her in a hovel.

Katherine Moriarty might be dead, but Katie Moore would go out and meet death head on.

At the moment it was too complicated for her fevered brain to sort out, for it seemed beyond reason that she was driven by a goading urgency, a timeless longing, to return to the trails she had ridden in happier days. She only knew she must die surrounded by the beauty of God's majesty.

If she still had breath when she reached the cliffs she'd step off into space. Better a body mangled by nature's rocky grandeur than a body desecrated by rats.

She made herself a pot of tea and packed a small bundle of food for Macha, who watched with anxious eyes. Then, taking her warmest cloak, she left the bothan as silently as a spirit leaves a dead body.

Chapter Thirty-One
The Earth Cowered

The earth cowered. The air sizzled. Lord Millhaven's beard smoked. "When did this letter come? Why wasn't I given it sooner?" His Lordship's voice was like the roar of thunder. A heavy walking cane, held by a white-knuckled, darkly-veined hand, vigorously thumped the marble floor in a way that suggested it was only awaiting permission before rushing off on its own to wreak havoc on somebody.

The workman, a tall, well-muscled carpenter who had been overseeing the redoing of the panelling in Millhaven's great hallway, cringed. If he were a bird he would have darted away from the man glaring at him with cold, vindictive eyes. Instead he tugged at his beard and tried to keep his voice steady. "Beggen your pardon, sir, it only showed up a few moments ago. One of my workmen found it when we pulled off the last of the wainscotting. I expect it slipped down behind it the day it came."

Lord Millhaven narrowed his eyes, lowered his brows, scowled fiercely at the workman who had handed him the letter, then slit open the envelope.

As he read the words written so long ago even the air around him seemed to burst into flame. His face had the tortured look of a man who has failed someone special to him.

Within the hour Millhaven's head steward was astride his Lordship's fastest horse, racing to catch the next boat to Cork with instructions to find Katherine Moriarty. "And be damn sure you explain that her letter only just reached me. And give her this money. With her husband gone and three boys to educate she must be near destitute. Meanwhile I'll be contacting people in high places to find out what I can do to get her husband returned to Ireland as a free man."

In due time the steward returned. But his news was grim. "Mrs. Moriarty left Grandon after her husband died en route to Australia. No one in Grandon knows where she went. Some think she may have died. Her two younger sons are said to be living with their grandfather in Dublin. However, there seems a bit of a mystery about the eldest boy, Andrew. He was reported to have been killed trying to stop a runaway carriage. Yet his funeral apparently raised questions to which there were never any clear answers. Rumours are still rampant."

Millhaven's steward, Ben Groves, ran a hand wearily over his dust-streaked face as he finished speaking, and at the same time stretched out his long legs as if that might ease the stiffness in his knees brought on by long hours in the saddle. It was facts, not rumours his employer needed. And facts seemed to be in short supply.

However, he had confirmed that the two younger Moriarty boys had indeed gone to live with their paternal grandparent in Dublin shortly before their mother disappeared. "Donal Moriarty is a wealthy old miser but he wouldn't lift a finger to help his daughter-in-law. Nor would he allow her to have any contact with her sons. If he knows where their mother is now he isn't saying. Yet he is said to be good to her boys. Evidently he has made them his heirs."

The steward, concerned that the news he brought might be too much of a shock for the ailing old man, who was his friend as well as his employer, said in a kindly fashion, "You will notice, sir, I said the oldest boy was 'reported' to have been killed.

"Do you remember Liam O'Brian? You and his father rode to hounds together in Ireland. Liam is now the horse doctor who checks the animals leaving Cove for England and the continent. He's very good at it too, from what I hear.

"It may only be a coincidence, but the day the Moriarty boy was reported to have been killed in Cork, an acquaintance of Liam's showed up in Cove carrying a badly hurt lad he said was his son. Liam said he never questioned the relationship. There was too strong a likeness between the two.

"Against all odds the boy didn't die. But although he recovered physically his memory was gone. He remembered nothing prior to the accident. Liam doubts he ever will."

"Damn, it man! Why are you telling me all this? I'm not interested in boys who are supposed to die but don't." Millhaven's look was fierce, his voice abrasive. "It's Katherine Moriarty I'm interested in. If she is alive I need to know. So I'm ordering you back to Ireland tomorrow, my friend. When you get there, spare no expense. Find her. If she's alive I must help her. It may be the last good thing I do in this life."

"Ah! But would your Lordship be interested in the lad if you knew he had a crook in his little finger? A dagger-shaped birthmark on his chest? That the man claiming to be his father was Patrick Tully, who was once head groom for Katherine's father?"

A man usually arrogantly sure of himself suddenly looked stunned, as if haunted by unbidden flashes of long-forgotten memories. Lord Millhaven normally wasn't one to rush his fences but now he jerked himself to his feet, saying brusquely, “I shall go at once and see him.”

“Sorry sir. That won’t be easy. Tully took him to America as soon as the lad was well enough to travel. Liam advanced them the money for a ticket to Canada. Tully paid it back as soon as he got a job in Montreal. Since then nothing has been heard from him and Liam believes he may have died.”

Millhaven, looking fierce and rocklike, pivoted as if he had just made an unequivocal yet long-standing bargain with destiny. “Then we must find the boy. I’ve failed Katherine. I mustn’t fail her son.”

Chapter Thirty-Two
A Rescue

Katherine's body burned with fever, her face was pinched with pain. Concentrate. She must concentrate. Lift one foot, move it ahead, put it down. Raise the other and repeat. Do it again. And again. Keep doing it.

Water ran in rivulets down her nose, dripped off her chin, puddled between her breasts. Her clothes were soaked. Her legs were chafed. Sometimes she stopped for a drink of tea. It was cold now, but still refreshing. Sometimes she drank thirstily from tiny streams. Always Macha watched her from anxious doggy eyes. Sometimes he whined and reached up his cool black muzzle to lick her burning hand. Sometimes she sat down to rest, but always there was the goading urgency to keep going. Get away from the haunts of gluttonous rats, and the cadavers they feasted on.

The sun was a red ball of fire as she staggered towards Beech Corner. Today she couldn't see the branch that could de-cap unwary riders. But she knew it was there. Just as she knew that beyond it she would shut her eyes and walk into merciful oblivion in a way befitting a Pirate Queen.

Stooping to pat her little dog one last time, Katherine staggered and fell. There was no Macha to pat. He had vanished. Vaguely hurt that her last friend should have deserted her just when she so needed to feel his wiggly doggy love one more time, she told herself he must have flushed a rabbit. She could hear him barking somewhere off in the distance. Except this wasn't his rabbit bark. This bark was demanding, bordering on hysterical. But she was too dazed to notice. If the drumming of racing hooves had registered on her mind she would have said she was hallucinating. Remembering the horrors of a race she hadn't really won. Her heart throbbed as a terrible lethargy spread through her, but somehow she had to get up off the ground and keep walking. It couldn't be much further.

Katherine's mouth was stiff with concentration, her eyes held a feverish glitter as she moved closer to the cliff. Her mind had shut down, blocked out everything except the shackled resolve to keep walking. She had an urgent appointment in another world, and must not be late.

The sunset was dying. Soon she would be too. A few more steps and her body would be hurtling into merciful oblivion. Instead she was jerked roughly backwards to fall with a sickening jolt on the rocky roadway. The rope encircling her chest, locking her hands to her sides threatened to cut off her breath, but she knew nothing of this. The fall had jolted the wind out of her.

When she slowly opened her eyes a rough little tongue was licking her hand. Dark and anxious eyes were watching her face. Fingers, tanned by the winds of life, were loosening the rope and massaging her arms with a woman's gentleness. "Mrs. Moriarty, ma'am! May I ask what in tarnation you thought you were doing?" His voice was stern. And puzzled. But it held such tenderness Katherine wanted to cry.

Instead she said severely, "I'm not Mrs. Moriarty. She's dead. I'm Katie Moore. Soon I'll be dead too. You shouldn't be here. And you mustn't touch me, or you'll get typhus." Then her mouth quivered, and she sank back exhausted. But she fought to continue. “Everyone is dead. There’s no one to bury me, so I have to walk off a cliff. So the rats can’t eat me.” Then, because that was all the explanation she had the strength to give, she gave a tiny sigh and slipped into the peace of oblivion.

For a moment Tim Watson held her in his arms, looking as if he had just been handed a precious gift. Then reality took over. *Damn it, man, the woman’s burning up with fever. You can’t let her die like this. There’s a canteen of water on your saddle. Use it.*

Leaping to his feet, he reached his horse with long purposeful strides, untied the canteen and whipped out a handkerchief. Then with strong fingers he quickly unfastened Katherine’s blouse and sponged first her face, then her neck and breasts with the look of a man lost in thought. When her eyelids finally fluttered he raised her head, put the flask to her lips, and urged her to drink. “There. That’s a good girl. Now I’m going to take you home where I can nurse you properly.”

Her barely comprehending eyes followed the movement of his hands as he carefully laid the wet handkerchief over her firm breasts and rebuttoned her clothes. Then cradling her as if she was a child, he remounted Khemsahib and with Macha hurrying to keep up, raced towards the Dunraughton estate.

“Tim, it’s not fitting for you to be nursing that woman the way you’re doing. There’s servants as can do the job. What will people say? No gentleman goes into a woman’s bedroom unless he’s her husband.”

“Evelyn, you’re my sister and I love you, but you’re a crotchety old maid too caught up in the mores of a society whose shallow values I hold in contempt. You forget I've helped birth a woman when there was no one else to do it. Neither she, her husband, nor I have felt the worse for it."

His dry grin suggested that here was a man in complete control of himself no matter what the situation. "Now if you'll kindly go downstairs and tell cook to send up a thick chicken broth, I'll see if our patient can be coaxed into taking a little."

Katherine managed a wan smile for the man gently easing her into the crook of his shoulder and saying in a voice that brooked no argument, "You're to drink this broth cook sent up. And after that there's a hot cup of tea to follow it."

"Faith, Tim, are ye trying to drown me then with all this liquid?" The words were the weary whisper of an autumn breeze.

"By the Lord Harry I'd even have tried a mite of drowning if that's what it took to get you on the road to recovery. I was fair worried about you for a while, but the fever seems gone today and the spots have turned from bright red to brown. So that's a good sign. In no time at all you'll be out riding Ebony again. And then I'll show you the most beautiful scenery in Ireland."

She was suddenly aware of a fluttering sensation in the pit of her stomach at the disturbing proximity of this man whose broad shoulder was pressing against her own. A man whose force of will had dragged her back to life against her better judgement. Now she looked at him and said levelly, "Katherine Moriarty is dead, you know. I have no right to be alive."

The look in the eyes watching her seemed to demand some further explanation. "I didn't want my sons to know their mother died destitute in a hovel. So I got word to their grandfather that Katherine Moriarty had died of typhus and was buried in a country cemetery. I couldn't write to my sons because if the old man found out he'd have turned them out without a penny. You see," she added as if there was a desperate need to keep talking, "after Peter died and the *Queen O'Malley* was shipwrecked, and I couldn't get work as a governess, there was no money to educate the children. Their grandfather promised to provide for them, but only if I agreed to never see them again. After the geldings were killed and Ebony aborted I was tempted to dress like a man and try to get work as a groom, but by that time I felt too ill." She had started speaking in a rush as if there was an urgent need to unburden her mind to someone she trusted, but now she closed her eyes. Her strength was exhausted.

The protective arm around her shoulder tightened. His face darkened into a fierce scowl. But his voice was infinitely gentle. "Life has dealt you a lot of hard knocks, little lady, but you've had the courage to handle them. 'Tis just glad I am that your wee dog brought me to you in time. I started back to Ireland as soon as I got my sister's letter, over a year old by the time it reached me, telling of Peter's conviction and death. When my boat finally docked in Cork I was afraid you might have left the district and I'd never be able to trace you. Or that you had remarried.

"I felt like a man granted a reprieve after Evelyn told me she had recently heard from you. But when I found your cottage empty, as were the neighbouring ones, and fresh mounds in what had been a potato patch, I was so sunk in gloom my life seemed empty too. It was then I heard a little dog barking in such a wildly excited manner he had to be trying to tell me something. So I followed him. Thank

God I did, and reached you in time to make the luckiest throw of my life."

Then he grinned a slow, very masculine smile with a hint of wickedness around the corners. "I've always said someday I'd rope myself a pretty filly. One with no man's brand on her, but by George, I never expected to be doing it under such extraordinary circumstances. I knew if I missed this throw I'd lost my reason for living."

His mouth brushed lightly against her cheek as he finished speaking. "What I'm trying to say in a clumsy fashion, Katherine, is that when you are well enough I'd like you to marry me. If it's too soon after Peter, I'll wait. But why not come back to America with me? There's healing in that vast and rugged country that makes one forget the past.

"I know, because after my wife died, I thought I'd never forget those months of hell. Nor would I ever risk asking another woman to marry me. Our marriage wasn't a happy union. We were both too young. She had the body of a goddess but the mind of an army slut. I was proud, arrogant, and impatient. When she ran off with her gypsy lover I didn't bother to go after her. When I heard she'd died, I actually felt glad, relieved that now I was completely free again. And that was the way I intended to keep it. Until I met you."

His fingers gently pushed back the damp hair that clung around Katherine's delicate face, a face that carried an air of sadness coupled with fierce durability and soft elegance. A face that tore at his heart and made him want to give her a long passionate kiss that would sweep over her and drive away all traces of sadness. But he wasn't one to rush his fences.

He had found her a fascinating anomaly the day he stumbled on her sitting on a rock. She had put him in mind of a moon goddess riding aloof and alone across a midnight sky, controlling the tides, influencing all who walked in her cool white light, yet knowing none of it. That fascination had begun to turn to love at Lady Highips' dinner party. God! How many times since then had he longed to kiss her the way a man kisses the woman he wants beside him for the rest of his life.

Perhaps it was weakness, or maybe it was surprise, that caused Katherine to listen and say nothing. Now she raised her head with a look of infinite sadness. "Lord Dunraughton, that was no filly you roped. You best cut your lasso and let me go. I have borne another man's brand. Worse than that, I came to him a tarnished bride. Do you want a woman like that to be the mother of your children?"

"Damn it, Katherine! It's not children I'm wanting to marry you for, but if they come I'll not be moaning. Nor do I put any stock in the belief there's seed from previous matings lurking in your womb waiting to pounce on mine. To my mind that theory was concocted to bolster the male ego."

The warmth of this man's breath on her cheek, the reassurance of his arm around her, the honesty in the eyes holding hers, the tenderness in his face, spoke a timeless language as old as the world itself. When he held her the pain of life's tragedies melted into the past.

Then she shuddered, as if fate had suddenly dealt her a blow so crushing, so catastrophic, that the world was disintegrating around her. Her eyes were tragic with unspoken guilt. "And now I've given you typhus."

Gently he reached for her wrist and ran one finger over the tiny scar from a healed scratch. "How did you do this? And when?"

"That scratch? It's nothing. I did it on an old bucket I found in the cottage when I went to scrub it out. Before I moved in."

A satisfied expression glowed on Lord Dunraughton's face. "Just as I suspected. It's the scratch that did it. Fleas spread typhus, but it takes a series of bites to do it. You're not the sort to harbour fleas so there had to be some other explanation." When Katherine raised startled eyes to his, he smiled, lifted her wrist to his lips, and kissed it with an air of authority before replying.

"That scratch allowed typhus-carrying dust particles from flea faeces into your bloodstream. So you can put all thoughts of giving me typhus out of your pretty head. That is not something I have on my agenda. I expect to be far too busy. After nursing a courageous lady back to complete health, I plan to court the woman of my dreams until she agrees to marry me. Then I'll carry her off, take her far away from the haunts of rats, the hunger, and the dying that has Ireland in its grip, to a land where we can start a new life as one."

Katherine suddenly felt as close to this man as if they were making naked love somewhere out in the New World he spoke so much about. Something warm and exquisitely exciting washed over her.

She knew now with infinite certainty that wherever she went with Tim Watson she would be safe. And she would be loved. She raised her mouth to his and he kissed her tenderly as if she was very fragile, very precious. Then the kiss grew hard and hungry, and her hunger matched his.

The courting had begun.

MARQUIS
MEMBER OF SCABRINI GROUP
Québec, Canada
2007